Santa Monica Pu

I SMP 00 05

D0458978

Santa
Monica
Public
Library

**4 — WEEK
LOAN**

IT IS AGAINST THE LAW
to cut, tear, write in, mark, deface,
break, or injure library property.
Misdemeanor. Cal. Ed. Code 19910

RENEWALS
451-1866   *Date Due*

DEC 2 6 1995	
OCT - 7 1996	
OCT - 6 1997	
FEB 2 2 1998	
MAR - 8 1999	
APR - 2 1999	

SANTA MONICA PUBLIC LIBRARY

NOV   1995

THE OGRE

Aug 29/89.

Also by Michel Tournier

THE FOUR WISE MEN
GEMINI
FRIDAY AND ROBINSON: LIFE ON ESPERANZA ISLAND
FRIDAY

MICHEL TOURNIER

· · · · · · · · · · · · · ·

THE OGRE

TRANSLATED FROM THE FRENCH
BY BARBARA BRAY

PANTHEON BOOKS, NEW YORK

SANTA MONICA PUBLIC LIBRARY

English translation
Copyright © 1972 by Doubleday & Company, Inc.

All rights reserved under International and Pan-American Copyright Conventions. Published in the United States by Pantheon
Books, a division of Random House, Inc., New York. Originally
published in France as *Le Roi des Aulnes* by Editions Gallimard.
Copyright © 1970 Editions Gallimard. First American edition
published in 1972 by Doubleday & Company, Inc.

Library of Congress Cataloging in Publication Data

Tournier, Michael.
The ogre.
(Pantheon modern writers)
Translation of: Le roi des Aulnes.
Reprint. Originally published: Garden City, N.Y.:
Doubleday, 1972.
I. Title.
PQ2680.083R613   1984   843'.914   83-23655
ISBN 0-394-72407-0

Manufactured in the United States of America

468975

To the slandered memory of
Staretz Grigory Yefimovitch
RASPUTIN
healer of the Tsarevitch Alexis, murdered for
his opposition to the 1914 war.

Contents

I
Sinister Writings of Abel Tiffauges

To find something interesting, you merely have to look at it long enough.

Gustave Flaubert

January 3, 1938. You're an ogre, Rachel used to say to me sometimes. An ogre? A fabulous monster emerging from the mists of time? Well, yes, I do think there's something magical about me, I do think there's a secret collusion, deep down, connecting what happens to me with what happens in general, and enabling my particular history to bend the course of things in its own direction.

And I do believe I issued from the mists of time. I've always been shocked at the frivolous way people agonize about what's going to happen to them after they die and don't give a damn about what happened to them before they were born. The heretofore is just as important as the hereafter, especially as it probably holds the key to it. As for me, I was already there a thousand, a hundred thousand years ago. When the earth was still only a ball of fire spinning around in a helium sky the soul that lit it and made it spin was mine. What's more, the dizzying antiquity of my origins explains my supernatural power: being and I have traveled side by side so long, we're such old companions, that while we may not be especially fond of one another, by dint of being together almost since the world began we understand one another and can't refuse each other anything.

As for being a monster . . .

To begin with, what *is* a monster? Etymology has a bit of a shock up its sleeve here: "monster" comes from *monstrare*, "to show." A monster is something that is shown, pointed at, exhibited at fairs, and so on. And the more monstrous a creature is, the more it is to be exhibited. This makes my hair stand on end: I can't live except in obscurity, and I'm sure I live at all only through a misunderstanding, because the mass of my fellow creatures don't know I'm there.

If you don't want to be a monster, you've got to be like your fellow creatures, in conformity with the species, the image of your relations. Or else have progeny that make you the first link in the chain of a new species. For monsters do not reproduce. Two-headed calves are not viable. Mules and hinnies are born sterile, as if Nature wanted to cut short an experiment she considered unwise. And here I link up with my eternity again, for with me eternity takes the place of both relatives and progeny. Old as the world, and as immortal, I can have none but putative parents and adopted children.

I've just read over what I've written. My name is Abel Tiffauges, I run a garage in the Place de la Porte des Ternes, and *I'm not crazy*. What I've just written should be taken completely seriously. So? So the essential function of the future will be to demonstrate, or more precisely to illustrate, the *seriousness* of the above.

January 6, 1938. The winged steed of "Mobilgas" outlined in neon on the damp dark sky is reflected briefly on my hands, then gone. The pink palpitation of Pegasus and an all-pervading smell of old oil combine to form an atmosphere which, though I hate it, gives me an unavowable pleasure. To say I'm used to it is putting it mildly: it's as familiar as the warmth of my bed or the face that greets me every morning in the mirror. But the reason I'm sitting down for the second time with my pen in my left hand, in front of this blank sheet of paper—the third page of my "Sinister Writings"—is that I sense I'm standing at a crossroads, as they say, and because to a certain extent I'm counting on this diary to help me escape from the garage and the paltry preoccupations that keep me here. And, in a sense, from myself.

All is sign. But only a piercing light or shriek will penetrate our blunted sight and hearing. Ever since my years of initiation at St. Christopher's, I've always been aware of hieroglyphs written across my path and a confused murmur of words in my ear. But till now I didn't understand them. It's true they did serve as repeated proof that the heavens are not absolutely void; but apart from that all they did was add to my already existing doubts about what to do with my life. Yesterday, however, the most banal circumstances produced the necessary flash of illumination.

A commonplace incident temporarily deprived me of the use of my right hand. I was trying to crank an engine that wouldn't respond to the battery when the starting handle kicked back on me—as it happened, at a moment when my arm was slack from the shoulder. My wrist bore the brunt of the impact; I'm pretty sure I heard the ligaments give. I almost vomited with pain. I can still feel a throbbing under the big elastic dressing resting against my chest. As I couldn't do any work in the garage with only one hand, I took refuge in the little room on the second floor where I keep my account books and old newspapers. And to occupy my mind I thought I'd try jotting down a few words at random with my uninjured hand.

It was then I had the sudden revelation that I could write with it! Yes, without any practice, quite fast and without hesitation, my left hand produces perfectly firm characters, not at all childish or clumsy, and, what's more, completely devoid of any resemblance to my ordinary writing. I shall come back later to this staggering event. I think I know its origin. But to begin with I had to set down the circumstances that have led me for the first time to take up my pen with the sole purpose of unburdening myself and proclaiming the truth.

Must I go back to the other, perhaps no less decisive circumstance of my break with Rachel? But then I'd have to tell a whole story, a love story, my love story. It goes without saying I loathe the idea, but perhaps that's only want of habit. For anyone as reticent as I am it's extremely disagreeable at first to pour out one's innards on paper. But once I've got started my hand runs away with me, and I doubt if I'll be able to stop. It may be that from now on there can't even be a sequence of events in my life without that verbal reflection called a diary.

I've lost Rachel. She was my wife. Not my wife before God and man, but the woman in my life, or, to put it differently though without stressing the matter unduly, the feminine element in my particular universe. I met her several years ago, in the same way as I meet everyone I know: as a customer in the garage. She drove up in a broken-down Peugeot four-seater, visibly pleased by the effect created by a woman driver, greater then than it is now. From the start she adopted a familiarity based on our common concern with cars. This familiarity so soon moved on to include everything else that it wasn't long before she turned up in my bed.

What first attracted me was the assurance and ease with which she wore her nakedness, with no more and no less self-consciousness than if it had been any other attire—a traveling suit or an evening dress. There's no doubt that the most uncomely thing in a woman is not to know it is perfectly possible to be naked—that there is not only a habit but also a *habitus* of nakedness. And I can tell at a glance, from a certain aridity about them and the strange way their clothes cling to their skin, the women who don't possess this knowledge.

Beneath her small head, with its aquiline profile and helmet of little black curls, Rachel had a round and powerful body, surprising in the femininity of its generous hips, violet-circled breasts, deeply hollowed back, and entire gamut of faultlessly firm curves too ample for the hand and making up a whole that was impregnable. Morally speaking she was a not particularly unusual example of the "bachelor girl" made fashionable by a recent best seller. She preserved her independence by working as a traveling accountant, visiting shops, workrooms and small factories to keep their owners' books in order. She was a Jewess, and I had occasion to notice that all her clients were Jewish too: the explanation being the confidential nature of the documents she dealt with.

I might have been put off by her cynicism, her destructive view of things, a kind of mental itch that made her live in constant dread of boredom. But her sense of the comic, her skill in detecting the absurd element in people and situations, a tonic merriment she managed to draw out of the dreariness of life, all had a beneficial influence on my own naturally bilious temperament.

Writing all this down makes me realize what she meant to me, and I have a lump in my throat when I say I've lost her. Rachel, I couldn't say whether we loved each other, but we certainly had some good laughs together, and that's something, isn't it?

As a matter of fact she was laughing, without a trace of malice, when she laid down the premises from which, by different paths, we both ended up at the same conclusion: our parting.

Sometimes she would dash in and hand her little car over to the mechanic for a repair or to be serviced, and we would take the opportunity to go up to my room. She always used to make some indecent joke or other, comparing the car's fate with that of its owner. On that particular day she said casually as she was dressing that I made love "like a canary." I thought at first she was criticizing my expertise, but she soon enlightened me. It was only my haste she was referring to, comparing it to the desultory thump with which the little birds acquit themselves of their conjugal duties. Then she musingly recalled one of her previous lovers, probably the best she ever had. He promised to take her as soon as they went to bed and not to leave her till sunrise. And he had kept his word, hammering away until the first gleams of dawn. "Of course," she added punctiliously, "we did go to bed late and the nights are quite short at that time of year."

This reminded me of the story of Monsieur Seguin's little goat, who made it a point of honor to fight the wolf all night and not let herself be eaten up till the first ray of sunlight.

"It would be a good thing, as a matter of fact," said Rachel, "if you thought *I* was going to eat *you* up as soon as you stopped."

Immediately when she said this I saw she looked rather like a wolf, with her black brows and flared nostrils and big hungry mouth. We laughed once more. The last time. For I knew her traveling accountant's brain had totaled up my inadequacy and located another bed to lie on.

Like a canary . . . In the six months since the phrase was uttered it has developed long and deep in me. I had known for a long time that one of the most frequent forms of sexual fiasco is *ejaculatio praecox,* the sexual act insufficiently held back and deferred. Rachel's accusation has wide implications: it tries to place me on the brink of impotence, and what's more reveals the great misunderstanding of the human couple, the enormous frustration of women, always being fertilized and never fulfilled.

"You don't give a damn about *my* pleasure!"

And I can't but admit it. When I engulfed and annexed Rachel with all my body, the last thing I thought about was what might be going on behind those closed eyelids, inside that little Hebrew shepherd's head.

"You sate yourself with raw flesh and go straight back to your car bodies."

It was true. And it's also true that a man eating bread doesn't bother about whether the loaf is satisfied or not.

"You reduce me to the level of a steak."

Maybe, if one meekly accepts the "virility code" women have evolved to protect their weakness. But, to begin with, there's nothing degrading about likening love to eating. Many religions make a similar comparison—first and foremost Christianity, with the eucharist. What really needs taking to pieces is the exclusively feminine notion of virility that measures it in terms of sexual power, the latter consisting simply in postponing the sexual act as long as possible. This makes it a matter of abnegation, so that the term *potency* ought to be taken in the Aristotelian sense of *potential,* the very opposite of the act itself. Sexual potency thus becomes the converse and in a sense the negation of the sexual act. It is the promise of the act, a promise never kept, the act indefinitely veiled, held back, suspended. Woman is power or potency, man is act. And so man is naturally impotent, naturally out of step with woman's slow, vegetative ripenings. Unless he meekly submits to her rule and her rhythm and slaves away hammer and tongs to strike a spark of joy out of the dilatory flesh presented to him.

"You're not a lover, you're an ogre."

By uttering this simple sentence, Rachel has conjured up the ghost of a monstrous child, both terrifyingly precocious and disconcertingly infantile, and the memory of him has taken sovereign and irresistible possession of me. Nestor. I always thought he would come back into my life in force. In fact he never really went out of it, but since his death he has left the rope slack, contenting himself with a little tug from time to time, unimportant, sometimes even amusing, just so that I shouldn't forget. My new sinister writing and Rachel's departure warn me his power is about to be restored.

January 10, 1938. I was looking recently at one of those

school photographs they take every year in June just before school closes. Among all those faces frozen into hangdog expressions the thinnest and most peaked is mine. Champdavoine and Lutigneaux are there, one grimacing under his clown's thatch sticking out in points like an artichoke, the other with eyes shut and sly face, as if meditating some mischief behind the pretense of taking a nap. Not a sign of Nestor, although the photograph was certainly taken while he was still alive. But actually it was just like him to get out of this slightly ridiculous ceremony, and especially to leave no commonplace trace of his life behind before he died.

I must have been about eleven and at the beginning of my second year at St. Christopher's. So I was not a new boy any more. But although my unhappiness was no longer that of the first uprooting and straying into the unknown, in this calmer, more considered and apparently final form it was all the more profound. At that time, I remember, I had counted all my woes, and looked for no gleam of hope from any direction. I had crossed out the teachers, and the world of the mind into which they were supposed to initiate us. I had got to the point—but have I ever been at any other?—of considering every author, historical personage or book, any educational subject whatever, as automatically null and void as soon as it was annexed by adults and dished out to us as spiritual nourishment. But here and there, leafing through dictionaries, picking up what I could in textbooks, watching out for fleeting allusions to what really interested me in French or history lessons, I started to build up a culture of my own, a personal Pantheon that included Alcibiades and Pontius Pilate, Caligula and Hadrian, Frederick William I and Barras, Talleyrand and Rasputin. There was a certain way of referring to a politician or writer—condemning him of course, but that was not enough, there had to be something else as well—which made me prick up my ears and suspect this might be one of mine. I would then start an inquiry, a sort of preliminary to beatification, carried out with all the means at my disposal, at the conclusion of which the gates of my Pantheon would either open or stay shut.

I was puny and ugly, with straight black hair framing a swarthy face that had a trace of both the Arab and the gypsy, a gaunt and awkward body, rough and clumsy movements. But above all I must have possessed some fatal trait that singled me out as the object for the attacks of even the most cowardly, the blows of even the weakest. I was the unhoped-for proof that they too might dominate and humiliate. As soon as the bell rang for recess I would be on the ground, and I was rarely able to get up again before we had to go back into the classroom.

Pelsenaire was a new boy, but his physical strength and the simplicity of his personality had at once won him a prominent place in the hierarchy of the class. He derived a large part of his prestige from an incredibly wide leather belt he wore around his black smock. I afterward learned it was made out of a horse's bellyband; it had a steel buckle with no fewer than three tongues. He had a square head with a blond cowlick, a regular-featured, expressionless face, and bright eyes with a very direct glance. He would walk among the groups of boys with his thumbs in his belt, impressively clumping the hobnailed boots which could on occasion strike showers of sparks from the granite cobblestones of the courtyard. He was a pure creature, devoid of malice but also defenseless against evil, and, like the savages of the Pacific who succumb immediately to the germs heedlessly brought among them by white men, he contracted unkindness, cruelty and hatred the very day I revealed to him the complexity of my heart.

"Tattooing" had suddenly become all the rage in school. One of the day boys did a trade in India ink and sharp pens with which you could mark the skin deeply without piercing it. We used to spend hours "tattooing" one another's palms, wrists and knees with letters, words and pictures—either just nonsense or vague symbols modeled on graffiti we'd seen on walls and in lavatories.

Pelsenaire felt the charm of our new pastime but lacked the imagination and skill to find a decoration for himself in proportion to his dignity. So he was interested right away when I nonchalantly flaunted a piece of paper on which I'd drawn as best I could a heart transfixed by an arrow. Blood dripped from the wound, and the whole thing was encircled with the words "Always Thine." I put the finishing touch to his enchantment by telling him I'd copied this wonder off the chest of a friend of mine who was a non-commissioned officer in the Foreign Legion. Then I offered myself as tattooist if he would like to bear these illustrious inscriptions on the inside of his left thigh, a site at once discreet and easily exhibited.

The operation took a whole evening study period. I sat on the floor under Pelsenaire's desk and worked away with loving care, screened from the attention of the master on duty by the books, satchels and bodies of the boys sitting near. The job was made more difficult by the pressure of the thigh on the bench, which altered its shape and made it convex.

Pelsenaire was very pleased with the result but rather surprised that the original words around the bleeding heart, "Always Thine," had become just "A T." I brazenly told him the members of the Foreign Legion always used this abbreviation. Pelsenaire seemed satisfied for the time being.

But the following evening, during the six o'clock break, he took me aside with an air that boded no good. Someone must have put him wise, for he attacked me right away about the initials.

"They're your initials," he said. " 'Abel Tiffauges.' Get rid of that nonsense immediately!"

I was unmasked. So I staked everything and did what I'd been dreaming of doing for weeks. I went up to him and put my hands on the famous belt, one on each hip, and slid them and myself very slowly forward until they joined behind his back. Then I put my head on his heart.

Pelsenaire must have wondered what was happening, because for a moment he didn't move. But then his right hand slowly rose, following the same tempo as that I'd adopted myself, and hit me flat on the face, and a sudden shove hurled me on to my back several yards away. Then he turned around and walked off, the nails of his boots sending up trails of sparks.

After that, having discovered the delights of mastery, he heaped humiliations and ill-usage on me. And I idiotically submitted. I was only too glad to let him have half of my portions at mealtimes, because I had no appetite, and it was with real, though concealed, happiness that I agreed to clean and polish his wonderful boots every morning. I've always loved touching shoes.

But these after all fairly reasonable demands were not enough. His infected soul required harsher satisfactions. So he decided I had to eat grass. Every day at the start of the midday break he used to push me into the sparse green patch surrounding the statue of our patron saint, and, sitting on my back, chin jutting out brutishly, he would thrust handfuls of weeds into my mouth, and I would munch them up as best I could so that they wouldn't choke me. A group of spectators used to watch this operation, and even now I still feel a flash of hatred and indignation when I think that not once did any of them, so quick when it came to catching me out and punishing me for something, ever raise a finger to put a stop to what was going on.

My servitude ended only by reaching its climax. It was at the beginning of autumn, when days and nights of rain had transformed the playground into a cesspool. The gravel and cinders were buried beneath a deceptively soft layer of mud and dead leaves. We were cold, undernourished, unwashed orphans, steeped in a damp that made our clothes stick to us like natural membranes, scales or carapaces. The effort to separate oneself

from this shell produced a horrible sensation, whether it came
from undressing at night or from an inner shrinking at any other
time: your flesh crept, your muscles knotted, your genitals
shriveled. That particular day our games were unusually violent,
almost desperate, as if by behaving like warriors or wild beasts
we were asserting ourselves against the gloom and harshness of
our condition. Fists thudded hollowly on faces, boys were tripped
and sent flying into the mud, others wrestled panting on the
ground. There were few shouts and no insults, but anyone who
fell grabbed handfuls of mud and flung it at his opponent to
make sure that he got dirty too. As for me, I skulked behind the
pillars around the yard, trying to keep out of the way of the con-
frontations—and there were many—that might be fatal to me.
For once I thought I need not worry about Pelsenaire; in this
grand melee he would not bother about so puny an adversary. So
I was not unduly terrified when I suddenly bumped into him in
avoiding a ball that came shooting at me as if out of a cannon.
He must have had a peculiar fall on to just one knee, for he was
covered in mud halfway up one leg, and otherwise untouched.
As I tried to slip off, he caught me by the arm, stuck out his
knee, and ordered me to clean it. I hastily knelt down and set to
work with a somewhat dubious handkerchief. But that wasn't
quick enough for Pelsenaire.

"Is that all you've got? Lick it off, then!"

His thigh and knee and the upper part of his calf were all
sculpted in shiny black mud, flawless except for a complicated
purple wound in the middle, under the kneecap. Out of it oozed
a bright red streak turning first to ocher, then to a darker and
darker brown as it mixed with the mud. I licked around the
wound, surrounding it with a gray halo. Several times I had to
spit out earth and bits of cinder. Blood went on welling out of
the wound. My eyes were right up against its whimsical geography—swollen pulp, whitish weals of abraded skin, inturned
edges. I passed my tongue swiftly over it once, not so lightly that

it did not cause a tremor, making the pad of muscle around the kneecap rise up in a kind of rictus. Then I licked it a second time, more slowly. Finally my lips rested on those of the wound and stayed there indefinitely.

I don't know exactly what happened next. I think I was seized with a fit of shuddering, convulsions even, and was carted off to the infirmary. I seem to remember I was ill for several days. But I have only a vague recollection of this episode in my life at St. Christopher's. What I am sure of is that the teachers saw fit to inform my father of my indisposition, and that the random explanation they thought up, with a grotesque irony of which they were unconscious, was that I had upset my stomach by eating too many sweets.

January 13, 1938. I used to tell Rachel: "There are two sorts of women. The woman-trinket that one can handle and manipulate and look at, and who is an ornament in a man's life. And the woman-landscape that one visits, enters into, may get lost in. The first is vertical, the second horizontal. The first is voluble, capricious, demanding, a coquette. The other is taciturn, obstinate, possessive, dreamy, and has a long memory."

She used to listen, frowning, trying to spot if there was anything detrimental to her in what I was saying. Then, to make her laugh, I'd put it differently. "There are two sorts of women," I'd say. "Those with a Parisian basin and those with a Mediterranean"—my hands indicating first narrowness, then width. She would smile at this, wondering with a trace of anxiety whether I did not put her in the second class—to which, beyond the shadow of a doubt, she belongs.

For this emancipated young woman so well able to fend for herself is undeniably a woman-landscape, a Mediterranean basin (her family actually comes from Salonica). She has an ample, welcoming, maternal body. I was careful not to tell her this for fear of making her angry—for her, speech is always either caress

or aggression, never a mirror of truth. I was even more careful
to keep to myself the thoughts that arose in me when, for example, I put my hand on her hipbone, which is highly developed,
like a promontory dominating all the rest of the landscape. Between the two ranges of the thighs the belly recedes, a chilly
coomb hollowed out with anxiety. I would reflect on the mystery
of the real sexual center in a woman. It certainly isn't the decapitated belly that may lay claim to the title, except by virtue of
the rough apparent symmetry between men's and women's bodies. A woman's real sexual center. It would probably be better
to look for it higher up, where the breast triumphantly bears its
two horns of abundance.

The Bible casts a strange light on this question. Reading the
beginning of the Book of Genesis, one is struck by a flagrant
inconsistency that disfigures the venerable text. "So God created
man in his own image, in the image of God created he *him;* male
and female created he *them.* And God blessed them, and God
said unto them, Be fruitful and multiply, and replenish the earth
and subdue it. . . ." This sudden transition from the singular to
the plural is downright unintelligible, especially as the creation
of the woman out of Adam's rib does not occur till much later,
in the second chapter of Genesis. But all is clear if one retains
the singular throughout my quotation. "So God created man in
his own image, that is, at once male and female. . . . And God
said to him, Be fruitful, multiply . . ." etc. Later he sees that
the solitude implied by hermaphroditism is undesirable, so he
puts Adam to sleep and takes from him not merely a rib, but
all his feminine sexual parts, and makes these into an independent being.

One understands then why woman has no sexual parts, properly speaking. It is because she *is* herself a sexual part—a sexual
part of man, too cumbersome for him to carry permanently and
therefore deposited outside himself for most of the time and
taken up when needed. Moreover, the quality that distinguishes

man from animals is this very power of equipping himself at any moment with an instrument, tool or arm that he needs, but that he can get rid of straight away, whereas the lobster has to drag his two pincers about with him everywhere. And just as man's hand is a sort of grappling hook that enables him to adjust a hammer, sword or fountain pen according to his needs, so his sex is the sort of grappling hook of the sexual parts rather than the sexual part itself.

If this is true, we can only condemn marriage's claim to knit together again as closely and indissolubly as possible what was dissociated. Let no man join what God has put asunder! A vain command! One cannot escape the more or less conscious fascination of the old Adam, armed with all his reproductive apparatus, having to live lying down, perhaps incapable of walking, certainly of working, a constant prey to amorous transports of unimaginable perfection, in which he was both possessor and possessed, except—who knows?—during the periods when he was pregnant by himself. And then what must our fabulous ancestor have been like, man-cum-woman become cum-child into the bargain, like one of those nests of dolls that fit one inside the other!

The image may seem laughable. But I, though I am so lucid about the aberration of marriage, am touched by it. It awakens in me a sort of atavistic nostalgia for a life that is superhuman, set by its very plenitude above the vicissitudes of time and old age. For if there is a fall of man in Genesis, it is not in the episode of the apple: on the contrary, the acquisition of the knowledge of good and evil is a step upward. No, the fall consists in the breaking into three of the original Adam, letting fall woman and child from man, and thus creating three unfortunates: the child, eternal orphan; woman, solitary and afraid and always in search of a protector; and man, light and alert, but like a king stripped of all his attributes and made to work at degrading tasks.

18 THE OGRE

Marriage's sole object is to turn the clock back and restore the original Adam. But is that ridiculous solution the only one?

January 16, 1938. When I left St. Christopher's, the soul of the old place had already deserted it four years before, and the whole religious, school and prison universe was peopled only by the shadows of children and priests. Nestor had died of suffocation in the cellar—dead for everybody else, but for me more living than ever.

Nestor was the only son of the school janitor, and anyone who has had any experience with that kind of institution will know at once the power his situation conferred on him. Living both with his parents and in the school, he enjoyed the advantages both of the boarders and the day boys. His father often entrusted minor domestic tasks to him, and he came and went as he pleased through all the buildings, owning keys to almost every door, and at the same time was free to go "into town" whenever he liked, outside of the hours for lessons and study.

But all that would have been nothing if he had not been Nestor. Looking back, I ask myself questions about him that never came into my mind when I was his friend. He was a monstrous creature with something of genius and something of magic about him. Was he a grown-up dwarf, whose development was arrested while he still had the stature of a child, or was he a baby giant, as his shape suggested? I couldn't say. Such words of his as I can recollect, perhaps only approximately, would bear witness to staggering precociousness, if it were certain that Nestor was the same age as the other boys. But nothing is less sure, and it may be that he was retarded, backward, fixed forever in childhood, born in school and doomed to remain there. One word emerges clearly amid all the uncertainties, and I shall not keep it back. It is the word "intemporal." I have spoken of eternity with reference to myself. So it is not surprising that Nestor, from

whom I undoubtedly derive, should, like me, escape the measure of time.

He was very fat, obese in fact, and this lent his gestures and
even his gait a majestic slowness and made him formidable in
fights. He couldn't stand the heat, dressed lightly even when
it was very cold, and perspired ceaselessly the rest of the year.
As if weighed down by his abnormal memory and intelligence,
he spoke slowly, with a studied, artificial, professorial solemn-
ity that was completely unnatural, often raising a forefinger when
he said something particularly sententious, which we would all
agree was marvelous though we didn't understand a word of
it. At first I thought he expressed himself solely in quotations
he had picked up in his reading, but then I entered his orbit
and realized my error. He held undisputed sway over all the
boys, and the masters themselves seemed afraid of him and
allowed him privileges that struck me as exorbitant at first,
before I knew who he was.

The first example I witnessed of his privileged position struck
me as irresistibly funny, because I was not yet aware of the
formidable aura that surrounded everything to do with him.
In every classroom a black-painted box by the teacher's chair
served as a wastepaper basket. Whenever a boy wanted to go
to the lavatory, he asked permission by raising two fingers in
the form of a V. When the master in charge nodded, the boy
would go over to the box, plunge his hand into it, and go to
the door with a handful of paper.

At first I didn't know Nestor dispensed with the V sign, because he sat at the back of the class. But I was immediately
filled with respect for the nonchalance with which he went over
to the box and the scene that ensued. He started examining
the various bits of paper at the top with meticulous attention,
then, apparently dissatisfied with the choice offered there, rum-
maged noisily in the box and brought up older balls and scraps
of paper, testing them at great length and even, apparently,

reading what was written on them. The attention of the whole class was irresistibly drawn to these goings on, and the teacher himself went on with the geography lesson in a slow, mechanical voice, with longer and longer silences. I ought to have been struck by the anxious quiet that hung over the whole class, when if any other boy had done what Nestor did there would have been a tremendous uproar. But there again, I was a new boy at St. Christopher's, and I bent over my desk and laughed till I cried, until at last the boy next to me gave me a few sharp digs in the ribs. I didn't understand why he was so cross, any more than I understood what he muttered between his teeth as Nestor finally selected a notepad covered with drawings. "It isn't the paper itself that matters to him," he said. "It's what's written on it and who wrote it." This couple of sentences —and many others I shall try to remember—pinpoint Nestor's mystery without revealing it.

He had an appetite out of the ordinary, as I had occasion to see every day, for though he ate with his family at night he lunched at midday in the refectory. Every table was set for eight and placed under a "head" whose job it was to see that everyone got fair shares. By one of those paradoxes which ceased to surprise me only after several months' initiation, Nestor wasn't head of his table. But he was all the better off, because the boy who *was* head—and all the rest at the table, for that matter—not only let him help himself to a good quarter of every dish but also surrounded him, like an antique god, with offerings of food.

Nestor ate seriously, laboriously and fast, stopping only to wipe away the sweat that ran down his forehead on to his glasses. There was something of Silenus about him, with his pendent cheeks, round belly and large rump. His life's rhythm was the trilogy ingestion-digestion-defecation, and these three operations were surrounded by general respect. But this was only Nestor's visible face. His hidden face, which only I suspected, was signs, the deciphering of signs. This was the main business of his life—this and the absolute despotism he wielded over all of St. Christopher's.

Signs and the deciphering of signs. What signs? And what did their deciphering reveal? If I could answer that question my whole life would be changed, and not only my life but also —I dare write it because I know no one will ever read these lines—the course of history. Probably Nestor had taken only a few steps in this direction, but my sole ambition is to follow in his footsteps and perhaps go a little farther, thanks to the longer time allowed me and to the inspiration emanating from his shade.

January 20, 1938. The viscous self. I hear a good, a very good piece of news and am filled with joy. Soon after, it is denied, and nothing is left of it, absolutely nothing. And yet there is! By a strange example of remanence, the joy that filled me and then withdrew has left behind a pool of happiness, just as the sea leaves clear pools of water that reflect the sky. There is someone inside me who has not yet realized that the good news was false, and who absurdly goes on rejoicing.

When Rachel left me, I took the matter lightly. And I still go on regarding the break as unimportant, even beneficial from a certain point of view, because I'm sure it opens the way to great changes, great things. But I have another self, the viscous self. It didn't understand the break at all at first. It never understands anything at first. It's a heavy, rancorous, moody self, always weltering in tears and semen, obstinately attached to its habits and its past. It took weeks to understand that Rachel wasn't coming back. Now it has understood. And it weeps. I carry it deep inside me like a wound, this innocent and tender being, slightly deaf, slightly shortsighted, so easily taken in, so slow to muster itself up against misfortune. Without a doubt it is my viscous self that makes me search the icy corridors of St.

Christopher's for a small inconsolable ghost, crushed by the general hostility and even more by a particular friendship—as though, twenty years later, I could take his sorrow on to my man's shoulders, and make him laugh!

January 25, 1938. St. Christopher's Academy, Beauvais, occupies the old buildings of the Cistercian abbey of the same name, founded in 1152 and suppressed in 1785. All that remains of the Middle Ages are the vaults of the restored abbey church. The main part of the school is housed in the huge abbey building put up by Jean Aubert in the eighteenth century. These details are not unimportant, because the atmosphere of rigor and austerity imposed on the pupils certainly had something to do with the origins and history of the walls surrounding us. Nowhere was this atmosphere more evident than in the cloister, an undistinguished piece of architecture dating back only to the seventeenth century, which served as a playground for the boarders in the morning before the day boys arrived and in the evening after they had gone home. We had to keep to the cloister itself and could only admire across the surrounding balustrade the little garden carefully tended by Nestor senior. It was planted with sycamores, which in summer shed a blue-green light; in the middle was a battered fountain, its basin filled with clumps of fern. The melancholy emanating from this place was rendered heavier, almost breathable, by the high walls that rose on all sides.

So in the absence of the day boys, who constituted our living link with the outside world, we gathered twice a day in the green prison that we referred to among ourselves as the aquarium. Noisy games and running about were forbidden there, and in any case the spirit of the place would have been enough to stifle any spontaneity. But we could walk up and down and talk, so that the aquarium, even more than the chapel, the refectory or the dormitories, was the normal meeting place

for the boarders, the point of convergence for a hundred and
fifty children shut up in the secluded and sequestered life of
school. Nestor appeared there seldom; nor, as I have said earlier, did he join us in the refectory in the evening. But he was
far from absent, and his two factotums, Champdavoine and
Lutigneaux, were charged with transmitting his messages and
orders. Their usual subject was a kind of trade in influence
which arose partly out of the ingenious system of punishments
and exemptions that operated at St. Christopher's, and partly
out of the occult power Nestor exercised in this important
sphere.

I knew the whole gamut of punishments at St. Christopher's
only too well—I ran through it continually from one end to the
other. There was "squad," a long file of boys who had to
walk in silence round the covered way of the playground for
fifteen minutes, half an hour, an hour, or even more; "sequestration," which forbade the boy being punished to speak except
in answer to a question from a master; and "erectum," which
meant you had to eat, standing up, at a separate table in the
refectory. But I'd have undergone any of these a thousand times
to avoid ever hearing the horrible phrase announcing the real
anguish and humiliation: "Tiffauges *ad colaphum!*" That meant
you had to leave the classroom, go up two flights of stairs and
along a deserted corridor, and finally open the door into the
outer office of the prefect of studies. There you knelt down at a
prie-dieu, strangely set in the middle of the room, facing the
door of the office, and rang a bell that stood within reach on
the floor. A prie-dieu, the kneeling, and the tinkle of the bell—
I can see that ritual now only as a diabolical parody of the
elevation in the Mass. For it certainly was not to perform an
act of worship that you went *ad colaphum!* After the bell had
been rung, the wait might vary from a few seconds to an hour;
it was this refinement that made the punishment so unbearable.
Eventually, sooner or later, the door of the office would be

flung open and the prefect would appear, his cassock rustling
furiously and holding a penalty-slip in his left hand. He would
dash at the prie-dieu, give the guilty party a series of hard slaps
on the face, shove the note proving he'd been disciplined into
his hand, and vanish.

These various punishments could be got out of by a system
of exemptions calculated with casuistical subtlety. The exemptions were little cardboard rectangles—white, blue, pink or
green, according to their value—which were awarded for good
marks or getting first place in tests. Thus we knew that for our
pastors and masters six hours of squad were equal to one day's
sequestration, two days of *erectum* or one *colaphus,* and could
be redeemed by being first in a test once, second twice, third
three times, or by getting more than sixteen out of twenty four
times. But often a boy would prefer to take his punishment and
keep his exemptions, because these would also buy a "little
exeat" (Sunday afternoon) or a "big exeat" (all day Sunday).

But the system remained almost always merely theoretical
and so to speak paralyzed, for in defiance of the communion
of saints and the revertibility of merits, the priests who ran the
school had decreed that exemptions were not transferable—the
number of the pupil each was awarded to was marked on the
back of the card—and so could benefit only those who had
earned them. And of course it was the very boys who collected
most of them—the clever ones, the grinds, the masters' favorites
—who needed them least, because some mysterious protection
seemed to hover over them and ward off squad, sequestration,
erectum and *colaphus*. It took all Nestor's genius to remedy this
imperfection.

February 2, 1938. All day I've been twisting an elastic band
around my fingers. Tomorrow I'm going to have to struggle to do
without this false and strange *presence,* rather like a wedding
ring, though more irritating and less symbolic. The elastic band

was like a little hand clinging to mine: it clenched and attempted
to hang on when you tried to pull it away.

February 8, 1938. Sometimes you have to touch bottom before you at last see a glimmer of hope pierce the clouds. It was
the *colaphus* that revealed to me for the first time the astonishing protection I was to be the object of, and which still hovers
over me.

There had been a lot of noise in the part of the classroom
where I was lurking, and I can't really remember what contribution I made to it. But from the dais the horrible sentence had
fallen on my head: "Tiffauges *ad colaphum!*" and the inevitable
shudder of sadistic pleasure had run down the aisles. I got up as
in a nightmare and made my way to the door through the tainted
silence of forty held breaths. It was December, the brink of what
seemed a winter which would last forever. I was still rather battered after my troubles with Pelsenaire, who appeared to be unaware of my existence since I had come out of the infirmary.
The courtyard was filled with damp twilight: beyond the black
lattice of the chestnut trees you could make out, to the left, the
deserted playground, and, at the end, the urinal sticking up
boldly like the reeking altar of boy-ness. Someone had left a
ball on the covered way round the playground; I gave it an aim-
less kick. In the dusk some black smocks hanging on chipped
pegs looked like a family of bats. A refusal to exist rose in me
like a silent clamor: a secret cry, a stifled howl coming from my
heart and merging with the vibration of motionless objects. Both
they and I were being hurtled toward the void, toward death,
with a furious thrust that bowed me down. I sat down with my
feet in the gutter. I put my arms around my knees: at least solitude always left me these two twin dolls, with square, bald,
battered heads, that were me. I brushed my lips over a black
scab in the middle of the checkered skin, dirty in some parts,
dry and dusty in others. Then I breathed in again with relief the

familiar smell of polished tiles. I realized I had just hit the bottom of darkness, hit it so hard I was still dazed as I went up the stairs toward the ordeal. The prefect's outer office was in semi-darkness, and I certainly was not going to switch on the light. From the prie-dieu you could see, standing out distinctly against the white wall, a garish picture of Christ wearing the crown of thorns and being struck in the face by a soldier. The reading of signs—the great business of my life—was still so unknown to me that I didn't think of making the obvious parallel. Now I know that any human face, however vile, becomes the face of Christ when it is struck.

A bell rang in the distance. The floor creaked. A menacing ray of light filtered through under the prefect's door. I crouched over the prie-dieu, holding my breath. Minutes went by, but I couldn't bring myself to ring the bell *ad colaphum*. Where was the bell? I groped on the floor for it in the dark. It wasn't long before my fingers encountered the curved wooden handle of the heavy, treacherous little brass object. I picked it up as carefully as if it had been a sleeping snake and felt more at ease once my fingers imprisoned the clapper. It was made of lead, and its surface was hammered smooth as flesh, the rim worn away above and below. This bore witness to long years of service, and I was just thinking of the innumerable *colaphi* the bell had caused to rain down on boys' faces when it slipped out of my hand, hit the padded arm of the prie-dieu, and rolled thundering over the floor. Immediately the door of the office flew open and the room was flooded with light. I shut my eyes, petrified, and waited for the blow to fall.

But there was no blow. Instead I felt a sort of caress, something soft and smooth rustling over my cheek. At length I plucked up courage to look, and there was Champdavoine, wriggling and giggling as usual, and holding out the piece of paper he'd just touched against my cheek. Then he stepped back, performed a mock bow, and disappeared through a chink in the office door. A moment later his head reappeared and gave a last grimace; then the door shut behind him.

I looked at the paper: it was the penalty-slip discharging me, duly signed by the prefect of studies.

As I went back to my class, my head was singing worse than if I'd undergone a double *colaphus*. But of course I hadn't realized what was happening: I was far from suspecting I'd just witnessed the opening of the first fissure in the monolithic fate bearing down on me. From that memorable day onward, I might have stopped considering that fate as an inexorable and a priori hostile concatenation and recognized, as I've been led to do since, that it might admit of a certain complicity with my own little personal history—in short, that something of Tiffauges might enter into the course of events in general.

But the business of the *colaphus* was only a harbinger. I still had to wait a long time for the event that was to make a radical change in my position at St. Christopher's and introduce a new era in my life.

On Palm Sunday the boarders were always sent on a picnic to celebrate the end of the winter. I loathed ever having to leave the school premises. At least there my misery could coil up on itself in some semblance of warmth. But this particular excursion was especially hateful. We were divided into two groups. Those who owned bicycles formed an envied élite, like knights in an army: they went farther afield, led by a young priest on a motorcycle. I was one of the lowly footsloggers who tramped for miles in heavy boots, nagged at by a pack of grudging masters.

Just as the whistle was about to blow for our departure, something happened that caused a sensation throughout the school. Lutigneaux appeared wheeling a gleaming bicycle—Nestor's bicycle. It was a "Halcyon," garnet-red picked out in cream, with racing handlebars of chrome. On the left handlebar was an enchanting rear mirror, on the right a big bell that gave a double ring. It had whitewashed semipneumatic tires, and a luggage carrier fitted with a reflector. To crown all, it was equipped—this was very unusual at the time—with a three-speed gear.

We all expected to see Lutigneaux join the group of cyclists. But nothing of the sort. He walked right across the courtyard, the bike bouncing over the stones like a prancing horse, and came toward me, lost among the mere walkers. When he reached me he handed me the bicycle, saying simply:

"From Nestor. For the outing."

I was just as surprised as the rest of the school, though everyone immediately taxed me with unheard-of powers of dissimulation, their argument being that such an enormous favor could only be the result of a long and intimate friendship. This may seem a very tame occurrence; it would probably have passed unnoticed by anyone unfamiliar with what went on deep down in life at St. Christopher's. But even a quarter of a century later I can't refer to it without trembling still with joy and pride.

All through the week that followed, Nestor seemed to take no notice of me, and I knew enough about etiquette to realize I wasn't supposed to thank him. But the next Saturday, during the long five o'clock break after the day boys went home, Lutigneaux came and told me I was changing my place in class, and that he would help me move.

Needless to say, places were autocratically determined by the prefect of studies, who took care to thwart the boys' wishes as far as possible, separating friends and putting in the front rows the dunces and dreamers whose only wish was to be left in peace at the back of the class. Nestor alone could upset this order and substitute his own will for that of the prefect. He himself sat on the far left corner of the class by a window. In order to keep an uninterrupted eye on the courtyard he had even raised his desk on little wooden wedges and put in a pane of ordinary glass instead of the frosted glass in the rest of the classroom windows. Henceforth, by a decree which could have issued only from him, I was to sit in the same corner as he did, beside him on his right. After the sensation of the bicycle, this removal did not surprise anyone. Everyone expected it, in fact, masters as well as boys.

From then on I lived under a protection as discreet as it was effective. Not a week went by without my finding some treat in my locker. The rain of punishments appeared to be diverted from my head. The big boys who had bullied me before were mysteriously cut down to size overnight. But all this was as nothing compared to the way I was now exposed to Nestor's effulgence for the whole of lessons and study hall. His formidable bulk seemed to tilt the entire room toward the corner where he sat. For me, that corner was the real center of the class, much more than the teacher's dais with its succession of absurd and ephemeral orators.

February 12, 1938. A woman customer came in to see me. She had her little girl with her, a child of about five or six, who got scolded when they were leaving for trying to shake hands with me with her left hand. It suddenly struck me that in fact most children under seven—the age of reason!—naturally offer to shake hands with the left hand instead of the right. *Sancta simplicitas!* They know, in their innocence, that the right hand is soiled by the vilest of contacts: that every day it puts itself into the hands of murderers, priests, policemen and politicians as blithely as a whore hops into a rich man's bed, whereas the humble unobtrusive left hand keeps in the background like a vestal, reserved for sisterly clasps alone. Must remember this lesson and always hold out my left hand to children under seven.

February 16, 1938. Nestor was always writing and drawing, and I regret not having either had or kept one of his notebooks. Everything he said seemed marvelous to me, though I understood so little of it that now, a couple of decades later, I'm reduced to expressing what I can remember of it in words that are certainly not his. It is true that the time I spent with him—in fact quite a short time—is so deeply engraved in me, and so obviously connected with the tribulations I underwent later, that there is really no need to distinguish between what is really his and what ought to be ascribed to me.

Besides, if I wanted irrefutable proof that I was Nestor's heir, all I'd have to do is watch my hand gliding over the paper—my left hand, tracing letter by letter this "sinister" writing. For Nestor held that hand a long time in his own: his big, damp, heavy hand warmed my feeble fist, a bony little transparent egg which nestled there ignorant of the energies with which it was thus being charged. Nestor's whole strength, his whole dominating and destructive spirit, passed into that hand, from which flow day after day the sinister writings that are the work of us both. And the little egg has hatched. It has become this left hand with square hairy fingers and vast palm, apter for the miner's bar than for the pen.

Nestor used to hold my left hand in his right, and write and draw with his left. He may always have been left-handed. But I prefer to think proudly that he made himself write with his left hand just for me, just so that he could hold my hand without leaving off writing. What's certain is that I've never felt so close to him as on the memorable day, some weeks ago, when I realized with a shudder of holy dread that I knew how to write with my left hand—that my left hand, let loose on the paper, without experiment, training or hesitation, could cover it with a new writing quite unlike that of my right hand.

I thus have two sets of writing: one that is "adroit," pleasant, social, commercial, reflecting the masked character I pretend to be in the eyes of society; and one that is "sinister," distorted by all the "gauchenesses" of genius, full of flashes and cries—in short, inhabited by the spirit of Nestor.

February 18, 1938. Every time I see a medal of St. Christopher on the dashboard of a car left for repair, I think of the school at Beauvais and marvel at the things that constantly recur throughout my life. Some are fortuitous and almost absurd. But this one is fundamental: St. Christopher's Academy, Nestor, then, as the owner of a garage, coming once again under the patronage of the giant who was the Christ-Bearer. And that is not all. I inherited my swarthy complexion and straight black hair from my mother, who looked like a gypsy. I never had the curiosity to look into her family background—my life is cluttered up enough as it is with premonitions—but it wouldn't surprise me if there were horses and caravans there somewhere.

The same thing with my given name, Abel, which seemed just an accident to me until I came across the lines in the Bible telling of the first murder in human history. Abel was a keeper of sheep, Cain a tiller of the ground. That is, the first was a nomad and the second a sedentary. The quarrel of Cain and Abel has gone on from generation to generation, from the beginning of time down to our own day, as the atavistic opposition between nomads and sedentaries, or more exactly as the persistent persecution of the first by the second. And this hatred is far from extinct. It survives in the infamous and degrading regulations imposed on the gypsies, treated as if they were criminals, and flaunts itself on the outskirts of villages with the sign telling them to "move on."

True, Cain is cursed, and his punishment as well as his hatred for Abel is renewed from generation to generation. The Lord said to him, ". . . now art thou cursed from the earth, which hath opened her mouth to receive thy brother's blood from thy hand; When thou tillest the ground, it shall not henceforth yield unto thee her strength; a fugitive and a vagabond shalt thou be in the earth." So Cain is sentenced to what he considers the worst possible punishment: he must become a nomad, as Abel was. He greets this verdict with rebellious words and does not obey. He went out from the presence of the Lord and built a city, the first city, which he named Enoch.

Well, I maintain that this curse on farmers—who are still as hard as ever on their nomad brothers—can still be seen working today. Because the earth no longer feeds them, the peasants are obliged to pack up and leave. They wander in thousands from one region to another: and in the nineteenth century, when the right to vote was linked to a residential qualification, it was in the knowledge that this excluded a large and fluctuating mass of voters, rootless and therefore not right-thinking. Settling in the towns, they form the proletariat of the great industrial cities.

And I, hidden among the sitters but not really sedentary, not really right-thinking, I don't move about, admittedly, but I do repair motorcars, the instruments par excellence of migration. And I possess my soul in patience because I know the day will come when heaven will tire of the crimes of the sedentaries and rain down fire on their heads. Then, like Cain, they will be flung in disorder on the roads, fleeing madly from their accursed cities and the earth that refuses to nourish them. And I, Abel, the only one who will be smiling and satisfied, will spread the great wings I keep hidden under my garage owner's disguise and, with a kick at their shadowy skulls, fly up among the stars.

February 25, 1938. One day Nestor took a little square cardboard box out of his desk and put it to my ear. I heard a modulated, melodious hum, like that of an airplane flying at very high altitude. My friend looked at me through narrowed eyes: the lenses of his spectacles were as thick as magnifying glasses. He put the box down on the table. It at once rose on one of its corners and started to dance with a grace so slow it was majestic. The hum grew louder and deeper as the box twirled nearer the ground. Finally it sank down on one of its faces and after a few more turns on its own axis lay still. I went over and looked with interest at the printing on it: "Invented in 1852 by the famous

French physicist Léon Foucault to demonstrate the rotation of the earth." Nestor picked up the box, opened it, and explained gravely: "It's a gyroscope—the key to the absolute."

It was composed of two concentric steel rings soldered together at right angles. One ring formed the circumference of a heavyish disc of red copper, with a rod through the center forming a diameter of the other ring and enabling it to turn with the disc. There was a hole in the rod, and Nestor threaded a piece of string through it and wound it around the rod. Then he gave the string a violent jerk: it unwound with a crack, and the disc started to hum. Nestor shook out of the box a little metal stand in the shape of the Eiffel Tower and balanced the gyroscope on it. The graceful dance began at once. The little device, so simple, severe and geometrical, turned on its fixed point in an ever widening circle, the stately slowness of its revolution contrasting with the furious gyration of the disc inside it, just as hummingbirds seem to fly all the more slowly, and even stay in one place longer, the faster they move their tiny wings.

The vibration of the Eiffel Tower against the wood of the desk made a low buzzing sound that soon attracted the attention of the other boys and of the master in charge. Nestor took no notice. He was leaning on one elbow, half turned toward me, absorbed in contemplation of the gyroscope and its dance.

"A cosmic toy," he murmured, "a perfectly faithful little imitation of the gravitation of the earth. For, do you know, M'Abel, Abel mine, this motion you're looking at doesn't exist! It's you, it's St. Christopher's, it's the whole of France, that's dancing! A gyroscope can escape the earth's motion, and that's why it appears to turn. In fact, it's we ourselves who are turning. Here, hold it in your hand."

And he plucked it off its stand and held it out to me. I closed my hand around the little living mechanism and immediately felt in it, in my wrist and even in my arm, a great thrust, an irresistible wrench.

"It feels like a toad!" I cried.

"It's you who are the toad, pretty Fauges," said Nestor. "You're hanging onto a fixed point, but the earth wants to turn and you can't stop it. What you feel in your hand is the stillness of the gyroscope contrasting with the rotation of the earth whirling you around. Give it back. It's my base when things go wrong —my pocket absolute."

February 28, 1938. I don't know whether it's the result of this going back into my childhood the last couple of months, but I'm haunted by the foolish rhyme old Marie used to sing to lull me to sleep on a rainy day. It used to make my soul, numb with unhappiness, curl up in the depths of its darkest cave.

> *When I think*
> *My heart doth sink*
> *Like a sponge*
> *That you plunge*
> *In a gulf o'*
> *Sulphur*
> *Where you suffer such woe*
> *From top to toe*
> *That when I think*
> *My heart doth sink. . . .*

March 2, 1938. He had taken to speaking without moving his lips, probably more through love of dissembling than necessity, for he enjoyed such immunity from the masters he could afford to take much greater liberties than that. Sometimes he would gaze at me for a long time, his eyes narrowed shrewdly, and voice words whose very obscurity plunged me into a whirl of happiness.

"One day they'll all go away," he might say. "But I'll still have you left, though I shan't be here myself. You're not handsome or clever, but you're mine as no other boy at St. Christopher's has ever been. In the end you'll make me unnecessary, and that will be a good thing."

Or on another occasion, shrugging his shoulders:

"I've planted all my seeds in that little body. You'll have to look for a suitable climate for them to bloom in. You'll recognize that your life has succeeded by sproutings and blossomings that will frighten you."

But now I fully understand the prediction he made one day. He took me by the chin and made me open my mouth.

"Soon," he said, "these little teeth will grow bigger. M'Abel will have formidable fangs, and the gnashing of his jaws will sound in every ear like a terrible threat."

And perhaps I shall know later, in the light of events now preparing, what he meant when he said:

"If you keep on knocking long enough at the same door it always opens in the end. Or else there is a chink in another door nearby that you hadn't noticed; and that's even better."

And again:

"Alpha and omega must be linked with one stroke."

I only ever saw him read one novel, but he knew pages of that by heart and would suddenly start reciting it, without moving his lips, when a lesson became excessively boring. It was *The Golden Snare* by James Oliver Curwood. Nestor would lean over to me mysteriously and mutter into my ear, as if it were some heady secret:

" '*If you take a canoe over Lake Athabasca and steer north up Peace river, you get to Great Slave Lake; then, if you go up the Mackenzie river to the Arctic Circle . . .*' "

The hero of the story was Bram, a huge wild half-breed, part English, part Indian, part Eskimo, who wandered alone over terrible icy wastes drawn by a team of wolves. And to say he howled like a wolf was not just a figure of speech.

" '*He had suddenly thrown back his great head, sending up a cavernous roar from his throat and chest,*' " Nestor would recite. *"'At first it was like a peal of thunder, but it ended in a sharp plaintive wail that could be heard for several miles across the level plain. It was the call of the leader to the pack; of the animal-man to his brothers. . . .'"*

This wild cry was answered by the roaring of the north wind, but sometimes also by *"the music of the skies, the strange fantastic harmony which announces the Northern Lights. Sometimes it was a shrill whistle, sometimes quite a gentle murmur rather like the purring of a cat, and sometimes it resembled the metallic buzzing of a bee."*

Bram's cry, the howling of the wolves and the wind, the metallic music of the Northern Lights, all these brought into the confined, secluded, promiscuous life we led at St. Christopher's a whole other world that was virgin and inhuman, white and pure as the void. For me its appeal merged with the silent clamor I'd heard that December evening as I sat in the yard, on my way, as I thought, *ad colaphum*. But it enriched and amplified my own experience and filled it with the harsh charms of Nestor's stories. He told me rapturously of the blizzard howling among the black pines, of the icy gulfs you went over crossing a frozen lake, of the monotonous "zip,zip,zip" of snowshoes, of packs of wolves on the prowl in the chill night, and also of the log cabin, crazily built and half buried in drifts, where the trapper takes refuge at night and lights a big fire to bring back the warmth to body and soul.

Years have gone by, but I have not yet really escaped from that atmosphere of miasma and moldiness in which my childhood died. And for me Canada is still the beyond that makes the absurd troubles that imprison me seem as nothing. Dare I say I've not given up? One day, M'Abel, you'll see! One day!

March 6, 1938. Went to the police station to renew my driver's license. Sad resigned queues up to the counter, to be yapped at by bad-tempered ugly women. What we need is a nice tyrant to abolish, with a stroke of the pen, certificates, identity cards, passports, police records, registrations and documents of all kinds, all that nightmare of paper whose usefulness, if any, is out of all proportion to the work and trouble it gives.

And yet it is true that an institution rarely survives without the consent and even the positive will of the majority. Thus the death penalty is not a bloodthirsty survival from more barbarous times: all the public opinion polls show that the great majority of people are still blindly attached to it. As for all the administrative red tape, that must correspond to some requirement of the greatest number, or rather to an elementary fear— the fear of being a brute beast. For to live without papers is to live like a beast. People who have no nationality or who are illegitimate know only a paper reality. These reflections have led me to invent a little fable.

Once upon a time there was a man who had a brush with the police. When it was over there was still a file that might pop up at any moment, so the man decided to destroy it. But once he got inside police headquarters, of course he couldn't find his file, and the only thing to do was destroy the whole lot, which he proceeded to do by setting fire to the place with a can of gasoline.

The success of this exploit, together with his belief that papers were an out-and-out evil from which mankind ought to be delivered, encouraged the man to persevere. He used all his money to buy cans of gasoline and systematically went around all the police stations, town halls, and so on, setting fire to all the files and records and archives. And as he worked alone he was never caught.

But he noticed a strange thing: in all the districts in which he had operated, the people walked with a stoop and uttered inarticulate sounds instead of speech. They were beginning to change into beasts. Then the man realized that in his attempt to free mankind he had reduced it to the level of animals. And this because the human soul is made of paper.

March 8, 1938. We were allowed to talk in the refectory in the evening. There were only a hundred and fifty of us, but the noise rose steadily *proprio motu,* since everyone had to keep raising his voice to make himself heard. When it reached its full flowering the racket formed an edifice of sound that exactly filled the big room, and the master in charge would bring it tumbling down with a single blast on his whistle. There was something vertiginous about the ensuing silence. Then a murmur would run from table to table, a fork would jingle on a plate, a laugh be heard: the network of sounds started to weave itself once more, the cycle started all over again.

We weren't allowed to talk at the midday meal, when the half-boarders ate with the boarders, making nearly two hundred and fifty in all. Hours of squad rained down on the talkative; if they broke the rule twice they were condemned to the *erectum*. One of the boys stood at a lectern on a dais and read from some edifying work, usually one of the lives of the saints. In order to make himself heard in the huge room over the clatter of crockery and the hum of stifled conversation, he had to bawl the words out *recto tono,* i.e., on a single note, without any intonation. This resulted in a strange drone that pitilessly ironed out every shade of expression, whether interrogative, ironic, threatening or amused, and made every sentence equally pathetic, plaintive, aggressive and vehement.

The job of *recitator* was highly coveted and was awarded to those who were first in class and able to perform it. For it was no easy matter for a boy to have to declaim for forty-five minutes, without faltering or making a mistake, a passage never intended for such barbarous usage. So the current *recitator* was always surrounded by a certain prestige, increased by the fact

that he had his meal alone before the others, and it was tradi-
tionally a bigger and better meal than the rest got.

Needless to say, I was not the stuff *recitatores* were made of,
and it was with apprehension as well as amazement I learned
one morning I was to take the place of the current reader, who
to everyone's surprise had made himself unworthy of the honor
by getting a *colaphus*. At the same time, I was handed the passage I had to read. It was the life of St. Christopher from Jacopo
de' Varazze's *Golden Legend*.

I had no doubt Nestor was behind this overwhelming honor.
Today, having reread in the light of what I know now the passage I declaimed then in front of the whole school, I recognize
his signature in it. But will my whole life be long enough
to elucidate the deep-rooted connection between the legend of
St. Christopher and the fate of Nestor, that fate of which I am
the trustee and executor?

According to Jacopo de' Varazze, Christopher was a Ca-
naanite. He was huge as a giant and terrible of aspect. He was
willing to serve, but only the greatest prince in the world. So he
went to a powerful king who was supposed to be unequaled in
greatness, and the king welcomed him kindly and had him remain at his court. But one day Christopher saw the king making
the sign of the cross over his face after someone had spoken of
the Devil in his presence. When Christopher asked why he did
this, the king replied, "Whenever I hear the Devil spoken of, I
use this sign lest he obtain power over me and harm me." Then
Christopher realized that the king he served was not the greatest
or most powerful, because he was afraid of the Devil. So he
bade the king farewell and went in search of the Devil. As he
was crossing a desert, he saw a great multitude of soldiers, and
one of them, who looked very fierce, came and asked him where
he was going. Christopher answered: "I am seeking my lord the
Devil to be my master." And the other said: "I am him
you seek." Christopher, delighted, engaged to be his servant

forever and took him for his master. But as they went along together they came to a cross set up at the side of the road, and the Devil was afraid and led Christopher aside across rough country, only joining the road again farther on. Christopher asked why he had been so afraid, and the Devil answered: "A man called Christ was hanged on a cross, and whenever I see one I am filled with terror and flee." Christopher said, "Then I have worked in vain and still have not found the greatest prince in the world. Farewell! I leave you now to go in search of this Christ who is greater and more powerful than you."

For a long while he sought someone to tell him about Christ, and at last he met a hermit who instructed him in the faith and said: "This king you wish to serve demands that you fast often." And Christopher said: "But I'm a giant, and I get very hungry. Let him ask something else of me, for it is impossible for me to fast." Then the hermit said: "Do you know such and such a river where travelers are often in peril of their lives?" "Yes," said Christopher. And the hermit said: "You are tall and strong, and if you stayed by the river and carried over all those who came that way, you would be doing something very pleasing to Jesus Christ, the king you want to serve." And Christopher said: "Yes, I can perform that task, and I promise to do it for him."

He went to the river they had spoken of and built a little hut on the bank. Instead of a staff he used a pole to support himself in the water, and he carried across all the travelers who came that way, without respite. After many days had gone by he was resting in his little house when he heard the voice of a child calling, "Christopher, come out and carry me over." Christopher got up at once but couldn't see anyone there. Then, when he was back inside, he heard the voice calling him again. Again he hurried out but found no one. The third time he was called he found a little boy on the bank who asked to be carried across. Christopher lifted the child on his shoulders, took his pole, and entered the water. And the river rose and rose, and the child weighed as heavy as lead. The flood became so strong, and the weight of the child on his shoulders became so unbearable, that Christopher was in great fear of dying.

But by dint of great effort he came through, and when he had come to the other side of the river he set the boy down on the bank and said: "You have exposed me to great danger. You weighed so heavily on me that if I'd had the whole world on my back I do not know if I should have had a greater burden." And the boy answered: "Be not amazed, Christopher. You have had not only the whole world on your back but also him who created the world. For I am Christ your king, whom you have rendered this service. And to prove that I speak truth, when you get back on the other side, plant your stick in the earth by your house, and in the morning you will see it has flowered and borne fruit." And with this he vanished. When Christopher got back, he drove his stick into the ground, and when he rose next day, he saw it had put forth leaves and dates like a palm tree.

I was more than a little proud of having chanted all this without faltering once, and I expected Nestor to congratulate me when I sat down beside him for two o'clock study hall. He was absorbed in one of the highly colored and intricate drawings he used to spend hours over, his face almost glued to the paper. When he sat up, I saw he had drawn a St. Christopher. But on his shoulders the giant carried all the school buildings, with the boys hanging out of the windows. Nestor wiped his brow with his handkerchief in a familiar gesture and murmured: "Christopher found the absolute master he was seeking in the form of a boy. But what one needs to know is the exact relation between the weight of the boy on his shoulders and the blooming of the pole."

Leaning forward, I saw he had given the giant Christ-Bearer his own face.

March 11, 1938. The sort of diary-memoir I've been keeping sinisterly for over two months now has the strange power of placing the facts and deeds it relates—my facts and deeds—in a perspective that throws a new light on them and gives them a new dimension. For example, my name, Abel, strikes me quite differently since my entry of February 18. In the same way I feel I can redeem certain little private, vaguely shameful habits, by devoting a few lines to them here, though to all appearances they are indefensibly absurd.

Take for example the staglike roar I'd certainly have indulged in again this morning if my right wrist didn't still stab with pain every time I try to use it. What I do is at one and the same time a mime of despair and a kind of rite to overcome it. I lie down on my stomach with my feet turned out, raise myself on my arms and throw back my head and in that position roar like a stag, a sort of deep long-drawn-out belch that seems to rise from my innards and makes my neck vibrate. It exhales all the sorrow of living and all the anguish of dying.

But this morning, instead of roaring, I invented a new rite that I shall call the john shampoo or the caca shampoo, I don't know yet which. The impossibility of going on existing weighed me down pretty heavily at dawn as I struggled to wrest my carcass from its sheets. But even that was nothing, comparatively speaking: as every day, but worse than usual, there was the disappointment of the mirror. I've never been able to abandon the secret hope that in the night my usual mask may be replaced by a new face. One morning, say, the serious innocent countenance of a roe deer might look back at me from the starred glass out of its long almond eyes. And I'd make up for the unwonted impassiveness of my face by wiggling my mobile, expressive ears.

But no, there I was again—yellower and gloomier than ever, with my deep-set eyes, beetling sooty brows, low, obstinate, uninspired forehead, and the two deep furrows down my cheeks that look as though they were made by a constant stream of scalding tears. I'd slept badly, my beard pricked painfully when I ran my hand over my chin, there was a green scum on my teeth. No, it was all too much! "What a mug!" I cried. "Into the john with it!" and my hands got hold of my neck as if to twist my head off. Then, in fact, carried away by my fury, I did go to the lavatory. I knelt down in front of the toilet as if to vomit, but instead put my head right in, groping for the chain as I did so. The water flushed like a cataract, and a jet as cold and hard as a guillotine fell on the back of my neck. I stood up, drenched and a bit confused, but calmer. It had done me good, anyhow! I'd be surprised if I didn't try it again.

March 14, 1938. The long four o'clock recess was at its height. A single roar rose from the playground, seething with hundreds of boys in their red-braided black smocks. Nestor was leaning on a window sill; I was sitting on it, watching a new game that was fascinating in its brutality. The lighter boys sat on the sturdier ones' shoulders, and each steed and its rider tried to unseat the others. The knights stuck their arms out straight like lances aimed at their enemy's face, then changed them into a grapnel with which they hooked him by the neck and dragged him sideways or back. There were sudden descents into the cinders, but sometimes the fallen knight still clung with his knees to the neck of his mount, and from the ground grabbed with both hands at enemy horses.

Nestor had first of all glanced around the yard, basking in the superiority of looking on at the melee unmoved and unmoving. Then he said, as usual not actually addressing his words to anyone: "A playground is an enclosed space that allows enough play for play—a blank page for games to be written on like signs that have to be deciphered. But the density of the atmosphere is inversely proportional to the space that encloses it. If the walls closed in, the writing would be more crowded together. Would it be more legible? We might just arrive at the phenomenon of condensation. But of what? Perhaps the aquarium, or better still the dormitories, might give the answer."

At that moment an inextricably tangled group of riders and mounts fell to the ground and disintegrated. Nestor gave a shiver of eagerness. "Come on, M'Abel," he said. "Now we'll show them who we are!"

He went behind me, put his great head between my skinny thighs, and lifted me up like a feather. He held my wrists and pulled on my arms to get me firm in my seat, so neither of us had our hands free. He didn't mind this: he was counting on his sheer mass. And indeed he charged through the battlefield like a mad bull, overturning everyone in his path. Then he swung around and charged back the other way, but now the effect of surprise was over, and those who were still left standing confronted him bravely. The impact was terrible. Nestor's glasses were sent flying. "I can't see a thing," he said, letting go of my hands. "You'll have to guide me!"

I took hold of his ears and tried to direct him by tugging on one side or the other, as at the bit of a horse. But he soon adopted a different tactic and, to elude the enemy, began to twirl around at a speed that was amazing in view of his size. I for my part grabbed at whatever came within reach, toppling our assailants like ninepins. Soon we were the only two left standing. The others were painfully unscrambling themselves on the ground. We were surrounded by a circle of admirers, from which one small boy detached himself and respectfully handed me Nestor's broken glasses.

Nestor knelt down to let me get off, reminding me fleetingly of an elephant setting down its mahout. Then he stood for a moment without moving, smiling vaguely and dreamily, with an expression of happiness I'd never seen him wear before, even forgetting the usual gesture of mopping his streaming brow.

Still unable to see, he put his hand on my shoulder without making any attempt to put on his glasses. When we got back to the window from which we'd originally set out, his face still had the same expression of somewhat foolish ecstasy. For a long time he didn't say anything. Then he said, "I never knew, pretty Fauges, that to carry a child was such a wonderful thing."

March 15, 1938. One of my minor consolations is cleaning my shoes. Under my wardrobe there's a little box full of brushes, hard, soft and medium, rags of pure wool, and, most important of all, tins of polish of various colors, from black to colorless via every shade of brown. I like to change the color of a pair of shoes every day by polishing them with carefully varied combinations of shoe cream. I clean and put the polish on at night, and shine and shammy in the morning. That's the proper way to do it. But what I like best of all is to feel a shoe in my hand and to put my hand inside it. I've got huge hands, strangler's claws, sewerman's mitts, which feel their own ridiculousness when they find themselves on a white tablecloth or a sheet of paper, or when they have to manipulate a little silver spoon or a pencil that might snap between their fingers at any moment like a match. But with shoes everything is different.

A week or so ago I found a pair of shoes on top of a garbage can. They were broken, ragged, eaten away with sweat, and further humiliated by having had their laces removed, so that their tongues lolled out in a yawn and their empty eyelet holes stared. But my hands gathered them up affectionately, my horny thumbs flexed the soles in a rough but friendly caress, and my fingers sank into the intimacy of the vamp. The poor old beetle crushers seemed to come alive again at such a sympathetic touch, and when I put them back on the heap of rubbish I felt a distinct pang.

I keep a little shoe-cleaning kit in one of the drawers of my desk. It contains a tin of colorless shoe cream, a hard brush for cleaning, a soft brush for shining, and a woolen duster. Whenever a customer outstays his welcome and gets on my nerves, I don't hesitate. I get out my apparatus under his astonished eyes and methodically set about cleaning my shoes, if necessary taking them off and putting them on the desk. The great advantage of colorless shoe cream is that you can, in fact you should, put it on without a brush. The pleasure of plastering your fingers with the transparent white turpentine-smelling stuff and slowly rubbing it into the leather, nourishing every pore, smoothing out the creases, going into every seam! It would be wrong of the visitor to take offense at this liberty: it restores all my patience and good humor.

My hands love shoes. The truth is they can't really get over not being feet, just like those tall girls who spend all their life wishing they'd been born boys.

March 16, 1938. Nestor, hunched in his corner, holds my left fist prisoner in his right hand and looks at me smiling through his glasses, more monstrous than ever now they're roughly held together with bits of adhesive tape.

"Do you know the Baron des Adrets?" he asks me.

Of course I don't know the Baron des Adrets—how should I? But Nestor does not wait for an answer.

"I'll tell you about him," he says without moving his lips. "His name was François de Beaumont, and he had a château at La Frette in the Dauphiné. He lived in the sixteenth century, when the wars of religion bespattered the country with blood and strong men could work their will with impunity.

"One day, out hunting, Adrets and his officers brought a bear to bay, and its retreat was cut off by a precipice. The bear charged one of the men, who fired, hit it, and was soon rolling with it in the snow. The baron, who had seen what happened, sprang forward to help the man but suddenly stopped, transfixed by an unutterable pleasure. He had noticed that the man and the bear, intertwined as they were, were gradually slipping toward the abyss, and the baron stood frozen and hypnotized by this fall in slow motion. Then the black bulk toppled over into the void, the only stain left on the whiteness was a gray streak, and Adrets groaned with joy.

"A few hours later the officer reappeared, wounded and bleeding, but safe—the bear had broken his fall. He expressed respectful astonishment at the baron's slowness in coming to his assistance. The baron, smiling dreamily as at some delightful recollection, replied in a mysterious sentence heavy with threat: 'I never knew that a man falling was such a wonderful thing.'

"After that he gave free rein to his new passion. Taking advantage of the religious wars, he imprisoned Catholics in Protestant regions and Protestants in Catholic ones, and arranged for them all to 'fall.' He worked out a subtle ritual. His prisoners were blindfolded and forced to dance to the music of a viol on the top of a tower without a parapet. And the baron, breathless with pleasure, would watch them draw near, move away from, and draw near again to the void, until suddenly one of them lost his footing and fell shrieking through the air, to be impaled on a bank of lances stuck in the ground at the foot of the tower."

I never took the trouble to find out whether Nestor's story was historically true. Anyway, what does it matter? There is a human, I almost wrote "Nestorian," truth which infinitely surpasses the truth of fact. After he'd finished telling me the baron's murky story, he made no comment. But now I can't myself help connecting the story with something he said later, which I didn't understand at the time. He said: "There's probably nothing more moving in a man's life than the accidental discovery of his own perversion." And I remember his fondness for the word "euphoria," which struck me as erudite then. "Adrets," Nestor would say, "discovered 'cadent euphoria.'" And he would ponder over that strange assemblage of words, looking perhaps for other ways of putting it, other keys to curious pleasures.

March 20, 1938. This morning the papers say 2,783 people disappeared without trace in France during the past year. Many of them must have been simple cases of people vanishing deliberately to escape from wives or families they hated. But the rest must be perfect crimes, in which the *corpus delicti* was completely destroyed by fire, earth or water. If to that you add the fact that the most skillful murders are those disguised as natural deaths, you get a dim idea of the terrifying society we live in. There can be no doubt that in the majority of cases crime pays and murder succeeds. Every day we shake hands that have strangled or poured out arsenic. The cases that come to justice are failures by definition. But the fact that they amount to a mere dozen or so a year shows they are merely symbolic—just the necessary minimum to make believe we respect the sacredness of life.

In reality our society has the justice it deserves: a justice appropriate to the cult of the assassin which literally blossoms at every street corner, on all the street signs setting forth for public admiration the names of the greatest warriors, or in other words of the most bloodthirsty professional killers in our history.

March 22, 1938. Although the ruins of the original abbey church had been restored, school prayers and services were held in a recently built chapel designed and decorated in what might be called modern Byzantine. On ordinary days we went there twice, once for morning and once for evening prayers. But on Sundays and high festivals we had to go seven times: morning prayers, communion, high mass, vespers, compline, evening service, evening prayers. Each boy had his own little place there: he was at home, so to speak, in his pew, his pigeon-hole, with all its familiar sight-lines. Our society was ordered just as hierarchically there as in class, but differently. First of all there were the members of the choir, rather envied by the other boys because choir practice sometimes got them out of lessons and could be made to cover a multitude of sins. But their position in the gallery under the great pseudo-flamboyant rose window, around Father Pigeard and his harmonium, would have been more of a liability than an asset had it not been for the advantage of being able to observe the whole school from a station of superiority, and from behind. It was Nestor who drew my attention to this last point, wondering whether it mightn't be a good idea to wangle himself a place there; but afterward he appeared to lose interest. I wish I could remember what he said one day in my presence about the choir, comparing its ordered and almost architectural unanimity with the wild Dionysiac unanimity that rises from a playground.

The composition of the choir had been an occasion of slight scandal to me, in the most spiritual sense of the word. Nestor had laughed at me for it, and it led to an initiation in the ways of the world of which I stood badly in need. I had thought it went without saying that in a church school like ours the signal honor of assisting the priest at the holy office of mass must go to the finest flowers of the school, those who were first in their class or won prizes for diligence, the paragons of virtue and budding saints. But I soon perceived that while these criteria did play a certain part in the choice of those who might wear the immaculate alb, there were other and more important considerations that had nothing to do with beauty of soul. The unavowable and shameful truth was, though the holy fathers would have admitted it only on the pale or at the stake, that you couldn't be a choirboy if you didn't have a pretty face. And it was not just a matter of crudely excluding such eggheads as happened to look like gorillas: it was a subtle proportioning, around the steps of the altar, of fair and dark, thin and stout, chubby pink cherub and gaunt Mater Dolorosa, joyously animal innocence and mortified purity.

Nestor enlightened me. Of all he said on that and other days what I remember most is his blaming the priests for not knowing, though they were instructors of youth by profession, that a child is only good-looking in so far as he is *possessed,* and he is only *possessed* in so far as he is *served.* The infant Jesus on Christopher's shoulders is at once carried and carried away. That is what accounts for his radiance. He is carried off by main force, and then humbly and painfully held above the roaring waves. Christopher's whole glory consists in his being at once beast of burden and monstrance. The crossing of the river is at the same time kidnaping and drudgery. No doubt I make what Nestor said sound clearer and more forceful than it could really have been, but in doing that I'm following my basic vocation. But I think I'm right in remembering him as having traced this same ambiguity in the choirboy, and having wished to see the prelate kneel to his small incense-bearer.

It was in the Byzantine chapel that fate dealt its first blow and gave us a dress rehearsal of the tragedy that was to take place at St. Christopher's later in the year.

I was sitting as usual one seat in from the end of a row, with Nestor on my left by the aisle, made narrower at this point by a confessional. What was different this time was my right-hand neighbor, Benoît Clément, a young Parisian "put away" in Beauvais because his family couldn't handle him in the metropolis. He had rapidly acquired great prestige among the rest of us little bumpkins by producing a series of articles either violent or poetic, such as a revolver, a compass, a switchblade, a bottle imp and a golf ball. I wonder on reflection if it wasn't from him that Nestor got his gyroscope, his "absolute toy," as he called it. What was certain at any rate was that a sort of complicity, if not friendship, had grown up between the two of them, on the strength of which Clément affected a familiarity with Nestor that pained me, partly out of jealousy and partly because it seemed like a degrading concession on the part of my friend. They were often to be seen in a huddle, debating swaps and exchanges, and the only way I could reconcile myself to this was by telling myself Nestor must be exploiting the newcomer's resources to the limit, and that he would put him in his place as soon as there was no more to be got out of him.

Clément's position on my right had something to do with this commerce between them, for no sooner had mass begun than my two neighbors started bargaining over my head just as if I didn't exist. Of course I took in every word, especially as the business in question was not new and had been debated in my presence for the last few days. The object was a First World War grenade that had been made into a lighter. I seem to remember Nestor thought the price Clément was asking—ten blank exemption slips—was too high, and he insisted on at least seeing that the thing worked. "I know what it is with lighters," he said to me after one of their arguments. "They never work." But a certain amount of lighter fluid was needed for the demonstration, and Nestor was the only one who could get hold of it.

That was how matters stood that Sunday morning, and by the time we got to the offertory, agreement was so far advanced that I was called on to pass a little bottle of fluid from Nestor to Clément. Clément at once set about applying this to the cotton wool inside his grenade, a delicate operation that was constantly interrupted because of the seminarist prowling up and down on duty in the aisle. Nestor began by watching closely, for his responsibility was involved, and no doubt he would have prevented any accident if the Father Superior's sermon hadn't for once appeared to interest him so much that he seemed to forget all about Clément and the grenade and the bottle of lighter fluid. By dint of much hunting I've just found the opening words of the sermon in Montaigne's Essays. They are taken from an anecdote about the fifteenth-century Portuguese conquistador, Alfonso d'Albuquerque, who, as the preacher quoted unctuously, "in extreme peril at sea, took on his shoulders a young boy, that in their common fortune the child's innocence might serve him as warrant and recommendation to God's favor, to bring him safely through."

After this exordium the holy father easily made the transition to our patron saint, his marvelous adventure as the bearer of Christ, and the reward of the rod sprouting leaves and fruit. There was no indication, he said, that Albuquerque remembered the story of St. Christopher and tried in his extremity to imitate him, though of course Christopher was the protector of travelers and navigators. No—what was at once more probable and more exciting was that the conquistador and the saint both derived their destiny from the same source, that each independently of the other placed himself under the protection of the child he protected, saved himself in saving another, took on a weight, shouldered a burden, but a weight of light, a burden of innocence!

"Keep reciting," muttered Nestor. "You've written it all down in black and white and learned it by heart! That mumbo jumbo will make a good addition to my collection!"

The Father Superior now went on to relate us to St. Christopher and Albuquerque.

"Because all of you here are placed under the sign of Christopher, now and throughout your lives you must know how to traverse evil by sheltering under the mantle of innocence. Whether your name be Pierre, Paul or Jacques, remember always that you are also called Child-Bearer: Pierre Child-Bearer, Paul Child-Bearer, Jacques Child-Bearer. Then, ballasted with that sacred burden, you will go through not only rivers and tempests but also the flames of sin."

At that moment a train of flames shot under the rows of chairs and rose in a flickering curtain in the middle of the nave. Clément hadn't noticed that in filling his grenade he had spilled some of the contents of the bottle on the flagstones, and after striking the lighter he must have dropped it on the floor, where it flared up like a torch. Everyone rose in confusion except the seminarists, who thought it was an apparition and fell on their knees. Panic swept everyone toward the door, which was blocked by the crowd. Clément thrust the empty bottle into my hands so as to free himself to deal with the grenade, which still emitted spurts of burning fluid as it whirled about under the chairs. I turned to Nestor, but he had inexplicably disappeared. At last the voice of the preacher rose above the uproar, ordering us to keep calm and go back to our seats. In fact it had been much ado about nothing. The flames were as short-lived as they were brilliant, and the damage was limited to a few singed missals. But what about the culprits? The accusing finger of the preacher pointed to where we sat. Clément and Tiffauges were sequestrated until further notice and were to come out and kneel in the central aisle. A murmur of horror greeted us as we thus exposed ourselves, for we still held in our hands the instruments of our crime—Clément his grenade and I the bottle from which all the trouble had come. Then the Father Superior, to demonstrate that the incident was now closed, sang out the creed at the top of his voice. The chorus that followed him was hesitant and thin at first, then gradually got fuller and fuller.

When the time came for communion I saw the curtains of the confessional stir, and out came an easily recognizable shape that mingled with the groups of boys making their way past Clément and me to the choir screen. Nestor brushed past me on his way to the altar, his arms folded, his triple chin bowed on his chest, withdrawn into his own thoughts.

March 25, 1938. Every night I tried to hold on to myself by stealing from sleep as many hours as I could of reverie and rumination; this was the only interval of solitude I got in that community life where the racket of recess and dining hall was interrupted only by the covert exchanges of study hall and chapel. Getting up to go to the lavatory was not forbidden, so if I felt like it I could indulge in a nocturnal prowl. I did so in moderation, however, for fear of coming face to face with our sleepwalker—every dormitory had its sleepwalker just as every Scottish castle has its ghost.

That night the incident of the grenade, together with the danger that I might have to appear before the discipline committee and the isolation of being "sequestrated," kept me awake. I got up and started to roam about the aisles between the rows of beds. I thought I'd met the dormitory ghost when I heard the sound of quiet footsteps and saw a large shape flitting slowly here and there, bending over and inspecting one sleeper, then moving away to another. It did not take me long to recognize Nestor, swathed in a thick cotton track suit which made him look even more massive than he was. He must have recognized me, for my sudden appearance out of the blue had no effect on his proceedings. Even when I came right up to him he appeared to take no notice: he did mutter some things he might have wanted to let me hear, but then he often just talked to himself.

"Here," he was saying, "the concentration is extreme. Play is reduced to a minimum. Motion is frozen into attitudes that do change, but only very, very slowly. Never mind—they are just so many figures that have to be read. There must be an absolute alpha-omega sign here somewhere—but where? Because sleep is a false victory. They are all there, naked and unconscious, but in fact a whole part of them eludes me. They are there and absent at the same time. Their not seeing is proof of it. And yet don't these damp abandoned bodies constitute an ideal condensation?"

The blue night lights made the rows of narrow beds look like graves in the moonlight; some of the boys' breathing sounded like the rustle of wind in yew trees. The air was as thick and stuffy as in a stable, for the peasants of Picardy and Bray who ruled over us regarded drafts as the greatest danger to health. To my great surprise, Nestor led me to the lavatory, where he bolted the door and threw open the window. The roofs and steeples of the town stood out against the phosphorescent sky as if drawn in India ink. The bells of St. Stephen's plaintively struck three. By contrast with the stale atmosphere from which we had just emerged, the pure night air struck chill. Nestor breathed in deeply.

"Condensation is full of intriguing mysteries," he said, "because it is life. But there's something about purity just the same. Purity equals nothingness, and we find it irresistibly attractive because we are all sons of nothingness."

Then, turning to me in sudden excitement, he exclaimed: "Isn't it wonderful that this little pine door with its two-bit bolt should separate being from nothingness!"

The dark wooden seat was perched like a throne on a sort of platform at one end of the room. Nestor turned away from me and slowly mounted the two steps up to it, as if performing some ritual. When he reached the foot of his throne he let down his trousers, which spiraled over his feet. He inspected the inside of the toilet bowl, took down a stiff straw brush that was hanging in a kind of little sentry box, and set about scrubbing the toilet, flushing it several times. All I could see of him were his buttocks, straining with the effort. What astonished me about them was not so much their enormousness—that I expected—as what I might call their moral expression. How shall I put it? There was something tremendously naïve about this double half-moon obscured by rolls of fat. Or rather, something that at first sight seemed quite foreign to Nestor's character. It was kindness. Up till then I had been overwhelmed by Nestor's prestige and by his power; grateful for his protection and touched by the attentions he lavished on me. It was when I saw his behind that I first began to love him, because it revealed the element in him that was defenseless and awkward and vulnerable.

He stood up and turned around. The upper part of his track suit came down to his navel. Below, the three masses of soapy white flesh formed by the protruding belly and the thighs enveloped and dwarfed a tiny organ. He sat himself down on the throne, where he at once took on the appearance of a Hindu sage or a benevolent, meditative Buddha. He resumed his interrupted monologue.

"I have nothing against the seatless privies of the playground," he said. "They are perfectly suited to the daily defecation of the masses, which, while it may not be profane, is certainly laic. You see the distinction. The discomfort of the crouching involved is full of the virtue of humility. The attitude is a sort of kneeling in reverse, with the knees pointing to the sky instead of to the earth. What points to the earth is omega: it seems to aim at direct contact with the earth, as if the earth could assist by attracting toward it, by a kind of magnetism, that in the body which resembles it most."

He raised a finger.

"No: that in the body which is an exalted image of the earth, an earth seething with live germs and incubated for a long while within our animal warmth. A dunghill is nothing but earth to which animality has lent its own dynamism. But the seatless privy immediately delivers the animal earth we bring forth to the mineral earth. It knows only matter. But refined souls find a particular charm in contemplating the forms produced by omega, which is sometimes a sculptor or even an architect. It is a regal pleasure, linking the throne with the nocturnal calm and leisureliness that usually surround it."

There was a long silence. A gust of wind blew in through the window, shaking the enameled metal shade of the light and bringing with it the distant puffing of a train. Then silence fell again, until it was broken by someone rattling at the door to come in. I was terrified, and looked at Nestor in consternation. He remained completely unmoved. After a considerable time had elapsed he stirred himself at last, stood up, and peered down into the lavatory bowl.

"Tonight," he commented, "omega has been in medieval mood. Look, pretty Fauges—towers and turrets surrounded by a double rampart. Feudal as well as medieval! Last week we performed in flamboyant Gothic," he said dreamily, refusing the roll of toilet paper I proffered.

"No. It would be a shame not to celebrate tonight as it deserves. I've been saving up some special paper for a special occasion—a rare kind of paper covered with the signs of a superior mind. I didn't really think the opportunity would present itself so soon, but there's no doubt there couldn't be a better occasion than tonight."

Out of the back pocket of his trousers he took three sheets of paper, unfolded them and showed them to me. With terror I read the opening lines: "Albuquerque, in extreme peril at sea, took on his shoulders a young boy, that in their common fortune the child's innocence might serve him as warrant and recommendation to God's favor, to bring him safely through." It was the Father Superior's sermon, written out in his own hand! Nestor's hefty paws closed around the manuscript again and kneaded it to take off the sharpness of the gloss. Then he handed it back to me and waited, propped on his hands over the seat of the throne, for me to do my office.

Nestor didn't let me go yet, though. He led me into a labyrinth of back stairs and passages I'd never been in before. When we reached the ground floor he stopped in front of a little cupboard built into the wall and, opening it, revealed dozens of keys hanging in rows. Without hesitation he unhooked three of them and led me off again, this time to the basement. There were no night lights here, only pitch-dark, until my companion took my breath away by boldly switching on the light in one of the kitchens. Then he swung open one of the heavy doors of the icebox and spread a table with pâté, a leg of mutton, a lump of gruyère and a jar of apricot jam. He gestured invitingly in my direction, and without bothering further about me, started to devour, not stopping for bread or anything to drink.

I was scared and cold, the food revolted me, and I was tortured by the thought of the punishment hanging over me. But Nestor's presence lent everything an irresistible air of magic. I don't think children have a very developed aesthetic sense, and I believe some strange discoveries would be made if anyone thought to inquire into what they understand by "beautiful" and "ugly." But most children are sensitive to the prestige of power, and even more of them react to the secret, magical power that can find the weak points of gray reality, topple whole stretches of it, and make it yield up its hidden treasures. Nestor had this gift in the highest degree, and he held me under so strong a spell I didn't even dare ask him about his behavior in chapel or what was likely to happen to me over the business of the grenade.

When I got back at last to my narrow bed, it was still quite dark, but reveille was sounding in the yard of the neighboring barracks. I knew I still had another hour before the nameless horror of clangings and lights would rend my golden slumbers at half past six.

I realized Nestor couldn't really have helped me if he had been implicated in the business of the grenade along with Clément and me. By keeping out of it he retained his freedom of movement and power to act. Nevertheless, his sudden disappearance just when the fluid caught fire, and his silence since, had destroyed the sense of security I'd been living in since he had taken me under his protection. How could I forget that my role in the affair had been practically non-existent—that it really concerned only Clément and him, and that in fact I was suffering

in his stead? Our nocturnal encounter and the sight of his power
and supremacy comforted me somewhat, but I was shattered
inwardly when the prefect of studies told me the very next morning that the committee was to meet the following day and pro-
nounce the verdict on us after interviewing us both separately.
The isolation of being "sequestrated" added the last straw to my
desperation. I completely lost my head and yielded to a panic
impulse to flee.

It was inconceivable to the holy fathers that a boarder might
run away, and there was practically no supervision at the time
the day boys went home. I had little difficulty in slipping out.
I went past St. Stephen's, across the Rue Malherbe, and hurried
down the Rue de la Tapisserie toward the station. That was all
I knew of Beauvais. Luck was on my side, for the last train to
Dieppe was due to leave in a couple of minutes, so I couldn't
be overtaken. I bought a ticket to Gournay and collapsed into
a third-class compartment, convinced that all the other passengers could see written all over my face my double disgrace
as sequestree and runaway. The train stopped and shunted at
every opportunity: it took more than an hour to cover the
twenty miles between Beauvais and Gournay.

All that time I racked my brains to think how I was going to
explain my arrival to my father. But I didn't have to. They had
phoned him from St. Christopher's and he was waiting for me at
the station. For once his unwavering indifference toward me
was welcome. He brushed both my cheeks mechanically with his
mustache and told me that if there'd been another train back to
Beauvais I'd have gone straight back, but that, as it was, the
seven-fifteen next morning would get me there in time to appear
before the committee. All this was said quite coldly, without a
trace of anger or impatience. When we got home I was slightly
soothed by the familiar smell of the workshop, but the apartment
on the first floor reflected so strongly the habits of an aging recluse—a mixture of neurotic fastidiousness and sordid neglect—

that I felt as alien as I did at St. Christopher's, though I'd been born and grown up in the place. I had a frightful night in which nightmares alternated with long hours of sleeplessness. The flames that had suddenly sprung up around me in the chapel were one image that kept recurring like an obsession. These represented not only the flames of hell but also liberation, for if St. Christopher's went up in flames, if the whole world was burned to a cinder, my own misery would also be engulfed.

At dawn I'd just managed to get to sleep at last when my father came and woke me up. As soon as I was awake my *idée fixe* about St. Christopher's in flames took possession of me once more. It gave me a morbid pleasure to think of myself perishing in the disaster. As for the improbability of such a conflagration, it was strangely counterbalanced in my mind by the thought that no other solution could save me.

My father had said a seminarist would be at Beauvais station to meet me, but there was no one there. I took this as a good sign: for a while at least things were not going to follow their expected course. I slowly retraced my steps of the day before, scanning the faces of passers-by for some sign.

The street the school stood in was filled with a chattering crowd which the firemen thrust aside as they unwound their hoses. The red wagon with the big ladder had been sent in case of need but hadn't been used—someone told me the fire had broken out in the basement. I could see pungent clouds of black smoke curling lazily out of the vents of the boiler room. The windows of the lower classrooms just overhead were broken, and through them could be seen an indescribable chaos of half-burned chairs and desks and blackboards. The final touch of desolation was added by the water liberally poured in by the fire brigade. People pointed out a kind of black crater in the floor opposite the dais, where the fire had erupted like a volcano after having smoldered for some time in the cellar. Fortunately the fire had broken out very early—at a quarter past six, someone

said—when the classrooms were still empty. According to the
crowd, there hadn't been any casualties. But suddenly the school
gates opened and an ambulance made its way through the crowd.
As it passed by me I recognized the haggard and swollen face
of Nestor's mother sitting inside.

Before the gates closed I slipped through into the yard. All
the boarders were there, standing still, whispering, in little
groups. Those day boys who could go home had been asked
to do so. No one paid any attention to me, and thus that day gave
me my first experience of other people's incredible blindness to
the fateful sign which distinguishes me from everyone else. It
was actually possible not to see the obvious, the dazzling connection between the fire and my personal fate! These stupid people who were all ready to come down on me for a peccadillo (of
which I was innocent into the bargain) would never realize,
even if I bawled the truth in their faces, the share I had had in
the retribution that had just fallen on St. Christopher's!

I tried to find Nestor. Why had his mother been in the ambulance? I was completely shattered by what I was told. That
morning, not for the first time, Nestor senior asked his son to
go down and stoke the boiler for him at five o'clock. No one
ever found out exactly what happened, but just over an hour
later flames burst through into the lower classrooms. The first
firemen who could get through into the boiler room came up
again with Nestor's body. He was dead of asphyxiation.

March 28, 1938. This morning I woke with a strange start and
the feeling it was time to get up. The alarm said a quarter to
two, but it had stopped. I got up to look at my watch on the
table: it too had stopped, at ten past two. I telephoned to find
out the time: it was seven o'clock.

Outside in the street there was a thick fog. I had parked my
old Hotchkiss at the side of the road so as to get off to see a customer in Meaux before the garage opened. When I pulled the

self-starter nothing happened: the batteries were dead, probably because of the fog. So the dashboard clock had stopped: it stood at a quarter past two.

I'd be taken aback by such a series of coincidences if I weren't so used to it. But my life swarms with inexplicable coincidences, and I've come to regard them as so many reminders. It's nothing—just fate keeping an eye on things and making sure I don't forget its invisible but ineluctable presence.

Once, last summer, I was asleep with the window wide open. When I woke I switched on the radio to beguile the first minutes of the day with some music. And indeed the music rose up, sparkling, vivacious, fresh, reckless. Then my attention was distracted by a violent outcry on the roof above my head. Some birds, evidently fairly large ones, were fighting and reviling one another passionately. The noise grew louder, and I could tell the contestants were slithering about on the sloping roof. Finally a mass of bristling feathers hit my window sill and fell into the room. Two terrified magpies disentangled themselves from one another and with one accord flew back out the window to freedom. At that moment the last chords of the music died away and a woman announcer said, "You have just been listening to the overture to *The Thievish Magpie* by Rossini." I smiled into the bedclothes and murmured, "Good morning, Nestor!"

Sometimes it comes in the form of an answer—usually an ironical one—to some unseemly solicitation of mine. Because after all, surrounded as I am by signs and flashes of illumination, I suppose I may say I *am* lucky?

Six months ago, when I had some money difficulties, I bought a whole ticket in the National Lottery, uttering as I did so a short prayer: "Just for once, Nestor, eh?" Well, I can't say my prayer went unheard! It was even answered, by a kind of thumbing of the nose. The number of my ticket was B 953716. The number that won its owner a million francs was B 617359. My number backward. That would teach me to try to take trivial advantage of my special relationship with the springs of the universe. At first I was angry. Then I laughed.

April 4, 1938. The *Voelkischer Beobachter,* official organ of the German government, has launched the slogan, "Guns before butter." This is the lowest form of the great *malign inversion* at work everywhere. Guns before butter—or in nobler, or plainer, terms: death before life, hate before love!

April 6, 1938. Renault's are bringing out a line of wood-burning vehicles—one- to five-ton trucks, and buses that hold from eighteen to thirty-one passengers. They take only five or six minutes to start up, and there's a patent system providing good acceleration and continued efficiency going down hill. The motor is fitted with a simple mechanical filter which eliminates risk from clogged or torn fabric.

It's absolutely typical of our time that progress should now go backwards. Only a few years ago the introduction of cars using wood for fuel would have made everyone laugh. Soon the latest thing in technology will be an engine that runs exclusively on hay, and we shall end up being thrilled by the invention of the horse-drawn carriage.

April 8, 1938. I stayed at St. Christopher's till I was sixteen. My conduct was irreproachable; my marks were disastrous. I covered my face with a mask of innocence that I've retained ever since, but which the break with Rachel, the discovery of the sinister writing and certain other signs have shaken strangely. I made up my mind to be forgotten by a society from which I looked for nothing but evil. My soul, on the other hand, never learned how to disguise itself. It threw up everything the teachers tried to make it swallow in the way of culture. At the end of my secondary education I was superbly ignorant of Corneille and Racine, though I recited Lautréamont and Rimbaud to myself in secret; the only thing I knew about Napoleon was his downfall at Waterloo (I was furious that the English didn't hang the perjurer), but I knew all about the Rosicrucians, Cagliostro and Rasputin; and while I scrutinized my surroundings for every possible sign, I had ruled out all the sciences whatsoever.

At the end of the year before I should have taken my *baccalauréat* it was clear I wouldn't get through, and the holy fathers included me without regret among the pupils who are turned away each year from that kind of school to keep up the examination averages. So I found myself back once more in Gournay-en-Bray, where my father tried to initiate me into his own trade as a mechanic. His cold, taciturn presence had always reduced both my head and my hands to confusion. And I might add that if I was a hopeless pupil he was not much better as a teacher: he had always worked on his own and resented having to open his mouth to explain anything. Anyway, I soon went to work for his rival in the only auto-repair shop that Gournay boasted. My military service gave me a chance to "go up" to Paris, where I met an uncle of mine who owned a garage near the Ballon des Ternes, the monument to the balloonists in the seige of Paris. The warmth of his welcome owed something to his desire to annoy my father: they hadn't seen each other since they quarreled over the dividing up of my grandfather's estate. After I'd done my military service I became my uncle's chief assistant, and when he died five years later he left the garage to me. Chance had decreed that I work in a similar trade to that of my father, only at a higher level, as if it were my ambition to climb a few rungs in the social scale without betraying family tradition. How grotesquely far from the truth! In reality I do my work in the same way as I was a soldier, as I've had women, as I pay my taxes—like a zombie, like a sleepwalker, forever dreaming of an awakening, a break that will set me free and let me be myself at last. It is no longer enough to say I dream of such a rupture: as I've said, the mask already trembles on my face. And above all there's this left hand, first sign to emerge of the new Tiffauges, which for three months now has been writing new things in words my "adroit" right-hand writing would certainly never have summoned up. Spring is in the air. Spring, thaw, debacle.

April 11, 1938. Yesterday 99.09% of the Austrian electorate pronounced in favor of their country being united with Germany. This practically unanimous dash into the abyss is not the product of an external force sweeping away all resistance. No, evil is rooted in each one, and when the crowd is confronted with the alternative, life or death, it cries, "Death! Death!" just as the Jews answered, "Barabbas! Barabbas!" to Pontius Pilate.

April 13, 1938. I was small and puny up to the age of twelve. Then I started getting enormously tall, though practically without putting on weight, so that my thinness, which began by being merely unsightly, became first ridiculous and then alarming. At twenty I was almost six foot three and weighed one hundred and fifty pounds. In addition, galloping myopia forced me to wear thicker and thicker glasses: by the time I went before the conscription board they looked like a couple of paperweights. With no doubt unintentional cruelty, the policeman in charge of operations made me take them off before thrusting me naked into the reception room of the town hall. My entry occasioned rustic laughter among the Gournay worthies ranged behind the desk. What amused them most was the fact that my sexual organs were in no way proportionate to my size; they were those of a child under the age of puberty. The local doctor produced a technical term that set off the general hilarity once more, as everyone took it for a particularly racy obscenity. He said I was "microgenitomorphous." My case was debated at length. Finally I just missed being rejected and was directed into signals, a sec-

tion of the army that didn't make many physical demands on
its members.

Once more I'd been stupidly misjudged. As soon as I'd somehow got myself through my military service, my teeth, as Nestor
had prophesied, began to grow: every day my stomach was
gnawed by the most voracious appetite.

At the beginning it was always between meals that the pangs
seized me. Suddenly, right in the workshop or in my office, my
inside would go hollow, my hands and knees would turn weak
and trembly, drops of sweat broke out on my brow, and saliva
gushed up under my tongue. I had to eat something, anything,
at once, without delay. My first attacks sent me running to the
nearest baker's: he gazed at me bewildered as I stuffed my
mouth with brioches and croissants. Later, when it was winter, I
saw some hampers of oysters smelling of wet seaweed arranged
on a stall outside a wine merchant's. This was an innovation,
the object being to promote the sales of the dry white wine drunk
with shellfish; the idea has caught on generally since. I asked
for two dozen *portugaises* and a glass of Pouilly Fuissé. The
gluttonous delight I felt when I sank my teeth in the glaucous
mucosity, cool, salty and pungent as spray, of the soft shapeless
little bodies abandoning themselves to oral possession, was one
of the revelations of my vocation as an ogre. I realized that the
closer I approached the ideal of absolute rawness, the better I
should satisfy my alimentary desires. I made a great advance
the day I found out that fresh sardines, which are usually eaten
fried or sautéed, can also be eaten cold and raw, as long as
whoever prepares them will take the trouble to scrape off the
scales—it's difficult to remove the whole skin. But my major discovery in this field was steak tartare, minced horsemeat eaten
raw with yolk of egg and a strong seasoning of salt, pepper,
garlic vinegar, onion, shallots and capers. But even into the satisfaction of so rare a passion improvements could be introduced.
By dint of argument with the waiters in the only restaurant in

Neuilly where this rough and cynical dish was served, I got them to leave out, one after the other, all the spices and condiments that only mask the frank nudity of the flesh itself. But since I was dissatisfied as to quantity as well as quality, I soon took to buying quarters of fillet at a horse butcher's and mincing them for myself. In this way I came to understand the attraction I'd always felt for stalls and hooks displaying the fierce and colossal nudity of flayed beasts, the lumps of gleaming flesh, the viscous metallic livers, the pink spongy lungs, the scarlet intimacy between the enormous thighs of obscenely spread-eagled heifers, and above all the smell of cold fat and caked blood that floats over the carnage.

This newly discovered aspect of my soul doesn't worry me in the least. When I say I love meat and blood and flesh the only thing that matters is the word "love." I am all love. I love eating meat because I love animals. I think I could even slaughter with my own hands an animal I'd raised as a pet, and eat it with affectionate appetite. I'd eat it with even deeper and more enlightened enjoyment than other meat that was anonymous and impersonal. I tried in vain to explain this to stupid Mademoiselle Toupie, a vegetarian because she can't bear slaughterhouses. How is it she can't see that, if everyone were like her, most of the domestic animals would disappear? They'd disappear just as the horse is doing since the motorcar began to liberate it from its slavery.

In any case the virtues of my heart could be vouched for, if necessary, by another of my tastes: I mean my liking for milk. My sense of taste, restored to its original delicacy by uncooked, unspiced meat, and capable of discovering worlds of subtlety beneath the apparent insipidity of what is raw, found another field for its activity in milk, which soon became my only drink. But in Paris you have to go a long way to find a dairy where the milk hasn't been killed by the infamous practices of pasteurization or homogenization! In fact, you have to go right to the farm, to the cow, to the very source of this liquid synonymous with life and tenderness and infancy, on which health fiends, puritans, cops and other curmudgeons all come down like a ton of bricks. I personally like milk to smell of the byre and to have the odd hair or straw floating in it. They are signs of authenticity.

My five pounds of raw meat and gallon of milk a day did not fail in the end to modify my shape, and also my relationship with my body. Now, though I have a great aversion to my face, I get on very well with my body. My weight varies in the neighborhood of two hundred and sixty-five pounds, but in proportion my legs are still long and gaunt. This is because all my strength is massed in my wide hips and my rippling back. My dorsal muscles form a sort of double scrip around my shoulder blades, which looks crushingly heavy. My usual posture and walk make me appear bent under the weight of my own spine. In fact, when I want to, I can lift the front or back of a Rosengart or a Simca V as if it were a feather.

Rachel, who had scrutinized me microscopically, knew all my physical peculiarities—including, naturally, first and foremost, my microgenitomorphism—and never missed an opportunity to joke about them. "Really," she used to say to me, "you're built like a stevedore or a beast of burden. Or what do you say to a cart horse? Or a mule rather—they say mules are sterile."

She also liked to tease me about a hollow in the middle of my chest which the medical fraternity refer to as a "sternal funnel." One day I got fed up and told her a story about it that she listened to with open-eyed admiration.

"It was my guardian angel," I began. "I wanted to do something I shouldn't, he tried to stop me, and we had a fight. I tried to hit him, he countered with a punch in the chest. An angel's punch, dealt with a fist harder and heavier than marble. A fist of bronze. I fell backward, gasping for breath. If the blow had been purely material, it would have killed me. But it was angelic, enveloped in the white feathers of the spirit like a boxing glove in spiritual down. I was able to get up again. But ever since I've had the mark, this dent in my chest, on either side of which my pectoral muscles stand out like hard knotty lumps, like little dry and desperate breasts. And sometimes I have difficulty in breathing, and then it's as if the marble fist is still there, bearing down still with all its weight on my chest. To myself I call this respiratory distress 'angelic oppression,' or more briefly 'the angelic.'"

"But are you sure it was your guardian angel?" she said, with a seriousness which surprised me, coming from her.

"Sometimes I wonder, as a matter of fact," I answered. "I ask myself if it wasn't someone else's guardian angel with designs on me. Yours perhaps? Or that of a boy I was at school with who died."

"But what was it," she went on, "the thing you shouldn't have done that the angel tried to stop you doing?"

As for the angelic, it's the only illness I know—if it really is an illness. The various doctors I've consulted have examined me without finding anything abnormal and got lost in absurd conjectures. I asked one of them if there mightn't be some connection between my difficulty in breathing and my sternal funnel, but he denied it categorically.

"Perhaps not a cause and effect relationship," I explained. "But what about one of symbol and symbolized?"

Be that as it may, the angelic has charged my respiratory life with deep meaning. Thanks to it, my lungs have made the transition from glandular darkness to visceral dawn—even, in extreme instances, to the broad daylight of consciousness. These extreme cases include the great dyspneic distress that makes me lie on the ground and struggle against a murderous though invisible grip; but also the profound and happy inspiration in which the whole sky, full of the flight of swallows and the sound of harps, plunges its forked root directly into my lungs.

April 14, 1938. Need I explain to whom I owe this formidable and useless strength concentrated in my shoulders and back? It is clearly bequeathed to me by Nestor. If I had the least doubt about it, the terrible myopia that is his other legacy would clinch the matter. It is his strength that swells my muscles, just as it is his mind that guides my left hand. He also holds the secret of the obscure complicity linking my fate with the general course of things, manifested first in the fire at St. Christopher's, and since by almost always trivial outcroppings. They are all warnings, stirring up the deepest, darkest and most secret part of my life, until the time of the Great Tribulation comes which will bring it forth into the light of day.

April 15, 1938. Yesterday, mass for Maundy Thursday at Notre Dame. I never enter a church or go to mass without the *mixed* feelings that are appropriate. For, in spite of all his errors, Luther was right when he said Satan sat on the throne of St. Peter. The whole hierarchy is in the pay of the Devil and flaunts his livery in the world's face. You have to have your eyes put out by superstition not to see the grotesque pomp of Satan in all the ecclesiastical ostentation and display—those miters like dunce's caps; the croziers like so many question marks, symbols of skepticism and ignorance; the cardinals got up in their crimson like the Scarlet Woman of the Apocalypse; all the Roman paraphernalia, fly swatter and *sedia gestatoria,* cluminating in the basilica of St. Peter's with the Cavaliere Bernini's monstrous baldachin crouched with its four legs and mammoth's belly over the altar as if to shit on it.

And yet nothing can quite dry up the feeble spring flowing timidly under this rubbish heap, for though Satan got his claws on the heritage of the New Testament, all light comes from Christ, and the priests are obliged to appeal to him even while they flout his teaching. So, now and then, a ray of light filters through the forest of lies and crimes, and it is in the hope of that improbable gleam that I haunt religious services from time to time.

The mass yesterday was celebrated in the funereal shadow of Good Friday, and gained in inwardness what it lost in brilliance. After the gloria the bells rang for the last time before Easter Sunday. Then came the prayer, accompanied on the organ by variations on the theme of a Bach chorale.

God forgive me, but every time His official musical instrument, the organ, gives forth its solemn gilded voice, I am back on the wooden horses at the fair at Gournay-en-Bray. The merry-go-round grinds out its vehement, mournful old tune. The little boys' bare legs clutch the painted sides of the rearing steeds that menace heaven with their gaping jaws and mad eyes. The young cavaliers fly through the air a yard above the ground, swept along in the fanfare of that veritable music factory, with its valves and cylinders and drums and forest of pipes, and its wild-eyed big-breasted Fury stiffly beating time. Now memory, which spiritualizes everything dead, has transformed this cavalcade into a contrapuntal chorale, and it is in the light of stained-glass windows, against wisps of incense, that I watch the little boys of bygone years go round and round. . . .

I was so absorbed in my reverie I was surprised by the reading from the gospel and the mandatum that followed. Twelve choirboys sitting in the choir stalls one by one brought their little white feet out from the folds of their surplices; their bareness stood out movingly against all the solemn pomp. Monsignor Verdier knelt before each in turn. He poured on each foot a few drops from a silver ewer, dried it with a cloth, then, despite his dignity and his paunch, bowed to the ground to kiss it. Finally, by way of thanks, he gave each boy a roll of bread and a coin—like a Teuton warrior offering his young bride the *Morgengabe* after their wedding night. The boys reacted variously to this homage. One would look around in dismay, another lower his eyes as if in self-communion. But my favorite, who

had the face of an angel, compressed his lips to stop himself
from giggling.

It has entered into my heart forever, the picture of that old
man weighed down with crimson and gold, bent to the ground
to set his lips on the naked foot of a child. And no matter what
turpitudes the Church may exhibit before my eyes, I shall never
forget the answer she gave so profoundly and so nobly yesterday morning to the question Nestor asked twenty years ago, a
couple of days before he died.

April 20, 1938. Happiness? That entails comfort, organization, a constructed stability altogether foreign to me. To have
troubles is to feel the scaffolding that is happiness shaken by
the blows of fate. In this sense I am safe. Trouble cannot reach
me, because I have no scaffolding. I am a man of sadness and
joy, a completely different alternative to that of happiness-
unhappiness. I live naked and solitary, without family or friends,
keeping alive by a trade so beneath me that I need think about
it no more than I think about my breathing or my digestion. My
usual moral climate is jet-black sadness, opaque and somber. But
this darkness is often shot through by flashing joys, unexpected
and unmerited, which swiftly die out but leave my eyes full of
gold and dancing fireflies.

May 6, 1938. This morning all the papers have front-page pictures of the new government. What a rogues' gallery! Baseness,
abjection and stupidity are all variously embodied in the twenty-
two faces, which we've had the opportunity to admire a couple
of dozen times already in other permutations and combinations.
Most of them were in the last government as a matter of fact.

Must think up a "Sinister Constitution," the preamble of
which would include the following six propositions:

1. Sanctity belongs to the solitary individual and has no tem-
poral power.

2. Conversely, political power belongs entirely to Mammon. Those who exercise it take upon themselves all the iniquity of the social body, all the crimes that are committed every day in its name. That is why the most criminal man in any country is the one who occupies the highest position in the political hierarchy—i.e., the President of the Republic and, after him, the ministers, and after them all the dignitaries of the social body: magistrates, generals, prelates—all servants of Mammon, all living symbols of the murky mess called the established order, all covered with blood from head to foot.

3. The organs of this body are perfectly adapted to its frightful functions. To practice the most abject of trades, men are sifted out by a topsy-turvy selection into groups constituting the most quintessential sublimate of filth the country can offer. It is well known that a cabinet meeting, a church conclave or an international conference gives off a smell of carrion that frightens away even the most blasé vultures. On a more modest plane, a board meeting, a staff meeting, any gathering of a constituted body, is a thugs' get-together that any averagely decent man would steer well clear of.

4. As soon as a man lays down the law he places himself outside it, and thereby outside its protection. Thus the life of a man exercising any kind of power is of less value than that of a cockroach or a louse. Parliamentary immunity ought to be transformed by *benign inversion* to give every citizen the right to shoot at sight and without a license any politician who comes within range. Every political assassination is a contribution to moral hygiene and brings a smile to the lips of the Virgin Mary and all the angels in paradise.

5. An article should be added to the constitution of 1875 whereby all the members of a government that is overthrown are executed out of hand. It is unthinkable that men from whom the country has withdrawn its confidence should be able not only to go home again unpunished, but even to pursue their political

careers wearing the halo of their fraudulent failure. This arrangement would have the triple advantage of getting rid of the country's deadliest pus, preventing the same faces from turning up all the time in different governments, and introducing into politics the quality it lacks the most: i.e., seriousness.

6. Everyone should know that in voluntarily donning a uniform of any kind he ipso facto points himself out as a creature of Mammon and lays himself open to the vengeance of decent people. The law should list among noxious beasts that may be shot in season and out of season, cops, priests, park-keepers and even members of the French Academy.

May 13, 1938. Benign inversion. Benign inversion consists in re-establishing the meaning of the values that malign inversion has previously overturned. Satan, master of the world, aided by his cohorts of rulers, judges, prelates, generals and policemen, holds up a mirror to the face of God. As a result, right becomes left, left becomes right, good is called evil and evil is called good. Among the signs that show the Devil's domination over cities are the innumerable avenues, streets and squares named after soldiers, i.e., professional killers—all of whom of course died in their beds, for a touch of the grotesque is the invariable signature of the Prince of Darkness. Even the name of Bugeaud, one of the most abominable butchers of the nineteenth century, dishonors the streets of several French towns. War, an absolute evil, is inevitably the object of a satanic cult. It is a black mass celebrated in broad daylight by Mammon, and the blood-boltered idols before which the duped masses are made to kneel are called Country, Sacrifice, Heroism and Honor. The center of the cult is the Hôtel des Invalides, rearing over Paris its great gold bubble swollen with the emanations of the imperial carrion and of the various lesser killers rotting there. Even the stupid massacre of '14–'18 has its rites, its smoking altar under the Arc de Triomphe and its incense-bearers, just as it had its poets, Maurice Barrès and Charles Péguy, who devoted all their talent and influence to serving the collective hysteria of 1914. They deserve to be raised to the dignity of *Grand Slaughterers of Youth*—among many others, needless to say.

This cult of evil, suffering and death is naturally accompanied by an implacable hatred of life. Love, while advocated in the abstract, is fiercely persecuted as soon as it takes on concrete form and calls itself sexuality or eroticism. This fount of joy and creation, this supreme good, this *raison d'être* of everything that breathes, is hunted with diabolical resentment by the whole right-thinking rabble, both lay and ecclesiastic.

P.S. One of the most classic and deadly malign inversions has given birth to the idea of *purity*.

Purity is the malign inversion of innocence. Innocence is love of being, smiling acceptance of both celestial and earthly sustenance, ignorance of the infernal antithesis between purity and impurity. Satan has turned this spontaneous and as it were native saintliness into a caricature that resembles him and is the converse of its original. Purity is horror of life, hatred of man, morbid passion for the void. A chemically pure body has undergone barbaric treatment in order to arrive at that state, which is absolutely against nature. A man hagridden by the demon of purity sows ruin and death around him. Religious purification, political purges, preservation of racial purity—there are numerous variations on this atrocious theme, but all issue with monotonous regularity in countless crimes whose favorite instrument is fire, symbol of purity and symbol of hell.

May 20, 1938. Went to see Karl F., who has a strange German contraption that records on tape, and plays back, all the sounds picked up by a microphone, which can be moved about on a long lead. He played me all sorts of animal cries. I was particularly struck by the belling of rutting stags, which would have been very evocative if I hadn't seen it first and foremost as an allusion to one of my own private rites. He told me he played his recordings of bird songs to a professor of ornithology from the Natural History Museum, and the only ones he could identify with certainty were imitations done by a music-hall artist. The real bird songs, obtained with great difficulty under natural conditions, were described by the professor as muddled, uncharacteristic, and in short a complete failure.

Karl F. little suspected the impression that would be made on me by the tape he kept till last as a special treat. It was just the mounting murmur of a crowd that was first impatient, then displeased, then angry, and finally furious. Was it possible that that many-headed monster was not really there under F.'s windows, shouting its rage, howling for murder, sending up a clamor of hatred mingled with the light tinkling of the first stone-shattered panes of glass? Above all, was it possible that that tide of execration was not rushing in against me alone? I broke out in an icy sweat; I must have gone pale. Eventually F. noticed, and asked if I wasn't well. Until I left, which I did as soon as I could, he looked at me in some perplexity.

How could I explain that I survive only because of a misunderstanding—that people see me as an obscure garage proprietor at the Porte des Ternes, and that if they suspected the dark power of which I am the bearer I'd immediately fall a victim to lynch law? Even I myself find it hard to conceive the secret of my fate: that one day when I was a boy I was touched by a magic ring that partially transforms beings of flesh into statues of marble. And that ever since I go through the world half flesh, half stone: with an affable heart, right hand and smile, but inside me something hard, pitiless and cold, against which anything human that touches me will inevitably be broken. It is a sort of ordination in which I have been the half-consenting ordinand, passionately obedient and repeating my acquiescence every time there has been a sign.

October 3, 1938. I neglected this notebook for over four months, and didn't expect to open it again except for some extraordinary event. But what happened this morning is of such significance it must be set down here, and as exactly as possible.

I got up at about six feeling extremely low. I thought of having a roar and then giving myself a john-shampoo, but felt so fed up I hadn't the strength to apply such desperate remedies. What's so awful about these states of depression is the lucidity, or at least apparent lucidity, that accompanies and reinforces them. Despair seems the only genuine response to the meaninglessness of life. Any other attitude, past or future, seems to belong to intoxication. Life is only bearable in a state of intoxication—alcoholic, amorous, religious. Man is the creature of nothingness, and can confront his inconceivable tribulation, these few years of being, only by getting himself dead drunk.

I refused to shave. I put on my overalls and went down to the garage without even bothering to go into the kitchen for coffee. To the frightening hostility of things I had to oppose the armor of a robot, without human weakness. This morning I would be the boss of the Ballon garage, nothing more, nothing less. Poor old Ben Ahmed was the first to feel the effect of it. He has an absolute genius for anything mechanical, but he can't read or write and works "by instinct," without method or calculation. He was checking the valves of a Georges Irat—the engine is identical with that of a light II CV Citroën—and he'd put them in the special grinder and was finishing the seatings. But he couldn't bring himself to check their fit by marking the edges with pencil marks two or three millimeters apart to correspond with the grooves on the cylinder head. It was probably having to use a pencil that put him off. I shouted at him and shoved him away from the car and started to do the job myself. A bit later Jeannot got yelled at for coming in late, and I sent him straight to the bench with a dozen inner tubes that needed their connections adjusted. Then I shut myself up in the glassed-in compartment I use as an office, to make out a pile of bills. At seven-thirty Gaillac brought in his 402 B to have the lights checked, and after that the postman came. The day was getting started up somehow.

It was a quarter to nine and I was talking to Mademoiselle Toupie about her Rosengart when Ben Ahmed, who had finished the Georges Irat, started up the engine. With one ear I listened to Mademoiselle Toupie, and with the other I auscultated the engine of the Georges Irat, which seemed to be running perfectly. The way Ben Ahmed kept pressing on the accelerator began to irritate me. The engine was purring like a fat cat—why did he have to race it? You'd have thought he took pleasure in the roar, and in the exhaust fumes with which he was filling the garage. Finally there was a silence. Mademoiselle Toupie was telling me about St. Dominic's, the convent school where she teaches philosophy. I was asking questions out of genuine curiosity, for I've always been attracted by places where people "live in," and I often wonder what life in a girls' school must be like. At that point the Georges Irat let out a fresh howl that drowned what we were saying. Then, in the middle of the furious crescendo, I distinctly heard a sharp metallic bang. Ben Ahmed heard it too, and took his foot off the gas. From where I was standing I saw Jeannot put his hand to his brow, bend forward over the bench, fall to his knees, and then topple over backward. I realized at once that a fan blade must have snapped off and hit him with terrific force. I was at his side in a single bound and lifted his thin unconscious body in my arms.

It was then something swooped down on me of unbearable and heart-rending sweetness. I was struck by a bolt of benediction from on high. My eyes were fixed on the limp body in my arms, on one side the gaunt bloodstained face under its tufts of brown hair, and on the other the thin pair of knees and the heavy boots dangling clumsily in the air. Ben Ahmed looked at me in astonishment. I didn't move. I could have stayed like that till the end of time. The Ballon garage with its cobwebbed beams and grimy glass roof had vanished. The nine choirs of angels surrounded me with a bright invisible glory. The air was full of incense and the sound of harps. A river of sweetness flowed majestically through my veins. Finally Ben Ahmed acted.

"Look!" he said, pointing to a dark patch spreading over the mud floor. "He's bleeding!"

At these words, a long silence trembling with happiness closed around us again.

At last I managed to speak.

"I'd never have believed," I said, "that to carry a child was such a wonderful thing!"

And that simple sentence awoke in my memory a long and profound echo.

It was Mademoiselle Toupie who broke the spell. She took charge, got me and my burden somehow bestowed in the back of her Rosengart, and drove us off to the clinic at Neuilly.

Jeannot isn't badly hurt—a bad gash in the head and a touch of shock. No sign of any fracture. I drove him back still half unconscious to his mother, who nearly fainted at the sight of his enormous turban of bandages. I'm still the greater casualty of the two, and still haven't finished ruminating over the dazzling discovery I was precipitated into by today's accident.

October 6, 1938. The first word that crops up under my pen seems banal and weak but turns out to be very fruitful. It is *euphoria.* Yes, it was a sort of euphoria that enfolded me from head to foot when I took Jeannot's inanimate body in my arms. I say from head to foot advisedly, for unlike ordinary pleasure, narrowly and obscenely localized, the wave of beatitude I'm speaking of now covered me entirely, flooding my deepest depths and uttermost extremities. It was not a lewd and limited titillation, but a total joy of all my being. And here I come back again to my biblical meditations, to the original Adam before the fall, woman-bearer and child-bearer, constantly in an erotic trance, both possessor and possessed, of which our ordinary loves are but a pale shadow. Could it be that my superhuman vocation might in certain circumstances allow me to attain the ecstasy of our great androgynous ancestor?

But I must try to shake off such speculations and come to grips with the concrete. The most objective element in the other day's experience was Jeannot's *weight,* a thing that can be expressed as accurately as desired in pounds or kilos. I took up that weight. Hence—euphoria!

Sensation of well-being, says the dictionary baldly. But the etymology is more enlightening. *Eu* gives the idea of good, happiness, calm and balanced joy. And *phoria* comes from the Greek word, "to carry." Someone euphoric is one who carries himself with happiness, who is well. But more literally still one might say it is someone who simply *carries* with happiness. At this, a shaft of light suddenly falls on my past, my present, and, who knows, perhaps my future too. For this fundamental idea of portage, of *phoria,* is also found in the name of Christopher, the giant Christ-Bearer; it is also illustrated in the legend of Albuquerque; and yet again it is embodied in the cars to which I reluctantly give the best of myself, but which even in their triviality are nonetheless instruments for the bearing of men, anthropophoric and therefore *phoric* par excellence.

I must stop. This series of revelations is making my eyes smart. But I just want to set down one more thought. The euphoria of October 3 was brought about by the weight of a child added to my own. Jeannot certainly isn't fat, but he must weigh about ninety pounds, and these were added to the two hundred and forty-five pounds, approximately, of my own weight. And yet it is by a feeling of lightness, of lightening, of winged joy, that my "phoric ecstasy" is best characterized. A sort of levitation caused by an increase in weight! What a paradox! The word "inversion" appears beneath my pen. There has

been a kind of change of sign: plus has become minus, and vice
versa. Benign, beneficent, divine inversion . . .

October 20, 1938. I couldn't sleep last night, and as the sky
was mild and luminous I went and drove about the streets in
my old Hotchkiss. The Champs-Elysées, the Place de la Con-
corde, the streets along the river. I was soon brought to a halt
by the caravans of carts and trucks blocking the approaches to
Les Halles. I left the car and went on on foot, soon getting lost
in the midst of that deluge of fruit and vegetables that creates in
the heart of Paris a kind of super kitchen garden and orchard
with sharp sweet smells and crude colors brought out by the
metallic light of acetylene lamps. At first one is reminded of a
gargantuan feast, but gradually the very abundance makes any
idea of actual eating ridiculous and discourages greed. I
walked around pyramids of cauliflowers and mountains of
kohlrabi; I just escaped an avalanche of leeks that shot down on
the pavement from a barrow backed into the curb.

It isn't to be thought that the enormous quantity of all these
things reduces their value. On the contrary, it heightens it by
making them unusable, by destroying in advance any idea of
utilization. That being so, those were essences spread out before me—the essence of apple, the essence of pea, the essence
of carrot. . . .

Except for a charming seller of fresh-water fish, shining fresh
and flashing with scales like a water sprite, the women were all
bulky and raucous. But the porters, the "strong men" of the city,
intrigued me because of the affinity I felt between them and myself. Their broad backs, enormous hands, and the quick short
steps they use when carrying a side of beef or a cask of herrings,
all these are, of course, me, from a certain point of view. But
theirs is a trivialized *phoria,* brought down to the level of lesser,
commercial utility. And I immediately imagined a true *phore*
of Les Halles, proud and generous, bearing triumphantly on his

formidable shoulders a horn of plenty which poured forth at his feet an inexhaustible treasure of flowers, fruit and precious stones.

October 28, 1938. Looking through a dictionary, I see that what Atlas carried on his shoulders was not the earth, as is usually depicted, but the sky. Moreover, geographically, Atlas is a mountain, and while to compare a mountain to a supporter of the sky makes sense, to make the reference apply to the earth is absurd. This is a notable example of malign inversion inflicted on one of the most outstanding *phoric* heroes. He upheld on his shoulders the stars and the moon, the constellations and the Milky Way, the nebulae, the comets, the dissolving suns. His head, rising into sidereal spaces, merged with the heavenly bodies. But that all had to be changed. Instead of the blue and gold infinity which both crowned and blessed him, he was burdened with the terrestrial globe, a lump of murky mud which bent his neck and blocked his view. And so the hero is debased and fallen.

But the more I think of it, the more it seems to me that Atlas uranophorus, Atlas astrophorus, is the mythological hero toward whom my life must tend and in whom it must at last find its fulfillment and apotheosis. Whatever I may bear in the future, with whatever precious and sacred burden my shoulders are laden and blessed, my triumphal end will be, God willing, to walk the earth carrying on my shoulders a star brighter and more golden than that of the Magi.

October 30, 1938. Hervé came in this morning to take delivery of his new open sports Renault Viva. My dislike of this sort of movie star's car was naturally tempered by the nice little commission I got on the sale. Hervé was very excited about his new acquisition. It made him more than usually expansive and sure of himself, as regards both his social success and his virtues, which of course he thinks of as indistinguishable. He is just thirty-six and told me that was the age of most possibility and poise, the highest point in a graph that has been climbing upward since birth and will now go down again toward death.

In fact it seems to me he's been thirty-six all the ten years I've known him, and that he was probably thirty-six before that— ever since he was born, very likely. Only up till now he has been too young for it, just as from now on, and increasingly from year to year, he will be too old.

Every man must throughout his life have an "essential age" that he aspires to till he reaches it and clings to after he's passed it. Bertrand has always been essentially sixty, and all his life Claude will be a young fellow of seventeen. As for me, my eternity sets an impassable distance between me and the tragedy of growing old, and I look on at the ebb and flow of generations with detachment tinged with melancholy, as a boulder in a forest may watch the coming and going of the seasons.

But when I see Hervé so fresh and optimistic, another idea occurs to me: he is *overadjusted*. The medical profession might well look into this new notion of hyperadaptation, and schools should take care that in trying to keep children from being mal-adjusted they don't go to the other extreme.

An overadjusted person is happy in his environment, "like a fish in the water." And a fish is a typical example of hyperadap-tation: the more complete its happiness, the more precarious. If the water gets too warm, or too salty, or if the level drops . . . So it's better to be just simply adapted, or even only fairly adapted, to water, like amphibians, which are not completely happy either in the wet or in the dry, but can accommodate themselves reasonably well to both. I don't wish Hervé any harm, but I think that if something in his brilliant setup were to give way, if fate had some blow in store for him, he would find it very hard to recover the poise he's so proud of. Whereas we amphibians, always at odds with things, accustomed to the makeshift and the approximate, we know from birth how to face up to all the treacheries of our environment.

November 4, 1938. Every time my comings and goings take me near the Louvre I reproach myself for not going in more often. To live in Paris and never go to the Louvre is the most inexcusable folly. So, after more than two years, I went this afternoon. And the clearest thing I got out of the visit was the realization of the change I'm going through. And this was brought home by the change that's taken place in my preoccupations.

I don't see how anyone can be exposed to the radiance of all those masterpieces without his eyes filling with tears. The magic of that antique Apollo from the island of Paros! The fascinating contrast between the hieratic formalism of the body, round as a pillar, thighs fused together, arms merged with the torso, and the enigmatic smile illuminating that countenance, emanating gentleness and made moving by the scars which mark the stone.

I started to imagine what my life would be like if this god lived with me, were possessed by me night and day. But no—to tell the truth, I was unable to imagine how I should endure the incandescent presence of such a meteor fallen beside me after a descent through twenty centuries. This statue is the best possible illustration of the essential function of art: to our hearts made sick by time—by its erosion, by the universal work of death, by the inexorable annihilation hanging over all we love —the work of art brings a little eternity. It is the sovereign remedy, the haven of peace for which we all long, a drop of cool water on our fevered lips.

I lingered longest in the Greco-Roman rooms by the busts. One never tires of examining those faces so vivid with intelligence, ambition, cruelty, self-satisfaction and courage—and, more rarely, goodness and nobility. One never tires of asking them the same question, a question that will always remain un-answered: of what sight, what life, what universe are you the secret cipher?

I strolled without paying much attention through various other rooms, only stopping in front of certain pictures—the same ones I've always stopped at for fifteen years. I was paying them a sort of visit, hearing their news and using them as mirrors in which to scrutinize my own image. Here I encountered an experience that used to be one of Nestor's preoccupations. He used to try to follow its variations in different places at St. Christopher's: it is called *atmospheric saturation*. In that atmosphere saturated with beauty I felt an intoxication that had a distant affinity with phoric ecstasy. Here was another piece to add to the great jigsaw I am patiently putting together.

As I went out through the turnstile, I noticed a boy having a heated argument with the attendant. I soon saw the problem, and the hopelessness of the dilemma. The boy had a camera, and he had to pay fifty centimes to take it in with him. As he hadn't got fifty centimes, he was supposed to leave it in the cloakroom, but that was an absurd suggestion as the cloakroom cost fifty centimes too. So he gave up and walked away, disappointed, and I of course took a hand—offering not the ridiculous adult solution of fifty centimes for the camera, but the bold, romantic, smuggler's solution. We both went back through the turnstile, I with the subject of debate bulging beneath my jacket.

Etienne was eleven, small for his age and delightfully dirty. His fine, thin, irregular, sensitive face made an exquisite contrast with an awkward body and knobbly round knees. The books spilling out of his pockets, his fiercely bitten nails, showed him to be one of those children who are surprisingly intellectually mature, who seem to have read and understood everything from birth, but whose physical backwardness gives an air of ingenu-ousness to all they say.

As soon as we got among the pictures he showed an astonishing familiarity with them and led me straight to Guido Reni's David, which he proposed to photograph. How had this stout lad, this greenhorn full of bounce, with his broad cheeks, his guileless eyes, his absurd plumed hat, and the skin tunic that covers him so skimpily, managed to win Etienne's heart? Through his rather muddled explanations I seemed to make out that for Etienne this David was the incarnation of that fascinating race who have never had any doubts about anything. Etienne had found that out! There are certain limited beings of dazzling but shallow beauty whom, to be frank, we should be quite justified in despising if it were not for the fact that they present us with the spectacle of a flawless adaptation to existence, a miraculous equivalence between their desires and the things within their reach, between their words and the questions they are asked, between their abilities and the professions they exercise. They are born, live and die as if the world were made for them and they for the world, and the rest—the doubters, the troubled, the angry, the curious, Etienne, I—watch them go by and wonder at their "naturalness," their unaffected spontaneity and ease.

In the midst of all this I had almost forgotten my recent preoccupations, when they were vividly brought back to me by the cast of a statue that is in the Vatican Museum. The inscription on the plinth would have been enough in itself to put me on the alert: Herakles Pedephorus. It was a representation of Hercules bearing seated on his left arm his little boy Telephus. Pedephorus means child-bearer . . . Hercules the Child-Bearer . . .

Etienne looked at me, unable, of course, to understand my astonishment. Then I laughed, bent down, and slipped my left arm behind his knees. He played along and sat on my arm, and I straightened up, pretending to rest my right hand on a cudgel, like our Herculean model. A little farther on we could have taken the same pose from the Hermes of Praxiteles, who carries the infant Bacchus seated on his left arm. But we were more tempted by two copies whose originals are in the National Museum in Naples. One shows a satyr playing the cymbals, his head turned up toward the infant Dionysus, who sits astride his neck. The child holds on with his left hand to the satyr's hair, and with the right offers him a bunch of grapes. It was fortunate we were alone in the room, Etienne and I, for, having perched my chance companion up on my shoulders, I danced around like the satyr to the imaginary clashing and banging of the cymbals, while Dionysus clutched my cheeks between his bare and grimy thighs. But it was the other Neapolitan statue that really gave us the chance to show what we were made of. It depicts Hector carrying off his little brother Troilus, who has been wounded. But *how!* He has thrown the child over his shoulder like a sack, so that he hangs head down with his left leg waving in the air while his brother holds on to him by his right calf. I looked at Etienne in questioning invitation, and he answered by simply holding out his left foot. I lifted him up so fast by the ankle that there was no danger of his head hitting the ground, and swung him choking with laughter over my shoulder, my apparent casualness secretly contrasting with the immensity and tenderness of my phoric vocation. How marvelous it felt! What a river of honey flowed majestically within me!

Etienne and I parted at the exit, and probably I shall never see him again. When that thought occurred to me I had a little silent sob in my throat, but I know for certain, with knowledge from an infallible, imperative source, that it is not for me to enter into individual relationships with this child or that. What would such relationships be, anyway? I think they would inevitably follow the facile beaten tracks of either paternity or sex. But my vocation is higher and more general. To have only one child is not to have any. To lack one is to lack them all.

November 10, 1938. All night the angelic made me gasp for

breath, made me dream of drowning and being buried in sand or earth or mud. I got up, my chest still racked, but glad to be finished with the phantasms which magnify a reality difficult enough in itself. Coffee so bitter it was undrinkable. A big roar. Two big roars. No relief. The morning's only consolation was of a fecal nature. Unexpectedly and impeccably I produced a magnificent turd, so long it had to curve at the ends to fit into the bowl. I contemplated fondly the fine chubby little babe of living clay I'd just brought forth, and my zest for life returned.

Constipation is a major source of moroseness. How well I understand the seventeenth century's mania for clysters and purges! What man finds it most difficult to accept is being a bag of excrement on two legs. The only remedy is a good, copious, regular defecation—but how stingily that favor is granted us!

November 12, 1938. Rachel and the pure act (power = 0). Jeannot and eu-phoria. What the Bible says about the original Adam. All these parts combine in my mind to form a coherent whole through which I see emerging the six letters of a name: Nestor.

The need to dominate. That is the phrase that best defines his personality. It seems to me now that to achieve his ends, to establish his ascendancy over others, there were two methods open to him. One was limited to the closed world of St. Christopher's, the school life in the center of which he crouched like a spider in his web, the buildings to which he had all the keys, inhabited by children who admired him blindly and adults who trembled before him. With careful vigilance he measured the atmospheric density of this closed world, which varied according to place—weaker in the playground than in the chapel, heavier in the refectory than in the aquarium, and at its very richest in the dormitories in the middle of the night.

As for the other method, he certainly anticipated it, he even attempted it a little, but only toward the end, and he didn't ex-

plore it far. I'm speaking now of the *phoric method*. Christopher
and Albuquerque, the fight of the horsemen, and even his wonderful bicycle—the schoolboy's phoric instrument par excellence
—all show he knew about this approach. And here I should like
to put forward a hypothesis which may be rather fragile but
which the future will confirm or deny. I wonder whether the two
methods are not mutually exclusive, in the way that two paths
cannot both be followed simultaneously even though they both
lead to the same end. The confinement of school life ruled out
the possibility of phoria, except as a useful preparation exercise
for some future unconfined. Thus phoria would belong to an
open environment, of very low density, and might be compared
to the oxygen mask that air pilots have to put on to fly at high
altitude.

All this is speculation, but it is simply an intellectual effort
on my part to understand the raw data that force themselves on
me.

Thus the idea of "atmospheric density," completely forgotten
since my schooldays, has cropped up twice in a few days, first
allusively in the Louvre, and again, and very violently, this
morning.

It was in the Rue de Rivoli, number 119 to be exact. A passage leads off there into the Rue Charlemagne, not far from
the school of the same name. I went along this dark alley, which
leads through two courtyards, on my way to see a supplier of
mine in the Quai des Célestins. School must just have ended, for
I suddenly found myself met head-on by a flood of children,
who rushed yelling down the narrow channel, fanning out into
the two courtyards, then jostling each other once more toward
the Rue de Rivoli. I held on my course like a salmon in a mountain stream, shoved and elbowed but deliciously happy too, with
the happiness of a little flower braving with all its stamens the
assault of a pollen-laden squall. It was a winged happiness, just

like that which had come upon me when I picked Jeannot up
after he'd been hit by the fan blade. But this time it was a multitudinous, tumultuous joy: all it needed to be better than phoric
ecstasy was the definitive seal of *totality*.

For I see now why a few lines from Descartes suddenly
seemed to stand out one day in letters of fire against the dullness
of a philosophy lesson. I was dimly aware that rule out of
the "Discourse on Method" had some connection with Nestor's
chief preoccupation. The rule was: "Make everywhere enumer-
ations so complete and reviews so general as to be sure of leaving nothing out." The great virtue of a world closed in on itself,
without any opening on the outside and obeying only its inner
self-given laws, is that it facilitates the observance of that fundamental rule.

But I live in an open environment, banished far from the
Nestorian citadel and its enumerated subjects. I grope my way,
comforted only by the certainty that an invisible thread guides
my footsteps toward a mysterious fulfillment. "Look at Christopher and step out boldly."

When I got back to the garage, I tried to find out how many
children there are at present in France. I fixed on twelve as being the age of the child par excellence, when he reaches his full
maturity as a child, his fine flowering, and also, alas, the brink
of the disaster of puberty. Here are the figures I was given by a
journalist friend who's an expert on demography:

BIRTHS IN FRANCE

	Total	Boys	Girls
1926	767,500	392,100	375,400
1927	743,800	379,700	364,100
1928	749,300	383,600	365,700
1929	730,100	373,000	357,100

So this year, 1938, is a particularly good year. The external atmosphere, now at its maximum strength, has a density it will not reach again for a long time, because the number of twelve-year-olds falls in 1939, and after having recovered a little in 1940 dwindles further still in 1941.

November 15, 1938. Yesterday evening the Hervés overcame my resistance and succeeded in getting me to go with them to see Mozart's *Don Giovanni.*

I knew already I hated opera, but now I also know why. It's because it shows us a world in which the sexual natures of the characters are broadened to the point of caricature. The men's virility borders on bestiality, the women's femininity is so acute hysteria appears to be its usual form. And I can't explain why, but that *freshness* which for me is the most important quality of all—in comparison with which the rest are just dud checks and dupery—is the quality opera is least suited to exhibit. Courage, greatness, majesty, a certain form of beauty—noble, proud, stormy—profundity, cruelty, love . . . yes. Freshness, no. Neither the music nor the sets nor the plot, still less the characters, leave the slightest room for it. In fact opera, whether we're speaking of the stage or the auditorium, is for me one of those stifling places where, naturally, children are excluded. Ugh!

As for the performance last night, I must admit it pierced my heart like a thorn, for the simple reason that Don Giovanni is myself. Oh, of course, painted and made up, masked and disguised, as is inevitable if I'm to be transposed into a universe from which freshness is excluded, so that everyone is taken in and the character remains unidentifiable to anyone but me. But the scene where Leporello gives a list of his master's conquests, a hundred and forty in Germany, two hundred and thirty in Italy, four hundred and fifty in France, and a thousand and three in Spain, is a good example of the *desire for exhaustive-*

ness that I'm only too familiar with. Rachel might have said to Don Giovanni as she said to me, "You're not a lover, you're an ogre!" And since I have eyes to see and ears to hear, I saw the meaning of the terrible epilogue, which was just my own death recounted in terms of the story. For I have no doubt that one night a visitor sculpted in gravestone will knock at my door with his marble fist, take the hand I hold out to him, and carry me off to the shades whence none returns. But his face won't be that of a father flouted and murdered. It will be my own.

I know now what my end will be. It will be the final victory of the man of stone that is in me over what remains to me of flesh and blood. It will come on the night when my destiny has entered into complete possession of me, and my last cry, my last sigh, will die away on lips of stone.

December 2, 1938. Just now, as I was watching the children coming out of the elementary school in the Boulevard de la Saussaye, I had a vision of a huge net suddenly scooping them all up. Most of them it would nab against the wall by the gate, but it would have to mop up the sidewalk to get those who were first out. And it would present me with a wriggling haul of black smocks piped in red, bare legs and laughing faces.

December 9, 1938. The papers are full of the arrest, at his house called La Voulzie at La Celle-Saint-Cloud, of Weidmann, a German suspected of having murdered seven people.

December 12, 1938. This morning there was a thin layer of snow all over the city, an event rare enough to justify a little photographic expedition. So I slung my Rolleiflex over my shoulder and went up the Avenue du Roule. When I got to the playground of the Collège Sainte-Croix, I stopped for a minute to watch. The strange ballet of the children's rushings to and fro, the figures ceaselessly formed and dissolved and re-

formed, must have some meaning. What? Groups, combinations, ensembles, arrangements, breakings apart—all here is
sign, as elsewhere, more than elsewhere. But sign of what?
That's my eternal question in this world covered in hieroglyphs
to which I haven't the key.

I went up to the railings, the grid separating the playground
from the sidewalk, and through the bars I took a spate of photographs, with the intense and guilty joy of a hunter shooting zoo
animals in their cages. I shall examine these pictures at leisure.
I shall compare the successive states of this little society, recorded second by second unawares. Surely I'm bound to discover something there! To put children in cages . . . My ogre's
soul ought to get something out of that. But this goes further
than a mere play on words. Every grid is an aid to deciphering;
all you need is to know how to apply it.

December 15, 1938. Midday break. Opposite me, sitting
reading with his left hand in his brown mop, is Jeannot. If he's
interrupted he puts his finger on the line where he left off or, if
he has to stop reading altogether, gets a stump of pencil out of
his pocket and makes a cross in the margin.

He's reading *Pinocchio* by Collodi, an Italian. I picked it
up and looked through it, shrinking in advance from the atroci-
ties children's stories are full of. As if children were dull brutes,
dim and insensitive, who can be moved only by fearsome tales,
real literary rotgut! Perrault, Lewis Carroll, Busch—sadists with
nothing to learn from the divine Marquis.

Pinocchio reassured me at first. The story of a puppet suddenly endowed with life goes back to a very old and gentle fairy-
tale tradition. But this first reaction only made me all the more
shocked when I came to the horrible episode where Pinocchio
and his friend Lampwick are changed into donkeys because
they are bad at their lessons. They go down on their knees,
clasp their hands, beg to be forgiven, but gradually their voices

become grotesque neighs, their little hands turn into hoofs, their faces lengthen into muzzles, and their trousers bulge and split with a horrid noise to let through a shaggy black tail. I really can't think of anything more horrible. Even the story of Donkey's Skin, making herself ugly to discourage the incestuous attentions of her father, seems to me less dreadful than what these two little boys go through.

But I realize their tribulation is an old acquaintance. Every day I encounter the wicked fairy who with her magic wand turns the coach into a pumpkin and the little boy into an ass: she is the fairy Puberty. A child of twelve has reached an unsurpassable point of balance and bloom that makes him the masterpiece of creation. He is happy, sure of himself, confident in the surrounding universe, which seems to him perfectly ordered. His beauty of face and body at that age is such that all human beauty is only a more or less distant reflection of it. And then—disaster. All the hideousness of virility—the hairy squalor and cadaverous hue of adult flesh; the rough cheeks; the shapeless, stinking, exaggerated, ass's sex—all descend at once on the little prince, hurled down from his throne. He has become a hungry cur, shifty-eyed, pimply and stooping, greedily guzzling up all the trash of the movies and the music hall. In short, an adolescent.

The drift is clear. The flowering time is over. Now he must become fruit, seed. The snare of matrimony will soon seize the simpleton in its jaws, and there he'll be, yoked with the rest to the propagation of the species, forced to contribute to the great demographic diarrhea the human race is dying of. It makes you sad and angry. But what's the good? And won't this dunghill soon produce other flowers?

December 18, 1938. Preliminary investigations have begun in the case of Weidmann, murderer of seven. He's nearly six foot three and weighs two hundred and forty-five pounds. Exactly like me.

December 21, 1938. This morning in the Avenue du Roule I was just going past the playground of the Collège Sainte-Croix and on to the series of repair shops and gas stations leading to my own garage when I was all at once rooted to the spot by a long cry that suddenly rose above the hubbub of the children at recess. It was a sustained guttural note of extraordinary purity, like an appeal welling up from the depths of the body, and it ended in a series of modulations at once joyous and moving. It gave an astonishing impression of simultaneous rigor and plenitude, balance and excess.

I at once turned back, sure I'd see something or someone in the playground that was exceptional and astonishing. But no, there was nothing. That crystal note enriched with all the harmonics of the flesh still rang in my ears, and the children just came and went as before, as if that aural miracle had never happened. Which of these little men had drawn forth from himself that pure and happy plaint? To me they all looked equally ordinary—i.e., each as essential as the other.

I stood there for some time, lulled by the fading echo of the "cry," which conjured up the memory of St. Christopher's, but which was being gradually drowned and effaced by the manifold, tonic music of the children playing and fighting. Then a bell rang and they lined up to go back into their classrooms. I walked away at last from the now deserted playground.

But before I went back to the garage I made a note of the date and time when I'd heard the "cry," absurd as it might seem to think a miracle could recur according to a pattern.

December 23, 1938. A single large plain building in the Boulevard de la Saussaye holds both the nursery classes and the boys' and girls' primary schools. It has become a habit of mine now to be there when the children are let out at six o'clock in the evening. What first attracted my attention was the rocket of sound fanning out behind the high wall one day when I passed at recess. I stopped, deliciously enfolded in a vast chorus, both single and manifold, irregularly interspersed with silences and exclamations, pauses and *mezza voce* repeats. I was waiting to hear again the "cry" that so touched me the day before yesterday outside the railings of Sainte-Croix, for I'm sure that was not the particular manifestation of an individual voice but the very essence of childhood in aural form.

I didn't hear the "cry" this morning. A powerful passionate unison was suddenly followed by a delicate trill, a shrill pizzicato as fine as lace and at once mocking and caressing, which made my eyes smart with tears. I made up my mind to ask Karl F. to lend me his recording machine. I'll go back every day and register every recess on tape, and listen to them quietly at home as many times as is necessary to decipher the thread of the symphony. And who knows, perhaps I'll learn to sing with it, to know it by heart, and to conjure up the memory of afternoon recess on November 25 or morning recess on December 20 just as I can summon up a Beethoven quartet or a Chopin étude.

While waiting to acquire this new kind of musical connoisseurship, I note with a surprise new every day the way the boys rush out into the street when let loose after long hours of confinement. It's always the same ones who come out first, always the same ones who linger. I know and recognize these better than all the others struggling and shouting to get through the gate together.

Out of the other door flows a twittering troop of little girls, whom I observe with passionate curiosity. It's impossible to express the harm done in our childhood by the segregation of boys and girls. Men and women are so foreign to each other, it's so difficult for them to arrive at a life in common, that it's stupid and criminal not to accustom them to sharing everything from childhood. And yet it's well known that a cat and a dog will live together in peace only if they've been reared on the same bottle!

December 28, 1938. The fathomless sadness of schools and playgrounds emptied by the Christmas holidays. How can one live without those little islands of reviving freshness, those little oxygen bags that enable one to forget for a few moments the pestilence of adulthood? I realize the children's freedom is the worst possible thing for me. When they're scattered to the four winds, the atmosphere they leave behind is so rarefied it's unbreathable.

It was in this downcast mood that I went this morning to the mass dedicated to the Holy Innocents, massacred by order of King Herod. How could I fail to relate this great and terrible slaughter to the symphony of children's cries I feast on every day? When they read out the account of the crime from St. Matthew's gospel I got behind a pillar and sobbed with pleasure and pity.

December 31, 1938. In a few minutes the year 1939 will begin. Men and women in clowns' hats are throwing confetti at one another. As for me, I get up out of a bed made arid, dull and inhospitable by insomnia and walk the brink of solitude like a sleepwalker on the edge of a roof. The certainty that the year will not end without a downpour of fire and brimstone fills me with fear and sadness. I open the Bible, but it is a book written by nocturnals like myself and gives off only a dreadfully amplified echo of my own laments.

Mine eye also is dim by reason of sorrow, and all my members are as a shadow. . . .

If I wait, the grave is mine house: I have made my bed in the darkness.

I have said to corruption, Thou art my father: to the worm, Thou art my mother, and my sister. . . .

Dead things are formed from under the waters, and the inhabitants thereof.

Hell is naked before him, and destruction hath no covering.

He stretcheth out the north over the empty place, and hangeth the earth upon nothing.

He bindeth up the waters in his thick clouds; and the cloud is not rent under them.

He holdeth back the face of his throne, and spreadeth his cloud upon it.

He hath compassed the waters with bounds, until the day and night come to an end. . . .

. . . he hath set darkness in my paths.

He hath stripped me of my glory, and taken the crown from my head.

He hath destroyed me on every side, and I am gone: and mine hope hath he removed like a tree.

. . . he maketh sore, and bindeth up; he woundeth, and his hands make whole. . . .

And I know he will one day bring back the smile to my lips, and fill my mouth with songs of joy.

Then shall the earth tremble for joy, and the sea echo with laughter.

The fields will ripple with love, and the trees of the forest shake their leaves, whinnying like steeds that toss their manes in their pride.

March 2, 1939. I haven't written anything since the beginning of the year. In fact I've hardly lived! When I was a child the plunge into the dark, damp and cold of winter was identical, for me, with the misery of existence. It took me a long while to see that in fact it was only a matter of season. As I get older, time passes faster and faster with every year, so that I can cope

with longer and longer stretches of it. But winter has still not
shrunk small enough for me to be able to step blithely across it.
One day perhaps I shall, but for the moment my stride isn't big
enough: I fall into the ditch of January-February feeling I shall
never emerge.

The truth is I hate winter because winter hates the flesh and
flogs it like a puritan wherever it finds it naked. Cold is a moral
lesson of the most ferociously Jansenist kind. And, quite
naturally, since signs need flesh to make themselves manifest,
winter silences the voices and extinguishes the fires that usually
strew my path. So I heave to and hibernate with my face to the
wall and my hands over my ears.

But this morning gusts of warm wind were drying up the rain
that had beaten down all night on the glass roof of the garage.
An oceanic mood softened the sky. When I went out I suddenly
found myself surrounded by a crowd of schoolgirls, their bare
legs whitened by winter. But soon, M'Abel, we shall be seeing
white socks and blouses again, summer dresses and short
skirts! You can start furbishing up your machine for thieving
cries and sounds and your box for capturing images.

But be careful, too—it won't be long either before premonitions start hitting you in the eye!

March 4, 1939. Sixty-two cardinals, each supported by a con-
clavist and a noble guard, shut themselves up the morning before last in the part of the Vatican where conclaves are held.
They sang the "Veni Creator," but heaven was displeased and
drowned their voices with a violent storm. So the fine flower of
the cosmopolitan ecclesiastical scum was walled up by Prince
Chigi, marshal of the conclave, and all the exits were guarded
by papal troops and officials of the Rota.

One trembles to think of the sabbath held by those hundred
and eighty-six old men, disposing of an absolutely unprecedented atmospheric density! Only the whorls of black smoke

coming out of the chimney of the Sistine Chapel bore witness
to the devilry which that assembly, drunk with their invulner-
ability, got up to.

At half past five in the afternoon, Cardinal Caccia Dominioni
presented himself on the central loggia of St. Peter's, which the
ceremony-mongers had thrown open, and which they had hung
with the great tapestry bearing the arms of Pius IX.

"I bring you glad tidings," he declared. "We have a Pope,
in the person of the Most Reverend Cardinal Eugenio Pacelli."

The crowd immediately sang the "Te Deum."

I don't know who this Pacelli is. His Christian name is
Eugene, the same as Weidmann's. And I've seen his photograph
in the papers. He looks like the mummy of Ramses II, only more
desiccated and less human. Just what's called for by the apocalyptic times that lie ahead: an anti-pastor ravaged by all the
demons of Purity.

March 15, 1939. I noticed, coming out of the elementary
school in the Boulevard de la Saussaye with a group of friends,
a little girl of astonishing beauty—she looks to me very much a
woman already, in spite of her flat body and grazed knees. I
said I noticed her, but it would be more accurate to say
she noticed me. It was bound to happen. I've been going there
for weeks, either with my camera, or with Karl F.'s recording
machine hidden in my old Hotchkiss, with only the microphone
emerging on top of a sort of vertical aerial I've fixed up between
the two doors of the car. Sometimes I take both the camera
and the recorder, using the second during recess and the first
when the children are let out of school.

I know her name is Martine because I've heard her friends
call her that. The question I ask myself is: what about phoria
in the case of a little girl? The exclusively bachelor education
I got at St. Christopher's makes the female infant a terra
incognita I'm dying to explore.

March 21, 1939. This first day of spring has been marked for me by one black milestone and one white, as if from now on good and bad omens were to balance one another along my path.

The black was I saw in the paper that Weidmann—I follow the details of his case every day—was born in Frankfurt on February 5, 1908, and he is an only child. I am an only child, and I was born on February 5, 1908, at Gournay-en-Bray. So it was not enough that the killer of seven was the same weight and height as I; he had to be born on the same day as well. This sort of coincidence upsets me more than I can say.

The white stone was the four-thirty recess yesterday, the recording of which ought to become a great classic of its kind. For the first time I was present at a shift from purely instrumental symphony toward dramatic action; in short, toward oratorio. And there it is, all coiled up on the spool. I've listened to it about twenty times and I don't think I'll ever get tired of it.

It's introduced by a triumphant spray of sound that absorbs everything else and creates a silence around itself. Then the apparently homogeneous mass cracks into a thousand little cries that diversify and weaken it at the same time. Then your heart is suddenly brought to a standstill by a terrific, breath-taking pause. And then comes another sheaf of sound, but this time the little cries have become words, a multitudinous murmur in which the dominant note is an anguish repeated and reflected a thousand times by a thousand different facets. Finally a word stands out in big shiny letters against this quivering background: PIG! Ah, every time I listen I await it in trembling, this long-prepared, richly set-off insult; and when it at length bursts out I've already been crouching for several seconds in my chair in anticipation of the shock. Afterward, inevitably, the mass of sound breaks up; independent centers form. People who like program music might explain these as a game of football or puss-in-the-corner, a row between two children, or a group of them chanting a counting rhyme. But such literary interpretations are to be rejected: the breakup is the attempt of a collectivity to differentiate itself and even, at the greatest danger to itself, to give birth to separate individuals. But then all is resolved once more in a fulmination of shouts and groans, a silver blur that shimmers with sad or smiling faces until the dome of sound is attacked by the rapid reverberation of the bell, which undermines it on all sides until it is reduced to nothing, and all that is to be heard is the tramp of boots on the ground.

Winding back the tape for the twentieth time, I marvel at how the clear and striking detail of these fifteen minutes went completely unnoticed as I was actually recording it. All I perceived at the time was a moving but chaotic hubbub. Its real nature emerged only gradually as I kept on playing it back.

The wall of our blindness and deafness can be penetrated only if signs make a repeated assault on it. All we need to understand all the symbols and parables in the world is the faculty of infinite attention.

April 6, 1939. Albert Lebrun has been re-elected President of the Republic by 506 out of 910 senators and deputies gathered to vote in the Palais des Congrès at Versailles. They made a highly discriminating choice. Lebrun is the only man who manages to be both insignificant and abject.

April 14, 1939. This evening Martine had tied a black silk scarf over her head, making a narrow frame for her triangular face. Stripped of the garrulous and trivial commentary of her blonde curls and reduced to its essential lines, her countenance had the purity of a Madonna, enlivened, in spite of her seriousness, by her childlike air. How pretty she was! She looked at me intently but did not smile.

May 1, 1939. When I range about the streets in my old Hotchkiss, I'm never quite happy unless the camera case slung around my neck is properly wedged between my legs. I enjoy being equipped with a huge leather-clad sex whose Cyclopean eye opens like lightning when I command it to look, and closes again inexorably on what it has seen. It is a marvelous organ, seer and remembrancer, a tireless hawk that swoops on its prey to steal from it and bring back to its master that which is profoundest in it and most deceptive—appearance! I am intoxicated by the constant availability of this fine compact object, so mysteriously hollow, swinging on its strap like the censer of all the beauties of the earth. The unused film with which it is secretly lined is an immense blind retina, which will see and be dazzled only once, but will never forget.

I've always liked photography, including developing and printing, and as soon as I came to live at the garage I made a darkroom out of a little room with running water from which the light could easily be excluded. Now I realize how providential this hobby was, and how it lends itself to my present preoccupations. For it is plain that photography is a kind of magic to bring about the possession of what is photographed. Anyone who is afraid of having his or her photograph "taken" is only showing the most elementary common sense. It is a method of consumption usually resorted to for want of a better: needless to say, if beautiful landscapes could be eaten they would be photographed much less.

One cannot avoid a comparison with the painter, who works openly, patiently and patently laying down on the canvas, stroke by stroke, his own feelings and personality. The act of photography, on the other hand, is instantaneous and occult, like the wave of a magic wand transforming a pumpkin into a coach, or a maiden who is awake into one who is asleep. The artist is expansive, generous, centrifugal. The photographer is miserly, greedy, avid and centripetal. In other words I am a born photographer. As I don't possess the despotic powers to procure me actual possession of the children I've decided to get hold of, I make use of the snare of photography. And I hasten to add that this is not at all a second best. Whatever the future has in store for me, I shall always love these images, bright and deep as lakes, into which I dive with abandon on certain lonely evenings. In them is life, smiling, plump, on offer, imprisoned in the magic paper, a last survival of slavery, that lost paradise I have not ceased to mourn. Sorcery makes use of the half-amorous, half-murderous possession of the photographed by the photographer. But for me, though I do not reject the power of magic, the object of the act of photography is something greater and higher. It consists in raising the real object to a new power—the *imaginary power*. A photographic image, which is indisputably an emanation of reality, is at the same time consubstantial with my fantasies and on a level with my imaginary universe. Photography promotes reality to the plane of dream; it metamorphoses a real object into its own myth. The lens is the narrow gate through which the elect, those called to become gods and heroes *possessed,* make their secret entry into my inner Pantheon.

That being so, it is clear I don't need to photograph *all* the children in France and in the world in order to satisfy the need for exhaustiveness that is my torment. For each photograph raises its subject to a degree of abstraction that automatically confers on it a certain generality, so that every child photographed is a thousand children possessed.

So on this fine sunny first of May, having breakfasted gaily and briefly, I set out image-hunting, my camera lovingly stowed in its genital position. My eyes were already nothing but view finders, collecting possible pictures from branches, sidewalks, even from inside the cars I passed. The pedestrians of the first of May, the dogs of the first of May, walked with a Sunday gait along streets made peaceful by the holiday. The world filed in procession past my windshield. The world was a window marvelously dressed by an ingenious window dresser called the First of May. The cops who spend their May Day regulating the traffic made friendly signs at me with their white sticks.

I left the old Hotchkiss by the river near the Pont Alexandre III. Gray gulls, motionless fishermen, deserted yachts, a few clerks washing their cars at the water's edge—perhaps the happiest moment in the week for them. A waterman worked away furiously at the pump of a barge, and at each effort a yellow ejaculation streamed out at the water line. I jumped into a boat and, at the risk of falling in the river, maneuvered into my view finder the yellow jet, the sharp black outline of the hull, and above, against a patch of blue sky, the little chap jumping up and down to bring all his weight to bear on the arm of the pump. On the quay a boy was amusing himself dazzling passers-by with a mirror. I asked him to flash his beam toward the camera and already imagined the photograph that would emerge: a white explosion surmounted by a shaggy head with a great gap-toothed grin.

On the esplanade in front of the Palais de Tokio there were some boys roller-skating and others playing ball. The skaters never stopped skating. The others never skated instead of playing ball. The two groups never mixed; they seemed separated by an almost biological difference. It made one think of ants, some of which are winged and others not.

I particularly noticed two of the skaters, very dark, brothers probably, and alike in dress as well as in face and physique. They differed only in age and height, as faun and faunlet. They swooped about, making swift arabesques, jumping down several steps at once. I asked them to hold hands and skate around under the huge relief that shows Terpsichore and a nymph dancing against an Arcadian background. I took a photograph of the double couple, the little one of flesh and the big one of stone, so unaware of each other yet so well attuned. Then I told the boys Terpsichore was a Greek goddess, one of the Graces, the patroness of roller skaters. After a while everyone's attention was attracted by a young cyclist who had fixed his front wheel to a roller skate. This surprising invention combined a schoolboy's two essential but in theory incompatible attributes. The front wheel of the bicycle didn't go around but slid with a metallic clatter over the flagstones.

After a moment the others resumed what they were doing, chasing each other, vaulting, leaping, dancing thunderous farandoles. One farandole broke up into a leap down several steps. One of the boys tripped, bounced down the rest of the stairs, and ended up at the bottom a poor little motionless heap. I recognized him as the younger of the two brothers, the faunlet. He turned over slowly, sat up, then bent forward over his right knee. He didn't cry, but his face was crumpled up with pain. I knelt beside him and slipped my hand under his knee, into that damp, tender, trembling hollow; a strange sweetness gripped my insides. His wound, caused no doubt by the edge of one of the marble steps, was magnificently clean and sharp: a flawlessly oval ruby slit, a Cyclops' eye with bordered lids and narrow corners, gouged indeed and blind, but scarcely bleeding—just oozing, as if with its own vitreous humor, a slow albuminous trickle of lymph that ran down the calf into the wrinkled sock. A couple of boys undid his skates while I fixed the necessary attachments to my lens and view finder. The casualty now had to stand up and keep standing up for at least a few seconds. I set him on his feet, but he tottered, lime green. "He'll fall," said one of the others. I wasn't going to have that. I slapped him hard and propped him up against the wall. Then I took one shot —but it would come out flat in that direct light. I needed an oblique angle to catch the purple depths of the socket. I twisted the boy around ninety degrees. On to the gouged Cyclops' eye my camera bent its crystal robot's eye. It was a basic confrontation between wounded flesh, reduced to passivity, suffering, open, unable to do anything but be seen, and the pure, possessive, definitive vision of the weapon I was armed with. Kneeling in front of that small statue of suffering, I finished the film in a kind of drunken happiness beyond my control. Then at last came the moment I awaited with jubilation. I let the camera fall on its strap, slipped my right arm under the boy's knees and my left under his armpits, and stood up with my fragile burden.

I stood up, and my shoulders touched the sky, my head was encircled by archangels singing anthems in my praise. Mystic roses poured forth their sweetest perfume. For the second time in a few months I'd lifted a wounded child in my arms and been enfolded in phoric ecstasy. That alone was enough to prove I'd entered upon a new era.

The children around me could not understand the light transverberating my face. I must step back into time, take up the thread of ordinary events again, pretend to be just one more of the great human family. . . .

I went over to my car and put the faunlet in, with the faun beside him to look after him. I dropped them both at a pharmacy in the Place de l'Alma and drove off singing, caressing between my thighs my image box full of new treasures. I knew in advance their beauty would exceed my expectations.

May 4, 1939. This morning I was strolling about St. Peter's Church at Neuilly, under cool vaults lit up by a ray of sunshine shining through a stained-glass window. An infant wail drew me to the side chapel that contains the font. There a group of friends and relations stood around a tall dark man gravely bearing in his arms a baby that looked as if it were swathed in a bridal veil. *The godfather bears his godson over the baptismal font*—for the first time I understood the Tiffaugian meaning of the sacrament of baptism: it is a little phoric marriage between an adult and a child.

Of course, this is only a secondary interpretation of an

institution whose main significance lies elsewhere—and it may be noted in passing that I've never been asked to be a godfather. But I like to observe that such a thing *could* fit in with my vocation. I see in this a sign, if not a proof, that a somewhat rough but not destructive conversion of things might be enough to turn toward me that facet which already bears my imprint.

May 7, 1939. Developing films and seeing the negatives involves both a temptation and a regret. For when you look at the negative transparencies they have a unique charm, and it is all too clear that printing them and restoring the positive image is a kind of debasement. But the richness of nuance and detail, the depth of tone, the nocturnal luminosity that lights up the negative image—all these would be nothing without the strangeness produced by the inversion of values. A face has white hair and black teeth, a black forehead and white eyebrows, and while the white of the eye is black, the pupil is a little pinpoint of light; a landscape has trees like swan's feathers standing out against an inky sky; in a naked body, the parts that are softest and pearliest in reality here appear darkest and murkiest. And this perpetual denial of our visual habits seems to introduce us into an *inverse* world, but a world of images and therefore without real malignity, one that can be put right again whenever we wish and that is thus literally *reversible.*

It is in the red night of the darkroom that the negative really stands out supreme. Yesterday I shut myself up there about seven o'clock and, as always, soon lost all notion of time. I emerged pale and trembling with fatigue in the middle of the night. There's something of the black mass about manipulating so recklessly such a personal emanation of someone else, just as there's something of the tabernacle in the enlarger, of hell in the gory light one works in, and of alchemy in the pans of developer and the stop and fixing baths. The odors of bisulphite, quinol, acetic acid and hyposulphite only add more evil spells to the already heavy atmosphere.

But it is from the enlargement of the image, and the possibilities this offers of inversion, that the most singular powers of the photographer derive. For it is not merely a matter of metamorphosis from black to white and vice versa. There is also the possibility, if you put the negative in the projector the wrong way around, of switching left and right. When the photograph is developed you thus get a double inversion—old cameras even actually "take" the picture upside down as well. The magic element, whether beneficent or maleficent, in photography is amply brought out by these minor but characteristic details.

I have a whole boxful of negatives derived from my gleanings in the fields of empiricism. And there are all these children, available at any moment, unresisting and good as gold. Whenever I like I can put any one of them into the enlarger, and at once he fills the room, spreads all over the walls, the table, me. I can reproduce any part of his body or face on a gigantic scale, and as often as I please. For while the great world itself is an unlimited hunting ground and the despair of whoever seeks exhaustiveness, my own little tank of images, though rich, is finite: my stock of children is counted and numbered, and all its possibilities are duly known to me. Finally, the fact that I have a finite number of negatives is neatly balanced by the fact that from each of them I can produce an infinite number of positive images. The empirical infinite, first reduced to the finiteness of my collection, becomes once more a possible infinite, but only through me. Through photography, wild infinity becomes domesticated.

May 14, 1939. The Ambroises. I've let three rooms to them on the ground floor. Ambroise acts as concierge and watchman when the garage is closed. Madame Eugénie doesn't do anything; she probably never has done anything in her whole life.

Ambroise told me his story. Forty years ago they met, Eugénie and he, at the Gare du Nord. He was just starting out as a cabinetmaker. She was a girl in deep mourning just up from Brabant in Belgium. She must have been one of those fair, flabby, plaintive beauties whose only strength is an unshakable power of inertia. She had left everything to come and settle the estate of her father, who had died in Paris in the arms of his son—a priest. The father had been well off and the brother would divide the property fairly between himself and his little sister. At least, this was what Eugénie told the young Ambroise while they were still in the station. He was already gaunt and scraggy in his black shiny cotton suit, but he was eager and enterprising and thought he had scented good fortune in both senses of the word. So he took charge of her two cases and, as she had nowhere to stay, offered there and then to put her up at his place—with strictly honorable intentions, he promised. And, as he said to me one day in a burst of helpless indignation, "I've been carrying those two cases for forty years!"

For as soon as she was settled, and without any difficulty seduced, Eugénie dug in her toes and stuck obstinately in Ambroise's modest lodgings. She weighed all the more heavily on him as her hopes as an heiress soon went up in smoke, either because the priest cheated her (that was *her* version) or because her father didn't leave anything. I imagine Ambroise and Eugénie have been performing for forty years the same duologue they now act out under my roof. He, tough and gnarled as a vine, twists his white mustache and fulminates everlastingly against his own stupidity and the vegetable sloth of his wife (though in fact they never actually got married). She lies flopped in a chair, huge, white and spongy, her gray hair falling in spaniel's ears around her big doleful face, and never stops blessing her kind Monsieur Ambroise—a real saint, who does not only his own work but also the cleaning, the shopping, the cooking and the dishes as well. An onerous love affair if ever there was one!

Eugénie talks a great deal, in a gray, uniformly plaintive voice, a kind of monotonous *lamento* that tirelessly goes over and over the awfulness of people and things and the weather. For a long time I paid no attention to this faucet of bitter, lukewarm water that murmured at me every time I had occasion to call on the Ambroises. Until one day I noticed that her voice, usually at the end of a verse, often rose an octave and was ornamented with silvery harmonics, vernal twitters, pastoral tinklings. Then I began to take pleasure in waiting for this sudden change of register, this transition I privately called her "cowbell effect," and came to realize the sense these tinklings and twitterings always had. Without exception they referred to some sordid slander, malicious aspersion or damaging insinuation, led up to by the usual long, morose gabble. In this way I found out that Jeannot pilfered from the department store; that Ben Ahmed "kept" a local Berber prostitute; that the Italian garage hand who helped out when we were busy didn't limit himself to his percentage and tips; and above all that my photographic expeditions had not escaped my informant's vigilant and spiteful eye.

One day when I'd arrived back after a particularly productive outing, swinging my camera on its strap as one might let a hound gambol about after he had especially distinguished himself in the chase, I heard someone saying something as, drunk with love and delight, I went past the Ambroises' window.

"There goes Monsieur Tiffauges back from the market with supplies of raw meat. Now he'll shut himself up in the dark to eat it. There are some things one can't do in broad daylight, aren't there?"

It was Eugénie, with a whole orchestra of glockenspiels in her voice.

May 18, 1939. For a long time I sneaked my photographs; that is, took them unknown to whomever I was photographing. It's a good, convenient method and also one that allows for the touch of cowardice that always grips me when I'm about to ravish an image. But it's really only a second best, and I realize now that, terrifying as it may seem, a confrontation with the person photographed is always preferable. For it's a good thing that the actual taking of the snap should be reflected in one way or another in the face or attitude of the subject: as surprise, anger, fear; amusement or flattered vanity; buffoonery or obscene or provocative gesture. A hundred years ago, when anesthesia was first introduced into the operating theater, some surgeons protested. "Surgery is dead," said one of them. "It rested on a union in suffering between patient and doctor. Anesthesia reduces it to the level of dissecting corpses." It's rather similar with photography. Telescopic lenses that enable one to operate from a distance, without any contact with the subject, kill what is most moving about taking pictures: the slight suffering that is experienced, together and from opposite poles, by the person who knows he is being photographed and by the person who knows he is known to be committing a predatory act, to be hijacking an image.

May 20, 1939. In the black-white inversion the grays also undergo a permutation, but a lesser one, and one that grows smaller as they approach a medium gray in which the black and white components exactly balance one another. This medium gray constitutes the pivot, immutable and absolute itself, around which inversion revolves. Has anyone ever tried to define and produce that *absolute gray* that resists all inversion? I've never heard about it if they have.

May 25, 1939. All the children had gone, and I was waiting, disappointed, because I hadn't seen Martine. Finally she came

out, alone, last. I went up to her, attempting a smile to mask
my agonized shyness. I said hello as if we'd known each
other a long time and in an access of boldness offered to
drive her home in my old Hotchkiss. She didn't answer, but
she followed me, and as I held the car door open for her she
got in and pulled her short skirt down over her legs with a deliciously feminine gesture.

I was tongue-tied and didn't exchange three sentences with
her throughout the journey. She didn't want me to drop her outside her own door—how pleased I was at the slightly guilty complicity that was set up between us!—and asked me to stop on the
island of the Grande Jatte in the Boulevard de Levallois, in
front of a building almost finished but still under construction.
She ran off light as an elf, and I was surprised to see her go on
to the deserted site and disappear down the stair leading to the
cellar.

May 28, 1939. Martine's father works on the railway. When
she told me she had three sisters I trembled with curiosity. How
I should like to meet these other versions of Martine, four years
old, nine years old, and sixteen, like a musical theme taken up
by different instruments and in different keys! Here again I encounter my strange inability to confine myself to one individual-
ity, my irrepressible inclination to turn a single formula into
variations, into a repetition without monotony.

She always has me drop her by the apartment building under
construction. She says that by going through the cellar she takes
a short cut to where her family lives, over in the Boulevard
Vital-Bouhot.

May 30, 1939. It's a funny thing, but ever since I started
concentrating so much on children I seem to have less appetite.
The windows of creameries and butchers' shops don't excite
my voracity as they did. I've even given up raw meat and milk

for a more ordinary diet. And yet I'm not getting thin! It's as if contact with children appeased more subtly and so to speak spiritually a hunger that itself seems to have become more refined, and closer to the heart than to the stomach.

June 3, 1939. Every day I read the reports of Eugene Weidmann's trial. Not only does the sight of all society seeking the destruction of this one man, weighed down with crimes, arouse a feeling of sympathy in me for the accused, but it's as if fate were going out of its way to make him and me alike. This morning I found out he's left-handed and committed all his murders with his left hand. Sinister crimes, if ever there were any! Sinister, like my writings.

Fortunately the mere thought of Martine is enough to drive away my obsessions.

June 6, 1939. The skin with its texture, its network of squares and diamonds, the varying scale of its blemishes, its tight or relaxed pores, its soft or bristling hairs, in a word the whole *epidermic grid*—that's a field where photography shows itself at its best, and which is completely different from painting.

June 10, 1939. The image I like best to conjure up is that of Martine's family—her three sisters and mother and father gathered together in the evening in the lamplight. I who never had a family, how I'd love to sit down among them, shut myself up in that closed cell whose atmosphere must be so special and dense! It's to be noted that my hunting expeditions, whether photographic or otherwise, though their quarry is always, necessarily, a particular individual, all lead me eventually to a closed community. I'm struck by a comparison which, though obviously ogreish, does throw light on my case. After centuries of gathering wild plants, man discovered agriculture. After centuries of hunting, he discovered cattle rearing. I, weary of coursing the icy steppes, dream of enclosed orchards where the finest fruits fall into my hand, of great herds meek and willing, shut up in warm steaming stables where I could sleep with them in comfort the winter through.

June 16, 1939. The vile Lebrun has just rejected Weidmann's appeal. The number of murders Weidmann has committed is unknown, perhaps even to himself. Just the same, is any crime more abominable than that of the man bedizened with honors and sitting behind a vast desk free from any kind of pressure, who refuses to make the tiny gesture that would prevent the perpetration of legal murder?

June 17, 1939. Some obscure force against which I struggled in vain made me yield to the entreaties of Madame Eugénie, who wanted me to take her and some of her neighbors to Versailles yesterday evening to see Weidmann's execution. The women's indecent excitement would have been enough to put me off such an expedition if by any aberration it had occurred to me, but some fatality seemed to force me to this rendezvous with the giant slayer of seven at the moment of his death, just as every day it had set before my eyes articles in the paper about the investigation of his crimes and his trial.

We knew the execution was to take place at dawn, but Madame Eugénie and her friends insisted on starting out at nine in the evening to make sure of getting good seats. Ambroise had refused point-blank to take part in this dubious excursion. He told me he was glad of the opportunity to spend the evening without his wife. From the start I was irritated by the trivial and venomous jabber of the four old gossips overloading the car. Every so often I would hear Madame Eugénie's cowbell effect, and each time I could detect the poisoned dart.

As soon as we reached the outskirts of the town, we could tell something unusual was up. Not only did the crowd you al-

ways get on a special evening fill the streets and sidewalks, but
also a sort of foul connivance floated in the air. All these men,
women and children were here for the same thing, and they
knew it. And I was one of them. Who was I to talk?

With some difficulty I managed to park the car in the Rue du
Maréchal Joffre, and we continued on foot. The mob got bigger
every minute. The streets were jammed with traffic. The Place
d'Armes opposite the château and the Place de la Préfecture
were being used as parking lots. The two stations disgorged
floods of people every time a train arrived. But even so cyclists
were the most in evidence, including a large proportion of tan-
dems with men and women alike dressed in knickers and turtle-
neck sweaters.

At midnight a long-drawn-out exclamation greeted the ex-
tinguishing of the gas lamps. The darkness, pierced by headlights, flashlights and acetylene lamps, was full of laughter, oaths
and chortles. Sometimes the sound was dominated by a smutty
remark from some smart-aleck, sometimes it was smothered by
a chorus of automobile horns. I let myself be hauled along,
grumbling, by my rope of four old women, led by a Madame
Eugénie whom there was now no holding back. This grotesque
crew made its way to the Place Saint-Louis and its three bistros,
lights all aflame. Madame Eugénie's skill and determination
got us a table and five chairs at one of the sidewalk cafés. But
this was not enough. Our chieftainess would not rest until she
had hoisted her chair on the table and we had somehow hoisted
her up on to it. Now she was enthroned above the melee, like
the divinity of the hangman's deeds that were about to take
place. I and her three friends had our work cut out protecting
the table, which was nearly toppled over by every movement of
the crowd; we couldn't really see anything except Madame Eugénie's elephantine ankles and buckled felt slippers. All around
us it was one vast picnic. People were unwrapping food and
munching; sandwiches and bottles of lemonade were handed

around over people's heads; there was a heavy smell of frying. At about one in the morning the beer gave out practically simultaneously in all three bistros. There was a moment of anger, then everyone fell back on coarse red wine out of a tanker that they queued up for. Madame Eugénie extracted from her shopping bag two thermos bottles, a pair of opera glasses, and a huge shawl in which she wrapped herself. Then she handed around hot coffee.

At two o'clock a few gendarmes tried to clear the space in front of the prison of St. Peter's where the scaffold was to be erected. The scuffle was short but rough; one woman got trampled. The gendarmes withdrew, but the reserves took their place, and finally the sacred square was occupied by the soldiery. The violent reactions provoked by all this spread as far as our terrace. Chairs were overturned; two men wild with waiting and wine rolled about among the tables, clutching at one another. Several times we had to make a wall with our bodies to prevent Madame Eugénie's observatory from coming to grief. But all the good humor had gone. The crowd was cross and didn't see why it was being kept waiting. It wanted its money's worth. Suddenly three syllables, chanted sporadically at first, were taken up in furious rhythm by thousands of throats: "Get started, get started, get started."

Was I really the only one to feel crushed by these people's infamy? Why didn't the soldiers surrounding the scene of the crime shoot into the crowd, or better still clean up all that human purulence with flame throwers? At last an immense, long-drawn-out "Ahhhhh!" succeeded the chanting. This, explained Madame Eugénie to us from her eminence, was because a black van drawn by an old horse was clattering over the cobbles. A gas lamp stuck on a post and shaken in the wind threw wavering shadows of two men, who took planks from the van and started to assemble the guillotine. There was an awful silence, broken by the hammering of mallets and the creaking of bolts. I put my head on the imitation marble table and was in agony. But I still had to hear Madame Eugénie's voice letting fall words heavy as rocks: "Balance, sawdust box, lunette, knife." Then came the announcement that a light was flickering somewhere in the black mass of the prison buildings, and that at last they were going to sound as loud as they could the death of the great solitary at bay. But no—there was more waiting. The crowd began to mutter again, surged back and forth, and threatened to sweep all before it.

The sky was beginning to pale in the east when the doorway of the prison was lit up. A group of small black men came out, thrusting before them a giant whose white shirt made a luminous patch in the twilight. Weidmann had his hands tied behind his back and could only edge forward because his legs were shackled. A great sigh of satisfaction swept through the crowd. The little black men were standing at the foot of the killing machine. Weidmann was carried on to the scaffold by four men, like a great medieval effigy. When he was set down on his feet the light shone straight into his white face. It was then that Madame Eugénie's ringing voice arose in the general silence, like an acolyte's bell at the elevation of the host:

"But, Monsieur Tiffauges, he's just like you! Anyone would think he was your brother! He's like you, Monsieur Tiffauges, exactly like you!"

At a sign from Henri Desfourneaux, the four assistants got hold of the big pale statue again and shoved him head first toward the neck rest. But what was happening? The routine gestures of death didn't seem to be going right. They bustled around the victim. The balance wasn't properly adjusted. In its fall the great body had missed the lunette where his head was supposed to rest, and he was lying half curled up on the balance. They got hold of him by the ears and dragged him by the hair. It was grotesque, unbearable. You could hear the click of the knife rising jerkily between the posts. Then a hiss. The blood spurted out in floods. It was 4:32 A.M.

Crouching beneath Madame Eugénie's throne, I vomited bile.

June 20, 1939. The miscellany of nightmares, hallucinations and devastating bursts of lucidity that filled the night for me was dominated by the tall and radiant form of Rasputin. Up till now I'd seen him as the man who, having caused a scandal by preaching the innocence of sex, opposed with all his considerable influence the warmongering of the Tsar's entourage. June 28, 1914, is usually considered the date of birth of the Great War, because that was the day the Archduke Franz Ferdinand was assassinated at Sarajevo. But who remembers that on that very same day, perhaps at the very same hour, Rasputin was stabbed in a small Siberian town by a prostitute in the pay of the Russian nationalists? He was out of action for several weeks and, despite the imploring messages he sent the Tsar Nicholas II from his hospital bed, was unable to stop him ordering general mobilization and thus unleashing the war.

In the sobbing darkness of last night, Rasputin appeared to me no longer as prophet and martyr of benign inversion, but invested with the attributes of his third and supreme distinction —that of the greatest phoric hero of our time. For his miraculous hands had the power to snatch the sickly body of a child away from illness and to carry it toward life and light. Last night my anguish found refuge at the foot of his severe and radiant form, a huge black candelabrum bearing aloft the fair flame, bowed by suffering, of the sleeping Tsarevitch Alexis.

June 23, 1939. From now on, no tobacco or alcohol. Children neither smoke nor drink. If you can't recapture freshness except through predatoriness, at least spare yourself the shabby vices that reek of adulthood.

June 25, 1939. For the last four days, unbudgeable constipation. Apart from the sort of anal itch I always get on such occasions, my belly feels all heavy and swollen, and I see myself as a bust of human flesh standing on a plinth of feces.

June 27, 1939. Impossible to recover my balance after the murder of Weidmann. The angelic presses a leaden weight on my chest. I keep trying to yawn to flood my lungs with fresh air, but in vain—I can't trigger the redeeming reflex, and tears stream down behind my glasses.

I lean on the sill of the open window and gasp for air like a fish on dry sand. In despair I think of consulting a doctor, despite the repulsion I feel for members of the dreadful profession that consists in laying bare and touching without love the bodies that have most need of it. Not to mention souls! How can one think without horror of the asylums where they shut up those possessed by the Devil whom the false priests, brought forth in profusion by Rome, neither will nor can exorcise—the people labeled "mentally ill" so that they can be handed over to the mercy of doctors behind padded walls?

If I went to see a doctor it would have to be the humblest, the poorest, the least "clever." I'd sit in his waiting room among crowds of tramps and whores, and it would be first and foremost in his look that I'd find healing for my wounds.

But I have a better idea. A vet looks after hummingbirds as well as elephants—so why shouldn't he take on a man? I'll go and line up at the nearest vet's, between a barren cat and a rheumy parrot, and when my turn comes I'll beg him, on my knees if necessary, not to refuse me the care he lavishes on our four-footed friends. I'll go about it so that he'll have to treat me the same as a guinea pig or a pomeranian. If I can't have human warmth, at least with him I'll find animal warmth, and he at least won't try to make me talk.

July 3, 1939. How could I have been so crazy as to believe this loathsome society would let an innocent live and love in peace, hidden among the crowd? The day before yesterday the mob made up its mind to besmirch me and drive me to despair; malice and stupidity sounded the death of the just and the lover. But already salvation is in sight—menacing for them, promising for me.

Keep calm, M'Abel, stifle your anger, bite back your imprecations. You are sure now that the great tribulation is being prepared, and that your humble fate has been taken in charge by fate itself!

I'd gone to meet Martine from school as usual and dropped her on the island of the Grande Jatte in the Boulevard de Levallois, by the building site. She tripped off gaily, giving me a little mocking wave of the hand before going down into the cellar. I lingered, my elbows on the steering wheel, contemplating the mauve evening sky at the end of the street, and, within me, the gentle ebb of the tenderness that filled me in Martine's presence.

I don't know how much time went by like this before I was frozen to the marrow by a bloodcurdling shriek coming from the building. This was not the modulated cry, rich in harmonics, of the playground at Sainte-Croix! It was the cry of a wounded animal, a rending of the air that petrified me for a moment, then made me leap from the car and go tearing across the rubble and down the cellar steps. The darkness made everything invisible, but I was guided by long strident sobs from inside the cellar, at the end of which I could see the luminous square of another exit. Soon my eyes got used to the dark, and I saw Martine. She was lying on her back, her skirt up over her thin thighs, in the middle of the rubbish and puddles that covered the floor. I spoke to her, but she seemed not to hear; she had her arms crossed over her face and only drew breath in order to renew her childish lament. I took her by the wrist and made her sit up with all the gentleness at my command. Then she suddenly uncovered her grimy face and shouted, "Help! Leave me alone! Oh, he hurt me!"—this in the direction of the door, where I now saw the outline of a man.

There were cries, running footsteps, and I was suddenly dazzled by a flashlight. A voice asked Martine, "Who was it hurt you?" and the heavens fell on me when I heard her say, "Him! Him!", pointing at me. At that I lost my head. I rushed for the other exit, but someone tripped me and I fell. When I got up I was surrounded by a threatening circle of men; two women were fussing over Martine. My arms were seized by many hands; black faces spat base insults into mine. Then, shoved in front of them with one arm twisted behind me, I had to go out and face the street, where someone had set off a police alarm.

I felt a certain relief when I was thrust into the police wagon. At least I was safe there from the crowd that had already gathered around me, yelling its hatred. I thought everything would be straightened out at the police station at Neuilly, which was where they were taking me. But during the first interrogation I realized with horror how feeble my denials seemed when confronted with the damning circumstances, and above all with Martine's outright accusation. Had the child gone mad? Or did she really think it was I who had attacked her in the darkness of the cellar? Or did she perhaps think that saying so was a good way of getting rid of me? I've often noticed the lies children tell are only a kind of simplification, to convey to adults a situation too subtle for them to understand. In short, perhaps I was just the victim of a bold short cut!

I spent the night at the police station and in the morning was taken in a wagon to the Quai des Orfèvres, to the vice squad. In the afternoon I was questioned by a divisional superintendent, or rather—the distinction is worth making—he noted what I said.

His correct though distant demeanor gave me a certain amount of reassurance after the scenes of the previous evening and the infernal night I'd spent among pimps and drunks. For the first time I was being treated humanely, that's to say politely. But that only made his cold blows the more deadly. He told me the evidence collected that very morning established the fact that for no good reason I hung about the schools in the Boulevard de la Saussaye. A search of the garage had resulted in the confiscation of my photographs and recordings. What little I could gather of Madame Eugénie's statement made me fear the worst. Then, changing the subject abruptly, the superintendent informed me of the conclusions of the medical examination, which left no doubt that the child really had been raped. Finally he summarized in two words what I emerged as from all this: a dangerous maniac. Then suddenly the door opened, and in came Martine. Oh, they'd arranged everything beautifully so as to finish me off completely! What I'd endured so far was nothing compared to the crazy, detailed, obscenely precise accusations that she-devil made against me. My pen refuses to put down a hundredth of the lies, intermingled with little bits of truth, that she piled one on top of another to destroy me. Lastly, the superintendent informed me that, under the terms of article 332 of the penal code, rape committed against a child of less than fifteen was punishable by twenty years' forced labor.

"I imagine your lawyer will tell you to plead insanity," he said, getting up. "That means you should make an absolutely clean breast of everything to my people. You'll be taken along to the inspector, who'll copy down your statement. Until the examining magistrate actually brings a charge, you're only . . . what shall I say? . . . a special witness."

Pleased with this witticism, he handed me over to a policeman, who took me up three floors to the top of the building. There I was made to dip my fingers in printer's ink and press them on a card. Then I was photographed in full face and in profile—I, the stealer of images! Absurd and malign inversion! And then the serious business began.

There were three of them in a room that was small, overheated, ugly and undistinguished as hell itself. One small, one fat, one medium. The medium one was working at a decrepit typewriter that stuttered like a machine gun. The fat one affected good humor. The small one exuded hatred. The fat one began by telling me it was only a formality. Because it was a case of *flagrante delicto* and all the witnesses were in agreement, all I had to do was sign a deposition that we would now compose together. I at once objected that, on one essential point, the special witness, Abel Tiffauges, was not in agreement, since he denied having committed the rape. At that he leaned back in his chair with an unspeakably sweet grin on his face.

"I'm going to tell you a story," he began. "Once upon a time there was a man who kept a garage and lived alone in the Place de la Porte des Ternes . . ."

And he glibly proceeded to go through my whole file, with details I hadn't yet heard about: the scene at the Palais de Tokio, reconstructed through the photographs; Jeannot's accident, recounted by Madame Eugénie. And from this complex combination of circumstances, each separate item of which was undeniable, the rape of Martine followed with inescapable rigor. My obstinate denial was senseless and would only annoy the jury when I came to trial.

I went on denying for six hours by the clock, bathed in sweat, tottering with fatigue, and showered with blows and insults. Finally the little one dragged me across to a mirror over a washbasin. "Look at the face you're going to show the jury," he said. "A real murderer's mug." I looked in spite of myself. For the first time he was telling the truth.

Then he went on to say he had a daughter the same age as Martine, and that it would give him great pleasure to impale scum like me personally. As I was head and shoulders taller

than he was, he made me sit down again. I thought he was going
to hit me and took off my glasses so that he shouldn't break
them and leave me unable to see. But he didn't hit me. He spat
in my face. When I really understood what had happened, when
I felt his spittle running down my cheek, I stood up. They all
hastily got out of the way, no doubt expecting violence. How
mistaken they were, yet again! I had just been filled with a great
and almost happy calm. As I no longer had my glasses on, I was
surrounded by a fog of soft and toned-down colors. Under my
feet I could feel something resembling the seismic trembling
that tells passengers the engines have at last started to pant
below, the anchor is up, and the deep and multitudinous
conspiracy that makes the ship move has just been entered
into, to last for some time to come. Fate was on the march and
had taken in charge my poor little personal destiny. A distant
image came back to me: Nestor's gyroscope, his absolute toy,
whose minute trepidation gave him direct and concrete proof of
the earth's motion. I felt the dim heartbeat of the world in my
every bone.

I smiled. I said I thought the interrogation was over. With a
meekness that would have been astonishing in any other circumstances, the fat one called a cop and had me taken back to
my cell. That night I couldn't sleep for happiness. There's nothing more to worry about. The great stewpot of history has
started to simmer, and nothing can stop it, and no one knows
who will come out of it or who be thrown in. The school is going
to burn down, as it did twenty years ago in Beauvais. But this
time the conflagration will be in proportion to Tiffauges the giant, and to the terrible threat that hung over him.

July 12, 1939. Maître Lefèvre, the lawyer officially appointed
for my defense, came to see me. He warned me against what he
considers delusive optimism. My file's such a bad one he's thinking of pleading mental defectiveness. I told him not to waste his

time with me: there will be neither trial nor pleading. History is on the march. The trumpets of Jericho will soon bring down the walls of my prison. As I spoke, I could sense his decision to plead madness growing stronger. He asked me if, in addition to the pencil and paper I was provided with on my second day here, I wanted any books for the holiday period, when legal activity comes to a standstill. I was going to ask him for a Bible, and then I changed my mind. The thing I need is a copy of the penal code.

July 16, 1939. I mustn't hide from myself the fact that all these men who hate me through a misunderstanding would hate me a thousand times more if they really did understand me, if they *knew.* But then again if they knew me *perfectly,* they would love me infinitely. Like God, who does know me perfectly.

July 30, 1939. The penal code. What a study! Society with its pants down exhibits its most shameful parts and most unspeakable passions. Concern number 1: the protection of property. No crime is punished more savagely than offense against ownership. Assault brings only a light prison sentence. But burglary is punishable by death if the thief was in possession of any sort of weapon, even if he left it outside in the car. And the stupid ferocity of most of these laws makes them quite inapplicable. One might have expected that the person who makes the law, working in the abstract in the quiet of his office, would try to frame his texts so as to moderate the vindictive instincts of judges and juries forced to deal with crime face to face. But it is the reverse. The laws have obviously been conceived by a bloodthirsty madman, and the good sense of judges and juries has to be relied on to mitigate their idiotic severity.

Some men are guilty a priori in the eyes of the law even

though they haven't done anything. Article 277: "Any beggar or vagabond taken carrying arms even though he has neither used nor threatened to use them, or having upon him files, picklocks or other instruments . . . is liable to from two to five years' imprisonment." A woman convicted of adultery can be imprisoned for up to two years, and only her husband can cancel her punishment by consenting to take her back (Article 337). A man has the right to kill his wife and her lover taken *in flagrante delicto* in the conjugal home. Needless to say, the wife has no such right in similar circumstances (Article 324). Not a word about incest. As a result a man may live conjugally with his mother or daughter, grandmother or granddaughter, and present a fine large family to the world without molestation.

I can't go on. This murky brew of stupidity, hatred and cynical cowardice leaves indignation dumb.

August 3, 1939. My carceral nights take me back to the long hours of wakefulness at St. Christopher's. Nestor's absence is no impediment, for in a way he lives again in me; I am Nestor. All my past life stretches out before my closed eyes, as if I were at the point of death.

I try to derive some lesson from my misadventure with Martine. I still adore children, but with the exception now of little girls. To begin with, what is a little girl? Sometimes a little boy manqué, as they say; more often still, a little woman. A real little girl doesn't exist. That's what makes schoolgirls look so charmingly comic: they are dwarf women. They trot along on their little short legs, flaunting little skirts differing only in size from the clothes of grown-up women. And this is true also of their behavior. I've often seen very young girls—three or four years old—act toward men in a way that is typically and comically feminine; there is no parallel in the attitude of little boys toward women. So why talk of little girls, since there aren't any?

It's all a mirage of symmetry. Nature cannot resist the soliciting of symmetry. Because adults are either men or women, Nature thinks it necessary for children to be either little boys or little girls. But a little girl is like a fake window—something belonging to the same order of deception as men's nipples or the second funnel on some big ships. I have been the victim of a mirage. *That's* the explanation of my being in prison.

September 3, 1939. I write these lines at home, in my office at the garage, which has been closed for two months and will stay closed a good deal longer. I was let out at the end of this morning. At nine I saw the examining magistrate, who said, more or less:

"Tiffauges, your file is against you, very much against you. In normal times, it would have been my duty to make a charge and bring you to trial. But the country is mobilizing, war's going to break out at any moment. I see from your cards you'll be one of the first to be called up. And after all you haven't admitted anything, and young Martine may have made it all up, as girls of that age often do. So I'm going to dismiss the case. But please don't forget it's only the war that has prevented your appearing in court, and make sure you redeem your sins by your conduct on the field of battle."

In other words I'm to go and get a bayonet stuck through my gizzard—he couldn't have put it better. But what does it matter? The school has burned down once again, the whole of France is seething like an ant heap and getting ready for the fray. Not, I may add, with the enthusiasm of 1914! This time no Péguys or Barrès have infected the ranks of youth with their patriotic pox. The men who've been called up don't even seem to have any very clear idea of why they're going to fight. How should they? Only I, Abel Tiffauges, otherwise known as Child-Bearer, microgenitomorph and last scion of the race of phoric giants, only I know, and with good reason. . . .

The cops have turned everything topsy-turvy here. Never mind. They've taken away all the photographs and all the recordings, but I found my "Sinister Writings" scattered over the floor. Probably the illiterates were put off by the writing, the "gaucherie" of which makes it difficult to read. And yet it's there they could have found the explanation of everything.

September 4, 1939. It's all very well for me to be smart while the sun's shining, but in the middle of the night the waiting for the great tribulation to come fills me with terror. While sleep enfolds all my brothers, my face stares horrified into the darkness.

A word came stealthily to me, and my ear caught the whisper of it. My every bone trembled with fear, and my every hair stood on end. A shade passed by me, and my staring eyes recognized its shape. The earth shook at each of its terrible steps.

As God's my witness, I never prayed for an apocalypse! I'm a gentle, harmless giant who thirsts for affection and stretches out his great hands joined in the shape of a cradle. And you know me better than I know myself. Before a word leaves my tongue, it is already known to you. So why this sky heavy with malice and rent by lightning, why this earth reeking with blood, why this charnelhouse smoke hiding the stars? All I asked was to bow my woodcutter's shoulders over great dormitories dark and warm, and to carry on them little laughing tyrannical riders. But your trumpets shatter the soft silence of the night, your visions terrify me, you flutter my dreams like a cloud of butterflies, you drag me by the feet and hair down your staircases of light!

I took communion this morning, with secret transports, in a side chapel at St. Peter's at Neuilly. Reviving freshness of the panting flesh of the Infant Jesus, beneath the transparent veil of the dry little host. What words can describe the infamy of the Roman priests who refuse the faithful communion in both kinds, reserving for themselves the succulence the flesh must gain from being moistened in its own warm blood?

II
The Pigeons of the Rhine

At the Elysée Palace the President of the Republic turned to the Field Marshal, representative of the highest military authority.

"Well, sir," he said, "how do you explain this unprecedented debacle?"

Monsieur Albert Lebrun had asked the key question. We listened even more intently than before; the whole strategic problem of the war was involved. And I can still hear the marshal's answer. "Perhaps we relied too much on electrical communications. They've been cut. Perhaps we gave up pigeon fanciers and carrier pigeons too soon. Perhaps we ought to have a pigeon loft in the rear through which General Headquarters could be in constant communication with the battle areas." We looked at each other, speechless.

Laurent-Eynac[1]

Abel Tiffauges was called up on September 6 to the mobilization center at Neuilly, where, thanks to his unusual dimensions, he was fitted out without difficulty from head to foot. The first-comers had grabbed all the average-size uniforms, and there were none of these left, but what remained was enough to rig out all the dwarfs and giants on earth. Three days later Tiffauges was directed to Nancy, attached to the 18th Regiment of Engineers and posted to a signals training squad.

As soon as he came in contact with the Morse Code, he felt distinctly, and for the first time in many years, the inner click that had poisoned his childhood and adolescence, and that signified the locking of his intelligence and memory when confronted with a new subject. To stimulate the men's enthusiasm, the officer in charge of the squad, a product of the Ecole Polytechnique, had decided they could have leave to go into town only if they could claim a perfect knowledge of the telegraphic alphabet. Tiffauges easily resigned himself to never leaving the barracks. For him the call-up which had got him out of prison, was only a continuation of his captivity in another form. In reality it was a waiting period. Its monotony would be broken by certain memorable upheavals, but its length and aridity would be proportionate to the triumphant rebirth to which it was the prelude.

The training they were given soon reduced all the trainees to one level. This was because the instructors, wishing to turn

in as impressive a report as possible every evening, preferred
to operate the transmitter themselves. Under their avalanche
of signals, the best the apprentices at the receiving end usually
could muster was the distress signal, meaning "Please repeat
more slowly." So Tiffauges contented himself with turning
the handle of the electric generator, a modest and monotonous
job that pleased him all the more because every day he saw
his friends in the infantry crawling about in the mud or panting
along interminably on the double. In January 1940 his inability to master the conventional signs—abstract, futile, and
without any fateful significance—resulted in his failing to qualify
as a corporal, so it was as a private that he was sent to Erstein,
about twelve miles south of Strasbourg, between the Rhine
and national highway 83.

His company, which included twenty telephone operators
and twenty telegraphists, was supposed to turn the post office
of the town, most of whose six thousand inhabitants had been
evacuated, into the nerve center of the division, linking command, which had been set up in the town hall, with the three
infantry regiments garrisoning the Rhine fortresses, a recon-
naissance group of Spahis, the field artillery, the heavy artillery,
the engineers and the services in the rear.

For weeks Tiffauges tramped up and down the roads and
lanes of the area, pushing a drum on wheels bearing field cables,
or carrying a lighter contraption on his chest, while two companions with ladders and forked poles draped cables along
walls, from tree to tree and from telegraph pole to telegraph
pole. He compared himself to a big spider inexhaustibly spinning out her thread behind her, and he enjoyed the long walks
across the wintry countryside, which were bracing but left the
mind free. Soon the Erstein post office itself was like the center
of a spider's web, with its forty overhead lines fanning out in
all directions—an easy target for a hit-and-run plane, as Second

Lieutenant Bertold pointed out. He was always making snide remarks about the telephone operators.

For there was a hidden rivalry between the telephone operators and the telegraphists, the latter considering their own technique both more modern and less grossly material, since it did not involve the laying and maintenance of cables. A short while before Christmas, events seemed to prove them right. The German loudspeaker at Ottenheim, which showered the French garrisons with news and slogans across the muddy waters of the Rhine, greeting units by their numbers and officers by name, asked them to be kind enough to contratulate the telegraphists who had just set up the Erstein network. A detailed description followed of the installations and their capacity. The matter would no doubt have ended there, if a French lookout hadn't spotted the horn of the loudspeaker mounted on a truck on the right bank of the river and seen fit to blast it to smithereens with a shot from a telescopic rifle. This was going directly against the tacit agreement for peaceful coexistence, and called down reprisals.

These materialized at dawn the following day in the form of a single Stuka dive-bombing the Erstein post office. As soon as the first machine-gun bullets stuttered over the tiles, Tiffauges and the six other men on duty clattered down to the cellar, which was shored up with tree trunks. The plane zoomed about a bit and dropped a string of small bombs which fell in various gardens. There would have been practically no damage if the stove, overstoked and forgotten during the alert, hadn't started a small fire, which partly destroyed the nearest telephone switchboard.

This incident assumed considerable proportions in the monotonous life of the sector. In the first place it gave rise to passionate discussions about the shrieking noise emitted by the Stuka during the dive bombing. Advocates of a siren specially installed to produce a psychological effect argued furiously against those who maintained the noise was only the plane rearing up again after its dive, to avoid crashing. The whistling sound, which grew shriller as the plane approached, became lower as it receded; hence the sirenlike effect. Tiffauges was present at these discussions, though he took no part in them. They gradually strengthened him in the idea that the war was nothing but a confrontation of ciphers and signs, a purely audiovisual tussle where the only possible risk was obscurity or misinterpretation. It might seem that no one was better prepared than he for the problems of transmission, reception and deciphering. Yet they remained a mystery, for without that warm, living, sanguine element that for him was the signature of being, they merely floated about in an atmosphere that was abstract, contemplative and gratuitous. He awaited confidently and patiently the union of sign with flesh, which for him was the final end of everything, and particularly of the war. This union presented itself a few weeks later in a form that, though absurd, was nonetheless a harbinger of later fulfillments.

The fears at General Headquarters concerning the vulnerability of their communications had unexpected consequences for Tiffauges. Their immediate effect was a short-lived triumph for the telegraphists. But the vast extent of the sector, plus the lack of personnel and equipment, meant that transmitters were too far apart for them all to be in touch with one another. In addition, the efficiency of enemy intelligence—demonstrated daily over the Ottenheim loudspeaker—made it necessary to use cipher, which slowed down everything and made the lack of suitable personnel even more acute. It was at this point that Second Lieutenant Bertold, a passionate pigeon fancier, suggested setting up a pigeon loft near headquarters at Erstein. Commander Granet was a veteran of Verdun and had fought beside Commander Raynal during his heroic defense of Vaux, which had kept in touch with General Pétain by means of carrier pigeons. He supported Bertold's suggestion enthusiastically.

But the lieutenant needed a handyman to help him. Tiffauges was chosen. He was available because no one wanted to keep him.

*

The whole of January was spent building and fixing up a pigeon loft on top of a strange sort of tower by the side of the town hall; the ground floor served as a tool shed for the municipal road menders. A narrow flight of stairs led steeply up to a circular room with slits in the walls, perhaps originally loopholes. These openings were fitted with little hatches, which could be set in any one of four positions: shut, exit only, entry only, or open. The room itself was partitioned into two, for, as Bertold explained, it was important to separate the pigeons attached to this loft by habit and a mate from those belonging to another loft, to which they would fly back with a message when released. This second category of pigeon must be kept only for a limited period and segregated according to sex; otherwise they would adopt this loft as their own and become members of the first category. With the aid of a carpenter they put up seventy compartments, each of which would hold either a single pigeon or a pair. This made a maximum capacity of one hundred and forty—"Just a beginning," said Bertold, obviously dreaming of a war consisting exclusively of the comings and goings of huge flocks of birds. Thirteen little boxes in a corner on the ground floor contained the whole range of official army pigeon food: barley, oats, millet, flax, rape, maize, corn, lentils, vetch, hemp, horse beans, rice and peas. There was also a box of salt earth, made of bricks, rubble, ground-up oyster shells and little bits of silica and clay, the whole bound together with salt water.

By January 20 everything was ready to receive the little winged soldiers, as Bertold called them in his tender moments, and Colonel Puyjalon signed a requisition order whereby all pigeon owners in the area had to make themselves known by

letter and hand over for a fixed sum those of their pets selected
by the recruiting officer. It thus came about that, at the end of
the month, Tiffauges set out over the roads of Alsace at the
wheel of a truck full of special wicker baskets, each fitted with
harnesses to hold six pigeons.

Bertold had trained him, mainly out of Captain Castagnet's
*Handbook for Candidates for the Certificate of Army Pigeon
Fancier*. He knew that a good military pigeon, capable of covering from seven to nine hundred kilometers a day and of handing
down to its descendants its own brilliant physical and intellectual qualities, must have a rounded head; a strong beak; a
rapidly blinking eye with quick and sensitive ciliary muscles
and a look that in the male is open and stern and in the female
more gentle; a well-feathered neck strong in the male and more
flexible in the female; a wide protruding breast; strong shoulders;
powerful well-feathered back; a sound sternum arched in front
and tapering behind so as to reduce the belly to a mimimum;
wings firmly attached at the shoulder and, when spread, slightly
incurved, with feathers closely overlapping like the tiles on a
roof; a wide firm back ending in a rump well covered with fine
silky feathers; twelve tail feathers, short rather than long and
reinforced at the base by numerous smaller feathers, to form
a rudder at once mobile, supple and strong; sinewy thighs; and
dry claws with sharp well-set talons. He had also learned that
the qualities needed in a pigeon fancier are gentleness, patience,
prudence, cleanliness, thoughtfulness, observation, firmness
and discipline. Bertold made him quote from memory the lines
famous in every army pigeon loft in France: "Passionate love
of pigeons is a talisman that confers the majority of these virtues on the sapper as soon as he enters the pigeon loft. The
most boisterous and quick-tempered pigeon fancier becomes
gentle and patient in the presence of his pigeons; the most
negligent keeps his birds cleaner than he keeps himself."

Thereafter Tiffauges was to be seen plowing through fields

and woods, making his way into farmyards, confronting roving
bulls and mastiffs, arousing sleepy hamlets, knocking at cottage
doors, ringing at the gates of big houses. And always, letter in
hand, he asked to see and handle the pigeons that had been reported. The ease with which he got used to taking hold of and
feeling them did not surprise him. He would raise both hands
slowly above the bird, then gradually bring them down over it.
Then he took hold of it, his left hand holding its hindquarters
with the feet stretched out under the tail between his index and
second finger, the thumb and index joined holding the wings
crossed over the tail, while his right hand supported the bird's
breast as it faced to the right. When he wanted to use his right
hand he held the pigeon against his chest, so as to keep it level
and not let it slip out of his left hand. He knew the technical
names of all the colors: Vendôme blue with black bands on the
wing, lead blue, brick red, speckled brown, floury, silver, mosaic.
And he knew that, other things being equal, one should always
choose the bird with the darker plumage, because it is less sensitive and therefore usually tougher. He could tell the difference
between "open" birds—those whose pelvic bones had a centime-
ter at least between them—and "joined" ones, in which the bones
touched, and "narrow" ones, in which the bones almost touched.
With his eyes shut and at a single feel he could tell a bird's age
and sex, when it had last molted and when it would molt next.

When he got back to Erstein in the evening with his cages,
Bertold went into long disquisitions about the merits of the
birds he had acquired, fitting around the left leg of each a metal
ring bearing a registration number, the last two figures of the
year of its birth and the initials F.A., signifying that it now belonged to the French Army. Then the newcomers were put in
their cages, where a tasty mixture of seed awaited them.

*

Because of his extraordinary size and strength, Tiffauges could
be reserved, standoffish and indifferent to the ordinary preoccu-

pations of his fellows. Where anyone else would have been accused of pride, he was thought of as stupid, or at best surly,
but with no harm in him. He didn't care. He knew the unbridge-
able distance his special vocation set between him and them.
This war, the "phony war" as it was called at the time, into which
they'd all been hurled pell-mell and in which they stared at each
other in jovial or peevish bewilderment as the case might be,
was his thing, his personal affair, even though it frightened him
and was infinitely beyond him. And he knew the tribulations had
scarcely begun, that his fate held in store other disasters and
other historic cataclysms. Even his being assigned to the pigeon-
fancying section of the regiment formed part, as he saw it, of a
general plan concerning him, and was just a preliminary sketch
for a higher vocation.

For he'd soon been converted to Second Lieutenant Bertold's
hobbyhorse, and pigeons now constituted the element of warmth
and affection in his life. His vast tours of the Alsatian countryside, which at first had been just pleasant distractions from the
monotonous lack of privacy of the section, soon turned into passionate hunting expeditions. The pigeons, instead of being merely
a welcome pretext for getting away, became little creatures loved
and desired, each with its own irreplaceable personality. It was
with trembling impatience that he went through the letters that
came every morning from pigeon owners reporting to the military authorities, and when, at the end of an expedition, he had
come to some isolated farm or estate secluded behind its ancient
walls, he was speechless with emotion as his big hand closed
around the little palpitating bodies, knowing he could carry
away whichever he chose. He had come to the conclusion that
many pigeon owners were not doing their patriotic duty, were
turning a deaf ear and, not so much out of negligence as out of
jealous attachment to their birds, were failing to write to the
Erstein headquarters. It was just these birds he longed to see

and touch and possess: as they were the most loved, they must also be the most desirable.

He began to neglect more and more the offers that came in to him spontaneously and to conduct a permanent inquiry among policemen and shopkeepers after the clandestine columbaria withheld from his cupidity. He got in the habit of always keeping an eye open to spot a single pigeon flying overhead, and he would then try to trace it back to some secret loft.

Thus it was that one fine morning in April—April 19, to be exact: the date became engraved in his memory—after driving along the bank of the river Ill to just beyond Benfeld, he had a vague impression that a streak of silver had crossed the sky over his head, heading in the direction of a sparse curtain of pines. He approached and started to examine the trees one by one with the aid of a pair of field glasses he always carried with him. He did not have to search long, for the bird's silvery plumage stood out vividly against the dark tangle of the branches. It was a marvelous creature, all wings, with a very small head proudly set above a snow-white crop that swelled out like the prow of a ship. It was pecking idly at last year's pine cones, but casually and only as if to occupy itself during its brief halt. Then it took off again and flew swiftly over the roofs of a group of houses. "If it's migrating," thought Tiffauges with a pang, "I'll never see it again."

He drove straight back into Benfeld and questioned the vet, whom he located by the plate on his door. No, there was no pigeon loft worthy of the name in the district. But there was a widow, Madame Unruh, to whose house he gave directions, who had a little pigeon run in which she raised a few rather strange birds.

Madame Unruh, who had not responded to the requisitioning order, received Tiffauges with a mixture of disdain and suspicion. It was true she had a few pigeons, but they were rare pedigree birds carefully selected by her husband. Professor Unruh,

who was an expert in genetics, had started experimental breed-
ing to observe the transmission through successive generations
of certain hereditary characteristics. Then he had got caught up
in it and begun to collect birds exceptional for their beauty,
purity of type, or even for their peculiarity. It was difficult to
distinguish, in the collection he left behind at his death, the part
that belonged to science and the part that belonged to pleasure.
His widow was equally indifferent to both but went on looking
after the remaining pigeons because she regarded them as a sort
of living bequest from her husband.

She spoke volubly and coldly, not at all in a hurry to ask
Tiffauges in and take him to the pigeon run. He had to make a
determined move in that direction himself before she consented
to lead the way.

It was a comfortable house that would have been quite ordinary if it had not been filled with stuffed pigeons of all sizes and
colors. There were ash-gray ring doves, bronze stock doves,
ginger pigeons from the Landes, rock pigeons, ruffs, feather-
legged swallows, and even a Chinese ruff and a tambourine.
Each one sat on a perch in an attitude thought up by the taxi-
dermist and had a label giving its genealogical and genetic particulars. Tiffauges and Madame Unruh went through two large
rooms like this, in which walls covered with outspread wings
and darting beaks contrasted with the bourgeois stiffness of
furniture and furnishings. The two universes of the professor and
his wife had obviously run parallel but never mingled during a
whole lifetime, like oil and water forming different layers in a
glass. Then they came to a veranda opening on to a tiny garden,
so small that a trellised dome was enough to turn it into an
aviary. There, on a skeletal tree, on bamboo rings, and on the
sills of a row of boxes, a living fauna as strange as the dead one
inside disported itself: it included a tumbler, a black, a carrier,
a capuchin, and even two pouters with enormous legs and heads
hidden behind immensely swollen crops.

Tiffauges was looking with some uneasiness at this partly exotic, partly monstrous collection when he noticed, huddled against a box, a perfectly ovoid heap of reddish feathers, its head and legs invisible. He went over to it curiously and stretched out his hand. The egg immediately disintegrated into two magnificent pigeons, the color of dead leaves and perfectly identical. Tiffauges got hold of them both at once and examined them with a connoisseur's eye, looking in vain for a detail that might distinguish one from the other. When he looked up, he was surprised to see Madame Unruh's stern countenance lit up with a gentle smile.

"Monsieur," she said, "I can see by the way you touch them you're a real pigeon-lover. It takes years of being close to them to get like that. And a genuine vocation, too. Even my husband wasn't better at it than you. As for me, though I did my best to help him with his experiments, he despaired of ever initiating me into that sweet and secret art. . . ."

Tiffauges stood with a pigeon in each hand, putting them together and setting them apart like the two halves of one simple harmonious object that has been accidentally broken. Every time the two russet brothers touched, they formed an egg by an automatic reflex that intermingled all their parts. It was as if they were drawn and held together by a magnetic force.

"They look quite ordinary," said Madame Unruh, "but in fact they're the most curious items in the professor's collection. They're artificial twins. My husband was interested in and reproduced the experiments of the Japanese master, Morita. The introduction into the egg of small fragments of frog or mouse tissue produces cellular irritation that may result either in two or three separate individuals or in double monstrosities. We had some birds with two heads, but they didn't live."

Before going off with the twins, Tiffauges asked Madame Unruh about the silver pigeon he had originally started to look for. She at once became mistrustful again and was evasive about it, though without actually denying its existence. Tiffauges was at the door and just about to say good-by when a loud flapping of wings attracted his attention toward a scrawny quince tree growing against the wall of the house. The silver pigeon had just alighted on it and sat there cooing gently and preening itself. It looked as if it were fully aware of its own splendor, with its long fine head and big violet eyes and tuft of white feathers, its tapering body revealing its strength through the jointing of the wings, and above all the metallic, platinous plumage that seemed to belong to the mineral rather than the animal kingdom.

Tiffauges held out his hand—a hand, he had noticed without surprise from the start, that did not frighten pigeons—and took hold of the bird. It at once spread out its twelve tail feathers in a fan over his wrist, a sign of submission, a homage from bird to fowler. It was then he noticed Madame Unruh's ashen face and trembling lips.

"Monsieur," she managed to bring out at last, "I can't stop you taking that one too. But I must tell you that while for you it only adds one more to your army pigeon loft, for me it's the dearest thing I have in the world since the professor died. My husband wanted it to be the dove symbolizing our union and our love. It's much more than just a bird, it's . . ."

She stopped when she saw Tiffauges imperturbably undoing the strap of the basket he carried over his shoulder. He slipped the bird inside and looked Madame Unruh in the face. Then she understood that if the platinum bird was a symbol for her, it was much more for Tiffauges, and that her supplications would be vain against a predatory impulse that of all his qualities was the most inflexible and least humane.

*

The more the pigeons invaded his life, the deeper Tiffauges buried himself in an increasingly forbidding solitude. He had never had much to say for himself; now he became completely silent. He had never joined in the talk and amusements of his companions; now he disappeared for whole days without anyone caring. Recruiting and looking after the pigeons should have given him more time off than any other job if he'd wanted to take advantage of it. But he spent every free hour either on the roads, joyfully seeking new quarry, or, more happily still, in his pigeon loft, amid a downy, cooing quiet where he forgot the outside world and from which he emerged, covered with droppings and feathers, with an expression of happiness on his face. His pigeon fancier's solicitude found perfect material to work on at the end of April, when he picked up from the muddy road a young pigeon half dead with hunger and cold, a precocious fledgling that had probably fallen out of the nest. Tiffauges put it, all sticky with mud, between his shirt and his skin, and set about saving its life with unwavering devotion.

He made it a sort of nest in a covered box and attempted to feed it several times a day. This was no easy matter, for though the young bird swallowed avidly whatever was put in its ever open beak, it was much more discriminating when it came to digestion, and several times at the beginning Tiffauges had to treat it first for constipation, with sodium sulphate, then for diarrhea, with nothing but rice. In the end, led by a dim but infallible instinct, he realized he should give his protégé only food he himself had chewed, exposed to saliva, and rolled around on his tongue for a considerable time in a sort of oral predigestion. So day and night, with admirable perseverance, he would reduce bowlfuls of beans and vetch—and later balls of chopped meat—to a perfectly smooth gruel at blood temperature, which he let trickle out of his lips into the pigeon's open beak.

It eventually grew bigger and able to take its place with the rest, but it remained sickly, and its black plumage was never as glossy as that of its fellows. But Tiffauges had a special fondness for it: he thought he could see in its eyes the look of a mind deepened and disillusioned by premature experience of loneliness and sorrow.

*

One of Commander Granet's chief worries was the hotheadedness of Colonel Puyjalon, which he was not always able to keep within bounds. Granet had a secret that revealed itself only after some time, and then only to the most observant. Everyone wondered at first why, instead of choosing somewhere more comfortable and impressive to live, he'd preferred a modest brick villa on the outskirts of the town. Then the little mystery was forgotten. The answer was in fact to be found behind the house, in a rectangle of earth measuring about a thousand square yards, which Commander Granet first cleared patiently with his own hands, then laid out with plants and seeds. He had a passion for gardening, especially kitchen gardening, and he spent the happiest hours of his life in the evening, with a spade or a hoe in his hand.

The fiery Colonel Puyjalon, on the other hand, dreamed only of vast movements of highly trained troops. All he talked of was switching units around. He told everyone he couldn't bear "stabilized situations." In every mess in the sector people repeated what he'd said to a captain before sending him on detachment to Strasbourg: "I want all the coordinates of my command to have variable parameters." All the plans and ideas put up by Puyjalon were carefully suppressed by Granet, whose worst fear was having to change sector before he could pick his young carrots and peas.

The events that started gathering momentum after May 10 sharpened this antagonism. Puyjalon, convinced that the Eastern Army Group, massed uselessly behind the Maginot Line, was going to be called to the rescue of General Georges, who was being driven back in the north, kept all his men ready to move at any moment. Granet, on the other hand, let it be known he had reasons for expecting Von Leeb to attempt a breakthrough from the other side of the Rhine. The capitulation of the Belgian army on May 28, followed by the series of collapses that ended in the entry of German troops into Paris, brought the threat of encirclement from the south and made the colonel afraid that Headquarters at Nancy, which was sending out fewer and fewer instructions, might fall back without warning the post at Erstein. He determined to get to the bottom of it, and fitted out a car for a brief intelligence sortie, taking with him Ernest, his faithful driver, and two staff officers. At the last moment, in case he should get cut off from Erstein, he decided to provide himself with emergency liaison by pigeon. And so it came about that Tiffauges took his place in the back of the car on the morning of June 17, carrying a basket with four pigeons in it. He had a presentiment that he would never see the pigeon loft at Erstein again, so he followed the promptings of his heart and chose the little black one, the big silver one and the twins that were the color of dead leaves.

The sun shining in a cloudless sky, the meadows gay with flowers, the bright trees and murmuring leaves, all seemed as if they were trying to make a triumphant and tender setting for the fall of France. Tiffauges, curled up on his seat with the basket on his knees, his left hand inside stroking the fronts of his birds, which he could tell apart without looking, wondered what aspect the retribution invited by the weak and cruel plebs was going to wear, a year to the day after the murder of Weidmann at Versailles.

The answer came at Epinal, through which they had to detour, the direct road to Nancy being barred for incomprehensible reasons by military police who remained unmoved by the colonel's gold braid. The little town was submerged beneath a confused flood of pedestrians, horses, cycles and cars; it was like a nightmare of the end of the world. Gas and provisions having given out, the merchants had all decided to shut up shop, and there were no supplies of any kind to be had. The harassed and short-tempered crowd had come from Nancy, where the imminent arrival of the Germans had been announced the previous day. In an unthinking instinct of flight, they were making their way to Plombières. A bus had stopped in front of a closed bistro, and several men, tired of beating on the iron shutters and calling for water, were trying to break down the door, using tables as clubs and battering rams. Puyjalon made a move to intervene, but the crowd turned on him, and he retreated hastily, telling the driver to head north along the Moselle. Tiffauges was divided between terror and jubilation, but for the moment what struck him most were the jeers of a youth who stuck a grinning, tousled head through the window of the car and said, looking at the basket: "Homing pigeons, eh? Going home then, are they?"

They covered five miles in two hours, going against the dense and motley stream of refugees. At Thaon they came to a complete halt. A woman lay shrieking on the ground, struggling with some invisible enemy; the crowd around her made it impossible to pass. Some whispered she'd drunk water from the Moselle that had been poisoned by fifth columnists. Others talked of epilepsy. A peasant with a long drooping mustache said she was a fraud and all she needed was to be spanked. Finally a spasm threw up her skirts, and between her spreadeagled legs emerged the skull of a dead child.

The colonel, fuming, ordered the driver to turn right and cross the Moselle to get free of this glutinous humanity. The bridge was intact, and that proved, according to him, that the Germans were still a long way off. After the frightful mob on the main highway, the little secondary road winding through fields of young wheat and barley plunged the travelers into an atmosphere of calm and rustic happiness. They drove swiftly through the village of Girmont, drowsing in noonday warmth, then through cool refreshing woods full of birdsong. At the top of a gentle hill the car came out among a group of houses around a big inn the Cordial Fountain: and by an ample coaching porch a brass fountain gaily poured its waters into a heart-shaped granite basin. The colonel gave the order to halt and vanished purposefully into the inn. He came out again almost at once with a pale fat man who must have been the innkeeper and who made exaggerated gestures to signify helplessness and destitution.

"The inn's closed," explained the colonel. "There's still some drink left, but nothing to eat. I suggest Tiffauges and Ernest go and buy what they can from the local inhabitants, and meanwhile I'll try to get through on the phone to Erstein."

When Tiffauges returned to the inn three quarters of an hour later, after knocking at every door in the village, which was called Zincourt, he brought with him a tin of peas, a loaf of bread and a half pound of butter, for all of which he had paid three times the proper price. The colonel was sitting with the officers at a table in the main dining room with several bottles of Traminer in front of him. He was in a good humor.

"Peas!" he exclaimed. "What could be better! They'll be perfect with the pigeons!"

Tiffauges didn't get it at first, but he had a dark presentiment as he went toward the kitchen. The basket was on the table. There was only one bird left in it. The tiled floor was covered with russet and silver feathers, and over a bright wood fire three little naked corpses, oozing fat, turned sadly on a spit.

"The colonel's orders," explained Ernest. "He wanted us to leave one just in case. You never know, he said. I decided to keep the black one—it's the thinnest of the four."

Then when Tiffauges, stunned, said nothing, he added: "Still, three pigeons won't go very far between five people!"

Tiffauges set out his provisions in silence. Then, after a last look at the basket, where the black pigeon crouched in terror, he went back to the other room and sat down at a distance from the officers, who were drinking and shouting and bawling.

"Three pigeons between five? Not likely!" he thought in a

fury. At least one of those present wouldn't eat anything—he, Tiffauges, who had raised his pigeons lovingly to be faithful messengers, living, throbbing sign-bearers. Then he had another idea. Wasn't he in fact the only one who *ought* to eat the little murdered corpses? To begin with he was dying of hunger, and he interpreted these pangs as a responsibility, almost a duty, to indulge in such a solitary and superabundant feast. What was ignoble was to carouse in the company of those drunken soldiers. But the silent, devout ingestion of the three little murdered warriors would be something almost religious, the best homage that could be paid them. Tiffauges felt a violent and growing hatred for the loud-mouthed Puyjalon, to whom the two staff officers listened with such servile deference. As for Ernest, it was a sure thing he had suggested the sacrifice of the pigeons to the colonel to save himself the trouble of going through the village in search of food. Once again Tiffauges found himself alone, face to face with coarse men who despised him because he was awkward and taciturn. But in fact he was the better man, the strongest, the only one elect and innocent, and thanks to fate he would get the better of this drunken rabble.

He had reached this point in his glum reflections when the inn door opened suddenly and silently, letting in a burst of sun. The innkeeper rushed over to the colonel's table.

"Watch out! The Germans!" he said in a whisper, but with such intensity that he seemed to have shouted it at the top of his voice.

The three men leaped up, buckling on their belts. Ernest' frightened face appeared through the kitchen door.

"They're coming on motorcycles from Hadigny. You'd better run for it! . . . But not in the car," said the innkeeper "They'd machine-gun you on sight. Make your way across the fields and try to get to the Bois des Fiefs. I'll show you the way."

And he went out again into the blazing afternoon sun, followed by Ernest, Puyjalon and the two officers.

Tiffauges, left alone, got up slowly, smiled, and took a deep breath. The earth, which had been trembling ever since the cop spat in his face at the Quai des Orfèvres, was going to split open again. He remembered Puyjalon's celebrated phrase, "I can't bear stabilized situations!" Well, the colonel had got what he wanted now! Tiffauges crossed the dark silent room and went toward the kitchen. The last pigeon, a black shadow, was fluttering about in the basket. Tiffauges put it under his arm and was just about to leave when he changed his mind and put the basket down again on the table. The three other pigeons, nicely browned, were there in a little row on the spit. Tiffauges spread a bit of waxed paper on the hearth, wrapped up the birds, and put the parcel in his haversack. Just as he was about to go out with the basket under his arm, he bumped into the innkeeper.

"Are you still here?" said the other. "The Germans are entering the village. I don't want them to find a French soldier in my place. You've still got time to join your friends. I'll take you."

Tiffauges followed him indifferently. The street was deserted. The village seemed to have been emptied by the sun. Only the heart-shaped fountain still chattered away endlessly. The two men went along a stony alley between houses, then into a vegetable garden. Tiffauges thought of Granet. For him at least the war had had some definite, undeniable meaning, but now the debacle would reduce him to the same fate as all the rest. Whereas he, Tiffauges . . .

They had come to a track that led in among some trees. The innkeeper signaled to Tiffauges to follow it as fast as he could and stood and watched him for a few moments before turning back to the village. "Off to cool his wine for the Germans," thought Tiffauges. "For him it's the debacle, not the war, that has a meaning."

He walked for one or two miles in a direction he took to be south, crossed a tarred road and a little river, and soon came to what must be the outskirts of the Bois des Fiefs. Ernest suddenly rose up out of a ditch where he'd obviously been keeping watch. The colonel and the two officers were hiding nearby in a charcoal burner's hut, waiting to see what turned up. When Ernest and Tiffauges joined them, Puyjalon said he was glad to see Tiffauges hadn't left behind his basket and its last inmate.

"I'm happy, my boy, that in such trying circumstances you didn't throw down your arms, humble as they are. I must remember to recommend you for a citation. And I know what— since we still have means of communicating with Erstein, I'll dictate a message for you to send if we're taken prisoner."

Tiffauges meekly got out of the basket the special pencil and book of very thin paper used for pigeongrams. The colonel walked up and down the hut, tapping his leather leggings with his cane, and dictated an eloquent address to the men in his sector:

"Men, your colonel has fallen into enemy hands after fierce resistance. You gave me such proof of your valor when you were under my command that I can trust you now, in the midst of the misfortunes that have overtaken our country . . ."

Meanwhile Tiffauges was writing down a completely different message addressed to Second Lieutenant Bertold:

"Dear Lieutenant. We are prisoners. The white and the two russets have been murdered by the colonel. The black will have had a long journey in the heat. He must have plenty to drink, but only tepid water, and as he'll be a bit weak give him two pills of cod-liver oil a day. The big white's eggs were addled again; she really only likes other females. The six Vendôme blues need a laxative. Give each of them two pills of castor oil on an empty crop. I think the light speckledy is getting a lump on his left wing—I noticed a little yellow swelling. Try painting it with iodine. . . ."

Two closely written pages bore witness to Tiffauges's affection and solicitude for his little sign-bearers. The colonel had finished for a good minute, and Tiffauges still went on scribbling feverishly. At last he signed it, hastily folded it in three, rolled it up, and fitted it into its tube before the colonel could ask him to read it back. As soon as it felt the weight of the tube on its left leg, the black pigeon came out of its torpor and showed impatience to be off. But Tiffauges put it back in the basket.

The sun was just going down when the five men were taken prisoner in a clearing in the Bois des Fiefs not far from Girmont. They were surrounded by a patrol led by a sergeant major. At the order, "Throw down your arms," three revolvers plopped onto the ground. Tiffauges opened the basket, carefully withdrew the pigeon, and tossed it gently in the direction of the revolvers. The bird spread its wings and fluttered down. Its little round eye bent toward the butt of one of the guns; its dry claws slipped on the steel of the muzzle. Then it crouched, took flight, and flapped noisily away over the heads of the Germans.

Tiffauges bent down and deposited the empty basket at his feet. Just as he was about to straighten up he received a furious kick in the behind; the pain spread right up his spine. As he grimaced and clutched at his back, the colonel helped him get his balance.

"Excellent, my boy," he said. "You put one over on them! My message will get to the lads at Erstein tomorrow at the latest. Are you in much pain? I'll put you up for a medal."

*

The next day Tiffauges was separated from the three officers and found himself in a factory yard in Strasbourg together with a few hundred companions in captivity. He knew at least one of them—Ernest, the driver. But he was not inclined to have dealings with anyone, let alone Ernest the pigeon killer. The first

night Tiffauges had eaten one of the three roast pigeons. H
was sure it was the silver, partly no doubt because of the weight
but there was also a certain flavor that seemed to have som
affinity with what the bird had smelled like when it was alive
The two others enabled him not only to escape the hunger hi
companions suffered from, but also to feed his soul throug
intimate communion with the only creatures he'd loved for th
last six months.

The prisoners were entirely without news and clutched a
even the vaguest rumors. As the armistice had been signed be
tween France and Germany, they had no doubt they would soo
be set free. They only had to wait for means of transportatio
to be restored and for the civilian refugees to return to thei
homes. Tiffauges did not share these illusions, not because h
was more perspicacious than the rest, but because he knew hi
truth lay in the east, and that for him to return to his garage i
Paris was an inconceivable absurdity. His personal destiny ha
always been too solidly structured for him to believe in suc
digressions. So when on June 24 they were taken out in group
of sixty and marched across the Rhine over the pontoon bridg
that replaced the one destroyed at Kehl, he felt a solemn and
secret joy in keeping with the importance of the event. Some o
his companions admitted this was the end of their dreams o
liberation and fell into silent despair. Others tried to keep u
their illusion with harebrained ideas that they passed to and fr
like false coins: they were being sent to Germany to help wit
the harvest and would be allowed to go home afterward; o
they were being taken to a temporary river port from whic
they would be sent home by water.

As they left Strasbourg the sun was already high in the sky
and the men were beginning to feel thirsty. Girls came out o
the houses at the side of the road and gave them drinks; th
German soldiers guarding them turned a blind eye. Tiffauges'
group was held up by an argument between an old Alsatian wh

had set up a pail and glasses on the sidewalk outside his house, and a German corporal who objected. Under cover of the slight confusion that ensued, a woman darted out of her house, dragged Tiffauges back inside by the arm, and offered, incoherent with haste, to hide him and provide him with civilian clothing. There had been no roll call before they set out; the absence of one man out of sixty is not easily noticed. There was every likelihood such a bid would succeed. Tiffauges had to condemn the irony of fate that selected him for this one chance of escape. He accepted a glass of milk, thanked the woman with genuine emotion, and went back to his place in the convoy. Soon after, the men's tired tread could be heard crossing the planks of the temporary bridge: through the gaps the waters of the Rhine could be seen below, the waves overlapping.

"We're entering Germany," said Tiffauges to his neighbor, a short dark man with black eyebrows.

It was such a solemn moment he'd had to say it, in spite of his usual silence.

"If I wasn't sure I'd be home for Christmas I'd throw myself in," answered the other, his jaw twitching.

Tiffauges was overflowing with a joy all the more piercing because he was certain he'd never see France again.

III
Hyperborea

All that passes is raised to the dignity of expression; all that happens is raised to the dignity of meaning. Everything is either symbol or parable.

Paul Claudel

Tiffauges slid into captivity without offering any resistance, with the sturdy optimistic faith of the traveler who abandons himself to rest at each halt, knowing he will awake with the sun a few hours later, the fatigues of the previous day gone, regenerated, ready to set off again once more. He had dropped Paris and France and everything to do with them behind him like soiled garments, worn-out shoes, sloughed skins—including, in the foreground, Rachel, the garage, the Ambroises and, on the horizon, Gournay-en-Bray, Beauvais and St. Christopher's. No one was more conscious than he of his fate—an imperturbable and inflexibly straight line, ordering the greatest world events in accordance with its own ends. But this consciousness also implied an implacable lucidity about what was merely accidental and episodic, all those trifling baubles common mortals become attached to and to which shreds of their hearts remain clinging when they have to leave them. Out of his downtrodden childhood, his rebellious adolescence, and the ardent youth long concealed beneath the most commonplace appearances but later unmasked and scoffed at by the mob, there had arisen, like a cry, a condemnation of an order that was criminal and unjust. And heaven had answered. The society under which Tiffauges had suffered had been swept away, with its judges, its generals and its prelates, its codes, its laws and its decrees.

Tiffauges was now traveling toward the east. They had been sixty to a car in an asthmatic train that kept stopping and shunt-

ing. A few die-hards who still clung to their illusions clustered
around a sergeant in the engineers who had a compass, and
every time the train went around a particularly sharp curve, or
even when it backed into a station, they tried to persuade themselves this meant they were not heading northeast but perhaps
south, perhaps even west. But Tiffauges knew without needing
to consult a compass that they were traveling toward the light.
Ex oriente lux. What light? He didn't know, but he was going
to find out, patiently, day after day, with long periods of secretly fruitful winter darkness, with revelations of dazzling
suddenness.

They were discharged from the train at a little industrial
town called Schweinfurt, parked in quarantine huts, and next
day put through the processes of disinfecting and delousing.
Some wept with humiliation at being paraded naked from yard
to hut, shorn, covered in black soap, showered, and then exposed for hours in all the pitifulness of their anatomy in a field
surrounded by barbed wire. But Tiffauges had no objection: for
him the whole thing took on the form of a rite of purification.
He even enjoyed the unexpected superiority conferred on him
by nudity: his height and muscularity annihilated the puny and
defective shapes of his companions, all sex and hair. But he
hoped he would soon be able to throw away the uniform
handed back to him, shrunken and still steaming from the steri-
lizer. The day he donned another kind of dress, in harmony at
last with his real dignity, then he would know, and so would
everyone else, that the days of obscurity were over.

Two days later they resumed their journey, still toward the
northeast, across Thuringia, Saxony and Brandenburg. They
saw pass through the narrow skylight of their car the Wartburg
of Eisenach, the towers of the castle at Gotha, the flowery fields
of Erfurt, the residence at Weimar, the Zeiss factories at Jena.
At Leipzig they were allowed to get down on the platform and
scatter over a part of the station specially shut off. The

stop lasted several hours. Soup was distributed in the third-class waiting room, and afterward they tried to group themselves according to the unit or place they came from, or just near the people they liked.

Tiffauges would have been left on his own if Ernest, the driver, hadn't stuck obstinately by him. Though he didn't resent this fidelity it surprised him, especially as he thought he detected in Ernest a deference that couldn't be explained by any difference in their rank. He got him to talk. In civilian life Ernest was a valet, a now rare profession that Tiffauges regarded as of dubious distinction, because of the cold duplicity and calculated obsequiousness that must cover the disparity between the smart circles in which it is exercised and the humble origins of the men who exercise it. He'd forgiven Ernest for his share in the sacrifice of the pigeons; in this, as in almost all the events in his life, he had come to recognize a kind of fatality that made it both innocent and understandable. He ended up by adopting the man who seemed to have chosen him as a master.

When the train started off again in the middle of the night, the guards bolted the doors and skylights of the cars. From all the stopping and starting and shunting that interrupted the train's progress, the men who remained awake deduced they were crossing Berlin. Then the pace of the convoy became regular, and the tightly packed bodies were rocked by an even rhythm. They must be crossing a vast plain, its endlessness mitigated only by the darkness.

Dawn seemed earlier and colder than usual. The sliding doors ground open. There were orders and shouts. Dazed, the men jumped out of the cars, to be immediately struck by a cold and cutting breeze. The landscape was so flat that the big black wooden shed of the station seemed almost imposing against it. A wooden board on two posts rattled to and fro in the wind. On it was written, in Gothic lettering on a white ground, MOORHOF. All around, as far as the eye could see, was an expanse of ponds and fields that obviously turned into marshes in the autumn. Here and there a clump of firs served to give the scale, bringing out the vastness of a horizon hidden by the drifts of mist floating about the reeds and high grasses. Tiffauges, who, apart from Paris, was familiar only with hilly and wooded country, was staggered by the grandeur of the place. The limitless view on all sides, plunging among the mists and soaring over the heather and sheets of water, gave him a feeling of freedom such as he had never known before. He couldn't help smiling at this paradox as he fell in behind the line of exhausted marchers, urged northward by the objurgations of a sergeant major.

They came on the camp suddenly a few hundred yards off the road; the village of Moorhof remained obstinately invisible. As they were to find all the time in this apparently open landscape as flat as the palm of your hand, houses, barns and even the observation towers of the camp became invisible at any distance, as if sucked up by the denseness of the soil and its carpet of vegetation. It was a comparatively small camp, consisting of only four double wooden huts built on low piles with tarpaulin roofs; each hut held two hundred men. The full complement of eight hundred, which was only reached a few weeks later with the arrival of more prisoners, suited the work to be done but not the interests of the prisoners themselves. The numbers were too low to give rise to a complex organization or a wide choice of company, or for a recluse to be able to lose himself in the crowd. The four huts were surrounded by a double barbed-wire fence with entanglements between. The camp area must have measured about an acre; there was an observation tower at each of the four corners.

As they entered their new domain, the men saw only discomfort in the flimsy huts, hostility in the fence, and vigilant hate in the towers. But Tiffauges found himself strengthened in the sense of freedom and unconstraint that had descended on him on leaving the train. Everything seemed designed to make the plain always immediately present to the inhabitants of the camp. Tiffauges remembered certain big farms in Picardy where every window opens on to an inner courtyard and all the outer walls are blank. Here it was exactly the opposite. The barbed-wire enclosures were transparent walls. The towers seemed to invite you to scan the horizon.

In the hut to which he was allocated, Tiffauges chose an upper bunk away from the stove but from which, by turning his head, he could see out through a skylight over all the east of the plain. He threw himself straight on to his bunk, exhausted by the disordered days and chaotic nights he had been through. For the first time since he was uprooted by his arrest at Neuilly he felt he had arrived somewhere, that some security was offered him. Europe was left far behind to the west, in the throes of deserved retribution. Above all, there was the formidable yet sweet appeal of all this empty space, this silvery gray earth with its somber facing of heather and its single slender birch, these sands, these peat bogs, this great flight eastward which must lead as far as Siberia, and which drew him like a vortex of pale light. He found out from those already at the camp before him the exact position of Moorhof on the map of East Prussia. The village, which had a population of four hundred, was about seven miles from Insterburg in the west and Gumbinnen in the east, on the bank of a stream called the Angerapp which flowed into the Inster at Insterburg to form the Pregel.

As for the work they were to do, the newcomers learned, after a regulation rest period of twenty-four hours, that they would be daily consummating their marriage with the black and water-logged earth. They were to be used on a huge project for draining the fields along the Angerapp, in which the inadequacy of the equipment was made up for by a cheap and more than ample labor force. Every evening at seven the prisoners were locked up in their huts: their trousers and shoes—or rather the wooden clogs they had been issued—were taken away from them. Then for each one began the long imaginary journey of the night, lit only by five kerosene lamps. They were so tired it did not occur to them to be bored. In the morning they were turned out at six and given a quart of *Waldtee,* a mysterious brew made of fir, birch, alder and blackberry leaves, together with the day's provisions of a slice of bread and a handful of boiled, and of course cold, potatoes. In the evening a clear soup awaited them, hot this time.

They walked in groups of ten, with one German guard, to the part of the drainage system assigned to them, an area of about twelve hundred acres mostly belonging to a big farm some distance from Moorhof. The scheme provided for a network of trenches eight feet deep with a sort of conduit at the bottom made out of two vertical stones crowned by one horizontal stone. The trench was filled in first with brick rubble, then with loose soil. The drains sloped very gradually downward to a main channel that emptied into the Angerapp. Most of the men were employed digging the trenches with spades. When a trench was dug, two men, one on either side, dragged a plane over the bottom to level it out. The construction of the conduits, the fixing of levels and the layout of the canals was entrusted to German laborers.

*

The complete lack of privacy of life in the hut ended by fusing separate individuals into a single little balanced community in which each had his place. For many, having to share everything with companions of different social, regional or professional origin came as a surprise—sometimes an enriching and sometimes a painful one. Some, torn away from their usual family or geographical environment, fell into a daze symptomatic of dangerous moral and intellectual regression. But for others this uprooting was a liberation that set them free to fulfill their greatest longings. Some shut themselves up in silent rumination which, though it might often be mere animal speechlessness, might also be fraught with rebellion and calculation. Some never stopped talking but confided in everyone their feverish plans and schemes. Thus a small haberdasher, Mimile, of Maubeuge, who had gotten married too young to too respectable a wife, never stopped giving vent to his dual obsession, women and money. He had no doubt that the two things were connected and kept dreaming up profitable schemes, which at first were restricted to the camp and later spread in theory to the whole region, the idea being to find a German mistress who would be his protector and "front," and through whom he would buy goods and a house and perhaps even land.

"All the men around here are in the army," he kept on arguing. "All that's left are women and property. Women, property and us! All we have to do is draw the practical conclusions from the situation we find ourselves in."

But Phiphi, from Pantin, the youngest in the hut, who got on everyone's nerves with his puns and his grimaces, objected that only Frenchwomen, Parisiennes, were worth thinking about. How could anyone fall for the rough and stolid charms of the Gretchens with braids and woolen stockings they'd had a few glimpses of since they came to Germany?

Mimile shrugged and appealed to Socrates, a graduate in Greek who observed the motley society of prisoners through his spectacles as he puffed placidly at his pipe. Socrates emerged from his usual silence only to utter oracular judgments that would begin with common-sense platitudes and then somehow turn into disconcerting paradoxes.

"Everything depends on the length and outcome of the war," he said one day. "If we're freed by Christmas, Phiphi is right. We should stay faithful to our own place. But if, as is more likely, Germany wins and goes on to cement her conquests with the corpses of several generations of young men, then let's set the advantages of comfortable defeat against the honors of fatal victory. And while the last surviving Germans watch over the boundaries of the Thousand-Year Reich, we'll fertilize its soil and its women with our sweat and our seed."

This sort of talk aroused only a gleam of mistrust and disapproval in the little peasant eye of Burgeron, a farmer from Berry with a drooping mustache. But it produced the characteristic whinnying laugh from Victor, "Mad Victor" as he was called, who had distinguished himself during the phony war and especially during the debacle. He was maladjusted, asocial and a manic-depressive, and had been in and out of all the mental homes in the Ile de France, his brief periods of liberty always terminating in some excess that got him shut up again. He happened to be out just when the war started, and at once volunteered for the infantry. Thereupon his excesses began again, but as they took the form of bold attacks on enemy lines and heroic acts during his regiment's disastrous retreat, he'd got himself covered with medals and citations. Socrates had explained his case: he was seriously maladjusted to a peaceful and ordered world, but absolutely right for the disorders of war, especially when war became complete rout.

Tiffauges stood apart from the little group in his hut, despite Ernest, who was always anxious to be friends with everybody. But he was not completely alien to his companions, and would even sometimes notice in one or another of them something resembling himself. They all had their own solutions to the problem of captivity, but these were all more or less related to his own solution, which he could not yet have defined clearly but knew to be an impending absolute. Mimile's dreams of carnal and material appropriation, for example, found an echo in him, and so even more did the madness of Victor, crushed by the social order but swimming like a fish in the murky and tumultuous waters of war.

But the others complained about the zeal he brought to his work. He dug and delved with a vigor that couldn't be explained just by his physical strength. How could he make his companions understand that he expected something of this place—a sign, a portent, he didn't quite know what—and that foraging in the earth seemed a way of expediting a message addressed to him alone?

He also enjoyed entering by main force into the richness and intimacy of a land he was beginning to love. This was revealed to him the day that, thanks to the connivance of one of the sentries, he was allowed to fulfill a desire he'd had ever since he arrived and climb up one of the observation towers. The towers were made of logs, twenty feet high, with a covered platform on top reached by a ladder. Tiffauges took only a brief look at the camp itself: its rigid layout and new, geometrical buildings contrasted with the all too human and dilapidated figures of the prisoners wandering about. He turned to the plain, toward that northwest that seemed to be the goal of his great migration, begun nearly a year ago now. The country was so flat he could see immensely far despite the comparative lowness of his observation post. It consisted of a series of almost white fields of ripe rye, cut across by the dark line of a pine forest; of steely ponds surrounded by light sandy beaches; of dark peat bogs against which glittered the silvery trunks of birches; marshes reflecting milky clouds and edged by a dark fringe of alders; fields of black corn alternating with patches of white flax. "A black and white country," thought Tiffauges. "Not much gray, not much color—a white page covered with black signs."

Suddenly the sun burst through the mass of clouds and lit up the mists rising from the marshes and the smoke from the houses in Moorhof. A window caught the light and sent out flashes as if transmitting Morse. And Tiffauges at last saw the village, its low shingle-roofed houses clustered around a squat and solid church—whitewashed walls and a low, massive steeple with a flat roof and what seemed to be a gallery around it underneath. Beyond the village, the gleams that shone through the tall grass suggested a swamp; beyond that again, on a morainic slope, a Dutch windmill reared its sharp but dilapidated outline. A flight of herons crossed the sky, their wings beating gently; a bell scattered its disjointed, mournful music into the wind. Tiffauges felt a strong bond uniting him to the place. To begin with—and perhaps for a long time—he was its prisoner, and it was his duty to serve it with his whole body and with his whole heart. But this would be only a probation period, a betrothal; afterward, by one of those fundamental inversions that ordered his life, he would become its master.

*

Perhaps it was something to do with all the rich black earth he shifted day after day, but ever since he'd got to the camp, and despite the indifferent and inadequate food, he'd lived in great fecal felicity. Every evening before the second and last curfew he went to the latrines and stayed there as long as possible. It was perhaps the best moment of the day and brought back vividly the years in Beauvais. It was an interlude of solitude, calm and meditation during an act of defecation performed generously and without excessive effort, by a regular descent of the turd into the lubricated sheath of the mucous membranes.

But the place did not really lend itself to the rite of meditation. It was just a ditch bordered by a narrow horizontal plank, supported every six feet or so by a log; it supplied its clients with no more than an uncomfortable perch. Tiffauges recalled Nestor's criticisms of "wasted" defecations. Here the fact that the latrines were emptied every ten days supplied an unexpected and not uninteresting corrective. The operation was carried out by means of little tubs on wheels, which a man filled with the help of a bucket on a stick, a sort of giant ladle just like those used in the camp kitchens, a fact that gave rise to everlasting jokes. Tiffauges had been aware that the trolleys were emptied into a drainage moat that fertilized the whole plain impartially. But fear of public opinion had kept him from volunteer-

ing unduly often for the job, and later the affair of the latrine
guard finally put him off the latrines. For it had soon been noticed that the prisoners didn't always bother to go all the way to
the latrines but just stopped where laziness or urgency dictated. So the Germans had introduced a sentry system: a
prisoner, who was relieved every four hours, kept watch. He
had to wear a tin label around his neck on which was written
the degrading legend latrine guard. That put an end to the solitude and reflection necessary to the fundamental act, and
Tiffauges soon came to use only portable and personal latrines
set up over his various places of work.

His reputation as a demon for work meant he was not very
closely guarded, and it was not rare for him to be left on his own
for several hours at the spearhead of a ditch being dug. Then he
was free whenever he liked to choose the auspicious spot
where a couple of strokes with his spade and the setting up of
the two planks he always carried with him created the altar on
which he consummated his secret and fruitful union with the
Prussian soil.

But later a staggering discovery gave a new meaning to his
hours of liberty. One day when he was helping to mark out a
prospective trench, he all but fell into a dried-up drain completely hidden by the tall grass. The starting point of this underground alley was only a hundred yards or so from the place
where he was working. The next day he let himself down into
it and walked straight ahead to see where it would lead. The
floor was firm and flat. Over his head the flowering grasses
joined to form a light and shifting roof pierced by shafts of sun.
He flushed a hen pheasant, which scuttled wildly along ahead
of him down the narrow tunnel. Soon he felt as if he were going
up a slope, so he must be approaching a little wood of firs
which marked the limit of Moorhof's cultivated fields. He
walked for a long time, still escorted by the pheasant, itself now
preceded by two partridges and a big red hare. Then the grass

above grew sparser, for a few yards the strip of blue sky had no
border of vegetation at all, and finally tangles of brambles and
hawthorn announced a change in the terrain. Suddenly the
pheasant rose in noisy flight. A few yards ahead a wall of loose
earth marked the end of the trench.

Tiffauges scrambled up to ground level. The little wood of
firs, in fact only a thin screen of trees, was behind him. He was
on the edge of a gently undulating birch forest scattered with
thickets of buckthorn. It was as if he'd been transported into
another country, another world. This was due partly no doubt
to having escaped from the atmosphere of the camp, but also
partly to the strangeness of the half-subterranean route that
had brought him here. He followed a sandy path winding
through a carpet of heather, went down a dell and up a bank,
and found what he was looking for: in a clearing, where the first
mauve patches of colchicum were already to be seen, stood a
log cabin on a stone foundation. Its doors and windows were
shut. It seemed to have awaited his coming for all eternity.

He stopped at the edge of the wood, moved and dazzled,
and uttered a word that went back to his most distant past and
at the same time contained promises of future happiness.
"Canada!" Yes, he was in Canada. It was Canada that this
birchwood, this clearing and this shack re-created in the middle
of East Prussia. And he heard again Nestor's low voice as, with
head buried in a novel by London or Curwood, he conjured
up in the reeking stuffiness of study hall the pure snowy wastes
and forests around Hudson Bay and the great lakes, Reindeer,
Slave and Bear.

That day Tiffauges did no more than make a tour of his
house. He saw the door was secured with a brass padlock that
would be easy to pick. Then he went back down his grass tunnel. No one had noticed he'd been away for three hours.

*

The first heavy autumn rains had begun when Lieutenant

Teschemacher, who was in charge of administration, found out that Tiffauges was a motor mechanic and promoted him to be driver of the five-ton Magirus attached to the camp. So he began to drive about the district, at first accompanied by a guard, then more and more often alone or with Ernest as co-driver. His usual errand was to collect provisions for the camp, which meant visiting farmyards to load sacks of potatoes, a few quarters of bacon, or long sausages bundled up by the gross like firewood. The rain turned the roads into quagmires with ruts so deep it seemed the bottom of the truck would touch the ridges between. From the end of October, the prisoners were surprised to see the roads being gone over regularly with the harrow, before the first frosts and in preparation for the use of sledges. Sometimes the rain was so heavy and continuous that draining operations had to be interrupted. An oppressive melancholy would descend on the men confined to the camp, itself partly under water. But Tiffauges still drove along in his Magirus, his face glued to the windshield, which the wipers swept in vain. As he rocked to and fro in the heavy truck, surrounded by steam and spray, he sometimes felt as if he were on a ship in the middle of a stormy sea.

He grew familiar with the surrounding villages. Their names, all redolent of heath or wood or marsh—Angermoor, Florhof, Preussenwald, Hasenrode, Vierhufen, Gruenheide—soon came to sing a refrain in his head, illustrated in turn by their elaborate gilded inn signs, with curlicues and arabesques, each celebrating some such animal totem as the Golden Lamb, the Trout, the Roebuck, the Golden Ox or the Salmon. Sometimes he lingered in their smoky rooms, shaking his head uncomprehendingly when some client who recognized him as a French prisoner of war suddenly spoke to him; and he began to like the bitter little cigars of chopped straw that were offered him. He had occasion to go as far east as Gumbinnen, a small town still largely rustic and crossed by the river Pissa, an inexhaustible subject for jest. Every Wednesday, in the shadow of the town hall with its great stepped gables, there was a famous horse fair supplied by the great imperial stud at Trakehnen, some nine miles away. A little farther to the south the Heath of Rominten began, a huge reserve full of woods and lakes and overflowing with game of fur and feather, a paradise containing the finest stags in Europe. Tiffauges, mingling more and more often with civilians, thus got to know Germany, tried his hand at speaking German, and gradually penetrated deeper into a new world whose richness he guessed though he did not yet have the key to it.

With the winter the inmates of the camp had grown noticeably fewer: the labor office sent the men out alone or in distant small work parties that retained only an administrative link with the center. Most of the prisoners were distributed as woodcutters through the neighboring forests, but many were also sent, according to their preferences or qualifications, to workshops, quarries, sawmills or stock farms.

Whenever he could, Tiffauges went to Canada. He had convinced himself that as most of the foresters must have been called up he was unlikely to be disturbed there. He had forced the door and arranged the single room as best he could. He would light a big fire in the grate, go and sacrifice on the defecatory altar he had set up under a lean-to behind the cabin, and spend hours in dreamy meditation blessed by the unhoped-for luxury of solitude. At first his only occupation was collecting logs for the winter and piling them under the eaves. Then to complete the picture of a trapper's life he set a few rabbit snares in a nearby patch of ferns. At first he thought these met with no success, but later he realized, from some mangled remains, that a wildcat or a fox had got there before him.

One day when he'd been caught by the rain he stayed on far beyond the limits of prudence, lulled by the crackling of the fire and the murmur of the drops on the roof. He fell asleep. When he woke up night had fallen, and still the rain was thudding down. It was certainly after roll call, and curfew would also have been sounded. Perhaps he had been reported missing. He decided to leave it to fate and spend the night in his house. He would go back to camp when it got light. He threw as many logs on the fire as it would hold and rigged himself up a bed with the glee of a schoolboy playing hooky. Pleasure kept him awake a long time: he lay with his face toward the glowing hearth, a little incandescent theater presenting an opera without music, full of silent conspiracies that exploded in luminous cataclysms. He was not particularly surprised to find on returning to camp next morning that his absence had passed unnoticed among the comings and goings of the work parties. It was just one more stage in the strange liberating process that was taking place within his captivity.

This was not true of his companions: the winter was putting the finishing touches to their demoralization. The wails of migrating birds crossing the washed-out sky, the uninterrupted sobbing of the bitter wind among the huts, the gloomy country in which everything was hostile to them, and above all the winter closing in, swallowing up their hopes of liberation —everything conspired to drive to despair these simple people torn from the comfortable routine of their daily life by an incomprehensible squall. Only Socrates, who had got up a series of lectures on the history of literature, and Mimile, who looked mysterious when people teased him about his relations with the wife of the carpenter where he worked, still brought an echo of life into the hut. One evening Phiphi was so excited that his friends plagued him to admit he'd got hold of some wine. He denied it by a firework display of evasions, mixing together people's names, streets and bistros in Pantin, and grotesquely Frenchified German words he'd picked up since he'd been a prisoner.

"Well, anyway, you're one person the Prussian winter suits!" said Mimile. "It does a person good to look at you!"

The next day Phiphi was found dead. He'd hanged himself by his belt on a post in the fence around the camp. His suicide created a panic. It suddenly seemed plain that no one would emerge from the camp both living and sane: disease, madness or despair would choose their victims in the course of the coming months. Besides, it was obvious the huts were designed to last only a year, and it wasn't liberation that was going to empty them!

Escape plans were hatched. Every day Victor had a new idea for getting out of the camp: he told everyone about it, including the guards. Others collected food; some tried to get hold of marks by exchanging cakes of soap and packs of cigarettes with the guards or the few civilians with whom they came in contact. Maps were drawn up. One day Ernest revealed to Tiffauges an idea he and another prisoner had had for using the Magirus and Tiffauges's German pass for an escape attempt. With a bit of luck they should get to Poland, where probably a less strict watch was kept and where the people should in theory be ready to help them. Tiffauges only shrugged his shoulders. Later he had to deal with advances from Mimile, who thought the comings and goings of the truck provided a marvelous opportunity for creating a commercial network outside the camp. The prodigious percentages he offered Tiffauges left him indifferent, but Tiffauges did feel a slight pang to see the gulf that separated him from his compatriots getting wider and wider.

One morning the Magirus was missing, together with Ernest and Bertet, a chartered accountant from Grenoble in the next hut. The truck was found two days later, out of gas ninety miles south of the camp. Penalties were clapped down on the whole place, canceling out the slight improvement in conditions that had taken place a few weeks before, after the handshake between Hitler and Pétain at Montoire. Bets were laid on the fugitives' chances of success. This first escape was a sort of test case. If it succeeded, it would give hope even to those who would never have the courage to imitate it.

Ernest was brought back four days later, muddy, in rags, beaten up. He was accompanied by a covered stretcher on which lay Bertet's body. After they left their truck they had to get off the roads, which were patrolled by the provincial police, and take to the moors. They got lost in the marshes, and Bertet was drowned. Ernest finally gave himself up at a country garrison headquarters. He was put in solitary confinement for a week as an example, then sent to the military prison at Graudenz.

A lull in the autumn rain and storms enabled Tiffauges to go along his grass tunnel again; it had been impracticable during the bad weather. He treated himself regularly now to a night in Canada. Each time it was a feast of solitude and dreams, fostered by all the secret noises of the forest—the hoot of a hunting owl, the quaver of a doe hare in heat, the thump of a rabbit giving warning of a fox, sometimes even the sad and distant belling of a herd of deer. He had at last succeeded in trapping some young hares, which he skinned and roasted over his fire in childlike joy at really living like a trapper in the frozen North. The skins were stretched to dry on twigs against the chimney; they gave off a musky smell of old leather.

One night he was awakened by the sound of something rustling against the side of the house. It was as if someone were leaning, as he walked, against the walls and even the door. More scared than he cared to admit, Tiffauges turned to the wall and went back to sleep. During the days that followed he brooded about this nocturnal visit. His presence in Canada was bound to be discovered sooner or later. The smoke rising out of the chimney of the little house announced it to the whole neighborhood. But he couldn't do without the fire. He reproached himself for his cowardice. If the visit were to be repeated, it would be better to face up to it and try to make a deal with the intruder, rather than risk being given away.

Several weeks passed peacefully. It was a long autumn that seemed to hesitate to turn into winter. But one night Tiffauges was wakened again by heavy footsteps and rustlings around the house. He got up and stood by the door. Outside all was quiet once more. Suddenly the silence was broken by a kind of rattle that made Tiffauges's blood run cold. Then something scraped against the door. Tiffauges threw it open and staggered back before the monster that stood framed there. It was at once like a horse, a buffalo and a deer. It took a step forward and was immediately halted by its enormous antlers, with jagged tips, which got caught on the doorposts. Raising its head, it stretched toward Tiffauges a big round muzzle, its triangular upper lip quivering delicately like the end of an elephant's trunk. Tiffauges had heard about the herds of elk still to be found in the north of East Prussia, but he was taken aback by the mass of hide, muscle and antler that now threatened to invade the little house. But the plea of that upper lip stretched out toward him was so eloquent he went and got a hunk of bread from the table and offered it to the elk. The elk sniffed it noisily and wolfed it down. Then its lower jaw seemed to slip to one side, and it began a long and conscientious mastication. The elk must have been satisfied with this offering, for it drew back and disappeared into the night, a heavy, clumsy shape whose awkwardness and solitude wrung the heart.

Thus the fauna of East Prussia had just sent Tiffauges its first representative: a half-fabulous beast that seemed to emerge from the great Hercynian forests of prehistory. Tiffauges lay awake till dawn; the visit had brought back to him the strange conviction he'd always had of possessing immemorial origins, of having roots that went back into the deepest mists of time.

From then on, every time he went along the grassy tunnel to Canada he used to take a few lumps of turnip for the elk. One night when it came later than usual he was able to get a look at it in the light of dawn. It was at the same time impressive and pitiful, with its lumpy withers six feet high dwarfing its short neck, its enormous head with asses' ears and great clumsy antlers, its bony crupper supported on spindly irregular shanks. It tried to graze on some bilberry bushes, and because of its short neck had to adopt an absurd position with its front legs splayed in order to reach the ground. Then, its mouth twisted as it chewed, it raised its enormous head. Tiffauges saw that its small eyes were covered with two white films. The elk of Canada was blind. Now Tiffauges understood the begging demeanor, the awkward gait, the somnambulistic slowness; and because of his own awful myopia he felt close to the dark giant.

One morning he was struck by its being more than usually cold. A crude light came in through the whitened window. He had some difficulty in pushing the door open, and when he had done so he fell back dazzled. The black wet shadows of the day before had been transformed into a landscape of snow and ice, sparkling in the sun and curiously silent. The joy that welled up in him was not only due to the inexhaustible wonder this white magic always aroused in his childlike heart. He felt certain that such a startling change in the land of Prussia must herald a new stage in his own career, and decisive revelations. As he took his first steps, sinking deep into the snow, this was confirmed: the sign, infinitely small but significant, was in the tracks of birds, rodents and small carnivores that made a delicate shorthand over the great white page lying open at his feet.

He started to drive about in the Magirus with snow chains on the wheels, clanking and slithering across a landscape whose features were all accentuated by the winter. Its simplicity became almost elliptical; its blackness scarred the great immaculate plain with gashes of India ink; its houses were no more than small hummocks beneath the white mass of snow; the people themselves, all booted and with their heads wrapped up, were indistinguishable one from the other.

One day after he'd given a lift home to a farmer he'd over-taken plodding through the drifts at the side of the road, he was asked in for a drink. It was the first time he'd been into a German house, and the malaise he felt—a mixture of suffocation and a feeling of having encroached on privacy—showed him how shy he had become as a result of the war, captivity and, no doubt most of all, natural bent. A wolf or bear straying into a bedroom would probably have felt the same kind of panic.

The farmer made him sit near the fire. The enormous mantel was decorated with a pink paper fringe and a motley collection of souvenirs, wedding photographs, an iron cross on a bed of red velvet, a bunch of dried lavender, pretzels tied in bows, and a Christmas wreath of fir branches with four candles. Tiffauges was given bacon that smelled of peat smoke, smoked eel, runny anise-flavored cheese in a jar, pumpernickel, and a glass of Pill-kaller, a grain alcohol raw as hell. The man, thinking to please his guest, recalled his experiences as one of the occupying troops in Douai in the First World War, and ended up anathe-matizing the changes and chances of war. The guns on a rack in a glass-fronted cabinet set him off about the marvelous hunting in the forests of Johannisburg and Rominten, filled with fabulous five-prongers; and in the Elchwald to the north, where herds of elk prowled slowly to and fro, clumsy and hieratic, by lakes swooped down on by flights of black swans.

Alcohol sharpened the long-distance, detached, speculative vision Tiffauges described to himself as his "prophetic eye," the vision best suited to reading the lines of fate. He was sitting by a double casement window, between the two frames of which some sprigs of innocence were growing. One of the casements just framed the lower part of the village of Wild-horst, its houses whitewashed up to the first-floor windows, then paneled to the roof, the pretty church with its wooden steeple, a bit of road on which he could see an old woman pulling a baby along on a sled, a little girl chasing with a stick a flock of angry geese, a sled of pine logs drawn by two horses. All this, shut up in a little twelve-inch square, was so distinct, so well drawn and arranged, that it was as if he'd seen everything up to now in a vague blur, properly brought into focus for the first time.

In this way he was given the answer to the question he'd been asking himself ever since he crossed the Rhine. Now he knew what it was he had come to seek so far to the northeast: in the cold and penetrating hyperborean light, all symbols shone with unparalleled brilliance. Unlike the oceanic land of France, shrouded in mists, its lines blurred by receding shades, continental Germany, more harsh and rudimentary, was the country of strong, simplified, stylized drawing, easily read and remembered.

In France things got lost in impressions, vague gestures, incomplete wholes, in murky skies and infinities of tenderness. The Frenchman had a horror of position, uniform, strictly defined place in organization or hierarchy. A French postman always liked to remind people, by a certain unbuttoned look to his uniform, that he was also a father, a voter and a bowling enthusiast. Whereas the German postman, bundled up in. his smart uniform, exactly coincided with his role. Similarly the German housewife, schoolboy, chimney sweep and businessman were all more housewife, schoolboy, chimney sweep or businessman than their French counterparts. And while the French propensity led to the weakness of faded colors, spinelessness, dangerous laxities like promiscuity, dirt and cowardice, Germany was always in danger of becoming a theater of grimace and caricature, as demonstrated by her army, a fine collection of gargoyles, from the oxlike sergeant major to the corseted and monocled officer. But for Tiffauges, for whom the heavens, studded with allegories and hieroglyphs, resounded constantly with dim voices and enigmatic cries, Germany was

revealing itself as a promised land, the land of pure essences.
He saw it through the anecdotes of the farmer, and as circum
scribed within the little window—with its painted toy villages
full of totemic signs, laid out on a black and white landscape
its forests tiered like organ pipes; its men and women cease
lessly polishing the insignia of their calling; and above all it
emblematic fauna—the Trakehnen horses, Rominten stags
Elchwald elks, and the clouds of migratory birds covering the
plain with their wings and their cries—a heraldic fauna to be
found in all the armorial bearings of the Prussian Junkers.

All this had been given Tiffauges by fate, just like the fire a
St. Christopher's, the phony war and the debacle. But since he
had crossed the Rhine, fate's gifts had ceased to take the form
of ironic thrusts amidst an execrated order and had become full
and positive. The pigeons of Alsace had been a foretaste—mod
est, even absurd, but remembered by him with affection—of the
fortune that lay before him. Canada had established the fact tha
the land that was to be his, though new and virgin, would never
theless preserve the profound and secret remembrance of hi
childhood. And now it had been revealed to him that the whole
of East Prussia was a constellation of allegories, and that it wa
for him to slip into each one, not merely like a key in a lock bu
like a flame in a lantern. For his vocation was not only to deci
pher essences but also to exalt them, to bring all their qualitie
to the point of incandescence. He was going to give this coun
try a Tiffaugian interpretation, and at the same time raise it to
higher power, never yet attained.

*

The days began to get longer, but the cold tightened its grip
Unless a terrific fire was kept going in the hearth, the Canadia
nights became rather an ordeal, and Tiffauges made them les
frequent, though he appreciated their tonic purity all the mor
after the clammy contiguity of the huts. One morning whe
the stars, shaggy in the sharp frost, were still shining in the blac

sky, he was wakened by a knock at the door. Still half asleep, he got up, grumbling, and went and fetched a few slices of turnip from the mantelpiece. He knew it was no use trying to turn a deaf ear to the elk, whose demands were irrepressible once he'd sensed there was someone in the house. Tiffauges had to struggle a moment with the door, which was stuck by the frost. Then it suddenly flew open to reveal the tall figure of a man in boots and uniform. There was a moment of astonishment on both sides, then the stranger marched in, shut the door behind him, and walked purposefully over to the fire. He took a dry log from the pile, threw it on the hearth, and turned to Tiffauges.

"What are you doing here?" he asked.

Tiffauges had seen at first glance he was not a Wehrmacht officer. His age—he couldn't be far from sixty—his dark green uniform with heraldic antlers on the lapels, his triple-barreled hunting gun, all suggested he was one of the forestry officials— gamekeeper, district forester, master forester, state master forester, etc.—who, reduced in numbers by the call-up, still tried to protect and look after the paradise of fur and feather exposed to all the depredations of poaching and war.

He had taken off his cap, a skier's cap with earflaps. As Tiffauges made no attempt to answer his first question he tried again.

"Escaped prisoner?"

Then the Frenchman held out his hands and showed him the pieces of turnip.

"I feed blind elks," he said.

The stranger did not seem unduly surprised.

Tiffauges continued, "I'm at the prisoner of war camp at Moorhof. I'll be going back there soon. Signalman-pigeon fancier Abel Tiffauges, 18th Regiment of Engineers, Nancy, taken prisoner on June 17 in the woods at Zincourt."

"Pigeon fancier?" repeated the man in green in an interested voice. "The noblest service—after the cavalry, of course. Poor pigeons!"

He sat down by the fire and prodded the log, which had flared up suddenly and looked as if it might fall out of the grate. Tiffauges, at a disadvantage in German, could not make out whether there was something ironical in the nostalgic reference to pigeon fancying. He decided to see in it only a bond of sympathy with the stranger.

"From what you say, I gather you know the Monster?" the forester went on. Seeing Tiffauges didn't understand, he explained. "That's the name of a blind elk who's probably afraid to stay with the others because the males would stab him with their antlers. Everyone knows him in the woods where he spends the winter, because he goes and begs from passers-by. Unfortunately, as soon as spring approaches he emigrates a few miles south, and if he goes somewhere he's not known he's in danger. One of these days they'll shoot my Monster," he concluded gloomily. "Especially as he's not very prepossessing as you may have noticed. And he's also a sorcerer, a devil. He frightens people with his white eyes and the way he won't take no for an answer!"

"Here he is," said Tiffauges.

The characteristic scraping, first against the wall, then against the door, had in fact joined with the sputtering of the fire. When Tiffauges opened the door the forestry officer, though he had often encountered the Monster before, was surprised by the black hairy hulk looming there. Tiffauges had cupped his hands and offered some slices of turnip to the quivering muzzle. The elk picked them up carefully in its little tight lips, as accurate as a thumb and forefinger. Then they talked to each other. Tiffauges drew his fingernails up and down between the two long, amazingly sensitive and expressive ears, telling the Monster he was beautiful and gentle, strong and without malice and that the world was wicked and treacherous. The Monster answered with a modulated roar, so deep it sounded like the laugh of a giant ventriloquist; his ears twitched and waved about, unmistakably manifesting happiness and trust. Then the elk withdrew, and Tiffauges followed as if to escort him to the edge of his domain. The characteristic click-clack of the great beast's step could be heard getting fainter in the distance. When Tiffauges came back into the cabin the officer, who was standing with his back to the fire, looked at him a moment in silence.

"You're a French prisoner," he said at last. "Perhaps not escaped, but at least breaking camp. You've broken into a forest hut for which I'm responsible. To judge by the skins drying above my head you're in the habit of poaching. All that would be enough to send you to Graudenz. But you seem to have managed to win the friendship of grouchy old Monster. And then, the idea of a pigeon fancier in a prison fortress . . . No, that's really too much. . . ."

He stood up.

"Go back to the camp. Maybe we'll meet again. I'm the chief forester of the Rominten Heath."

He put on his hat, pulled down the earflaps, buttoned his tunic, and went out. But before walking away he stopped and turned to Tiffauges.

"Don't overdo the turnips in this cold! I'll have a few bales of hay and a sack of oats put up in the loft here. Perhaps that'll keep the Monster from going any farther south."

*

For Tiffauges the spring was marked by an incident which everyone in the camp had forgotten by the next day but which changed Tiffauges's image of himself and of his destiny in East Prussia.

The crocuses were beginning to pierce the last crusts of snow, and every night the laughing geese could be heard calling to one another as they gathered on the Bay of Courland, waiting for the spring breezes to drive them farther north. Several weeks before, Tiffauges had had to trade his faithful Magirus for an old Opel with a wood-burning motor; cars and trucks using gas were now restricted to combat troops. Rumor had it that this heralded a German offensive. Tiffauges didn't care about this: he saw the change only as introducing one more link between himself and the Prussian forest, whose wood would now provide the energy for his journeys. He also scented in this development, which was undeniably restrictive and retrograde, a first step in the breakup of Germany that would eventually bring that proud victorious country down to his level, put it within his reach, and—who knew?—perhaps one day at his mercy.

The huts needed repair after the winter, and Tiffauges was sent quite a long way north to collect a load of planks from the big sawmills at Elchwald. He easily recognized the landscape and atmosphere of which the Monster was the purest possible incarnation: a soil more sandy and shifting if possible than any he had come across since his arrival in East Prussia; the general dissolving of earth into water and sky into pale horizons; the whole place so unsubstantial that the horses were fitted with projecting wooden shoes, the wagons with wheels like steamrollers, and each farm was equipped with punts and barges to cope with the spring and autumn floods.

Still farther north came the line of the dunes, tirelessly shaped and reshaped by the wind; beach grass was planted in an attempt to prevent shifting, and sometimes the massive, archaic silhouette of a herd of elk would be seen filing across the top of them. Next came the Bay of Courland, a shallow lagoon of over nine hundred and sixty square miles, gradually filled in in the course of thousands of years by silt from the Memel, Deime, Russ and Gilge. This great salt lake with its dying waters was separated from the Baltic only by the Nehrung, a thin tongue of sand fifty-nine miles long and varying in width between four and five hundred yards. Tiffauges was never to go to these farthest confines of the hyperborean region. But he neve stopped dreaming of them, especially of a village with the winged name of Rossitten, in the middle of the Nehrung, inhabited exclusively by ornithologists who spent their lives observing and protecting the vast flocks of migratory birds that flew over twice a year and alighted on them like huge living nets of feathers.

Tiffauges's return from the incursion into the northern limits of his kingdom was strewn with incidents. At any moment the Opel's engine threatened to give out under the load of planks, which were stacked up higher than the cabin of the truck. But in the end it was the road that got the better of its panting perseverance. Emerging from a little wood, the track was covered by a stretch of water, into which Tiffauges launched himself gaily, sending up two big wings of spray. But suddenly he had the feeling the steering wheel was no longer responding, and he instinctively applied the brake. The truck skidded about twenty yards and stopped. When Tiffauges tried to start it up again the wheels slithered in the mud and sank deeper at every attempt. He walked into Gross Skaisgirren, the next village, and asked for help at the town hall, producing his warrant. Night was falling when he got back to the truck, accompanied by a farm laborer leading two horses. But the animals too slipped in the liquid mud; one of them fell and grazed its knees. Ropes were needed if the horses were to haul the truck out while remaining on firm ground themselves. Tiffauges had to put himself in the hands of the local police, who sent him to sleep in an uncomfortable little room. The next morning the truck was hauled out of the mud, but the engine refused to budge. Tiffauges had to spend another night with the police and set off two days after for Moorhof, forty-eight hours late.

Lieutenant Teschemacher greeted him with relief.

"Yesterday they took a corpse out of the peat bogs at Walkenau," he said, "and I was afraid it might be you. Especially as the description they gave me over the phone sounded rather like you. The surprising thing is that no one's been reported missing either from the camp or from the villages round about."

Tiffauges was too intent on signs and encounters to let this incident pass. He'd been told the unidentified corpse had been left at the school at Walkenau, which was empty because of the Easter holidays. It was a mile from camp. He went as soon as he got an opportunity.

*

"Note the delicacy of the hands and feet; the fineness of the face, with its aquiline profile in spite of the broad brow; the aristocratic air reinforced by the richness of the chlamys, which looks as if it was made of gold thread, and of the objects with which the dead man was surrounded for use in the afterlife."

Tiffauges's arrival in the classroom interrupted the account being delivered by Professor Keil, of the Koenigsberg Institute of Anthropology and Archaeology, to half a dozen people including the mayor of Walkenau, a little man with glasses who was surely the teacher and who was the person who'd notified the institute at Koenigsberg, the pastor, and a few other local worthies. Stretched out in front of them on a table was a half-naked corpse the color of peat, with a wrinkled skin that made it look like a leather dummy: the whole scene resembled an anatomy lesson. The emaciated, spiritualized face had a thin band over the eyes, drawn so tight it seemed to have sunk into the bridge of the nose and the nape of the neck. A six-pointed star of gilded metal was fixed to the band, between the eyes.

Tiffauges gathered from the professor's lecture that the man was one of those "peat-bog men" periodically exhumed in Denmark and the north of Germany in such a marvelous state of preservation, because of the acidity of the soil, that the country people take them to be the victims of some recent accident or crime. In fact they are ancient Germans who were subjected to ritual immersion in the shallow waters of the peat bogs as far back as the first century A.D. or the century before. Unfortunately very little is known about these tribes, and the only authority is Tacitus' *Germania,* which, Keil said, was a second-hand account and not to be relied on. Then he pointed out that the skin was so well preserved, in spite of being two thousand years old, that the police of the commune had actually taken its fingerprints to try to identify it. He himself had carried out an autopsy and could show from the state of the lungs that the man died by drowning. There was in any case no trace of any wound or violence. For what was to follow, the professor, smiling triumphantly, put on a mysterious air and looked at the dead man from before our era with knowing glances, as if he and the other shared a secret that was inexpressibly piquant and impossible to divine. After a calculated pause he went on, carefully enunciating each word.

"Ladies and gentlemen"—there were no ladies present—"I have examined personally the stomach, small intestine and large intestine of our great ancestor. These organs, though compressed, were intact and still held their contents at the time of death. So I have been able to reconstruct *scientifically*"—he emphasized each syllable—"the last meal of the Walkenau man, which was taken, and I am in a position to prove it, between twelve and twenty-four hours before death. It consisted of a gruel composed mainly of a kind of knotgrass, popularly called water pepper, mixed with various proportions of wild carrot, patience dock, bindweed and daisies. I don't really think vegetable broth was the ordinary diet of the ancient Germans, who were hunters and fishermen. I think it was more likely a ritual meal, a sort of anthumous communion taken before the sacrifice by the victim and a few of the faithful.

"As for the date at which death took place, it is of course impossible to fix with any accuracy. But the gold coins found near the body place it in the first century A.D., because they are stamped with the head of Tiberius. And here we come to the

most moving aspect of our discovery. It is not absolutely beyond the bounds of possibility that this last meal of a man who
must have been of some importance, probably a king, eaten
before a death that was horrible but freely chosen, took place
at the same time—the same year, perhaps even the same day,
the same hour!—as the Last Supper, the paschal meal shared
by Jesus and his disciples before the Passion. Thus at the very
moment when the Judo-Mediterranean religion was springing
into life in the Middle East, a similar rite may have been found-
ing a parallel religion here that was strictly Nordic and even
Germanic."

He paused as if overcome by emotion and by the importance
of his own words. Then he resumed less solemnly.

"I will just add that our ancestor was exhumed near here in a
little wood of alders, of the black variety common to marshes.
And here I can't help thinking of Goethe, the greatest poet in
the German language, and the ballad of *The Erl-King*,[2] at once
his most famous and his most mysterious work. It sings to our
German ears, it lulls our German hearts, it is the true quintes-
sence of the German soul. So I propose to you, as I shall propose to the Academy of Sciences in Berlin, that the man we have
before us should enter into the annals of archaeological research
under the name of 'The Erl-King.' "

Then he recited:

> "*O who rides by night thro' the woodland so wild?*
> *It is the fond father embracing his child . . .*"[3]

At that moment he was interrupted by a farm laborer rushing in and whispering something to him.

"Gentlemen," said Keil, "I am informed that a second body
has just been found in the same peat bog. I suggest we all go
there right away to welcome this latest messenger from the mists
of time."

They had taken the precaution of extracting the whole sod of peat in which the body, no doubt curled up on itself, was embedded. Only the head, or more exactly the right profile, was visible, as if encrusted in the mud and with no more thickness than the face on a medal. Its color was so like that of the peat itself it seemed merely modeled in low relief in the sod. It was a small face, emaciated, childish and sad. It wore a cap made of three pieces of material roughly cobbled together, which made it look like a prisoner or even a convict. The peat workers had waited for the professor to arrive before setting about the sod with trowels. Now they first uncovered the whole head, then the shoulders, which appeared to be wrapped in a sort of sheepskin cape. The whole garment emerged quite rapidly but seemed to be empty. When the remains of this "latest messenger from the mists of time" were placed on the grass and its shepherd's cloak could be unfolded, it was only to reveal that in fact the body had been entirely consumed: only the head had mysteriously survived the ages.

"So," said Keil, "we shall never know whether it was a man, woman or child. But judging by the results of similar excavations, I'm inclined to think it's a woman. It was not unusual for a personage of importance to descend to the shades accompanied by his wife—the ancient Germans being strictly monogamous, as you know. At any rate, that makes one more enigma concerning the Erl-King. It's like the band over his eyes with the gold star: it's impossible to make out its significance in the present state of our knowledge. But the further we advance in time, the nearer the past gets to us. Paradoxically, we know infinitely more about antiquity today than we did a hundred years ago. Soon, perhaps, new light may be thrown on the ancient Germans. But there will always be some veil of mystery around what is most sacred in the peaty eternity of the Erl-King."

Before returning to Moorhof, Tiffauges took a long look at

the frail, mournful little convict's head which the sun was caressing for the first time after so many centuries of muddy darkness. It was as if he were trying to engrave its features in his
memory so as to be able to recognize it if he met it again.

*

In the autumn of 1940 the inhabitants of the little town of
Rastenburg were surprised when they were forbidden to go into
the forest of Goerlitz, their traditional resort for dances, shooting matches, fairs and Sunday afternoon walks with their families. The Karlshof café, where everyone used to have tea, was
requisitioned; its staff was sent away; and a section of the SS
was installed. Then teams from the Todt Organization came,
and building firms like Wayss und Freitag and Dykehof und
Widmann; even trucks belonging to Seidenspinner, the landscape gardener in Stuttgart. The roads were widened, an airport
was built nearby, and the Rastenburg–Angerburg railway line
was closed to civilian traffic. In the papers the official explanation of all this was that a big subsidiary of the Askania Chemical
Works was going to be set up on the old Goerlitz estate, but this
explanation did not square with the number and luxuriousness
of the new arrangements. Despite the mystery surrounding
what was called the "new town," people talked of a barbed-
wire fence ten feet thick and five feet high, inside which was a
mined area fifty yards wide, patrolled day and night. Anti-
aircraft batteries and heavy machine guns guarded two other
defense perimeters beyond which visitors could penetrate only
by passing through a series of check points. In addition to a
dozen or so individual villas, the "town" consisted of an ultra-
modern radio station, a parking lot, a sauna bath, a heating unit,
a movie theater, assembly and lecture rooms, a casino for officers, and, to the north, an underground bunker luxuriously fitted
out under twenty-five feet of concrete and reached by an
elevator.

On June 22, 1941, the very day when Operation Barbarossa

let all hell loose on Russia, Hitler installed himself in his new "Wolf's Lair" with Bormann, his staff and his chief colleagues. The bigwigs of the regime immediately set up their own quarters as near as possible, Himmler in the Hegwald at Grossgarten, Ribbentrop at Steinort, Lammers, head of Chancery, at Rosengarten, and Goering, only too pleased at this unhoped-for opportunity, in his hunting lodge at Rominten.

That day two hundred and twenty German divisions supported by thirty-two thousand aircraft and ten thousand tanks hurled themselves on the Russian frontier, aided in the north by the Finnish army and in the south by the armies of Hungary and Rumania. From then on the soil of East Prussia never stopped trembling beneath the tracks of tanks; its sky shook constantly at the passage of squadrons of bombers. It was like some biological tropism, some center of attraction drawing irrestibly toward it a gigantic maelstrom of men and arms, horses and vehicles. The prisoner of war camps were stirred by a thrill of hope. It was a sign that something was happening, and that perhaps their own lot was going to change. But for Tiffauges this entirely external development occurred during the period of waiting and consolidation that followed the discoveries and revelations of winter and spring. His trips in the Opel, which gradually revealed to him Germany, the Germans and the German language, alternated with periods in camp relieved by visits to Canada. At the first breath of spring the Monster had vanished, no doubt on the mysterious southern migration the chief forester of Rominten had mentioned. It was as if the animal's allotted time in Canada were over, and his mission concerning Tiffauges accomplished. In any case, the immemorial message of the Monster had been only a harbinger of the much more moving one of the Erl-King and of his little prisoner, as Tiffauges called him to himself.

On October 3, in a speech at the Sports Palace in Berlin, Hitler announced to the world the launching of Operation Typhoon, which was supposed to result in the fall of Moscow and the final annihilation of the Red Army. And again the area was overrun with men and equipment, younger and younger men and more and more advanced equipment, all thrown pell-mell into the vast furnace of battle. So when the first birds started to migrate, high against the gray clouds, letting out mournful cries, Tiffauges thought sadly of all those young men cut down in their prime, and it seemed to him it was the souls of the dead that were fleeing up above, alone, terrified of the mystery of what lies after death, and lamenting that familiar mother earth they had had so little time to love.

The first frosts had already whitened the surface of the marshes when he was summoned to the labor office of the camp. A tall white-haired man in dark green uniform with antlers on the lapels was waiting for him. Tiffauges recognized the chief forester who had come upon him six months before in Canada.

"I need an assistant who knows about cars and can give me a hand in general at Rominten," he said. "So I thought of you. The authorities at your camp have made the assignment. But of course I don't want a slave. I'll take you only if you want to come."

An hour later Tiffauges had bade a rapid farewell to his companions and Lieutenant Teschemacher and was sitting beside the forester in a heavy Mercedes that ran on gas.

They drove about thirty miles southwest across a countryside frozen by war and an early winter. It was still daylight when they crossed the palisade around the Rominten Reserve through a log gateway over which was written in Gothic letters: Rominten Heath Wildlife Reserve.

IV
The Ogre of Rominten

He began to sniff about him, saying that he could smell human flesh.

Charles Perrault

They left the official Mercedes at a gatehouse and went on in a hunting gig drawn by a chestnut from Trakehnen. Thus nature remained unsullied as far as possible by motor vehicles within the enclosure at Rominten. Night had fallen by the time they stopped in front of the official residence of the chief forester, a villa with a veranda, covered with old tiles and with eaves decorated with stags' heads. Tiffauges had to unharness the horse and take it to the stable, an unaccustomed task that he discharged as best he could, under the critical eye of an old servant who had come running when he heard the gig on the cobblestones. Tiffauges was given a little attic room to sleep in. He ate in the kitchen, sharing the soup, bacon, red cabbage and black bread of the servant and his wife.

During the weeks that followed he went with the forester, on foot or in horse-drawn vehicles, on tours of inspection inside the Reserve. The job of driver-coachman-factotum had previously been filled by the son of the two servants; Tiffauges owed the change in his circumstances to the fact that this young man had just been called up for the Russian front. The boy's parents were hostile at first, but this soon wore off, and Tiffauges felt himself gradually becoming a sort of adopted son, treated with a kindness in proportion to the old people's fears for their real son.

When the great gates closed behind him and he plunged for the first time beneath the wild leafy canopy of Rominten, Tiffauges realized he was entering a magic circle as the protégé of a magician who, though minor, was recognized by the spirits of the place. The first of these to welcome him was a big golden lynx sitting on a tree stump, which, as it watched him go by, smiled under its thin, Asian prince's mustache and waggled the tufts of bright hair over its ears. Then he was escorted by a pair of beavers, followed by a white falcon and a big gray dog with slit eyes and sloping back—he was told this was one of the Siberian wolves that migrate in packs across the Polish plain. But it was the flora, sometimes maleficent, sometimes beneficent, whose connections with magic beings was most evident. The forester showed him the big mushrooms with red, white-spotted caps, under which elves and trolls sleep; the black hellebore that makes people mad, but which on Christmas Eve is covered with Christmas roses; the "trumpets of death" whose putrescent horns, though edible, are a sign of nearby carrion; belladonna, which dries up sweat and dilates the pupils; the devil's boletuses, with crimson tumefied stalks; and, above all, the rooty hollows in banks which are entrances to the dwellings of gnomes, those apparently ancient and decrepit creatures who speak with a voice of thunder and can halt any horse by throwing themselves at its head.

Tiffauges expected the forester to give him some fantastic initiation—take him down into caves where dwarfs wrested diamonds from the rock; lead him to a castle buried in saxifrage and brambles where a beautiful naked girl slept in a glass coffin; or teach him to pound up plants to make the elixir of youth or love philters. His credulous, childlike soul was surprised—though not disappointed—when the lord who reigned over this forest and its beasts was revealed to him. For though he met neither gnomes nor sleeping princess nor a king who had ruled through the ages from a throne in a hollow tree, he was soon brought before the ogre of Rominten.

The sixty thousand acres of the Rominten Reserve were

looked after by several foresters, whose villas were hidden away among the woods in their charge. But the most remarkable buildings were William II's hunting lodge and the hunting lodge of Hermann Goering, both in the middle of the Reserve about a mile apart.

The imperial hunting lodge, put together in sections by a Norwegian architect in 1891, was an astonishing little wooden castle bristling with turrets and balconies and painted dark red all over—a cross between a Chinese pagoda and a Swiss chalet. An attempt to stress the Nordic element had produced a final note of outlandishness: the ridge poles ended in Viking prows carved in the shape of dragons' heads. There were outbuildings in the same style, a chapel dedicated to St. Hubert, and a life-size bronze stag by Richard Friese, animal painter and sculptor to the Kaiser.

In 1936 Field Marshal Hermann Goering, who ruled over Rominten as both head of the Prussian government and Master of the Hunt to the Reich itself, had built his own hunting lodge nearby. Goering's hunting lodge, though it affected the utmost rusticity, eclipsed with its elegance the naïve display of the imperial hunting lodge. A quadrangle of low, reed-thatched buildings surrounded an inner courtyard which was half patio and half cloister. The gables were decorated with the ancient Masurian good-luck sign, and the power of the talisman was reinforced by sets of five-pronged antlers. Inside, a monumental stone chimney piece dominated a huge living room the size of a church, lit by high windows with small panes of colored glass set in lead. The lights were in the shape of crowns, and the wooden framework of the room itself was left uncovered to resemble the upturned hull of a great ship. Around this main room were the bedrooms, each paneled in a different kind of wood and named accordingly. There was the ash room, the elm room, the oak room, the larch room, and so on. The Master of the German Hunt had spread about him, in this forest setting, the same

luxury as was to be found in his town house in Berlin, at Karinhall in the Schorfheide, in his chalet at Berchtesgaden, and even
in his own personal armored train, the *Asia*, a veritable palace
on rails. His hunting lodge was a sumptuous mass of tapestries,
old masters, furs, objets d'art, china, silver, jewels—all the spoils
of a great pirate to whom war had thrown open the great houses
and museums of Europe. The arrival of Hitler and his staff in
the Wolf's Lair at Rastenburg, less than fifty-four miles away,
gave Goering an unexpected opportunity to reconcile his duties
toward the master of the Third Reich with his pleasures as a
hunter of stags and eater of venison. He kept open house at
Rominten, lavishly entertaining the highest dignitaries of the
regime and allied statesmen, on whom he bestowed the honor
of shooting a stag. The victim was always chosen beforehand
in consultation with the chief forester and in accordance with
the importance of the guest—but always from a much lower category than the regal quarry Goering kept for himself.

*

One of Tiffauges's first tasks arose from the complaints of
the farmers whose land adjoined Rominten's western edge:
their crops were ruined before they had time to harvest them
by wild boars from the Reserve. No enclosure weaker than a
stone wall can withstand the head of an old male boar bent on
forcing a way in for himself and his companions, and though
the gaps made in the fences and palisades were always conscientiously filled in, everyone knew it was useless. The only solution would have been to exterminate all the boars in the
Reserve, a solution favored by the foresters themselves, who
feared for their own seed beds and nurseries. But the Master of
the Hunt decided otherwise. He was too fond of the great beast
—brave, jovial, greedy, gulping down cereals, insects and carrion alike; its irregular and unforeseeable ways made a change
from the fastidious and pedantic habits of the deer and roebuck,
always faithful to the same runs, pastures and lairs. So he or-

dered the opposite solution: the eastern part of Rominten was to be made so delightful to the boars that they wouldn't want to leave it. This was to be done by feeding them the corpses of horses assigned to the slaughterhouse, but brought instead and killed on the spot and left for the boars to devour.

Tiffauges found this operation, in which he was given the role of slaughterer, a cruel ordeal, though undoubtedly it was charged with meaning and therefore beneficent. He had to take delivery of the horse in a neighboring village or stud farm—Trakehnen was only a dozen or so miles to the north—and then drive in a cart, accompanied by the owner, to the place of sacrifice. Often the poor old nag was so broken down, and had been given so little to eat since its fate was decided, that progress was painfully slow. Tiffauges had even been provided with a syringe and a bottle of stimulant to get the animal going again temporarily, if it showed signs of giving out altogether before they reached the Reserve.

He did the killing with a pistol shot behind the ear, fired from a distance of about eighteen inches. The animal collapsed at once, and its owner would immediately set about removing its shoes, and, if it was worth the trouble, its hide. Tiffauges nearly passed out at these horrific goings-on. It was like some gigantic crime committed in an out-of-the-way corner, especially as he soon detected the deep affinity linking him and the horse, the phoric animal par excellence. This lent a suicidal note to the slaughter. One day, returning to the scene of the crime, he came upon a whole crowd of boar wallowing with savage eagerness in the carcass of a mare. They had torn it open and scattered it all over the clearing. But that was nothing compared to another incident. A solitary old boar attacked a horse's corpse when it was still fresh—attacked it by the anus, which it enlarged to the size of its own head by the use of its snout and tusks. Under its furious thrusts the dead horse seemed to be struggling, waving its four legs in the air. And Tiffauges, deeply pained, felt something of this grotesque indignity rebound on to him.

*

The arrival of the Master of the Hunt, Field Marshal of the Reich, and Commander-in-Chief of the Luftwaffe was announced at the hunting lodge by an influx of provisions and a great bustle of servants. When the *Asia* stopped at Tollming-kehnen station, the Mercedes was waiting, pennant flying, to whirl the great man to the fairy chalet where a huge fire was burning on the monumental hearth. Butlers in white gloves arranged groups of candles on the long refectory table covered with fine linen and sparkling with gold plate. Valets warmed the master's great bed of silk and furs. In the kitchens the traditional stuffed boar, roasted over charcoal, oozed fat into the pan. The chief forester was one of the first to be summoned by the Master of the Hunt, whose voice, gruff with its slight Bavarian accent, rumbled orders ceaselessly all through the lodge. The old forester, dressed up in his best uniform, came away from these interviews with his head full of instructions and a wild look on his face. He would unburden his woes to Tiffauges, who was waiting for him in the stable with the chestnut horse.

The first time Tiffauges had occasion to see the field marshal himself was in the middle of the winter, because of an incident that gave immense pleasure to the master of Rominten.

Tiffauges was coming back from Goldap in a cart drawn by two big farm horses, with a load of beets and corn to be used as fodder for the deer. While the horses panted along, their spiked shoes ringing on the frozen ground, Tiffauges, wrapped up in a sheepskin coat, watched the frosty tracery of the bare branches passing slowly over his head. He was thinking that his long migration toward the east, into which he had been plunged by the Martine affair and the war it had caused, was accompanied by a pilgrimage into the past, marked from the reflective point of view by the appearance of the Monster and the peat-bog man, and from a more practical point of view by the abandoning, first of the ordinary, then of the wood-burning car, in favor finally of the horse. He suspected with a delicious anguish that his journey would take him still farther, still deeper, into the most venerable shades, and that he might finally arrive at the immemorial darkness of the Erl-King.

It was at this point that he saw an apparition that confirmed his belief that his thoughts had the formidable power of summoning up real beings. To the right, trotting briskly toward him among the branchless trunks of the tall firs, was a herd of enormous creatures, black and shaggy as bears and humped like bison. Tiffauges recognized them as bulls, but obviously of a prehistoric type, such as are depicted in neolithic cave drawings —that is, aurochs, with their short horns like daggers and withers rippling with a thick mane. Unfortunately Tiffauges was not the only one to see them coming. The horses broke from their placid amble into a gallop that soon became a wild bolt; the cart bumped about all over the road. Tiffauges didn't feel like holding them back: he was no less frightened than they were, especially as a second herd of aurochs threatened to cut off their retreat. He counted about twelve in the first group and ten in the second, roughly twenty-two in all, but the farthest away and least swift were mostly females and calves. Tiffauges and his team just escaped the second herd as it joined the first, forming a great tumultuous mass that crushed everything in its path. But the next turn in the road was the runaways' undoing. The cart went along for a few yards on two wheels, then fell on the outside of the bend, still dragged along by the horses, while Tiffauges was sent rolling in the snow. One of the horses was freed in the process and charged along, dragging the broken harness behind; the other, still attached to the cart, struggled and kicked against it. Tiffauges hastened to extricate this horse and got on its back before it, too, dashed away. When he looked behind him he saw the herd of aurochs peacefully gathered around the overturned cart, stuffing themselves with beets and corn.

At the time this incident occurred the father of the aurochs of Rominten was actually at the hunting lodge, where he was a frequent visitor. This was Professor Dr. Lutz Heck, director of the Berlin Zoo. It had been his idea to try, by careful crossbreeding of bulls from Spain, Corsica and the Camargue, improved by selection carried out through several generations, to re-create the original aurochs. The last representatives of the species had died out in the Middle Ages. He thought he had succeeded quite well, and the Master of the Hunt had given him permission to let loose in the Rominten Reserve what he called with pedantic joy *Bos primigenus redivivus.*

The huge black herd had spread terror through the Reserve ever since. A story was told of a patrol on bicycles who were attacked by an auroch and had to escape up the nearest trees. The animal had vented its wrath on the bicycles strewn all over the road. First it trampled them, then hoisted the remains on its horns and went off in triumph, crowned by trophies of mangled tubes and wheels.

When Goering heard of Tiffauges's misadventure his delight knew no bounds, and he summoned him to hear the story from his own lips. So Tiffauges presented himself at the hunting lodge the next day, freshly shaven and dressed in a green uniform and black boots, the legacy of a forest ranger who was about the same size. He was given a lengthy and magnificent dinner in the kitchen with the staff, who looked at him with respect mingled with fear as one on whom the eye of the Master of the Hunt had lighted. Then he had to await the pleasure of those who were confabulating around the monumental hearth with cigars and liqueurs. Finally he was sent for.

Although all the guests were in uniform, they were eclipsed by the size of the Master of the Hunt and the extravagance of his costume. His two hundred and eighty pounds overflowed a huge antique chair whose fretted and checkered back formed a fan-shaped nimbus around his head and shoulders. He was wearing a white shirt with a lace jabot and loose sleeves, covered by a sort of tunic of mauve suede from which emerged a heavy gold chain with an emerald at the end the size of a pigeon's egg.

This exhibition would have been unbearable for the Frenchman if the German language had not interposed between him and the rest a sort of translucid but not transparent screen, which took the edge off their grossness and enabled him to address the second most important person in the Reich in terms and in a tone that would never have been tolerated on the part of a German.

Tiffauges was required to give details of the time and place of the encounter, the number of aurochs, the direction they seemed to be coming from, the horses' reaction, his own attitude—and at every new fact the Master of the Hunt howled with laughter and slapped his thighs. Then Tiffauges was chaffed about his glasses: perhaps the magnifying lenses had made him mistake some rabbits for giant bulls. Thus for the first time Tiffauges discovered one of the quirks of the masters of the Third Reich—the hatred for men in glasses, who for them embodied intelligence, study and speculation. In short, the Jew. Professor Dr. Lutz Heck, father of *Bos primigenus redivivus,* explained that paradoxically his beasts would remain dangerous so long as they retained any traces of domestication. Born in captivity, they would take years to learn to fear man and to flee as soon as they suspected his presence. Whereas now, though not so much as at the beginning of their new wild life, they were puzzled at being abandoned in an icy forest without much to eat when the district was full of rich pastures and prosperous farms. More than once they had broken down fences, broken into stables and haylofts in search of fodder, sometimes mounting in passing some mild heifer. Their aggressiveness toward men had something of the resentment and bitterness of abandoned children, concluded Professor Heck. The incident with the Frenchman was the best possible proof of it.

*

But the king animal at Rominten was the stag. It was hunted by the only two methods the denseness of the trees allowed—stalking and beating—and was for the Master of the Hunt the object of a cult at once amorous, sacrificial and culinary. This cult had its own theology, whose esoteric element concerned the identification and interpretation of cast antlers and calculation of the "points" earned by the head. This was assessed by a jury of official huntsmen a week after the stag was killed; the antlers were dried in a heated room during the interval.

The winter was drawing to a close, and Tiffauges's work now consisted mainly of collecting cast antlers from woods and thickets. The task was of particular importance at this time of year because the older deer shed their antlers in February and March, while the younger ones sometimes waited until it was almost summer. What made things difficult was that there were usually two or three days between the shedding of the first and second antler, so that the discovery of one entailed a long search for the other, without which it was of no value. In spite of first the conscientiousness and then the growing passion with which he carried out his quest, Tiffauges would have been hard pressed without the help of two specially trained griffons which did wonders, and which had been brought from a neighboring district when Goering was not at the hunting lodge—one of his whims was to hate dogs and not allow them in his presence. More surprising still was the skill of the chief forester, who without hesitating would identify any antlers brought to him as Theodore's fourth head, the Sergeant's seventh, or the tenth of old Poseidon. The shed antlers were placed on a special board for each animal, above the heads of previous years, so that the whole formed a pyramid ultimately crowned at the eleventh or twelfth level by the complete head of the stag after it had been killed.

That day the field marshal was expected to arrive at the end of the morning, and a company of horn players was gathered in front of the hunting lodge to sound the hunt's-up when he got out of his car. Tiffauges and the chief forester had arranged on a table all the shed antlers collected since his last visit. These heads constituted a detailed and intimate chronicle of life at Rominten, and the deciphering of them gave rise to passionate discussions between the foresters and the Master of the Hunt. In particular, they made it possible to follow the stages of development of any King Stag, and to decide with certainty when he should be killed, because having then reached his peak he would inevitably start to "go down" the following year.

The Mercedes, flags flying, was just driving up the main avenue, and the musicians, stiffly at attention, were holding their instruments to their lips, when an aide-de-camp came running up in front of the car, calling out:

"No horns! No horns! The lion can't bear them!"

There was general astonishment. For a moment people wondered if "the lion" was some new appellation arrogated to himself by the "Man of Iron"; but in that case what was the explanation of this sudden dislike for his favorite music?

The great car glided to a halt, its four doors all opened at once, and out of one of the rear doors emerged a long fawn body, a lion, a real one, led on a leash by the field marshal, laughing and entangled in the leash and looking as round as a ball in his white uniform.

"Buby, Buby, Buby," he sang as he was dragged across the courtyard by the lion, crouching near the ground in alarm at its new surroundings. They disappeared into the house, the servants melting away in terror before them.

There was a feverish search for a room where the lion could be kept temporarily: finally Goering's own bathroom was trans-

formed into a menagerie, with a barrowload of sand in the
shower to act as a sort of litter box. Then the field marshal came
out of the house, took his place opposite the musicians, and listened at attention to the welcome they had been rehearsing for
several weeks. He made a gesture of thanks with his blue and
gold stick and disappeared into his suite to change his clothes.
An hour later he was conferring with the chief forester, looking
over the cast antlers on which depended the hunting programs
for the summer and autumn.

That evening Tiffauges glimpsed a sight that engraved itself
on his memory with the crude vividness of a colored woodcut.
Goering, dressed in an elegant pale blue kimono, sat at the table with half a roast boar in front of him, brandishing a leg of it
like Hercules' club. The lion sat beside him avidly watching the
piece of game being waved back and forth over its head, and
making slow and languid snaps at it whenever it came near
enough. Finally the Master of the Hunt sank his teeth into it,
and for a few moments his face disappeared completely behind
the monstrous joint. Then, with his mouth full, he held the leg
out to the lion, who bit into it in his turn. From then on the leg
passed regularly back and forth between the two ogres, who
gazed at each other affectionately as they chewed the lumps of
black, musky flesh.

*

The worst trial the chief forester had to endure was the allo-
cating of stags for guests, in accordance with their rank, to
shoot. It often caused storms that broke over his head alone.
Field Marshal von Brauchitsch was the cause of one of these
scenes, which arose because the Master of the Hunt was jealous about every deer in the Reserve. Brauchitsch, supreme
head of the Wehrmacht, had set out one day when it was still
dark accompanied by the forester of a neighboring district, who
had found tracks suggesting a five-pronger, probably the Bully.
The Master of the Hunt left a little while later with the chief

forester, in the direction of the covers of the two King Stags whose cast antlers pointed them out as the next victims. Night was falling when he came back to the lodge, bringing in the back of his car an old five-pronger and his equerry, a stag just turned five years old. Both heads were magnificently formed, that of the older animal like a candlestick, the other more open, like a three-fingered hand. The Master of the Hunt, radiant at his success, withdrew to his suite to get ready for dinner. An hour later Von Brauchitsch's car was heard returning.

The custom on such occasions was to have a ceremonial dividing of the spoils at midnight in the inner courtyard of the hunting lodge, by the light of braziers burning pine logs. So after a jolly feast the huntsmen gathered by the bodies of the three stags, arranged as usual in order of size. As soon as the Master of the Hunt saw them he bent over the biggest, the Bully, whose head had twenty-two points and weighed at least twenty pounds. He stroked the pearling along the horns, the burrs, the furrows. He tested with his finger tip the sharp points of the brow-tines, whose ivory whiteness contrasted with the charred brown of the beams. When he stood up all good humor had vanished from his baby face, and his lower lip jutted out resentfully.

"That's exactly the kind of stag *I* like to shoot," he said.

The twelve horn players were standing in an arc, and at a signal from the chief forester they sounded the mort. The forester, standing bareheaded, solemnly read out the names of the hunters and the stags who were their victims, concluding with a few words of thanks and farewell. The horns then took up again their hoarse, misty song to salute the end of the day's hunting, and Tiffauges, looking on unseen from the wooden cloisters, tried to identify the memories that wild and plaintive music awoke in him. He found himself back in the yard at St. Christopher's, listening to a deep and despairing murmur of death; then at Neuilly, in his old Hotchkiss, trying to capture a cry heard by chance and never found again, but which had pierced him like a lance. This evening's music contained harmonics that undoubtedly had some affinity with him, but it was an indirect, lateral, almost artificial connection. And yet he felt a dim certainty that he would hear that death chant later in its pure form, and that it would not be for stags that it arose out of the ancient soil of Prussia.

"That's exactly the kind of stag *I* like to shoot," repeated Goering threateningly.

And since he was face to face with the chief forester, he grabbed him by the lapels and hissed in his face:

"You let the guests kill the best ones, and I have to be satisfied with the second-raters!"

"But, your excellency," stammered the forester faintly, "Field Marshal von Brauchitsch is supreme head of the Wehrmacht!"

"Idiot!" said Goering, before he let go of him and turned his back. "I'm talking about stags! And there are two sorts of stag: the stags of the Reich's Master of the Hunt—mine! And the rest! Try not to mix them up any more!"

*

Without doubt one of the noblest stags of the Reich's Master of the Hunt was the Candelabra, whose record the chief forester kept up to date almost to the month, and who promised to become king of all the Rominten herds. One evening when Goering, swathed like a bear, was floundering about in the wet snow in search of wolf tracks that had been reported, the Candelabra suddenly emerged like an apparition against a tracery of frosty boughs. It was like a dark ebony statue, its twenty-four prongs borne high on its muscular neck, as regular as the ribs of an ice crystal. The animal was tall and straight as a tree, a living breathing tree with darting ears and eyes bright as mirrors who stood looking at the three men. The Hunt Master's jowls started to tremble.

"The finest shot of my career!" he said. "The finest head I ever saw!"

He had cocked the gun he had been carrying broken over his arm, and was raising it slowly to his shoulder. Then with an air of authority that amazed Tiffauges the chief forester interposed.

"Your excellency," he said, in a voice so loud the animal was bound to be frightened away, "the Candelabra is the best sire we have at Rominten. Let him be for one more season. He's the future of our Reserve!"

"But do you realize the risk?" bellowed Goering. "He weighs at least four hundred pounds and must have twenty pounds of antlers on his head! And he might get himself slit open by a mere brocket that's swifter and more eager than he is. And how do you know what his antlers will be like after he casts them next?"

"Finer still, your excellency," said the forester. "Nobler still —thirty years' experience tell me so. As for his life, I'll answer for it with my own. Nothing is going to happen to him!"

"Let me get him," insisted Goering, shoving the forester aside.

But when he had leveled his gun at last, the Candelabra had vanished, without a sound, without even a stir of the branches. It was as if he were an emanation of the high wood, which had gathered him back into itself. There is no telling what the Hunt Master's fury would have led to if the forester, skillful to avert the storm, hadn't made haste to bring him before nightfall to a dell a few miles away, full of tall heather and an almost impenetrable thicket of small hazel trees. Goering started to grumble when they had to crawl on their stomachs through a patch of brambles full of black spines, down a slope leading to a kind of arena. But he gasped in astonishment when a clear space enabled him to kneel and look at the bottom of the gully through his field glasses. There were a good thirty of them, side by side below the sharp slope, their breath rising in a slight mist through the chill air. Warning was given before the first shot by an old sterile doe who seemed to be their leader. The three men were upwind, but some sound must have reverberated off the opposite slope, for the doe, in error, made straight for them. The first shot brought down a two-year-old brocket but did not stop the flight of the rest—they could clearly be seen jumping over its body. The Master of the Hunt raised his gun, fired, and the cartridge case was ejected and spun to the ground at his feet. He looked, aimed, and fired again, laughing and chortling with glee. The five-pronger behind the doe was hit in the breast: it reared, gave a leap forward, then fell in front of the whole herd. Only then did they seem to understand that their retreat was cut off. They stopped, heads erect, ears laid back. Then, as another shot brought down a shaggy, loose-limbed young stag, they all turned and rushed back to the bottom of the gully. The shooting started again as the herd tried to scramble up the steep and frozen bank with a hail of terrified hoofs. One big stag, trying to get up a steep slope, was overbalanced by the weight of his formidable antlers and fell back on a doe, breaking her spine. Three young males, mad with panic, fought each other savagely, sometimes rearing and prancing on the same spot, sometimes falling back before violent thrusts, with roars that could be heard for several miles. In the end they got their antlers so entangled they could not break free, and all died together.

When the slaughter stopped, eleven stags and four old does lay reeking in their own blood. It was a good thing to do away with the females too old to bear young: they were the first to go in heat, and tired the males to no purpose. But the Master of the Hunt was only interested in the stags, and it was wonderful to see him running heavily from one to the other, waving his huntingspear. He parted the warm legs of the great, still palpitating bodies, and plunged both hands in. With the right he made a rapid sawing movement, with the left he groped

a the scrotum for the testicles, pink, opalescent eggs of living
esh. It is commonly believed that unless a stag is emasculated
s soon as possible after it is shot its flesh becomes musky and
aedible.

Tiffauges gave the credence it deserved to this incongruous
xplanation, especially dubious in the realm of venery, where
ll is cipher and immemorial rite. Watching Goering's enor-
ous white rump pointing skyward over the royal animal he
'as about to dishonor, Tiffauges wondered yet again what was
ae key to the stag and its apparently inordinate importance in
ae bestiary of East Prussia. As if to give an immediate answer
a this unspoken question, the field marshal stood up and beck-
ned to his companions to join him. The animal at his feet was
a "grotesque head" with antlers so asymmetrical as to be pain-
ully ugly. The right one was that of a stag just turned five years,
with a beam bearing six tines, three of them grouped in a tri-
ent at the top and forming a well-grown palm. The left, thin,
trophied and crumbly, was that of a three-year-old brocket—
ast a straight shaft ending in the beginning of a fork. Kneeling
gain beside the great fawn body, Goering pointed out to one
f his guests that the disequilibrium of the antlers was repeated
a the testicles, one of which was normal and the other atro-
hied. But it was the right testicle that couldn't be grasped and
aat formed an almost imperceptible swelling under the leath-
ry skin of the scrotum. The chief forester, standing apart with
'iffauges, explained that an injury to a testicle from a bullet or
arbed wire, or a wound from the antlers of another deer, or a
ongenital malformation, always produces some defect or
trangeness in the antler on the opposite side. Thus not only
vere a stag's antlers in reality but the free and triumphant flow-
cing of its testicles, but also, in obedience to that inversion that
lways accompanies symbols intensely charged with signifi-
ance, the exalted image they gave was one that was reversed,
s if reflected in a mirror.

The fact that antlers were so literally phallic lent huntin and the art of venery a disturbingly profound meaning. T bring a stag to bay, kill it, emasculate it, eat its flesh, and stea its antlers to glorify himself with them as a trophy—this was th procedure in five acts of the ogre of Rominten, official sacri ficer of the Phallophoric Angel. There was a sixth act, mor fundamental still, which Tiffauges was to learn about som months later.

*

In a moment of exasperation the chief forester had hinted t Tiffauges that Goering was not really a very great connoisseu of game. It would have been easy to find a good hundred hunt ers and foresters in Germany who were undeniably superior t him both in the art and in the instinct of the chase. But to giv the devil his due, one important thing had to be acknowledgee There was one field, and not an unimportant one, in which th field marshal showed a knowledge and talent that were unpai alleled. This was the interpretation of the droppings of game When it came to deciphering all the messages written in the de jecta of the animals, the Master of the Hunt revealed such pen etration and experience one wondered where and when h could have acquired them, and whether they might not simpl have their origin in his being an ogre.

Tiffauges had particular occasion to observe the master o Rominten exercising his coprological gifts one spring mornin when there was nothing that could be shot without infringin the ethics of the chase, but when the state of the ground wa especially favorable for the reading of droppings. Goering, wh asked nothing better than to parade his knowledge, soon cor centrated his attention exclusively on the signatures left by th animals at the foot of trees, in thickets and in the most fre quented runs.

He showed that the dung of stags consists of only one heav rod at a time, with some distance separating each, whereas th dung of the does consists of two, which are viscous and very black and unequal. In the winter these droppings are hard and dry, but the fresh grass and young shoots of spring soften them until they look like soft flat cow pats. Then the summer makes them denser again, turning them into golden cylinders with one concave and one convex base. In September they form a kind of string. When the does drop their young, their dung is often bloodstained. It must also be remembered that evening droppings are harder and drier than those of the morning, having been preceded by the long ruminations of the day. The field marshal didn't mind testing the consistency of his finds between thumb and forefinger, or even smelling them to judge their age, for the odor they give off becomes sharper with time.

But equally interesting and worthy of commentary were the droppings of roe deer, a single lump in winter but in summer a composite bunch as in the case of sheep; those of wild boar, long cylinders in winter and sloppy pats in summer; those of hares, the buck's dry and pointed, scattered and black, the doe's large, shiny and spherical; the ivory-white discs of the woodcock, with an olive-green speck in the center; pheasant droppings accumulated under their perches; those of the grouse, left on stumps of fir; even those of the humble rabbit.

Tiffauges couldn't help thinking of Nestor and his nocturnal defecation sessions and commentaries, when he saw this big fat man, his decorations jingling, running from tree to tree and bush to bush with joyful cries, like a child looking for chocolate eggs in the garden on Easter morning. And though he had now been accustomed for a long time to the arrangements fate made with him in mind, he was filled with wonder at the fact that the hazards of war and captivity had made him the servant and secret pupil of the second most important person in the German Reich, an expert in phallology and coprology.

*

Summer saw the arrival of an unusual guest—a civilian, small, nervous, eloquent, with a big nose supporting thick glasses. This was Professor Otto Essig, whose recent doctoral thesis on *The Mechanism of Symbols in the History of Germany Ancient and Modern,* presented at the University of Goettingen, had attracted the attention of Alfred Rosenberg. The official philosopher of the regime had got his protégé this invitation, though Goering, who couldn't stand intellectuals, agreed only reluctantly. Tiffauges saw him only once during his brief stay at Rominten, and even then the professor spoke so fast and so technically that Tiffauges couldn't understand half of what he said; but Tiffauges was sorry about this, for the odd and incorrigibly awkward character always talked about subjects that particularly interested him.

One evening Tiffauges heard him discussing various different ways of measuring stags' antlers—the Nadler method, the Prague method, the German method, the Madrid method—and applying these with astounding mental agility to whatever examples were submitted to him. Tiffauges observed that the Nadler method, the simplest and most classical, proceeds by adding up points gained under fourteen different heads:

—average length of the two beams (coefficient: 0.5)
—average length of both brow–tines (0.25)
—average circumference of the two burrs (1)
—circumference of right beam at base (1)
—circumference of right beam at tip (1)
—circumference of left beam at base (1)
—circumference of left beam at tip (1)
—number of tines (1)
—weight of antlers (2)
—span of antlers (0–3)
—color of antlers (0–2)
—quality of pearls (0–2)
—quality of palms (0–10)
—state of tops (0–2)

The Prague method also brings in the average length of the two royals and the quality of the surroyals (0–2). The German method does not use this last heading but adds an over-all coefficient from 0 to 3.

As he now knew the phallophoric meaning of antlers, Tiffauges was amazed at the arithmetic that brought such precision and subtlety into so secret a matter. The hunters, each taking from his pocket a tape measure he appeared to carry with him, handed cast antlers and those of shot stags back and forth, hurling figures at one another and recalling the fantastic measurements of some famous stag that had caused a sensation at the annual international exhibition at Budapest—the Torch, for example, who had 210 points Nadler, or Osiris, with 243 points Nadler, only just surpassed—and even then the facts were debatable—by the 248.55 of a stag killed in Slovenia, the most impressive head in the memory of any living hunter.

Professor Essig took advantage of the silence when everyone was getting his breath back to sketch out a philosophy of stags' antlers. He began by emphasizing that the three methods of measurement under discussion all took into account purely qualitative elements—color, the beauty of pearls and palms, and, in the Prague method, the beauty (not the length) of the surroyals.

This, he maintained, was the part of being that cannot be reduced to figures, that aspect of concrete reality which is accessible to no kind of quantification. If we look at it from the point of view of the animals themselves we see that the significance of the antlers goes beyond their use as fighting weapons. Those of a King Stag, judged from a purely practical point of view, are cumbersome and awkward. But though their weight and size make them inefficient as weapons, it is nonetheless true that it is very rare for an old five-pronger to be beaten by a brocket. The danger comes rather from the roebucks, for the massiveness of a great stag holds no terrors for a young roe,

whose horns can cause the larger animal irreparable injuries
But with the young stags the case is quite different, and here we
touch on the essential function of the most noble attires: it is as
if they inspire a kind of respect in the younger stags. Thus what
the old stag loses through them in offensive power, he recoups a
hundredfold in spiritual influence. And, bowing in the direction
of Goering, the professor drew a parallel between a stag's antlers and a field marshal's baton, which would be a poor weapon
but which makes him physically untouchable through the dignity it confers on him. So, he ended, while the genital virility
shamefully hidden in the lowest and most withdrawn recesses
of the body draws the animal earthward, its sublimated expression, raised toward the sky, enfolds the stag in an effulgence
that quells even the blind ardor of the youngest of the herd.

The little professor had put some enthusiasm into his exposi-
tion, and was not conscious of the coolness with which it was
received. He didn't yet know the hatred aroused in this society
by any kind of thinking or speaking that departed from the flat
and superficial. The question of weight was discussed next, in
particular the relation between the live weight of an animal and
its net or butcher's weight—i.e., when sold in pieces. Essig had
a theory on the subject and lost no time putting forward his
method of calculation. To get the net from the live weight, all
you had to do was take four sevenths of the latter, add a half of
it, and divide the result by two. Goering had him say it again,
then got out a pencil and did a quick calculation on a cigarette
pack.

"So, Professor," he said, "as I weigh two hundred and eighty
pounds live, I'd be a hundred and fifty pounds, at the most,
butcher's weight. I don't know whether I ought to find that hu-
miliating or a comfort!"

And he burst into a guffaw, slapping his thighs. The guests
followed his example, but their laughter was slightly scandalized
and somewhat disapproving of the little professor. Realizing

this, the professor decided to stand up for himself as boldly as possible. The conversation had got on to elks, and he saw fit to tell an anecdote about Sweden, where King Gustav V went on leading the chase in spite of the fact that he was eighty-two. Guests were discreetly informed that, since His Majesty couldn't see as well as he used to, it was wise, if anyone came near him in the course of the beat, to shout out as soon as possible, "I'm not the elk!" Toward the end of the hunt one distinguished guest acted accordingly but, to his horror, as soon as he'd called out he saw the old king raise his gun and aim in his direction. He was slightly wounded and carried off on a stretcher, but after the kill had a chance to sort things out with the king, who offered his apologies. "But, sire," said the victim, "when I saw Your Majesty I called out, 'I'm not the elk!' And yet it seemed to me it was when you heard that that Your Majesty aimed in my direction!" The king thought for a moment. Then he said: "You must forgive me—I don't hear so well now. I thought you said, 'I *am* the elk!'"

The professor had made an awful gaffe. Goering cultivated a great reverence for the memory of his first wife Karin, a Swede, who died in 1931 and was buried beneath his sumptuous house, Karinhall, which was more or less a mausoleum. Everything concerning Sweden had thenceforward been sacred to him, and the little professor's story making fun of Gustav V was heard in horrified silence. The Master of the Hunt got up and retired to his suite without a word to Essig. They were not to see each other again, for Goering had a meeting in Rastenburg the next day, and when he set off the professor had already been in the Ebershagen woods on the eastern edge of the Reserve for two hours, with a forester who, on Goering's instructions, was to have him shoot the oldest and sickest stag with the most grotesque and imperfect set of antlers in all Rominten.

The circumstances surrounding what happened that morning were never entirely cleared up. The effect on the little col-

ony in the forest was that of an earthquake. The lamentable
specimen assigned to the little professor, tracked by the forester
the previous evening, turned up as planned at the place where
the two men arrived in their hunting gig, just as the dawn was
starting to tinge the tops of the pines with pink. With touching
cooperation the animal even appeared on the edge of a little
clearing right in the line of sight of the hunters, thirty yards
away on an observation post among the outermost trees. The
forester, rather pleased with himself and relieved to see his task
so swiftly and happily concluded, signed to his charge to shoot.
The professor raised his gun but took so long to aim that the
forester began to be afraid the deer would disappear into
the thicket. But at last the gun went off. The stag was hurled to
the ground but bounded up again so quickly it could not have
been seriously hurt. Indeed, both men could see that the charge
of buckshot had shot away only the animal's single antler, which
in any case was thin and imperfect. Antlerless, with no more
dignity than a skinny donkey and still half stunned with the
shock of the impact, it stood rooted to the spot looking in the
direction of the observation post.

"Quick, sir, shoot him before he gets away!" implored the
forester, overcome with shame for his charge.

Then followed an uninterrupted fusillade that echoed throughout the forest. Earth sprayed up, dead leaves flew, branches
were shot off, trunks lost great lumps of bark. The only thing
that seemed unscathed was the stag, who trotted off among the
trees and had already been out of sight several seconds before
the volley came to an end. The forester stood up and shook
himself to get the circulation going again.

"After that row," he said gloomily, "it's all over for this
morning. We'll just have to go back empty-handed. And this
evening we'll get the *Rubbeljack*," he added, trying to smile to
hide his vexation.

The *Rubbeljack* was a joke much favored in East Prussia

It consisted of making the victim drink, through the uncleaned barrel of a gun, a mixture of schnapps and white pepper, poured into the breech through a funnel.

The forester was pawing the wet ground with impatience, waiting for the professor, who for some unknown reason had not yet come down from the platform. He was just shrugging his shoulders when he heard the professor shout: "There he is again! Over in the gap between the beeches! It must be at least five hundred yards! I'll use a bullet!"

There was one last shot. Then silence. Then the voice of the professor, who had exchanged his gun for his field glasses.

"Come and see, forester," he said. "I think I got him."

It was absurd, but the forester sighed and politely climbed up to join the guest on the platform. Sure enough, through the glasses you could see the body of an animal lying in a ride that ran through a beechwood toward the horizon. The distance was enormous and in theory ought to have put the deer out of range of even the finest shot. And yet there lay that patch on the ground, though darker-colored, it seemed, than the fawn of the stag the professor had blazed away at with buckshot.

They walked to the beechwood. The stag looked as if it were sleeping; its head rested peacefully on its front legs, its antlers rising in a magnificent spread of dark ivory color. Its strong compact body seemed sculpted in ebony. It was still warm. The bullet had struck it directly in the chest.

The forester nearly passed out. At first glance he recognized the Candelabra, the King Stag Number 1 of Rominten that all the foresters were supposed to guard and protect at all costs. And this fool Essig, lost to all dignity, was whooping and doing a scalp dance around its venerable remains! Nevertheless, standing orders were that guests of the Master of the Hunt were sacred to the staff on the Reserve. No matter what he had done, Essig must not suspect the enormity of his crime. So everyone made a great fuss over him when, bursting with pride, he got back to the hunting lodge—but the smiles were strained, and the cries of "Long live the hunter" came from choking throats that no amount of champagne could soothe.

"Buckshot's not my style," Essig kept saying to everyone. "Bullets for me!"

He couldn't get over the fact that the Master of the Hunt wasn't there to rejoice with him. Goering was due back the next evening, probably late, but everyone swore to the professor that he wouldn't be back for at least a week. They worked all night to get his trophy ready and packed him off the next morning, somewhat surprised at all this haste but radiant and taking loving precautions for the safety of the heaviest and most beautiful head—240 points Nadler—in the history of Rominten.

Goering didn't arrive until the middle of the night, but by ten the next morning he was sitting before a breakfast in which hare pâté, potted wild goose, marinated boar and roebuck pasty were harmoniously balanced by smoked salmon, Baltic herring and trout in aspic. In the midst of all this the chief forester presented himself in full uniform, his face blank, mastering his grief manfully. The sight of the big fat man in his brocade dressing gown, his little feet stuck in otter-skin slippers, presiding over this array of food, made him lose his self-possession for a moment.

"I heard some good news this morning," said Goering at once. "The little professor went home yesterday. You soon got rid of him. Did he shoot a stag?"

"Yes, your excellency."

"A grotesque, a broken-down mule, a sick old nag, as I ordered?"

"No, your excellency. Professor Otto Essig, of the University of Goettingen, killed the Candelabra."

The noise of crockery, glass and cutlery crashing on the tiled floor brought the butler rushing up, as cloth and all were swept off the table. Goering, his eyes closed, held his two podgy hands, covered with rings and bracelets, stretched out in front of him like a blind man.

"Joachim," he said in a faint voice. "Quick, the bowl!"

The butler vanished, and returned with a huge onyx bowl which he set down in front of the field marshal. It was full of precious and semiprecious stones, and Goering plunged both hands into it avidly. Then, without opening his eyes, he slowly kneaded the mixture of garnets, opals, aquamarines, tourmalines, jade and amber. He had been told they had the power of discharging the electricity accumulated in his body, and thus restoring his calm. As a morphine addict he was tempted by stronger remedies: this one had the double advantage of being harmless and catering to his love of luxury.

"Bring me the head," he said.

"The professor took it away with him yesterday," stammered the chief forester. "He wouldn't be parted from it."

Goering opened his eyes and looked at him with a gleam of cunning.

"You did wisely. It was better for all of you that I shouldn't see it. The Candelabra! The king of all the herds of Rominten! How on earth did that miserable runt . . . ?"

Then the chief forester had to relate the incredible story of how the professor tried to pepper the old stag without any antlers, of his forester's despair, of the last shot fired blind at an enormous distance, and of the Candelabra's inexplicable presence in the eastern part of the Reserve. Such a combination of improbable circumstances looked so much like the decree of fate that Goering was silent, shocked and vaguely uneasy, as if suddenly brought face to face with the mystery of things.

*

At the end of the summer of 1942 the only topic of conversation at Rominten was the big shoot that the Gauleiter of East Prussia, Erich Koch, was planning to hold over the three districts of the Masurian lakes, which the Master of the Hunt had granted him as a private preserve. It was to be a huge battue after hare, with three thousand beaters, five hundred of them on horseback. All the officers from Rastenburg and the local bigwigs were to be there, and the proceedings were to end in the crowning of a king of the hunt.

One evening the chief forester came back from Trakehnen leading behind his dogcart an enormous black gelding, rippling with muscles and with rump and hair as ample as a woman's.

"It's for you," he said to Tiffauges. "I've been wanting to get you on horseback for a long time, and the Gauleiter's battue is a good opportunity. But the trouble I've had getting a mount that can carry you! This one's a half-bred four-year-old thickened with a strain of the Ardennes. But despite his size, his rounded forehead and shimmering jet coat show his Barbary origins. He must weigh twelve hundred pounds and stand at least eighteen hands. He's really a classical coach horse—there's no danger of him flying, but he could carry three of you. I've tried him out. He doesn't shy at jumps, and he's not afraid of rivers or thorns. His mouth's a bit hard, but at a gallop he's like a tank."

Tiffauges took possession of his horse with an emotion in which the swelling of his lonely heart mingled with a presentiment of the great things they would accomplish together. From then on he went a mile every morning to old Pressmar's. Pressmar had formerly been a master of hounds to the Kaiser, and his place had a large stable, a forge and an indoor riding school. The big horse was stabled there, and Tiffauges learned how to groom and ride him, under the direction of Pressmar, delighted, as every horseman is, at the opportunity to exercise his vocation as a teacher. The pleasure Tiffauges felt at being so close to the great, innocent, warm body, which he rubbed down, curried and brushed, reminded him at first of the pigeons of the Rhine and the hours of downy happiness he had spent in the pigeon loft. But he soon realized that this recollection was superficial and rested on a confusion. In fact, when he was rubbing his horse's coat until it shone, he was really repeating the modest satisfactions of polishing his boots and shoes, raised to an incomparably higher power. For while the pigeons of the Rhine had been first his conquests and then his beloved children, it was really himself he was tending when he devoted himself to his horse. And it was a revelation, this reconciliation with himself, this affection for his own body, this still vague tenderness for a man called Abel Tiffauges which came to him through the giant gelding from Trakehnen. One morning when a sunbeam fell on the horse against the light, Tiffauges noticed that the jet-black coat had concentric circles of blue in it, producing the effect of watered silk. It was clear he must be called Bluebeard.

Pressmar's riding lessons were at first both simple and an ordeal. The horse had a saddle but no stirrups. Tiffauges had to jump into the saddle, then rattle around the ring at a trot. According to his teacher, this was the only method of acquiring a correct seat, and then only on condition that it was kept up long enough. The pupil emerged stiff all over, exhausted, with his rear rubbed raw.

At the beginning Pressmar gazed fixedly and critically at his pupil, speaking only to say something disagreeable. Tiffauges was tense and rode bending forward with his feet stuck out behind. He'd fall, and he had it coming. The rider had to sit well back with his behind tucked in and his feet forward, and counterbalance this by arching his back and shoulders. Tiffauges didn't let himself be put off by this harsh treatment, but he did regard Pressmar as an intimidating old fossil, shut up irrevocably in a narrow and dying universe that he couldn't even fully exploit. Tiffauges changed his mind, though, when he was with him one day in the tack room and heard him discoursing on the truth about horses. Then he saw this survivor from another age suddenly become intelligent and animated, and express himself accurately and vividly. Perched on a high stool, his meager

thighs crossed, his boot waving in the air, his monocle screwed
in his eye, Wilhelm II's master of hounds started by laying
down a principle: as both horse and rider are living beings, no
theory or method can replace the secret sympathy that should
unite them, and that presupposes in the rider the cardinal virtue
of equestrian tact.

Then, after a silence designed to bring out all the force of
those two words, he went on to talk about dressage. Tiffauges
listened with passionate interest, because it involved the rider's
weight and its effect on the balance of the horse, and so was of
obvious phoric interest.

"Dressage," began Pressmar, "is something incomparably
more beautiful and subtle than is generally thought. It consists
essentially of restoring the horse's natural gait and equilibrium,
after these have been disturbed by the weight of the rider.

"Compare the dynamics of the horse with that of the deer,
for example. All the deer's strength is in his shoulders and neck.
But all a horse's strength is in his crupper. A horse's shoulders
are fine and flat, just as a deer's hindquarters are thin and tapering. A horse's weapon is his kick, which comes from the
crupper; a deer's is his antlers, the force of which comes from
the neck. A deer moves by a sort of front-wheel drive; a horse
impels himself forward by the motion of his hindquarters. In
fact, a horse is crupper with organs attached to the front.

"So what happens when a rider mounts? Examine his position closely: he sits much closer to the horse's shoulders than
to the crupper. In fact two thirds of his weight is borne by the
horse's shoulders, which, as I said, are weak and light. The over-
burdened shoulders contract, and their stiffness spreads to the
neck, the head, and the mouth—and it is the softness, supple-
ness and sensitiveness of the mouth that give a saddle horse its
value. The rider has in his hands, then, an animal that is tense
and unbalanced, and responds only crudely to his aids.

"This is where dressage comes in. It consists in gradually

bringing the horse to relieve its shoulders by throwing the weight of the rider as much as possible on to its hindquarters. To do this it has to base itself more on its back legs and bring them as far forward as possible underneath—in short, to use a comparison that mustn't be overdone, to imitate the kangaroo, which rests all its weight on its lower members, leaving its front paws free. By various exercises, dressage tries to make the horse forget the parasitical weight of the rider, to restore naturalness by the perfection of artifice. It justifies anomaly by introducing a new organization in which anomaly has its place.

"Thus horsemanship, which is the art of governing the muscular forces of the horse, consists chiefly in getting control of the crupper, in which those forces are concentrated. The haunches must respond to the lightest pressure of the heel, the gluteal area must have that smooth flexibility which in imparting readiness to it imparts value to all the rest."

And the greast master of hounds stood there bowlegged, glowering at his own flat and bony crupper, gripping the flanks of an imaginary horse, then twirled about the room, beating the air with his crop.

Abstract and subtle as they were, Pressmar's contrasts between the deer and the horse were illustrated in the tracking and searching Tiffauges now engaged in on Bluebeard. Dogs were still forbidden by Goering, and the horse seemed to have come to understand what was expected of him: as if their two opposed natures were bound to fight each other, the horse scented out the tracks and traces of the deer as eagerly as a bloodhound.

One evening, as he was loitering in the golden shadow of the stables where the sweetish smell of urine hung on the air, and watching the gleaming hindquarters undulating in their stalls, Tiffauges saw Bluebeard's tail rise up slightly to one side and reveal the anus, small, projecting, hard, hermetically sealed, and pleated toward the center like a drawstring purse. And then

the purse turned inside out with the swiftness of a rosebud
filmed in accelerated motion, exposing a damp pink corolla in
the center of which Tiffauges saw brand-new balls of dung
emerge, wonderfully smooth and shiny, to fall one by one un-
broken on to the straw. Such perfection in the defecatory act
struck Tiffauges as the supreme justification of Pressmar's
theories. The whole of a horse is certainly in its crupper, so the
crupper makes the horse the Spirit of Defecation, the Anal Angel, and makes Omega the key of its essence.

By the same token Tiffauges saw the meaning of the ances-
tral fascination exercised on man by the horse, and the preg-
nancy of the couple formed by horse and rider. With obstinate
insistence, the rider superimposes on the gigantic generous
crupper of the horse his own sterile and flabby one. He vaguely
hopes that by a sort of contagion something of the radiance of
the Anal Angel will bless his own dejecta. But his hopes are
disappointed: his dejecta remain irregular, whimsical, sometimes dry, sometimes slack and slimy, but always nauseating.
Only complete identification of the hindquarters of the horse
with those of man would give the latter the organs for equine
defecation. This is the meaning of the Centaur, in which we see
man carnally fused with the Anal Angel, the crupper of rider
made one with that of the horse and happily forming its scented
golden apples.

As for the role of the horse in deer hunting, its meaning became very clear. It was the persecution of the Phallophoric Angel by the Anal Angel, the pursuit and putting to death of Alpha
by Omega. And Tiffauges marveled to see at work once again
the amazing inversion that made the animal that is timid and
large-hipped the principle of aggression and extermination
while it turned the king of the forest, whose virility burgeons
proudly on his head, into a tracked-down quarry, imploring
mercy in vain.

*

In September the big offensive that was supposed to hem in and capture Stalingrad forced Erich Koch to postpone his shoot. Then early frosts brought an unusually mild autumn to an end, and the first snow falls made it seem that life was going to lapse into its usual winter calm. It was then that the shoot was fixed for the beginning of December, and preparations for it were resumed. They had to be interrupted, however, because Goering, who was the principal guest, was sent to Italy to try and breathe some fresh ardor into Germany's faltering ally. In the end Gauleiter Erich Koch's big hare shoot took place on January 30.

Tiffauges set out on the twenty-fifth with the first contingents of the five hundred mounted beaters. The rallying point was the little village of Arys about seventy miles to the south, in the middle of the Masurian lakes. It took three days to get there. They were billeted with those inhabitants who had stabling for the horses. Tiffauges, fitted out in new clothes and boots, was amused at his requisitioning a room for himself among the civilian population, as if he were the occupier in a conquered country. Was the German still the victor? Was the Frenchman still a prisoner? He wondered, as his boots echoed along sidewalks where housewives muffled up in shapeless old clothes lined up in front of shops with empty windows. He was served at table with respect, and he held forth, surrounding his origins in mysteries made impenetrable by his outlandish accent and his undeniable connections with the Man of Iron.

But the true source of the new force and conquering youth within him was Bluebeard, the giant brother he could feel living between his thighs, who raised him above the earth and above other men. Sometimes, during the long ride that brought him to Masuria, he would rest his back by lying down on his horse's crupper to watch the pure pale sky moving to and fro above his face and feel under his shoulder blades the muscular swell of the working haunches. Or sometimes he would lean forward, put his arms around Bluebeard's neck and lean his cheek against his shimmering mane. Once while crossing a crammed village market place, the horse suddenly halted in the thickest part of the crowd. Tiffauges felt himself uplifted by the arching of Bluebeard's back and heard the sound of a cataract hitting the road. The splashed bystanders leaped out of the way, either laughing or grumbling, and the Frenchman sat there impassively, wrapped in the honeyed vapors that rose up from the ground; he had the intoxicating feeling that it was he, Tiffauges, proudly relieving himself in the faces of the yokels of his kingdom.

The role allocated to him in the shoot was a less glorious one. The beaters on foot covered the woods and hilly ground, while the horsemen were naturally enough assigned to the open plain and fields. The whole area amounted to almost a thousand acres, including several lakes. It was not a closed hunt: neither snares nor nets were used. It was a "roundup": the beaters and hunters set out in pairs, one to the left and the other to the right, every three minutes, joining up again later. They all formed a huge semicircle with the ends drawing closer and closer until they finally formed a ring which itself got smaller and smaller. At a given signal the hunters stopped firing into the circle—they were now too close to each other—and only fired outward.

Of all the slaughters Tiffauges had witnessed, this was the cruelest and the most monotonous. When the hares were started, they shot off like arrows, but only to meet others fleeing in the opposite direction. Bewildered, they swerved about all over the place, and the beauty of their natural trajectory, with all its range of cast-back, spurt, changing and doubling, was lost in a panic further increased by the shooting. The last picture Tiffauges carried away with him that day was of an immense carpet of fawn and white fur formed by the bodies of twelve hundred hares lying side by side—the bag. Alone in the middle of this cemetery of softness, Goering, crowned king of the hunt by virtue of his bag of two hundred, posed for his official photographer, belly outthrust, field marshal's baton held aloft in his right hand.

Next morning all the German papers announced, with heavy black borders, that Field Marshal von Paulus, together with twenty-four generals and the hundred thousand survivors of the Sixth Army, had surrendered at Stalingrad.

*

Armed with his route slip, which left him a certain amount of latitude in getting back to Rominten, Tiffauges avoided the direct route via Lyck and Treuberg and plunged north across Masuria, the most austere region of East Prussia and the one most charged with history. Over that desolate heath, dotted with bogs surrounded by sparse groups of alders and broken here and there by the erratic blocks under which the Sudavians, the last Slavs to struggle against German infiltration, used to bury their dead, there still seemed to hang the malediction of the battles which for a thousand years had steeped the place in blood. From old Stardo's last resistance against the Teutonic Knights, through the battle of Tannenberg in which Jagellon crushed the Knights of the White Mantle and the Knights of the Sword, to Hindenburg's last victories over Rennenkampf's army, the earth here had been nothing but a vast charnelhouse bristling with ruined fortifications and standards ripped by shot.

Crossing the narrow strip of land separating Lake Spirding from Lake Tirklo, Tiffauges kept on until he reached the village of Drosselwalde. He was driven forward by a solemn yet joyful presentiment that he was moving toward an unknown but for him decisively important goal. Since Stalingrad the hollow clanking of the history machine was once more stirring the depths of the soil. Tiffauges felt taken over, directed, commanded, and he obeyed with somber happiness. He went through a hamlet with the magnificently strange name of Schlangenfliess, "serpent's fleece." And then it hit him.

The great tablelike mass of Kaltenborn rose up on a mound

of glacial rubble that seemed enormous in this flat country. Coming from Schlangenfliess, Tiffauges saw only the southern face of the fortress, the one crowning a cliff-bordered promontory. The enceinte followed the shape of the mound, ending in a point with an enormous machicolated tower of rusty stone supported by a buttress that stood out against the surrounding emptiness. But behind the enclosing wall, protected at regular intervals with heavy abutments and jutting towers, Tiffauges could make out a mass of turrets, watchtowers, chimneys, gables, campaniles, terraces, weather vanes and roofs, all lent a vivid and triumphant air by a profusion of standards and banners. Tiffauges experienced the bitter and exciting certainty that behind those high walls was hidden an organized life all the more intense for being secluded.

He turned into the road that wound up toward the castle. The north frontage, which appeared when he got to the top, was preceded by a huge esplanade forming a glacis, where an old man in a peaked cap was sweeping the snow. The regularly placed narrow embrasures of the fort did not relieve its forbidding monotony, nor did the two round towers with low pointed roofs which dwarfed the cramped entry, defended by portcullises. It was a rough, graceless citadel all in reds and blacks, a weapon of war conceived of and built by men indifferent to joy and beauty. But the inside, contrasting with the crude and depressing approach, confirmed Tiffauges's feeling that a gay and youthful vigor was pulsing away behind those ancient ramparts. Roofs of multicolored tiles sloped down to terraces gleaming with modern weapons; clusters of red, swastika flags flapped in the north wind, which every so often wafted the burst of a trumpet or the strain of a song.

Tiffauges exchanged a few words with the sweeper, asking him to keep an eye on Bluebeard, whom he tied to a tree. Unable to go in, he set out to walk around the walls, at least as far as the buttress of the biggest tower which he had seen from be-

low. It was not an easy walk: a narrow path ran along by the
wall, but it was often interrupted by encroachments of rock or
masonry that entailed scrambling down on to the face of the
mountain and up again. Tiffauges couldn't have said what he
was after, unless it was some approval or confirmation or
sanction, something resembling the signature of fate, a kind of
hallmark guaranteeing Kaltenborn's Tiffaugian vocation. He
found what he was looking for at the very base of the buttress
of the big tower, though to reach it he had to get through a
thicket of brambles, elders, clematis and saxifrage made more
impenetrable still by the strands of ivy trailing from the wall.
Not even that was enough. When he got to the foot of the buttress he had to scoop away with his hands the soft snow that
had piled up there. But little by little the answer of Kaltenborn
was revealed to him: at this point the buttress was hollowed
out in a sort of niche, and the overhanging stonework was supported on the shoulders of a bronze Telamon. Twisting and
grimacing under the crushing weight, the black Colossus
crouched with his knees up to his beard, his neck bent at a right
angle, his arms raised and embedded in the stone. The composition was mediocre: the grandiloquent academicism of the last
German Kaiser was written all over it. No doubt the figure had
been added recently, under the great tower it seemed to support, together with the fortress as a whole. But its being buried
under the vegetation and the snow, and his having exhumed it,
proved to Tiffauges that the Titan had been let into the side of
Kaltenborn for him alone.

When he got back to Schlangenfliess, he sat down in the village inn, the Three Swords, in front of a table with a jug of beer,
and from the innkeeper found out the rest of what he wanted
to know about the castle and its owner.

The great East Prussian families took pride in tracing their
origins back to the Teutonic Knights, who received that far-
away pagan province from the Emperor Frederick II and Pope

Gregory IX on the understanding they would convert it to
Christianity. The pious inquiry into their own genealogy in
which every Junker family engaged was lent piquancy by the
fact that the Teutonic Knights were monks and as such bound
by the vow of chastity. Logically speaking, they could not have
any descendants. But the ambitions of the counts of Kaltenborn
were loftier still: they claimed to go back to the Knights of the
Sword, conquerors even older and bolder than the Teutonic
Order. The Knights of the Sword were originally a religious
community founded in 1197 by Albert of Apeldom, a member
of the University of Bremen, but they were made a military
order by Albert of Buxhoewden, Bishop of Riga. He gave them
their insignia: two swords of red cloth sewn on the left side
of their white habit. The Knights of Christ of the Two Swords
in Livonia—that was their full name—conquered Livonia, Courland and Estonia thirty years before the Teutonic Knights arrived in Prussia. But, weakened by the ceaseless struggle against
the Lithuanians and the Russians, they begged the Teutonic
Knights to be allowed to merge with them. The amalgamation
was ratified by the Pope in 1236 and consecrated at Viterbo in
the presence of the Grand Master of the Teutonic Order,
Hermann von Salza. While remaining an autonomous military
order with their own provincial governor for Livonia, the
Knights of the Sword now became one with the Teutonic Order,
though among themselves they preserved a secret but undying
awareness of their own even more venerable and glorious
origins. The arms of the counts of Kaltenborn were *argent, with
three swords gules erect on pales, with sable chief.* The three
red swords on the white ground recalled the two swords of the
Knights of the Sword plus the one sword of the Teutonic
Knights. The black band at the top made up, with the white and
the red, the three colors of the Prussian flag. As the innkeeper
pointed out, besides inspiring the inn sign the three swords
were also to be seen, larger than life size and pointing upward,

on the parapet of the largest terrace in the castle, the one looking out eastward by the Telamon tower.

The castle itself, one of the proudest in all East Prussia, had
at the beginning of the century seemed doomed to destruction,
despite the efforts of the counts, who kept on living in it and
filling in as best they could the breaches made by time. Salvation came with Wilhelm II, who liked this region because of
the hunting. In 1900 he ordered the restoration of the castle
of Upper Koenigsberg, near Selestat, as a challenge to the
hereditary enemy in the west. He then decided that another
fortress worthy of his reign should form the eastern confine of
his empire, facing the Slav invader. The work of restoration was
not completed until just before the 1914 war. Archaeologists
considered Kaltenborn overrestored, like Upper Koenigsberg,
which had been turned into a sort of smart, brand-new giant
toy. But Teutonic architecture suffered less severely than other
kinds from the whims of modern restorers, because the knights-
errant who originally created it put into it their mystic dreams
and memories of foreign lands, so that Saracen, Venetian and
German elements may all co-exist in a single building.

The renovated fortress of Kaltenborn attracted the attention
of Joachim Haupt, a chief of the SA (the Nazi Party army),
who from 1933 set about the creation of paramilitary schools
on the model of the famous imperial prytaneum at Ploen. The
schools were to produce the elite of the future Third Reich.
Called "Napolas," and usually installed in requisitioned castles
or monasteries, they grew more and more numerous every year,
in spite of Haupt's fall after the "Night of the Long Knives" on
June 30, 1934, and the suspending of the SA. Haupt's work
was taken over and continued by a high official of the SS (the
Nazi police force), General August Heissmeyer, who ensured
that Himmler's men had control over the forty Napolas then in
existence. The Napola at Kaltenborn was theoretically under
the authority of General Count von Kaltenborn, the last of his

line, who lived in one wing of the castle. But he was an old man. His attachment to Prussian tradition made him resistant to the attractions of the new order brought into being by the Third Reich—he didn't believe that anything good for Prussia could come out of Bavaria or Austria. And his interest in historical research and heraldry left him little time for playing any real part in the organization of the school. In any case, though the general had been given the title of commandant of the Napola in deference to his past and to keep a place for him still in his own castle, all practical authority was wielded by SS Commander Stefan Raufeisen, who imposed an iron discipline on Kaltenborn's thirty army instructors, fifty non-commissioned officers and men, and four hundred boys.

*

When he got back to Rominten, Tiffauges, profoundly impressed by the fortress of Kaltenborn, happened to mention it to the chief forester. He was then told that General Count von Kaltenborn had been present at Gauleiter Koch's big shoot, but in spite of all the details the forester gave him, Tiffauges could not remember him. He couldn't forgive himself, and though he still did all his tasks conscientiously, his mind and heart were now always somewhere else: they were drifting toward Masuria, around the high walls within which prison life seethed and sang.

An early spring of intoxicating mildness was filling everything with tenderness when Tiffauges went in April, as he went every month, to renew his German pass at the town hall in Goldap. He felt bounteous and weak, like the young grass starred with daisies, like the warm breezes caressing the birch and hazel catkins and making the pine branches scatter their powdery, saffron-colored seed. He almost wept with emotion when he saw a sparrow taking a bath in the warm dust of the road, and two little schoolboys laughing and jostling each other with their satchels strapped to their backs like snails' shells. The twittering that filled the sky still seemed to exist inside the austere town hall, which that morning had an unusual air of animation. Just inside the door, the bronze pegs of the cloakroom caught the eye with their brightly colored array of hoods and tippets, shawls and mittens. Underneath were scattered child-sized clogs, boots and galoshes. It was as if a conference was being held there of all the Little Red Riding Hoods of the forests of East Prussia. Tiffauges went up the wide staircase that led to the room where weddings were celebrated, drawn by an exquisite, fresh, springlike smell, redolent of pepper and seed. He stopped outside the imposing carved oak door: yes, it was in there. He could hear a sort of birdlike twittering; the waves of sweetness lapped about him. He turned the heavy brass handle and went in.

What he saw made him stagger with surprise and lean on the doorpost for support: a whole swarm of completely naked little girls lit up the huge dark oak-paneled room. Some were skinny as flayed cats, some pink and chubby as sucking pigs. There were tall ones like beanpoles, and dumpy ones round as dolls. Hair plaited or braided or coiled in earphones or hanging loose between the frail shoulder blades was all that covered the little not-yet-nubile bodies, smooth as cakes of soap. No one had noticed Tiffauges, and he pushed the door quietly shut behind him so as to restore the atmospheric density that only completely hermetic closure could supply. He half shut his eyes and drew in eager breaths of the spicy odor he had been following since the beginning of the morning, but which he now caught in its nascent purity. And in spite of himself he stretched out his hands as if to gather, as if to garner, all that warm and merry provender, East Prussia's latest gift.

"What are you doing in here? Go away at once!"

A Germanic goddess with severe and regular features, in immaculate nurse's uniform, was looking daggers at him. He stepped back, opened the door, and reluctantly started to with draw.

"Who let you in, anyway?"

"It's the scent," he stammered. "I didn't know the flesh o little girls smelled like lily of the valley. . . ."

The official who stamped his pass gave him an explanation of this charming assembly. Every year on April 19 all the children ten years of age went before a board before being in corporated into the Hitler Youth.

"The boys are on the other side of town," the man added "At the municipal theater."

"But why April 19?" asked Tiffauges.

The man looked at him incredulously.

"Don't you know April 20 is our Fuehrer's birthday? And every year the German people give him a whole generation of children as a birthday present!" He pointed proudly at the big colored photograph of Hitler scowling down from the wall be hind him.

When Tiffauges took the road back again to Rominten the Master of the Hunt, with his shoots and his trophies, his feast of venison and his coprological and phallological science, had dwindled to the rank of a little, imaginary, picturesque ogre out of an old wives' tale. He was eclipsed now by the other, the ogre of Rastenburg, who demanded of his subjects the exhaustive birthday gift of five hundred thousand little girls and five hun dred thousand little boys, ten years old, dressed for the sacrifice, or in other words naked, out of whose flesh he kneaded his cannon fodder.

*

The atmosphere had darkened at Rominten since Stalingrad and Goebbels' speech at the Sports Palace calling on the people to throw themselves fanatically into total war. New call-ups had thinned out the staff. People's thoughts ran less and less on the pleasures of the chase and of the table, and more and more on the great conflict which glowed lurid in the east, and which no one could be sure of keeping out of. Air raids were becoming serious, and as his armored train offered better protection than his hunting lodge, which had no air-raid shelter, Goering came less frequently to the Reserve.

One day the chief forester told Tiffauges that as the staff had to be reduced to the absolute minimum he would have to return him to the disposal of the labor office at Moorhof. But if Tiffauges had any request to make, the fact that he'd been on the staff of the second most important person in the Reich might carry a certain amount of weight. Then Tiffauges remembered the shoot in January at which General Count von Kaltenborn had been a guest, and his own short visit to the Kaltenborn fortress. He asked if he might be posted to the Napola as a driver or groom. The forester was surprised to hear his factotum, always so silent and obedient, express such precise wishes.

"After the last call-ups," he said, "I'd be surprised if the people at the Napola didn't jump at the chance of a worker recommended by the field marshal, and not liable for the army either! I'll fix it on the phone."

A fortnight later Tiffauges had his travel warrant for Kaltenborn, and he and Bluebeard left Rominten. Bluebeard had been assigned to Kaltenborn too.

V
The Ogre of Kaltenborn

O come and go with me, thou loveliest child . . .

Goethe

The reddish mass of the castle hid the horizon, and around it an irregular group of buildings covered the ten acres inside the ramparts with a close, compact little city. One of the two towers beside the entrance served as a tool shed; the porter and his wife lived in the other. Then, straggling along a sort of path leading to the main courtyard were an indoor riding ring and its stables; two gymnasiums; the infirmary; a garage and re- pair shop; a boathouse; the steward's house; four tennis courts; two villas each with a little garden; a football field; a basketball field; a theater-cum-cinema that could also accommodate a box- ing ring; a quadrangle fitted out as a training ground. Right by the castle itself was a kennel where eleven Dobermans greeted anyone who went by the cage with a chorus of howls; a block- house for arms and munitions; a generator; a prison. And all the walls spoke and cried out with mottoes and sayings and sang with flags and banners, as though the walls alone retained the faculty of thought. "Praised be that which hardens," pro- claimed one of the gym halls, to which the other seemed to reply, with a quotation from Nietzsche: "Drive not the hero from thy heart." Goethe and Hitler rubbed shoulders over the door of the assembly room. Goethe: "Disgrace is not to fall but to lie." Hitler: "Rights are not to be begged for. They are to be gotten by conquest."

Eyes stunned by this peremptory epigraphy, Tiffauges scarcely took in his first human contacts in the Napola. He was received by a second lieutenant-penpusher who inspected his army papers and his travel warrant and had him fill in a huge questionnaire more concerned with his parents and grandparents than with himself. Then he was passed on to a corporal who showed him Bluebeard's stall and his own attic. To get there they went through the castle armory and up a series of increasingly narrow and increasingly steep staircases, until they got to a corridor lit by tiny skylights off which opened the little rooms assigned to the non-commissioned officers of the SS.

"As you were recommended by the field marshal," said the corporal, "the commandant has been advised of your arrival. He'll send for you. Unless he forgets," he added with an indulgent smile. "At any rate the director's waiting for you."

The director was Commander Stefan Raufeisen. He had the oblong skull, receding chin and close-set eyes of the Frisian Germans about whom racial theorists were so enthusiastic. When the Frenchman was shown into his office on the ground floor of the castle, Raufeisen went on reading the file he had in front of him, not deigning to raise his blond greyhound's head until he'd finished the last page. Then he looked at Tiffauges with a wily expression for a few moments without saying anything, and finally let fall three sentences.

"Report to Captain Jocham in the Commissariat. Salute all members of the SS from the rank of captain up. You can go."

To his own astonishment Tiffauges was in no hurry to make the acquaintance of the children who were after all the whole raison d'être of this array of loquacious buildings and laconic men. But he felt their presence undeniably in the atmosphere of the citadel, which seemed to condense every so often in the form of a pair of boxing gloves on a chair, a forage cap on a post, a stray football left lying about, or a heap of red jerseys thrown on the green grass. He was acutely aware there was a barrier between him and them, and that he might have to wait a long time before it fell. His first days taught him painfully enough that this barrier consisted in the first instance of the SS staff who officered the pupils and ran the place: he had to learn by heart the ranks of the Black Corps, and the minute differences distinguishing one from the other on uniforms all identically macabre.

Thus he had to remember that the collar tabs of a mere SS man had no ornament, whereas they had one stripe in the case of a private first class, two stripes in the case of an acting corporal, a star for a corporal, a stripe and a star for a sergeant, two stars for a master sergeant, two stars and a stripe for a quartermaster, three stars for a second lieutenant, three stars and a stripe for a lieutenant, three stars and two stripes for a captain, four stars for a commander, four stars and a stripe for a lieutenant colonel, an oak leaf for a colonel, two oak leaves for a general, two oak leaves and a star for a brigadier general, three oak leaves for a lieutenant general, and three oak leaves and a star for a major general. The *Reichsfuehrer* SS alone— Heinrich Himmler—wore an oak leaf surrounded by an oak wreath.

Epaulettes were less varied but led the more easily to unfortunate mistakes. Up to the rank of captain they were decorated with six rows of silver thread. From captain to colonel these were tripled to form a single braid. The braid became double from colonel up.

Captain Jocham, who was in charge of the Commissariat, was a big ruddy man who ruled over a store bursting with sacks of dried vegetables, tins of beef, hams, Dutch cheeses and tubs of jam, not to mention piles of blankets, bales of clothes and even rolls of bandages—a solid collection with a smell indecipherably complex, which in those days of shortages seemed as rich as Ali Baba's cave. As the only two cars that were usable were reserved for the commandant and the director respectively, Tiffauges carried out his supply duties in a four-wheeled cart drawn by two horses, to which racks could be attached, or hoops to support a hood.

He had the same job as he had had at Moorhof, but he used more rustic means and attributed to it a meaning more profound. For he never forgot that he worked to provide for the needs of the children, and he felt this role of purveyor of food, of *pater nutritor,* as a piquant inversion of his ogreish vocation. As he unloaded his cart into the odorous stores of the Commissariat with its narrow, barred windows, it gave him pleasure to think that the sides of bacon, sacks of flour and blocks of butter he carried in his arms or on his shoulder would soon be metamorphosed by a secret alchemy into the songs, movements, flesh and excrement of children. His work thus came to signify a new kind of phoria—secondary and indirect, admittedly, but, until something better turned up, not to be despised.

*

There were four hundred pupils, the *Jungmannen,* divided into four groups of one hundred, each under the command of a centurion. The latter was assisted by a grown-up instructor who was an officer or non-commissioned officer of the SS. The groups were divided into three columns of thirty or so Jungmannen, subdivided into groups of about ten. Each column was under the command of a column leader; each group under that of a group leader. Every group had its own dormitory and its own table in the refectory.

"From now on," Hitler said in his annual party speech in 1935, "the young German will go up through one school after another. He will be taken in hand as a child and will not be let go until he retires. No one will be able to say that at any time of his life he was left to himself."[4] For the time being, however children of under ten years old were not drawn into the system because of the lack of qualified teachers; but from ten onward the little girls went into the *Jungmaedelbund* and the little boys into the *Jungvolk.* At fourteen they passed into the *Bund*

Deutscher Maedel (BDM) and the *Hitler Jugend* (HJ) respectively. The boys stayed there until they were eighteen, when they went into first the Labor Service and then the German armed forces, the Wehrmacht.

The Jungmannen in the Napolas went through a mill more continuous and so even more constricting. They joined at twelve years old and left school at eighteen, after an education partly traditional and partly intensively military, and angled according to choice on the army, the air force, the navy, or the Waffen SS. More than half the Jungmannen chose the latter.[5] Recruits for the Napolas were acquired in two ways—from volunteers and by prospecting among pupils in elementary schools. There would have been enough volunteers to fill all the Napolas, of which there were not more than about forty, but then the great majority of the boys would have been from the middle classes, the sons of army men and party officials, whereas the populist philosophy of the Reich demanded a wider intake from the lower strata of society. The statistics had to show a suitable proportion of sons of artisans, workers and peasants. So country schoolmasters were asked to present boys they considered possible candidates to a traveling recruiting board. They were then directed to centers where they underwent rigorous racial and physical selection—boys who wore glasses were automatically excluded—and mental and physical tests. But the chief requirement, which the recruiting instructions insisted on over and over again, was that a boy had to be outgoing, or in other words his instinct for self-preservation had to be as atrophied as possible. To any candidates who lacked a strong instinct for self-preservation, some of the tests were simply suicidal: they had to jump into the water from a height of thirty feet whether they could swim or not; climb obstacles that had some hidden trap—such as a ditch, wire entanglement, or water; fall from the second story of a house into a blanket held out by older boys; or dig themselves a hole and crouch in it while a continuous row of tanks thundered over.

The selection was severe enough to make the mental level well above average, but non-military instruction in the Napolas had been much impaired by the war. Successive call-ups kept thinning the ranks of the teachers, all originally SS officers, and soon after his arrival Tiffauges witnessed a change that sealed the fate of science and literature at Kaltenborn. This was the replacement of all military teaching staff by civilians. All the good will and competence of the retired schoolmasters and professors called in to fill the gap could not make up for their lack of prestige in the eyes of the pupils in this citadel bristling with arms and death-dealing devices. They were elderly; they taught subjects that seemed absurd in the urgency of war—one was a specialist in Latin, another in Greek. They were despised for their civilian clothes; they couldn't adapt to the breakneck rhythm of the Napola. So the boys teased them and hissed at them and wore them down. They all disappeared one after another, except for a seminarist in Protestant theology from the ecclesiastical training school in Koenigsberg, pupil-pastor Schneiderhan, who was impervious to any insult, dug in his toes, and finally won himself an acknowledged place in that wild boys' cage.

The day began at six forty-five with electric bells pealing furiously through the little dormitories. Then red jerseys started rushing down the stairs and into the main courtyard, where there was a morning workout. Meanwhile the shower room, where one group was followed by another every five minutes, steamed like a witches' kitchen. At eight everyone gathered on the glacis in uniform to salute the colors. Then ranks were broken, and the boys rushed to the refectory where a cup of ersatz coffee and two slices of dry bread awaited them. After that the merry-go-round started, deftly dealing out the various groups either to classrooms for lessons or study hall, or to the sports fields, the gyms, the places in the surrounding country and lakes where they were given training in riding, rowing, and the handling of arms, or to the shooting ranges or the maintenance workshops.

Tiffauges watched the way the ponderous machine worked. Because the discipline was iron and the boys so strictly selected, it functioned smoothly and at full speed, to the sound of trumpets, fifes, drums, and above all the thud of boots. But what struck Tiffauges most were the vigorous bursts of song in harsh clear voices which every so often seemed to be answering one another from various points in and immediately around the citadel. He wondered whether he would ever come to have a place in this child-mill where bodies and hearts were all set to serve the same cause. The very perfection of its functioning and the terrible energy that went into it were enough to exclude him forever, but he knew no machinery is safe from a piece of grit, and that fate was on his side.

While the force of circumstance still kept him on the fringe of the bustling life of the Napola, Tiffauges made a connection in Frau Emilie Netta, the housemother, who lived in one of the citadel's two houses and ruled over the infirmary. She had been a war widow since 1940 and had three sons: the two eldest were fighting on the Russian front and the third was a Jungmann in the Napola. By a Kaltenborn tradition rather than by the nature of her job she was always accessible either at the infirmary or at home, and no one needed permission or even a special reason for coming. She was ready to see anyone, and her door was always open. Tiffauges soon found his way to her little overheated holystoned kitchen with its smell of wax and red cabbage. He would go to his corner and sit there for a long while, not moving, not speaking, listening to the time go by in the rhythm of the weights of the clock and the simmering of the pan on the stove. Sometimes one of the boys would rush in, blurt out his problem—a stomach-ache, a tear in his clothes, an

urgent letter to write, some unjust and tiresome punishment—
and leave again with it solved. Frau Netta, the only woman in the
citadel, enjoyed an authority there that extended well beyond
the minor world of the Jungmannen. Officers and non-
commissioned officers obeyed her decisions, and everyone was
sure the director himself would never care to challenge her. At
any rate Captain Jocham never thought to reproach Tiffauges
for the amount of time he spent at her house.

He inevitably came to wonder what the place of a woman,
and this woman in particular, could be in this entirely war-
oriented community, whose spirit, blazoned everywhere, was
enough to turn the milk of human kindness sour. Emilie Netta,
like her husband, was of Slav origin. But—and this was another
proof of the privileged position she occupied at Kaltenborn—
her small stature and dark hair, usually imprisoned under a
brightly colored scarf, which ought in theory to have gone
against her in such a hotbed of racism, did no more than make
her look different from everyone else. She never said anything
from which Tiffauges could make out whether she believed in
the ideology of the Napola. But her whole behavior indicated
that she belonged to it body and soul. And yet she seemed
rooted in the most concrete aspect of life by her apparently innate knowledge of plants and animals, lakes and forests, which
made her irreplaceable as the leader of mushrooming and berry-
picking expeditions; and by the instinct she showed in the
infirmary for nursing and healing. Tiffauges only began to understand on the day news came that one of her sons was missing
after Kharkov was recaptured by General Koniev's armies. As
ill-luck would have it, he was there when she read the letter,
overflowing with delusive hopes and derisory honors. She
showed no emotion; her movements just became a little slower,
her gaze slightly more fixed. When she noticed Tiffauges watching her, she at last murmured in a toneless voice, like a prayer
learned by heart:

"Life and death are the same thing. Whoever hates or fears death hates or fears life. Because it is an inexhaustible fountain of life, nature is only a vast cemetery, the slaughterer of every moment. Franzi is probably dead now. Or else he *will* die in a prison camp. One mustn't be sad. The woman who bears a child must also wear mourning for him."

She was interrupted by an inrush of Jungmannen who surrounded her, all talking at once. Without betraying her sorrow, she did and said what was expected of her.

*

Three rooms on the first floor of the right wing of the castle were the domain of Commander Professor Doctor Otto Blaettchen, on detachment from the Institute for Research into Heredity. With his tapering black goatee, big velvety eyes, inky serpentine brows and swarthy skull, this Mephisto in white overalls was an exceptionally pure specimen of the laboratory variety SS. His career had taken a rapid spurt about a year before when Professor August Hirt, head of the department of anatomy at Strasbourg, had entrusted him, at the Institute, with a particularly delicate job. It had just been realized in high places that, since the Jews and the Bolsheviks were the sources of all evil, it would be useful to look for their common origin in some as yet undefined Judeo-Bolshevik race. So Blaettchen was sent to camps of Russian prisoners to collect those who were both Jewish and people's commissars—a paradoxical mission, since the Wehrmacht had strict orders to shoot without hesitation any Russian commissar they captured.

For a whole winter nothing more was heard of Otto Blaettchen, but just before Easter the directors of the Institute were astonished to receive a hundred and fifty numbered glass jars all labeled *Homo judaeus bolshevicus*. Each contained a human head in formaldehyde, in a perfect state of preservation.[6]

In addition to his commander's stars, this success also won Blaettchen the reputation of being an expert on the eastern territories—East Prussia, Poland and occupied Russia—and the Institute sent him on permanent mission to Kaltenborn, where he presided over, or thought he presided over, the selection of candidates. For Tiffauges soon saw that there was open antagonism between Blaettchen and the director. Raufeisen regarded the race expert as a vague parasitical creep, and Blaettchen treated the director as a boorish, drunken trooper. But as they were both of the same rank in the SS hierarchy, they were obliged to tolerate one another. The director, however, had the advantage of being able to call on all the Napola staff, whereas Blaettchen, shut up in his tower, was reduced to whatever help he could get from people in their spare time. He soon found out the possibilities offered by the French prisoner and tried to get hold of Tiffauges whenever his duties in the Commissariat permitted. In the end Tiffauges got to know the three rooms that made up the Kaltenborn Raciological Center quite well: Blaettchen's little bedroom, the office, and the big white-painted laboratory, for some unknown reason decorated with an imitation marble pool in which the professor lovingly tended a hundred or so goldfish.

"*Carassius auratus*, also called *Cyprinopsis auratus*," he said, wagging his finger, the first time Tiffauges went in. "The masterpiece of Chinese creative biology. You see, Tiffauges, these little creatures are here to remind me that if the Asiatic barbarians have been able by selection and crossbreeding to produce the golden fish, it is up to us to fabricate *Homo aureus,* the incomparable man who will rule the world. Anything you see me do here will always come down finally to searching among the children they bring me for the grain of gold dust that justifies selective reproduction."

Blaettchen's big moment was always the arrival at Kaltenborn of a fresh batch of recruits. He awaited them with greedy impatience. As soon as his name had been entered in the books, each new boy was turned over to him for the making up of his raciological card. The Commander Professor Doctor, now assisted by Tiffauges, would get out his array of callipers, spirometers, chromatic scales, color reactors and microscopes, and set about weighing, measuring, surveying, testing, labeling and classifying each specimen. To the hundred and twenty standard particulars in R. Martin's *Textbook of Anthropology* Blaettchen had not failed to add some characteristics of his own of which he was rather vain.

Thus Tiffauges learned that from the point of view of hair the human race can be divided into lissotrichous, kymotrichous and xulotrichous; that there are three main types of dermatoglyphs or fingerprints—whorled, scrolled and arched; that one may be brachyskelic or macroskelic according to whether one's legs are short or long in relation to the torso; chamaecephalic or hypsicephalic according to the height of one's head; tapeinocephalic or acrocephalic according to the width of one's nose, and leptorhinian or chamaerhinian according to its thickness. But what made Blaettchen wax really lyrical was talking about what he called, with emotion and respect, the "sanguine specter" of race. The four blood groups discovered by Landsteiner (A, B, AB, and O), plus Rhesus positive and Rhesus negative, opened up to him a combination of infinite subtlety. And all these particulars, dimensions and averages did not merely get bogged down in a poverty-stricken and amorphous objectivity. They were activated by a vigorous Manichaeism which turned them into so many expressions of good and evil. Thus when Blaettchen measured the horizontal cephalic index he was not content with just distinguishing round heads or brachycephalic heads from oval or dolichocephalic ones. He explained to Tiffauges that intelligence, energy and intuition belonged to dolichocephalics, and that all France's troubles came from having been ruled by round heads like Edouard Herriot, Albert Lebrun and Edouard Daladier. Respect for the truth obliged him to admit such exceptions to this rule as the good

Pierre Laval, as no head could be rounder than his, and the bad Léon Blum, about whose dolichocephaly there could be no doubt.[7]

So it was not surprising that Blaettchen's anthropological tables contained a certain number of characteristics that constituted radical defects. Such, for example, was the "Mongolian spot," a kind of bluish mole in the sacral area more visible in children than in adults. It is common in the yellow and black races but occurs only sporadically in the white; racialist theoreticians regarded it as a mark of infamy, a sort of devil's imprint. They took the same view of the hooked nose of the Semites; the Indians' prehensile foot; the flattened occiput of the Dinaric and Armenian groups, the line of whose head goes straight up from the nape; the arched fingerprints characteristic of pygmy races; and the agglutinogen B frequently found in the blood of nomads, gypsies and Jews.

While he noted down all these data in quantified form ready to be used in algebraic formulae, Blaettchen also made use of intuition, immediate, instinctive and infallible, though impossible to justify by demonstration or proof. His black eye would observe the children's gait, expression and general appearance, and draw from them conclusions that were always quite peremptory. But his real triumph was his raciological nose: he maintained that each race has its own smell, and claimed to be able to distinguish black, yellow, Semitic and Nordic with his eyes shut, just by the fatty volatile acids and alkalis secreted by their sudoriferous and sebaceous glands.

Tiffauges listened as he noted down the figures; he watched as he helped with the Broca's callipers or the dynamometer; he recorded; he reflected. It was true that the SS filled him with the most acute repugnance. But the Napola, whose discipline, uniforms and crazy songs went against all his inclinations and anarchist beliefs, forced him to make every possible allowance because it was so obviously a machine for both subjecting and exalting fresh and innocent flesh. Blaettchen's maniac erudition, on the fringes of sadism and crime, carried this subjection and exaltation to their highest pitch. The link with the phallology of the Master of the Hunt and Pressmar's theories about riding also helped to reduce Tiffauges to patience and silence. The consistency of his evolution, and above all the advance he had made in passing from stags and horses to children, proved he was following the path of his vocation. What he now had to do was be stronger than circumstance and find a way of annexing Blaettchen's domain and bending it to his own purposes, just as he had succeeded in extracting unforeseen and purely Tiffaugean fruits from Rominten. For although, for the time being, he shared in Blaettchen's work, he was sure the SS doctor was only an ephemeral figure, fated sooner or later to give place to himself.

It was in this spirit that, finding himself with a certain amount of leisure and comfort for the first time since the beginning of the war, he got hold of a school exercise book and resumed his "Sinister Writings."

*

S.W.   Went to Johannisburg this morning for a load of mattresses. Big military parade in the Adolf-Hitlerstrasse, don't know why. Big crowd. The half of it that was in uniform—i.e., that was made uniform, homogenized, all rolled into one under the same cloth, the same leather, the same steel—moved forward at a walking pace, a uniform walking pace, like a giant centipede unrolling its field-gray length along the road. This part of the crowd is in an advanced state of the metamorphosis that makes several million Germans into one great irresistible sleepwalker, the Wehrmacht. The individuals enveloped in the great entity, like a shoal of sardines in the belly of a whale, are already being crushed together and on the point of merging into one another.

In the other half of the crowd this process is only at an

early stage. The variegated and irregular foam of civilians comes and goes chaotically on the sidewalks and under the trees. But the digestive juices of the great green snake reach out in powerful waves toward these little individuals still for the moment free. That mournful obsessive music, the heavy tramp of the legions on the march, the air regularly filled by the same swell of voices, the swastika flags rippling in the breeze—all this ritual enchantment secretly works on their nervous systems and paralyzes their wills. A mortal pleasure grips their innards, brings tears to their eyes, freezes them in an exquisite and poisonous fascination called patriotism. *Ein Volk, ein Reich, ein Fuehrer.*

But the monolithic block of the Reich already has a large crack in it: the surprise I got on my way back was an almost comic illustration of it. It was at Seegutten, a little doll's village perched on Lake Spirdling. I had to pick up six sacks of potatoes from a farmer there. But the fellow made difficulties and insisted that my requisition slip be stamped at the town hall. All right. The town hall was a small new building in modern neo-classic. I tied up the horses and walked along by the wall toward the entrance. It was then I heard, through the open door, a familiar voice laying down the law in execrable German. I stopped to listen.

"All right, the trains go any old time, there's no more gas, and the bus that runs on wood has broken down!" thundered the voice. "But you ought to have thought of all that! You people at the front, you seem to imagine we're all living in clover back home! But we get bombed too, we're hungry and everything's disorganized. And now you come and ask me to vouch for you—you want me to authorize another twenty-four hours' leave. Well, my boy, that's something a mayor hasn't the power to do!"

Every so often this outburst was interrupted by a timid

attempt at defense stammered in a voice that sounded like a young peasant's, but this only started the mayor off again.

I knew as I went up the steps whom I had to deal with, and was delighted at the enormous practical joke fate had kept up its sleeve for me after the parade at Johannisburg.

"Tiffauges! Well I never!"

Victor, the madman of Moorhof, threw his arms around me and dismissed his petitioner with a tap on the shoulder. The young soldier in field gray hastily disappeared. Then Victor took me into his office and made me sit down. I began answering his questions with a rather circumstantial account of my stay at Rominten, but soon cut it short when I saw that in spite of his intent expression, piercing gaze and fixed smile he wasn't paying the slightest attention to what I said. Even the name of Goering, which usually had a magical effect, didn't get through that mask of artificial attentiveness. Anyway, what did it matter? It was *his* story that interested me.

Victor had been, in succession, a woodcutter in the Altheider Forest, a fisherman on the Meuer Sea, a groom in the stud at Frauenfliess, and finally a sawyer in Seegutten. Fishing and sawmills go together there: a huge carpenter's shop is devoted entirely to making packing cases for fish out of scraps of wood. Every day Seegutten dispatches an average of a thousand pounds of eel, perch, pike, and in particular half-smoked fresh-water herrings. Victor, suddenly lyrical, rushed at me and wrung my hands.

"Wood, my boy, wood—there's nothing to beat it!"

Then he told me how the firm owned two Kirchner reciprocating saws with up to fourteen blades, five circular saws, a cutter, a parquet-maker and a sharpening shop. He followed that up with stories of miraculous hauls of fishes, with two, three, four and even five boats bringing back thirteen tons of fish in one day! He owed it all to wood and fish that he had become the real master of Seegutten.

To wood because every evening in the hostel he braved the laughter and rude remarks and devoted himself to a master-piece of marquetry work: an absolutely faithful model of the Hindenburg mausoleum at Tannenberg. Was Victor's sub-sequent good fortune the result of chance, sound intelligence work, or premonition? General Oskar von Hindenburg, the field marshal's son, was living in retirement at Koenigsberg, and one day he came to Seegutten. Victor got permission to give him his model, and was thereby transformed into a dif-ferent person.

His debt to fish was as follows. The previous winter he had gone angling on the ice, which was rather unsafe because of a momentary thaw. So he was the only adult present when eleven-year-old Erika, his boss's daughter, who had rashly gone skating with some friends, fell through the ice. Victor, happening to be on the spot with a rope, was able to save her.

His fortune was made. His boss made him his right-hand man, and, as he was mayor of Seegutten, Victor was ap-pointed clerk at the town hall. From then on, Victor's inde-pendence and power automatically increased in proportion as the men of the town left for the front and living conditions grew worse. It was Victor who now distributed ration cards and registered births, and when necessary, as I had just seen, scolded people who overstayed their leave. And as he told me all these wonders he kept hooting with his madman's laughter!

As he spoke I was filled with a twofold uneasiness. His insolent success is just what I myself have been after ever since I arrived in Germany, and the sight of it filled me with bitter jealousy. But most painful of all was to see that Victor owed his success to his madness. I remembered Socrates' diagnosis which had impressed me so much: that a man as crazy as Victor could fulfill himself only in a country turned upside down by war and defeat. But in the last analysis, aren't I another Victor? Isn't my only hope that the blows of fate may put Kaltenborn at the level, and at the mercy, of my own form of madness?

*

Whether in protest against what he considered the exaggerations of SS uniform or against his own minor role in the Napola, General Count Herbert von Kaltenborn usually appeared wearing a frieze cape and a Tyrolean hat. Admittedly he never looked more of a soldier than when he affected civilian dress. He gave the impression of being tall, though in fact he was below average height, and his square face, simplified by its Franz Joseph mustache, wore an expression of affable sympathy that had nothing to do with the harsh and limited ideas he lived by.

The first time he saw him Tiffauges was grooming the horses by the wall of the stable. The count exchanged a few sentences with him in French, obviously pleased to have the opportunity to show off his knowledge. Then he seemed to forget all about Tiffauges, until a day in September when Tiffauges had to drive his cart to Loetzen to collect half a heifer from a butcher.

He found the shop closed and locked. He was told the butcher had been arrested for black-market activity. Tiffauges, driving about the country, was witnessing week by week its disintegration under the disasters of war. For a long time the fact that bombing raids affected only the western part of Germany had made East Prussia a privileged area: the K.I.V., the department in charge of evacuating children from the war zones, sent whole trainloads of children there from the devastated cities in the west. But since the spring an even heavier threat than bombers began to hang over the east, and East Prussia felt itself becoming, slowly but inexorably, the doomed part of the Reich. In spite of the Gauleiter's decree forbidding evacuation or any preparation for departure, the richer and more mobile part of the population moved toward the west. As they couldn't take everything with them, a busy traffic had sprung up between those who expected the worst and those who kept on hoping. The police reaction was wild and unsystematic. There were denunciations, rumors, campaigns in the press. The prisons filled up. The party heads fulminated. But nothing could stem the tide of dismay swelled by the fall of Mussolini and Italy's capitulation in the west, the falling back of the Wehrmacht in the Ukraine in the east, and above all the black blocks of casualty lists in the daily papers.

But the Masurian countryside had never been so radiant as it was that autumn. Tiffauges, since he couldn't do what he had been sent to do in Loetzen, dawdled back by Lakes Loewentin, Woynowo and Martinshagen. The water was so limpid the diving birds flying above it and the silver fishes swimming in its depths seemed to be moving through the same element. The boats moored to the docks were suspended in the void like captive balloons. Tiffauges was followed, surrounded and preceded by a joyous and peaceful escort made up of a huge humming of bees rifling a field of colza in flower, the tranquil whirr of a threshing machine in a farmyard, the clank of an anvil, even the hammering of a woodpecker on the trunk of a larch. This glory was not inconsistent with the poisoned atmosphere Tiffauges had found in Loetzen. It seemed natural to him that, as Germany's ruin loomed up, nature should prepare for him a victor's apotheosis.

It was while he was in this triumphant frame of mind that he saw the commandant's ancient black limousine parked at the side of the road a few miles from the citadel. The car had broken down, and the old man sat in it, waiting motionless for his driver to return with help. Tiffauges respectfully invited him to join him on the seat of the cart and drove him back to the castle. He didn't remember his brief replies to the few questions the commandant asked him during their short journey. So he was surprised when a few days later the general summoned him to his office and, after having dealt with some trivial matter, said:

"On the way back the other day I asked you about your general impression of Prussia. You said it was a country that was black and white. What did you mean?"

"The firs, the birches, the sands, the peat bogs," said Tiffauges, hesitating.

The general took him by the arm and led him to a wall covered with weapons and standards.

"The Prussian soil is black and white, as you say," he said. "And the colors of the East Prussian flag are black and white, an obvious allusion to the Teutonic Knights and their white cloak quartered with black. But don't forget the Knights of the Sword, without whom Prussia would have remained cold and sterile."

"Yes, sir," agreed Tiffauges. "They were the salt of the Prussian earth."

And he reeled off the innkeeper's lecture about Albert of Apeldom, Albert of Buxhoewden and the distant empire uniting under the two crimson swords Livonia, Courland and Estonia. Then he went on to Gothard Kettler and the merging with Hermann von Salza's Teutonic Knights which was to seal the greatness of East Prussia.

The commandant was enchanted.

"That's why," he said, "one mustn't forget to add the red of the Knights of the Sword to the black and white of the Teutonic Knights. The red symbolizes all that is alive in the sands and peat bogs you spoke of."

And Tiffauges remembered that, after having subjected him to the black earth and snow of Moorhof, Prussia had sent him a continuous stream of warm, quivering creatures: the Monster of Canada; the migratory birds; the Rominten stags; Bluebeard,

an alter ego; the little girls at Goldap; and lastly the Jungmannen
of Kaltenborn, that dense, vibrant mass of serried ranks which
he heard singing with one pure metallic voice and pounding
with a single step the enclosed courtyard at the foot of the
tower.

The commandant led him through the chapel to the terrace,
and they stopped by the bronze swords that made three formidable gashes in the quiet undulating horizon of forests and lakes.

"Each of these swords bears the name of one of my ancestors," explained the commandant. "Here in the middle is
Hermann von Kaltenborn: the Virgin Mary appeared to him
on the eve of the battle in which he was slain to tell him
his place was prepared in the knights' paradise. To the west is
Wiprecht von Kaltenborn, a real athlete of Christ, who baptized
ten thousand Prussians in a single day with his own hand. And
on the east is my father, Veit von Kaltenborn, who was in command here in August 1914 under Field Marshal von Hindenburg and freed his own land from the Slav invader."

And he stroked the verdigrised metal of the superhuman
blades with a respectful and affectionate hand. From the courtyard the voices of the Jungmannen in singing unison rose in
aggressive waves:

"Let the worm-eaten bones of the old world tremble!
The battle is on. We have conquered fear. Victory awaits us!
We shall march, march, march, and smash all beneath our tread!
Today Germany is ours, tomorrow the whole world!"

*

S.W.   I often wonder how I, who used to be so intolerant
and easily aroused to indignation in France, always cursing
and swearing, came to be so meek and patient as soon as I
set foot in Germany. It's because here I'm always face to face
with a *significant reality* which is almost always clear and
distinct; or, when it does become difficult to read, that's be-

cause it's growing more profound and only losing in obvious-
ness what it gains in richness. In France I was always coming
up against crude manifestations of blasphemy arising out of
a blank and expressionless desert. It's not that everything that
happens here goes in the direction of what is good and just—
far from it! But the material offered me here is so fine and
so solemn at the same time that I've neither time nor
strength to get angry if it strikes me rather roughly.

Blaettchen, for example, does everything possible to fret
me, with the most odious insistence. One of his obsessions
is to transform foreign place names and family names—in
this case Polish and Lithuanian ones—into words that sound
unmistakably pure German. He has a maniac's flair for detecting some impure source in the most innocent-sounding
place names, and is always writing off to the Fuehrer to point
them out and suggest what he at least considers more
euphonious replacements. And now, if he hasn't got carried
away and started on *my* name! Only in this case, he says, it's
not a question of replacing Polish or Lithuanian by German.
He has convinced himself that Tiffauges is a modified form
of Tiefauge, and conceals a distant Teutonic and so even
more venerable origin. He now calls me Herr Tiefauge, or,
in moments of euphoria, ennobles me into Herr von Tiefauge.

"What proves the purity of your blood," he says, "is that
you have to the most marked degree the particular sign from
which your patronymic ancestor got his name: Tiefauge
means deep eye, an eye set deep in its socket. And the meaning of the name is so plain just to look at you, Herr von
Tiefauge, one might almost wonder if it isn't a nickname!"

But the other day he went further still, and I all but exploded. Everything was going wrong. The boy we were examining had nothing but eastern characteristics: he was short,
and doomed to remain so, judging by his strong, knotty
muscles; hyperbrachycephalic (88.8); chamaeprosopic;

dull-complexioned; and his blood group was AB. Blaettchen
was fuming about the selectors' lack of discernment. I kept
making mistakes in the measurements and finally broke a
bottle of Rhesus reactor. Then Blaettchen insulted me. Oh,
he did it very discreetly! He just inserted a letter into my
name.

"Watch what you're doing, Herr Triefauge," he said.

I know enough German to know that *triefauge* means sick,
tearful, or, to be precise, rheumy eye! My terrible myopia
and the thick glasses without which I can't see anything make
me liable to this sort of insult. I went up to the Professor
Doctor, close enough to touch him, advanced my face toward
his, and slowly took off my glasses. And my eyes, which are
usually screwed up and slitlike behind their heavy lenses,
opened wide, filled their sockets till they nearly leaped out of
them, and fixed the Professor Doctor with a vacant, basilisk-
like stare.

I don't know where I got this idea. It was the first time
I'd tried it, but the result was so good I shall do it again.
Blaettchen turned pale, drew back, muttered an apology, and
didn't say another word until we'd finished examining the
boy.

                                    *

Tiffauges had always thought the fateful significance of each
step in his career was fully attested only if it was not merely
surpassed and transcended, but also preserved in the subsequent stage. So he was anxious for the acquisitions he had
gained at Rominten to find their fulfillment at Kaltenborn. He
got his wish in October when supplies became so difficult that
extreme measures had to be resorted to. The director was away
for several days and explained when he came back that he had
been conferring with the Gauleiter in Koenigsberg. Erich Koch
had promised arms and munitions enough to provide for the
Jungmannen's military training and an anti-aircraft battery

against the increasing air raids. He had also given immediate
authorization for the taking of game in the whole district of
Johannisburg, to improve the food situation in the Napola. The
director decided that Abel Tiffauges was to be responsible for
obtaining the game, in his dual capacity as assistant in the Commissariat and former hunt servant to Goering. But the Gauleiter
had specified that he wasn't actually granting hunting rights: no
guns were to be used. So the quarry had to be brought to bay
and dispatched with side arms or else simply trapped. This was
giving with one hand and taking back with the other. But
Tiffauges adapted himself to this restriction by asking for the
use of one group of a hundred boys, with whose help he very
effectively snared the warrens and runs of the Sostroszner. Frau
Netta took another group of a hundred and organized mushrooming in the forest of Drosselwald. The autumn was dry and
cool with mainly east winds. This climate, though it worked
against Frau Netta's expeditions, favored those of Tiffauges.
The morning frosts were early that year, and the first snow fell
in early November and did not melt.

*

S.W.   This morning, after a great burst of sun, the plain sud-
        denly went dark. A big, metallic, preternaturally black cloud
        rolled slowly toward us from the west. It was a passage of
        that cosmic anguish, that atavistic thrill, which I know so
        well—but for once it overflowed from me to other people,
        animals, everything. And suddenly the air was full of thou-
        sands and thousands of white flakes spinning gaily in all
        directions. A spectacular inversion of black into white, in
        keeping with this landscape so devoid of nuances. So the
        cloud of lead was only a sack of feathers! Who is the Greek
        cosmologist who spoke of "the secret blackness of the snow"?

*

The evening of Christmas Day brought a storm from the
northwest that seemed to be trying to wipe out the memory of

a year that had been on the whole calm and sunny. At noon
the whole sky was covered by a lid of lurid clouds. Sea birds
flew over at a vast height, crying out in fear and swept on a gust
of panic. The sleeping plain suddenly seemed to stir and struggle against the grip of a nightmare. The snow laid down in
silence through calm and quiet nights rose up and advanced
over the country like an army of white shadows. Squalls of wind
drove branches, stumps, trunks and even rocks over the surface of the frozen lakes. Standing there on its promontory, the
citadel became the instrument of the storm, a huge Aeolian
harp singing in all its vestibules, passages, turrets, campaniles
and vanes. The weathercocks shrieked in human voices, doors
banged against walls, packs of invisible wolves galloped howling down the corridors.

All the Jungmannen were gathered in the armory around a
glittering Christmas tree, for the ceremony of the Yule festival.
It was not the birth of Christ that was being celebrated, but that
of the Sun Child, risen from his ashes at the winter solstice. The
sun's trajectory had reached its lowest level and the day was
the shortest of the year: the death of the sun god was therefore
lamented as an impending cosmic fatality. Funeral chants celebrating the woe of the earth and the inhospitableness of the sky
praised the dead luminary's virtues and begged him to return
among men. And the lament was answered, for from then on
every day would gain on the night, at first imperceptibly but
soon with triumphant ease.

Then the director read out greetings sent to Kaltenborn by
the forty other Napolas scattered throughout the Reich: Ploen,
Koeslin, Ilfeld, Stuhm, Neuzelle, Putbus, Hegne, Rufach, Anna-
berg, Ploschkowitz, and so on. And at every name one of the
boys stepped forward from the semicircle of his comrades and
added a candle to the tall fir tree. There was a lull in the howls
of the storm, and the director, as if seized by sudden inspiration,
cried out:

"Heaven lies in the shadow of the sword!"

Then in a quiet voice he explained how every type of man is expressed in a special tool that is also a symbol. There are men of the pen whose natural function is writing; peasants, who are revealed in the share of their plow; architects, whose emblem is the T-square; smiths, whose image is an anvil. But the Jungmannen of Kaltenborn were doubly vowed to the sword, first as young warriors of the Reich and secondly by virtue of the castle's arms. All that was not of the sword must be alien to them. Recourse to anything but the sword was cowardly and treacherous. They must always keep in mind the story of Alexander and the Gordian knot. On the Acropolis at Gordium, in Phrygia, in the temple of Jupiter, the chariot of the first king of that country was preserved. According to an ancient oracle, Asia would belong to whoever could undo the knot joining the yoke to the pole; the ends of the knot were invisible. Alexander, eager to rule Asia and impatient at the difficulty of the test, sundered the two pieces of the chariot with a blow of his sword. Thus every problem had two solutions: one long, slow and difficult; the other that of the sword, crushing and immediate. The Jungmannen must, like Alexander, draw their swords whenever any Gordian knot stood in their way.

As he was speaking, the storm went on battering at the walls, making the little flames dance on the tree. Then they went out altogether, leaving the children enveloped in thunderous darkness, as the big armory window was shattered by a cataclysmic gust. A single star, like a yellow eye, pierced the dense roaring shadows toward the east.

*

S.W.   It took me some time to jump on this great flagged merry-go-round, noisy and gaudy, with its cargo of children and handful of adults. Now that I'm on it I understand better what makes it work. It is clear that the trajectory of time here is not linear but circular. You live not in history but in the calendar. So it's the undisputed reign of the eternal return—the merry-go-round image is exact. Hitlerism is resistant to any idea of progress, creation, discovery, or imagination of an unknown future. Its virtue is not rupture but restoration: hence the cult of race, ancestors, the dead, the soil. . . .

In the peculiar martyrology of this calendar, January 24 is the eternal anniversary of the baleful year 1931 and the death of Herbert Norkus—patron saint, because of his age, of all the youth organizations.

Once again, in spite of their protests that they had seen it before, the Jungmannen were shown the film based on Schenzinger's novel on Norkus' life.

I was surprised at the choice of actor. It was a boy much younger than the real Norkus, frail and a bit girlish and namby-pamby, obviously destined from the outset for the sacrifice. The young socialists who were to bring about his fall, on the other hand, were presented as precocious young brutes dressed up as men, with a bent for tobacco, alcohol and women. The pure and tender paschal lamb of the film was far indeed from the boy celebrated by Hitler as "tough as leather, slim as a greyhound, and strong as Krupp steel." I was surprised the film director should have arrived, ten years before I did, at the vision, so opposite to the official version, of a German youth not bursting with vigor and conquest, but doomed from the beginning to a massacre of the innocents.

After the film came the vigil. The drums beat out interminably the doleful call of the Black Corps: two long beats by the majors of the right, two short beats by the majors of the left, answered by the rest with five short beats, followed by another three, then another two. It was a mesmerizing and funereal tomtom that mimed the massive dance of destiny on the march. The litany was suddenly broken into by the blare of trumpets. Silence. Then an adolescent voice sounded through the darkness. Another answered. Then a third.

"Tonight we celebrate the memory of our comrade Herbert Norkus!"

"We are not keeping watch by a cold coffin. We gather together around a dead comrade, saying:

" 'There was one who dared before to do what we are trying to do now. His lips are silent, but his example lives!' "

"Many fall around us, but at the same time many are born. The world of living and dead is vast. But the noble deeds of our forebears live again in the fight of those who follow."

"He was fifteen. The Socialists stabbed him to death on January 24, 1931, in the Beusselkietz district of Berlin. He was only doing his duty as a Hitler youth, but that earned him the hatred of our enemies. His corpse will be a barrier between us and the Marxists forever!"

Then they sang "A young nation rises to go into battle . . ." Their voices rose in the air, clear as ice crystals, while the swastika standard writhed around its pole like an octopus burning in the narrow beam of an arc light.

*

STEFAN RAUFEISEN

I was born in Emden, in East Friesland, in 1904. It was a cozy little Dutch-type village, half of its activities mercantile, the other half deriving from the two canals that linked it to Ems and Dortmund. My father kept a butcher shop in a working-class district, and as the poor don't eat much meat we were poor too. He had a brother, my Uncle Siegfried, who was also a butcher, but at Kiel in Schleswig-Holstein, near the navy office. Siegfried died in 1910, and we moved to Kiel to take over his business.

I was too young to notice clearly the difference in atmospher
between the drowsy, spick-and-span little North Sea town an
the naval port on the Baltic, its air vibrating with revolt an
struggle. But in fact I grew up in a very heated political climat
The Kaiser had decided that the future of Germany lay on th
sea, Kiel was his favorite town and he often visited it. But th
great occasion was Kiel Week at the end of June, when he cam
and presided in person over the international regatta.

In 1914 my father was called up to serve on the submarines
He and his U-boat went down together in 1917. In accordanc
with history's usual cruel logic, it was from Kiel that the severes
blow was struck at the Kaiser's throne. The naval mutiny i
November 1918 sounded the death knell of the Second Reich
In another of time's revenges, the armistice and the peace, b
abolishing the war fleet and banning the German flag from all th
oceans, meant sudden death for Kiel and its docks and ship
yards. Our butcher shop was dying too. I didn't care. I wa
fifteen. Since I couldn't get pigs, I made my sausages out of th
horses of the now defunct imperial cavalry. But my heart wa
elsewhere. I had heard the call of the Wandervoegel. . . .

The Wandervoegel movement, named after the migrator
birds, was first of all an act by which the younger generation cu
loose from its elders. We didn't want anything to do with th
defeat, the poverty, the unemployment, the political agitatior
We threw back in our fathers' faces the sordid heritage the
were trying to fasten on us. We refused their ethic of expiation
their corseted wives, their stifling apartments stuffed with drape
and curtains and tasseled cushions, their smoky factories, thei
money. We went around in little groups with our arms linked
singing, in rags but with flowers in our battered hats, our only
baggage a guitar over the shoulder. And we discovered the grea
pure German forest with its fountains and its nymphs. Thin, dirt
and lyrical, we slept in lofts and mangers and lived on love and
cold water. What united us first and foremost was belonging t

the same generation. We kept up a sort of freemasonry of the young. It's true we had masters: Karl Fischer, Hermann Hoffmann, Hans Blueher, Tusk. They wrote stories and songs for us in little magazines. But we understood one another too well to need a doctrine. They never came to Kiel.

It was then that the miracle of the vagabonds happened. The 'League of Vagabonds," which was just like us but with a Nazi ideology, revealed to us wandering schoolboys that our ideas and way of life were not necessarily doomed to remain outside a society strong in its organization and its inertia. The Vagabonds were Wandervoegel possessed of a revolutionary strength that directly threatened the social edifice.

The time for dreaming was over. The struggle in the streets was beginning. My butcher shop immediately took on significance: I became the party organizer of my guild. We stuck up posters, daubed the houses of those who didn't agree with us, stopped the anti-militarist film *All Quiet on the Western Front* from being shown in Kiel. The municipal authorities reacted by clamping down indiscriminately on both Nazis and Socialists. One day the Hitler Youth uniform was banned. All the butcher's assistants in my group paraded the streets in their working clothes and terrified the bourgeoisie with their great blood-stained aprons and the huge knives stuck in their belts. The Socialists, called Sozis, had a fife band that acted as their rallying call. We had one too, and after a number of fights the fife became the signal of the Nazis.

But the really unsurpassable day was October 1, 1932. Baldur von Schirach had chosen that date for the first Nazi youth rally at Potsdam. The Party had hired thirty-eight giant tents that could hold in all a thousand people. More than a hundred thousand girls and boys turned up from every province in the Reich. They came by the trainload, on foot, on bicycles and on packed trucks bristling with flags. Incredible chaos! Marvelous medley of friendship! There were no food supplies. Everyone was half dead with fatigue. We all lived on our nerves, drunk with songs, shouts, marching and countermarching. Yes, marching became our myth, our opium! *March, march, march.* It was a symbol of progress and conquest, and also of assemblies and rallies. It made our legs hard, dry, dusty as wheels or piston rods, and turned them into the main political organs of our bodies!

Sixty thousand boys were camped on the Schuetzenwiese, fifty thousand girls in the stadium. It took us seven hours to file past the official stand. But we, the boys from Kiel, were the handsomest and wildest. We had rolled our sleeves up and our socks down, we were so proud of our muscles of bronze. When we had marched past the stand in a strident thunder of fifes, one of the Fuehrer's aides ran after us.

"The Fuehrer sent me to ask who you are!" he said.

"Tell him we are the Hitler youth of Kiel, to serve him and to die!"[8]

The joy, the thirst for sacrifice there was in that answer!

Four months later Adolf Hitler became Chancellor of the Reich.

*

S.W.   This morning Blaettchen handed me a circular letter from the general inspectorate of the Napolas about the choice of candidates. "Selection should take into account," it said, "the slow rate of development normally found in children of Dalic or Nordic race, both from the physical and from the psychological point of view. The selectors must not be misled by the apparent sleepiness and lack of intelligence of these boys in comparison with East Baltic and Alpine types of the same age. In fact, quick intelligence and a ready sense of repartee are often the signs of a precociousness that is incompatible with the purity of the German race. A thorough examination will almost always reveal corroborating anthropological characteristics."[9]

"Well, Herr von Tiefauge," said Blaettchen, "whoever wrote that note deserves full marks for perspicacity and courage. Have you noticed how every nation claims as its first virtue the very quality it lacks most? What is French courtesy, in fact, but a cover for inveterate caddishness, especially toward women? And the sense of honor the Spaniards are so touchy about is belied by the Iberian races' irresistible propensity for treason and corruption. As for Swiss honesty, their consuls spend most of their time trying to get their fraudulent compatriots out of jail. English phlegm?—blind and crazy hatred! The cleanliness of the Dutch?—the reek of their cantonments! As for Italian gaiety, just go and see for yourself! The rule even applies to Germany. Ever since you've been here you must have been deafened by descriptions of our rationality, our sense of organization and our efficiency. The truth, Herr von Tiefauge, is that the German soul is a dark chaos. It isn't backwardness that makes the Nordic boy dull and dense. However mature he gets, he will never reach Mediterranean brightness. Reason is the invention of the ancient Greeks, a nation bastardized a thousand times over by heavily Balkanized Dinaric Alpines, with Levantine and Egyptian strains. In short, an indecipherable mixture of the dregs of Eurasia. *Purity is opaque,* Herr von Tiefauge, that's the truth we must have the courage to face! The Nordic boy has all the appearances of a noodle, but that is because he is in direct contact with the source of the vital energies. He drowses as he listens to the visceral murmur that rises from the depths of his being and dictates his behavior. No one else has the German's sense of the black springs that secrete the fundamental sap of things. This basic instinct makes him a drowsy brute most of the time, capable of the worst aberrations, but sometimes it produces incomparable creations!"

*

S.W.   In spite of the great progress I'm making in German

it's clear I came to it too late and shall never speak it as well as I speak French. I don't really mind. However much it is reduced, the gap between my thoughts and my words when I think, speak or dream in German has undeniable advantages. First of all this slight opacity of language makes a sort of wall between me and the people I'm speaking to and gives me an unexpected and very beneficial assurance. There are things I could never manage to say in French—harsh things, confessions—which escape my lips quite easily disguised in hard German speech. This, added to the simplification imposed by my imperfect knowledge of the language, makes the German-speaking Tiffauges a much rougher, more direct and brutal person than the French-speaking one. This is an infinitely pleasing metamorphosis—for me at least.

There are no liaisons in German. The words and even the syllables are set side by side without mingling, like so many pebbles. A certain fluidity gives a French sentence a pleasing continuity, but there is a risk of substance being eliminated altogether. German, being made up out of solid pieces like building bricks, lends itself to the construction of an infinite number of composite words, all perfectly decipherable. Any attempt to do that in French would soon end in a shapeless mess. So a German sentence that is rapid and imperious is also harsh and raucous—it would suit statues and robots. But we tepid, viscous foreigners prefer the soft parlance of the Ile de France.

What is really extraordinary are the sexes the German language attributes to things and even to people. The introduction of a neuter gender would have been an interesting refinement if it had been used with discrimination. But instead of that, it unleashed a baleful passion for universal transvestism. The moon becomes masculine and the sun feminine. Death becomes male, life neuter. A chair is masculinized, which is crazy; a cat is feminized, which is sensible enough. But the height of paradox is reached in German's systematic neutralization of women.

*

The oldest Jungmannen were seventeen or eighteen. Tiffauges's categorical demand for freshness was offended by the presence, alongside genuine children, of these adolescents and young men. It filled the refectory, the dormitories and the whole place with a virile, military odor that disgusted him and set up a regrettable barrier between him and Kaltenborn. But an obstacle so clearly opposed to his vocation was bound to tumble sooner or later. The arms promised by the Gauleiter would have made it possible to train the Jungmannen who were called up in Kaltenborn itself. The director dreamed of having a whole corps of young soldiers under him there, armed and trained. But in spite of his frequent reminders, the arms failed to turn up. On March 1 the inevitable happened. The two highest groups, aged sixteen and seventeen, were abolished and made subject to immediate call-up. The older boys went into the Wehrmacht, the younger into a crash training course. The ten SS non-commissioned officers were also to leave the Napola.

*

S.W.   The older ones who are being sent to the slaughter next week do their training on the glacis. They wear boots and trousers but are naked above the waist in the sharp early morning air. Stefan, who wants to combine strengthening exercise with team movement, has thought up the idea of making them juggle with beams of wood. Each beam is about thirty feet long, and a section of twelve boys holds one of them at arm's length, raises and lowers it, moves it from one shoulder to another, and throws it into the air, first vertically, then to the right, where it has to be caught by the adjoining team. If anyone made a wrong move there would probably be a broken skull or an ear torn off or a fractured shoulder here and there, but this risk doesn't bother the authorities here; on the contrary.

All these youngsters are between fifteen and eighteen, and the trace of the razor can be seen on most of their chins and cheeks. But one has to admit that their torsos are all of a touching tenderness, emphasized by the coarseness of their belts, trousers and boots. Not a hair on those white chests; even most of the armpits are smooth too. A few chains with medals add a childlike touch to those milky necks, more fit for a mother's kiss than a cut from a Cossack saber.

A twenty-year-old arm may be the carnal equivalent of a twelve-year-old leg, but one mustn't be taken in. Below the belt, infantile purity is over, and all that is left is blackness and cynical virility.

*

Shortly after the bloodletting which restored Kaltenborn's "infantile purity" but reduced its numbers by half and disorganized its staff, Stefan called a council of war attended by Tiffauges, who was hidden behind Blaettchen, the SS, and the surviving civilian teachers. The director explained that, to make up for the departure of the ten non-commissioned officers, the pupils would play a greater part in the practical organization of the place. They would work in shifts in the kitchens, laundry and stables, and a roster would be worked out for fetching wood and supplies. A more serious problem was that of recruitment. Kaltenborn had to keep its position as a first-class Napola by maintaining its enrollment; it mustn't let itself be turned from its vocation by the difficulties presented by the war. In principle, each Napola ought to have boys from every province in the Reich and avoid too local an intake. But the present situation called for emergency solutions. So the director asked all the officials present to prospect the area themselves for young men fit to fill the gap caused by the call-up of the two oldest groups.

He and Professor Doctor Blaettchen would examine all such candidates.

Tiffauges didn't give a damn for the class or vocation of the Napola. But though he had welcomed the elimination of those elements that were older and less fresh, and so appealed less to his tenderness, he was aware of an undeniable détente in the atmosphere: Kaltenborn had lost its fine rich resonance. So he ardently hoped that it would soon have a full complement again, though he didn't expect much result from the director's appeal. He realized that in fact it was really addressed to himself over the heads of the rest, all uninitiate and unaware, except perhaps for Blaettchen, whose knowledge of the mystery, such as it was, was vicious and perverse. And Tiffauges realized too that the time would surely come when fate would sweep away the mob and put back into his hands the keys of the kingdom for which he was born.

*

S.W.　　It was only to be expected: the departure of the ten non-commissioned officers and the boys' attempts to help run the practical side of the Napola has irremediably upset the smooth mechanism of which we were all prisoners. Apart from certain surviving points of reference, such as roll calls, saluting the colors, and other ceremonies, the whole time-table has been disrupted and its discipline undermined. For me, this liberation is inseparable from the spring, which the warblers greet at the tops of their voices, and which has set invisible streams gurgling under the crunchy snow. The year begins not on January 1 but on March 21. By what aberration has the human calendar got separated from the great cosmic clock that rules the round of the seasons?

Of course, I don't know where the year now beginning will lead me. But Blaettchen, who simply reeks of crime, makes me glimpse the possibility of an immense and rending revelation: who knows whether everything here that corresponds,

or seems to correspond, to my hungers and aspirations is no
in reality their *malign inversion?*

This morning Blaettchen wrote on the blackboard:

$$living\ person = heredity + environment$$

Under that he wrote a second equation:

$$being = time + space$$

Then he drew a ring around "environment" and "space"
and labeled it "Bolshevism," and another ring around "he
redity" and "time" and labeled that "Hitlerism."

"These are the terms of the great debate of the twentietl
century," he said. "The Communists deny the living perso
the patrimony of heredity. According to them, everythin;
must be set down to education. If a pig is not a greyhound
that's a social injustice—it's the fault of the person who raise(
it." He laughed. "And then they invoke the name of St. Pav
lov! The Jew Freud, who maintains everything in our lives i
determined by the fortunes and misfortunes of our earlies
years, says the same thing in a slightly more subtle way. It'
a philosophy of bastards, of nomads without tradition or race
of rootless urban cosmopolitans. Hitlerism is a doctrine o
farmers and sedentaries strongly rooted in the ancient soil c
Germany, and reverses the terms of the argument. For us
everything is in the hereditary equipment handed down from
generation to generation according to known and inflexibl
laws. Bad blood is neither treatable nor educable: the onl
way of dealing with it is destruction pure and simple.

"The aristocratic philosophy of the *ancien régime* fore
shadowed our ideas. For the aristocrat, one is either well
born or not wellborn, and no amount of merit can cause th
commoner's commonness to be forgotten. And the more an
cient a line, the greater its value. I am quite willing to recog
nize the precursors of our racism in men like Genera
Count von Kaltenborn. But they couldn't evolve. And no
biology must take over from the Almanach de Gotha. Title

must give place to chromosomes. The 'sanguine specter,' Tiffauges, the phantom of blood, that's the god that haunts us! For the armorial bearings of the ancient nobility we have substituted the throbbing, pulpy, blood-filled viscera, which are what is most intimate and vital in us! And that's the reason, too, why we must not be afraid of shedding blood. 'Blood and Soil' go together. Blood comes from the earth and goes back to it. And the soil must be watered with blood—it calls out for it, it wants it. It is blessed and fertilized by it!"

But I, as I listened to this mad speech, remembered that I was of the race of Abel, the nomad, the rootless, and that God said to Cain: "The voice of thy brother's blood crieth unto me from the ground. And now thou art cursed from the earth, which hath opened her mouth to receive thy brother's blood from thy hand."

*

At nightfall all the Jungmannen assembled on the glacis in ose formation, leaving an open square on the side toward the rtress. In the open space a low podium flanked by cressets and riflammes was to serve as an altar in the rite that was to be lebrated. On one side the young drummer boys waited in si- nce, their tall black and white drums poised on their left ighs; on the other side were the young trumpeters, the brass orns of their instruments resting on their hips.

There was a sudden strident clamor of trumpets. A thunder drums rising up into the darkness in successive waves, threat- ing and somber, then dying away as if lost in the distance.

A story of betrayal and death was related in accusing antiph- ny by single, impassioned voices:

"And now the fanfares fall silent, and the infinite columns of en withdraw into pious meditation, and the flags are slowly wered to salute the shades of those who died for the father- nd."

"At this hour we call up the memory of the first soldier o
the Reich, Albert Leo Schlageter."

"Schlageter came from a long line of peasants in Schoena
in the south of the Black Forest. And it is there that his bod
lies. He enlisted as a volunteer in the war and was wounded se
eral times. After the Diktat of Versailles he was in the Balti
Volunteer Corps and the frontier guards of Upper Silesia."

"But in the west the storm broke, and the thunderbolt struc
this exemplary fighter. Infringing both law and peace, Frenc
troops invaded the Ruhr. Resistance sprang up on all sides, an
Schlageter fought in the front line. By their bold actions h
and his comrades paralyzed the enemy's lines of communicatio
and supply."

"But through treachery he fell into the hands of the French!

"We young men who love Germany have inscribed on our fla
the word 'Combat'! All that is cowardly and vile must burn
Our right comes from blood and the soil. Bright flame wi
consume the halfhearted! Let us smash all that is rotten an
moldy! Free the Fatherland from slavery! Forge the German na
tion! We young men who love Germany have inscribed on ou
flag the word 'Combat'!"

"Schlageter did not hesitate for an instant at the call of hi
people in distress. He was a lieutenant at the front, a chief gun
ner in the Baltic provinces, a champion of the National Socialis
cause, a leader of the resistance in the Ruhr—always ready t
make the supreme sacrifice."

> "Do you see the dawn reddening in the east?
> It is the sun of liberty rising.
> We stand shoulder to shoulder, for life and unto death.
> Why doubt any longer? Let us end our quarrels,
> For it is German blood that flows in our veins.
> Let the people spring to arms.
> To arms, to arms, the nation is in arms!"[10]

"Schlageter appeared before a military tribunal for having attempted to blow up the Haarbach bridge at Kalkum, between Duesseldorf and Duisburg. After the occupation of the Ruhr on January 11, the invaders requisitioned all trains, mainly to transport the coal they stole. Schlageter resolved to prevent this pillage by attacking the railways. On February 26 the general of the French Army of the Ruhr ordered the death penalty against saboteurs. Schlageter was sentenced to be shot."

"At dawn on May 26, 1923, he was taken by a heavy escort to a quarry on Golzheim heath, where the cross now stands that bears his name. His hands were tied behind his back. They hit him to make him kneel. But when he was left alone facing the rifle barrels, Andreas Hofer's 'Never' echoed through his mind, and he determined to die, as he had fought, on his feet. He stood up. The death salvo shattered the silence of the dawn. One last time the body reared in the air, then he fell face down on the ground."

"Here lies destroyed on the stones one who was like us. The sun has gone dark, sorrow bows us down before the remains of all our hopes. Lord, thy ways are inscrutable! He was a hero. Our flags are clad in black, but he has gone to join his ancestors, full of his noble deeds. We are with him in his death. His will is ours, and ours his destiny. We may have lost him, but for the Fatherland he is immortal. And from the depths of the grave his voice says: 'I live!' "

*

The Kaltenborn officials' attempts at recruiting produced very feeble results. They were overworked, continually being thinned out by call-ups that made them live from day to day, and devoid of any phoric vocation. They weren't interested in getting new recruits for a place they would be leaving sooner or later, and which they expected to be shut down at any moment. Raufeisen, driven on by fanatical faith, cursed the shortage;

Blaettchen complained about the anthropological mediocrity of
the few specimens that were brought to him.

One day Tiffauges was coming back from Nikolaeken, where
he had taken Bluebeard to be shod. The rather late spring was
now bursting forth with such tender joy he was sure some piece
of good fortune was in store for him. The gelding, proud of his
sparkling shoes, clattered them on the surface of the road, and
Tiffauges thought, with a nostalgia that lent a halo of morbid
charm to even the saddest and cruelest episodes of his past, of
the thunderous hobnailed boots of Pelsenaire. By association
he was also thinking of Nestor's lovely Halcyon bicycle, the mem
ory of which still made him swell with pride, when about an
hour away from Kaltenborn, by Lake Lucknain, he saw six
bicycles propped against the trees by the water. They were
heavy German models with handlebars turned up like cows
horns, pedal brakes, and old-fashioned wood-handled pump
fixed to the frames. Between the branches of the trees came the
scintillations of light on water, shouting, laughter, and splashing.

He dismounted, left Bluebeard in a little flowery meadow
and two minutes later, with a leap, he too was in the midst of
the cool clear water with its light and its living movement. He
had calculated his jump so as to emerge right among the boys
who greeted him with shouts and laughter. They were from
Marienburg, three hundred miles away, and were using the
Whitsun holiday to bicycle through the forests and lakes of
Masuria. Tiffauges talked to them about Kaltenborn. He told
them about the citadel, the gyms, the shooting stands, the horses,
boats and guns, and the exciting life of the Jungmannen. He
invited them to dinner and to spend the night with hundreds of
friends their own age.

When Raufeisen heard the name Marienburg, he trembled
with joy and pride. It was the historical and spiritual capital of
the Teutonic Knights, and its castle, admirably preserved, was
certainly the proudest architectural masterpiece of East Prus

sia. It was there in the great hall of the knights that Baldur von Schirach, every year on April 19, made the radio speech to all the ten-year-old Germans which bound them forever to the Fuehrer. Blaettchen couldn't help crying out with enthusiasm when he examined the newcomers. He had never before seen at such close quarters such pure specimens of the Borreby East Baltic type, of which Hindenburg was the most illustrious example. Telephone calls were made and letters sent to the boys' families and the authorities in their home town. They were never to see Marienburg again.

After this masterly haul the director summoned Tiffauges. He admitted that up until then he had underestimated the Frenchman. But Tiffauges had just proved he was capable of bringing Kaltenborn something better than cheeses and sacks of beans. The director could not, of course, give him any official powers, but he gave him the job of searching the whole area for young recruits worthy of the Napola. He would circularize the districts of Johannisburg, Lyck, Loetzen, Sensburg and Ortelsburg to this effect; and others still farther away if necessary. Tiffauges was answerable to the director alone, and the director would judge him by results.

Blaettchen did not have time to congratulate his assistant on his promotion. There had lately been talk of a vast campaign known under the code name of Operation Haymaking[11] initiated by Himmler himself. The object was to select and deport into specially set up villages in Germany between forty and fifty thousand White Ruthenian children of from ten to fourteen years of age, taken from the areas occupied by the Army Group Center. Once again Alfred Rosenberg, minister for Eastern Occupied Territories, opposed this purely SS operation with the most obtuse lack of understanding. He objected that such young children would be a liability to the Reich rather than an addition to the labor force, and suggested that the intake be restricted to boys of between fifteen and seventeen.

Patiently but in vain Himmler's emissaries explained that this
was no mere transfer of manual workers, but a transfusion to
be carried out in the biological depths of the two communities,
one designed to weaken forever the vital forces of Germany's
Slav neighbor. In the end they had to decide to act independently
of the Ministry for the East.

Then someone remembered Otto Blaettchen and his bril-
liant record in the matter of the hundred and fifty Judeo-
Bolshevik heads. His knowledge of the borders of Russia and
Poland would no doubt be very useful now.

On June 16 Blaettchen bade farewell to the commandant and
the director, and, having put his goldfish—*Cyprinopsis auratus*
—in sealed gas cans, he went off, cursing about how little luggage
he could squeeze into the inferior Opel that had been sent for
him. Two days later, with the director's permission, Tiffauges
installed himself in the three rooms of the Raciological Center.

When he found himself monarch of all he surveyed, alone
in the "laboratory" among the anthropometric bric-a-brac left
behind by the Professor Doctor, Tiffauges was seized with a
fit of nervous laughter, in which triumph was mingled with a
stab of uneasiness in the face of this new twist of fate.

*

S.W.   This evening the columns broke up in silence in the
warm and scented dark, to go and light the solstice fires on
the Seehoehe, the banks of Lake Spirding, the other side of
Lake Tirklo, and all the places from which the Kaltenborn
fires would be visible and the fires of other columns could
be seen.

The secret sadness of this feast of the sun. Hardly has the
advent of the young summer been celebrated than it begins
to decline—not visibly and obviously, but by a daily gnawing
away of one or two minutes. Thus the child at his zenith of
health and beauty already carries the seed of decrepitude.
Conversely, Christmas, at the antipodes of the year, cele

brates the joyful mystery of Adonis' rebirth at the blackest and wettest time of winter.

The Jungmannen stood around the pyre in a square open on one side to let out smoke and sparks. The smallest boy came forward and walked toward the pyre. In his hand he carried a little point of fire, quivering and light as a butterfly and so wavering we were all afraid it would go out before the little fire-bearer could perform his task. It did go out when he knelt at the foot of the pile of resinous trunks from which faggots of kindling protruded. He jumped back as the flame leaped up with a roar. The clear voices rose in the flickering darkness:

> *"Nation goes to nation, as flame to flame!*
> *Mount to heaven, sacred fire,*
> *And leap roaring from tree to tree!"*

They broke ranks and came one by one to light their torches at the pyre. Then the square re-formed, made up now of dancing flames.

The fires of other columns could be seen in the distance. They were greeted by a frail solo:

> *"See how the threshold shines that will deliver us from night.*
> *Already, beyond, can be seen the dawn of a time of radiance.*
> *The doors of the future are open to those whose hearts burn*
> *with love for the Fatherland. Look at the sparks of light bring-*
> *ing alive the land that is still in darkness. Ancient, tragic*
> *Masuria answers our call and burns with a thousand fraternal*
> *fires. They foretell and hasten on the brightest day of the year."*

Three Jungmannen, each carrying an oak wreath, advanced to the fire:

> *"I sacrifice this wreath to the memory of those who died*
> *in the war."*

284 THE OGRE

"I place this wreath on the brow of the National Socialist revolution."

"I dedicate this wreath to the future sacrifices that German youth will gladly make for the Fatherland."

All the others replied in unison:

"We are the fire and the pyre. We are the flame and the spark. We are the light and the warmth which drive back the dark, the cold and the damp."

As the glowing trunks collapsed in a torrent of sparks, those in the square started to move. The Jungmannen filed around in a circle, and each in turn sprang forward and leaped through the flames.

This time there is no need for interpretation or for any deciphering grid. This ceremony, obstinately mingling the future and death, and throwing the boys one after the other into the live coals, is the clear evocation, the diabolic invocation, of the massacre of the innocents toward which we march, singing.

I'd be surprised if Kaltenborn had the chance to celebrate another summer solstice.

*

From then on Tiffauges on his big black horse covered Masuria from the heights of Koenigshoehe in the west to the marshes of Lyck in the east, with excursions southward as far as the Polish frontier. Armed with letters of introduction bearing the arms of Kaltenborn, he presented himself at the town halls, reconnoitered the elementary schools, talked to the teachers, and examined the children. Each tour ended with visits to the parents: a mixture of dazzling promises and veiled threats rarely failed to convert them to the idea of letting their sons join the Napola. Then Tiffauges would ride full tilt back

to Kaltenborn and report to Raufeisen, who would ratify his
decisions and make them enforceable. But sometimes he
came up against more or less open resistance, which was very
difficult to overcome in this country saddened by defeat. And,
of course, it was often the boys Tiffauges for one reason or
another most wanted to get, who turned out to be the most
difficult quarry.

He had found at the end of Lake Beldahn, a long, twisting,
narrow green tongue among the sands of Johannisburg, a pair
of twins whose parents were poor and lived in a fisherman's
hut. Tiffauges had always been fascinated by the phenomenon
of twins, which seemed to him to indicate a vital power at
a depth where flesh dictates to soul and makes it do its will. And
it is a caprice of nature by which one being is willy-nilly admitted to all the most intimate secrets of another by being made his
alter ego. In addition to this, Hajo and Haro were ginger as
fox cubs, white as milk, and covered with freckles. As soon as
he came across them one day gathering reeds on the shores of
the lake, he thought of the disturbing theory Blaettchen had told
him once—only to refute it with angry contempt—according to
which there are only two races: the redheaded, which is a race
apart right down to the level of the cell, and the fair- and dark-
haired, which results simply from infinitely varied combinations
of the same pigment.

Quite unexpectedly, the attempt to acquire the twins met
with a passive resistance on the part of their parents that was
almost insurmountable. At first the parents pretended they
didn't understand German: they spoke a Slav dialect among
themselves. Then they met Tiffauges's explanations with im-
becile dimness, repeating again and again that the twins were
only twelve and too young to be soldiers. Tiffauges applied to
all the surrounding villages in vain: none of the authorities
wanted to get involved in this doubtful affair, and all denied that
the lake came into their district. Raufeisen, urged on by

Tiffauges, had to get the district of Johannisburg to intervene,
and finally it was the mayor in person who brought the two boys
to Kaltenborn.

*

S.W.   I had a phone call to say the twins were definitely in
the bag. A car from the garrison headquarters at Johannisburg was bringing them to Kaltenborn, and they would be
here in an hour.

I was seized with a kind of fever I know very well—a
trembling like tetanus that shakes my whole frame and
comes chiefly from my jaw. I struggled as well as I could
against the trismic tremor that makes my teeth rattle and little
jets of saliva shoot up inside my mouth. I struggled against
it by instinct but soon abandoned myself to what is only the
expectation of too great a happiness. I even wondered
whether this expectation of a prey still absent, but absolutely
certain to come, was not the best thing life would ever bring
me.

They arrived. The district leader's heavy Mercedes swept
around the courtyard and stopped in front of the door. The
twins got out one after the other, so alike it was as if the same
child jumped down on to the flagstones twice. But they were
both there, side by side, both buttoned up in the black velvet
trousers and brown shirt with shoulder belt of the Hitler
Youth. It brought out strongly their own red and white.

I've been pondering for several weeks about the attraction
I feel so strongly, not so much for these two children in
particular as for the phenomenon of twins in general. It's
probably a special application of the rule by which the four
hundred or so miniature men of Kaltenborn together form a
collective mass whose density is immeasurably greater than
that which results from the mere adding together of their in-
dividualities. These multiple and contradictory personalities
largely cancel each other out, and all that remains is the naked

and massive mob. Personality, which is spirit, penetrates
flesh and makes it porous, light and breathing, as yeast spiritualizes dough. If personality disappears, the bullion of flesh
returns to its native purity and gross weight.

Twins carry the despiritualization of the flesh further. It is
no longer a matter of a contradictory tumult in which souls
neutralize one another. The two bodies really have only one
concept between them with which to clothe themselves in
intelligence and fill themselves with spirit. So they develop
with calm indecency, exhibiting their creamy complexion, their
pink down, their muscular or adipose tissue in an animal
nudity that is unsurpassable. For nudity is not a state but a
quantity, and as such infinite in theory, limited in fact.

The examination of the twins, which was carried out at
once in the laboratory, confirmed these views. Hajo and
Haro are of the lymphatic type, pulmonary, slow, on the fat
side. Brachycephalic skulls (90.5), wide faces with prominent cheekbones, pointed ears, flat noses, widely spaced
teeth, green rather slit eyes. In short, rather "low" faces, at
once dull and sly, expressive of a modest intelligence dominated by an intense instinctive life. The bodies strongly made
and of apparently unshakable poise. Shoulders rounded, pec-
torals poorly defined and visibly fatty rather than muscular.
The thoracic notch is wide and forms a full arch; the groins
and the supra-pubic groove form a pointed arch, closed by
the inverted fleur-de-lys of the genitals. Between these two
symmetrical arcs the three abdominal planes are astonish-
ingly clearly drawn in a body elsewhere so well covered. Beneath the wide nape a fleshy back, generously modeled and
white and oval as a big slice of bread, is divided in two by
the vertebral valley that disappears between the loins. The
saddle-shaped renal area heralds the excessive protuberance
of the buttocks. The hands have short square fingers and
muscular palms. The legs are heavy and thick-ankled; the

large flat kneecaps hyperextend easily, displacing the mass of the thigh so that it overhangs the foot.

On the extremely white skin the freckles are scattered in streaks and trails of varying density; on the arms and nape they even form irregular patches like maps. The inner surface of the thigh is crisscrossed by small blue veins, regular as the meshes of a net.

S.W.   In the hasty examination of the twins carried out on their arrival, with all the impatience of entering into possession, I failed to see the essential, the marvel of marvels, which leaped to my eye this morning with a blinding flash of happiness.

I was wasting my time on the rather futile problem of trying to find the difference, however minute, that would enable me to tell one from the other. Such a difference does exist, and after living with them for a few days I could distinguish Haro from Hajo at a glance. But this was not so much through any precise distinctive mark as through each child's general bearing, gestures and manner. Haro has a dash, drive and clarity in his movements that is not to be found in Hajo's slower and more meditative pace. One gets the impression that, between the two of them, it is Haro who takes the initiative and if necessary commands, though Hajo can always set up against his too near and too lively brother the defenses of dream and procrastination.

As for the precise and anthropometric decisive mark that can be expressed in a few words, I did find it, but at a level much finer, more abstract and more spiritual than the one I was wasting my efforts investigating. I had observed a long time ago that if you divide a child's face into two halves vertically, by a line passing through the bridge of the nose, the left and right halves, though they may be very alike on the whole, still present innumerable small discrepancies. It is as if the child were made of two halves based on the same model but corresponding to two different inspirations: the left turned toward the past, reflection and emotion, the right toward the future, action and aggression, and the two stuck together at the last stage of creation. At the other extremity of the trunk the raphe, the litle pebbled amber-colored protuberance that runs along the ridge of the perineum and the middle of the scrotum, from the front edge of the anus to the end of the prepuce, also suggests, in its rough and crude manner, that the boy is formed of two valves stuck together at the last moment, like a shellfish or a celluloid doll.

And now for the marvel that will make this a red-letter day forever: there is absolutely no doubt that Haro's left half corresponds to the right half of Hajo, and Haro's right to Hajo's left. They are *mirror twins* who can be superimposed on one another face to face, not one on top of the other like the others. I have always been extremely interested in the processes of inversion, permutation and superimposing; photography provided a special illustration of them, but only in the realm of the imagination. And now here I find the theme that has always haunted me actually written out in children's flesh!

I had made them sit side by side and was looking at them with the sense that I was confronting a secret to be penetrated. I get this feeling from the presence of any face or body, but this time I did not have the depressing certainty that the mask would only harden in answer to my scrutiny. On the contrary, now I felt I was going to find the answer. It was then I noticed that Hajo had a curl on his forehead that twisted clockwise, while Haro had one that twisted counterclockwise. This first faint illumination led me to perceive almost immediately afterward that the little scar or mole on Haro's right cheek corresponded to a similar mark on Hajo's left. Similar discoveries came in a torrent, but the most revealing of all was, of course, the distribution of their freckles.

I phoned the Anthropological Institute at Koenigsberg, which I had consulted before under Blaettchen, and told them of my discovery. They confirmed the existence of mirror-twins, a comparatively rare phenomenon due, it was thought, to a separation taking place not *ab initio* but at a later stage, when the embryo has already begun to be differentiated. The Koenigsberg people would come and see my twins when next they visited the area.

*

It was during the month of July that the Jungmannen were given the magnificent toy they had been promised months ago: an anti-aircraft battery made up of four heavy coupled machine guns, four light 200-mm. rapid-firing pieces (two to three hundred rounds a minute), a 3.7, and three 10.5s for long-range firing. There was also a sound detector, but they still had to wait for the last item, the searchlight battery. The "Flak" was camouflaged in a pinewood on a height overlooking the village of Drosselwalde, two miles from the citadel, from which it could cover the road from Arys, which would be the route taken by an invader from the east. The battery was commanded by two training officers and serviced by a roster of four columns taken from different groups of boys.

Every so often from then on, training shots would be fired, filling the sky with little white clouds, their triumphant thunder constantly recalling the nearness of the war. Sometimes shrapnel could be heard pattering down on the roofs of the castle. Tiffauges regularly took supplies to the columns on duty. He would find the boys either in shorts, dotted about the woods sunbathing, or else, wearing helmets with felt earflaps to muffle the noise, busy about the huge howling guns. They had never had such fun and were only sorry no enemy aircraft put in an appearance to act as a live target.

S.W.   Shocking though it may appear at first, the fundamental affinity that exists between war and boys cannot be
denied. The spectacle of the Jungmannen serving and feeding the monstrous idols of steel and fire that raise their
monumental jaws amidst the trees is irrefutable proof of this
affinity. And boys always insist on playing with toy guns,
swords, cannon and tanks, or tin soldiers and various kinds
of killer's outfits. It might be said they are only imitating their
elders, but I wonder whether the truth isn't really the opposite, for in fact grownups make war less often than they go
to the factory or office. I wonder whether wars don't break
out with the sole object of allowing adults to "act like children," to regress with a sigh of relief to the age of tin soldiers
and dressing up. When he's called up, the adult, weary of all
his burdens as head of department, husband and father, puts
off all his duties and virtues and sets about amusing himself
freely and carelessly with friends of his own age, manipulating cannon, tanks and airplanes which are only enlarged
copies of the toys of his childhood.

The trouble is that the regression doesn't work. The adult
takes up the toys of the child, but he no longer possesses
the instinct for play and storytelling that gave them their
original meaning. In his great clumsy hands they take on
the monstrous proportions of so many giant tumors, devour-
ing flesh and blood. The death-dealing seriousness of the
adult has replaced the playful gravity of the child, of which
it is a caricature or inverted image.

But what's going to happen now, when children are given
these hypertrophied toys conceived by a morbid imagination
and brought into being by the activity of madmen? We see
the answer in what is happening on the heights of Drosselwalde, in the Napola at Kaltenborn, and all over the Reich:
the phoria that expresses the ideal relationship between the
adult and the child is being established in monstrous fashion

between the child and the grown-up toy. The toy is no longer carried by the child—drawn, pushed, tilted, rolled, as an imaginative object in destructive little hands. Now it is the child who is carried by the toy—swallowed up in a tank, shut in the cockpit of a plane, imprisoned in the swiveling turret of a machine gun.

I now touch for the first time on what is probably a phenomenon of the first importance: *the overturning of phoria by malign inversion.* It was only natural, actually, that these two elements in my symbolical mechanism should react on one another sooner or later. The new figure that results from their conjunction is a sort of *paraphoria;* I say "a sort" advisedly, for clearly there must be other varieties of this kind of deviation.

A new piece has just been added to my system and I don't yet see it in all its aspects. I shall have to observe it in action and in different contexts before I can estimate its importance.

*

The second week in July was marked by a storm of unusual violence that burst over the whole area and nearly had tragic consequences for Kaltenborn. The accumulated heat of a summer charged with electricity had led the director to organize sailing exercises that day on Lake Spirding. A hundred little boats with four Jungmannen in each crossed from one shore to the other in search of messages scattered in numbered bottles over an area of several square miles. The object was to pick up as many bottles as possible and reconstruct the whole ciphered text out of the fragments contained in them. It was a wonderful sight to watch the little white skiffs, driven swiftly before the scorching and ever more violent gusts, swinging around adroitly as one of the boys leaned halfway out over the water to scoop up a sign-bearing bottle. But at about five o'clock the sky suddenly darkened and the surface of the lake was swept by a

squall. The director at once gave the signal to return to the landing pier. Four boats capsized, but no harm was done; the rest
clustered about the moorings, while torrents of rain sent everyone into the boathouses for shelter. It was then that a roll call
revealed that one boat was missing. Visibility was almost nil in
that leaden twilight hatched with fierce curtains of rain. The
director had all the chief villages on the shores of the lake
alerted by telephone, and set out to cover the whole surface
systematically in his motorboat. But in vain. Next morning the
sun rose on a lake as calm as usual, but deserted.

Then Tiffauges had the idea of searching the uninhabited
parts of the shore with the eleven Dobermans. The dogs were
familiar with the children's presence and smell and set out barking in joyful if discordant chorus, Tiffauges on Bluebeard panting in their wake. It was the dogs who finally found the four
boys, safe but freezing with cold in the rocky mouth of a stream,
where their boat had been wrecked.

Tiffauges applied the results of this experiment: since the
dogs knew and could find the Jungmannen, perhaps their instinct also extended to any boy of similar age with the qualifications required for joining the Napola. He tested it out by taking
the pack with him on his recruiting tours. When he reached a
village the dogs would scatter among the houses and gardens,
and when they halted and barked by a gate or a fence or a tree
it was rare for them not to be drawing the recruiter's attention
to someone of interest. Tiffauges took his long hunting whip
with him and stuffed bits of raw meat in his pockets, perfect-
ing the training of the dogs by punishing their mistakes and
rewarding their successes. This unforeseen assistance was all
the more useful because summer and the call-up of teachers
had emptied the schools and dispersed the pupils, and one man
couldn't keep his eye and nose on everything. The danger lay
in the lurid and brutal spectacle presented by the great black
baying hounds and their swarthy cavalier on his big night-

colored mount. Their intimidating appearance sometimes produced the desired result, but there was reason to fear violent
reactions, as was demonstrated by the attack of July 20.

It had been a particularly productive week, and Tiffauges
was returning from the village of Erlenau, where he had arranged for all the boys born in 1931 to be presented to the
director. He was just going at a walk through a plantation of
saplings when something whizzed past his ear, and a young elm
he was passing fell to the ground, cut down by an invisible
scythe. A second later he heard the sound of the shot leaving
the gun. Bluebeard shied and nearly threw his rider. For a moment Tiffauges thought of setting off with the dogs in the direction of the shot, but this would mean risking a second attempt,
this time at closer range, and anyway what would he do if he
came face to face with his attacker? He clapped spurs to his
horse and went back to Kaltenborn, resolving not to breathe a
word about the matter.

As he was dismounting in the courtyard, the director signaled
to him through his office window. He held out a sheet of cheap
paper which bore a roughly stenciled text:

**This warning is addressed to all mothers in the areas of
Gehlenburg, Sensburg, Loetzen and Lyck!**

BEWARE OF THE OGRE OF KALTENBORN!

**He is after your children. He roves through our country steal-
ing children. If you have any, never forget the Ogre—he never
forgets them! Don't let them go out alone. Teach them to run
away and hide if they see a giant on a blue horse with a pack of
black hounds. If he comes to see you, don't yield to his threats,
don't be taken in by his promises. All mothers should be guided
by one certainty: If the Ogre takes your child, you will NEVER
see him again!**

*

Shortly before he left, Blaettchen had said to Tiffauges, almost absent-mindedly: "Someone once told me about the son of some charcoal-burners in the forest of Nikolaeken. He has hair white as snow, violet eyes, and a horizontal cephalic index that must be in the region of 70. You ought to go and have a look around there. His name is Lothar Wuestenroth. His parents have never answered any of my summonses."

Tiffauges was in the district for the first time. It was the poorest in the area and very difficult to get to. He had to cross the arm of a lake on a makeshift raft propelled by a goiterous boatman who was cheerful but apparently deaf. After balking for a considerable time, Bluebeard finally leaped on board so desperately he nearly overshot the frail assemblage of logs. The boatman started up a little motor whose stutterings echoed all over the lake. Throughout the crossing the horse rolled its eyes wildly and kicked frantically against the logs with its hind legs.

Tiffauges remembered what Blaettchen had said when he saw a lot of men all black from their work going to and fro in the clearings around charcoal stacks so numerous they looked like a sort of dwarf village. He approached some of the men and mentioned the name Wuestenroth. They all affected ignorance, until one indicated a place called Baerenwinkel five or six miles to the east.

Tiffauges rode on through great clearings sparsely planted with saplings which led on to purple heaths and sands, where Bluebeard sank up to the pasterns and had to make great efforts to get along. Then came the charcoal forests and stacks again, with great clearings where the light hurt eyes grown accustomed to the green shade of copse and thicket. Tiffauges rode up to a group of men standing around a burning pile of charcoal. The first to notice his approach was a child, judging by his size, though he was wearing the same sacking tunic and trousers as the others. Tiffauges was going to question him, but there was no need. The child had raised his sooty face toward him, and his anemone-colored eyes made patches of mauve light in the black mask.

"Lothar Wuestenroth," said Tiffauges in a tone combining interrogation and statement.

The boy showed no surprise, though perhaps the anemones encroached a little further on the black mask. But he slowly pulled off his woolen cap, revealing a helmet of straight platinum-colored hair.

Tiffauges expected the negotiations to be protracted and uncertain. He knew from experience that the humbler the social milieu involved the more difficult it was to get recruits from it. While the middle classes fell over themselves to get their offspring into the Napolas, prospecting among the workers and peasants—the families most sought after by the authorities—came up against mistrust, fear and hostility. Yet to Tiffauges's great surprise the Wuestenroths agreed immediately to all his demands. They gave their consent so readily he began to wonder whether they really understood what it was all about. To avoid any misunderstanding he took them to the town hall at Warnold, the nearest commune, where the clerk translated what Tiffauges said and put the main points down on paper.

Riding back to Baerenwinkel, Tiffauges was borne up by choirs of cherubim singing hymns of thanksgiving, for at the last minute it had been agreed he should take Lothar to Kaltenborn that same evening, and he could already see himself galloping through the triumphant light of the setting sun, the boy with white hair and mauve eyes clasped to him beneath his cloak. But Tiffauges had to abandon this vision: Lothar had left the charcoal-burners' village during his absence. The men had seen him going in the direction of Warnold and thought he had stayed behind to tidy himself up and was now going to join his parents and the stranger. He was still nowhere to be found late that night, when Tiffauges resigned himself to going back to Kaltenborn with empty arms and a heart racked with sorrow and anger.

It had been agreed that the town hall at Warnold would keep in touch with the Wuestenroths and let Tiffauges know when Lothar returned. So Tiffauges got his place ready for him at the Napola, arranging which group he should be in, which table he should sit at in the refectory, which bed he should sleep in, and getting together his clothes, his blankets, and even the knife he would be solemnly invested with. But the days went by, and phone calls to Warnold were met with only vague promises and evasive silences. But instead of despairing or forgetting, Tiffauges looked forward in quiet confidence. Lothar's disappearance must be no more a matter of chance than anything else in Tiffauges's life. His disappointment had been as keen and inevitable as if he had seen a giant hand come down out of the clouds and snatch the boy with mauve eyes up from under his very nose. But if Lothar had eluded him that day, it was because his coming to Kaltenborn was too important for fate not to surround it with fabulous circumstances.

It was not until the end of August that all the necessary circumstances were assembled. That day a group had gone across the lake to go hunting in the forest of Johannisburg: they usually returned in triumph in the little skiffs, weighed down by stags and bucks whose heads hung over the side with their antlers skimming the surface of the water. Flanked on the east by Tiffauges, Bluebeard and the dogs, the boys beat the thickets and brambles, driving toward the lake all the fur and feather that consented to be raised. They had no guns, only their knives and clubs, plus a whole array of lassos and nets. Lack of method and experience was made up for by the number and agility of the participants; and the great abundance of game, which had not been hunted for several years, meant that these gaily improvised beats were practically never unsuccessful. But that morning the woods were still and silent, and the absence of small game seemed to indicate the presence of some large animal taking cover in the thickets. They went on beating for an hour without any result, until suddenly a big grouse took noisy flight and alighted on a beech. Knocked off it by a direct hit from a piece of wood, he ran toward a patch of brambles and was about to disappear into it when one of the Dobermans finished him off with a snap of his jaws. It was a superb creature as big as a turkey; they carried it slung on a pole between two boys.

They were getting near the shore of the lake, where the hunt would normally end, when everyone suddenly froze at the sound of little hoofs clattering along a gravel path. Tiffauges silenced the dogs and was distracted for a moment by Bluebeard, who stood there with his ears pointing forward, panting, muscles aquiver. Then, like a streak of fawn lightning, a five-pronger broke cover, followed by two does. There was a swish of lassos; some boys vainly attempted to run after the animals on foot. But they were soon outdistanced by Tiffauges, and their cries rapidly died away in the distance. Tiffauges, crouched on Bluebeard's neck, galloped along guided by the baying of the dogs, already out of sight.

The first hours had the gratuitous beauty of a game. The herd flew straight ahead, leaping nimbly across banks and paths. They were closely followed by the dogs, grouped like the fingers of a hand and sounding a fanfare from eleven burning throats. Tiffauges gave Bluebeard his head: the horse launched his whole weight at thickets, osiers, ferns and heather and bored furiously whenever he encountered the obstacles of ditch, stump or hedge. Sometimes his rider ducked and shut his eyes to avoid the flying pine needles or the low branch of an oak. The great burning, foam-flecked body whose movement he followed radiated a life so ardent and near that it could not but win his blind confidence.

He caught up with the dogs by an arm of the lake which the

five-pronger was swimming across, holding his antlers high above the water like floating candlesticks. The two does had vanished, and Tiffauges marveled that the dogs had not let themselves be distracted to follow them. The stag was climbing out, streaming, on the other bank when the dogs leaped as one into the shallow water, followed by Bluebeard, who was able to ford it. And the hunt was on again, the black pursuers flying howling with bloodshot eyes, shoulder to shoulder through the ever thinning trees. Tiffauges lost sight of them again when, after crossing a succession of fields, they plunged into a hazel thicket. Then came more little woods and fields of gorse with the hounds still in full cry, purple heaths, and sandy stretches pitted with warrens. Then suddenly Tiffauges realized that the course had ended and the quarry was at bay: he could still hear the dogs, but their voices seemed to have changed register and were louder now but deeper and more discordant. It was no longer the unanimous fanfare that accompanies the effort of pursuit, but the song of death that precedes the kill.

He urged on Bluebeard, who had slowed to a trot, as if he realized the dogs had halted. Rounding a corner of wood, he came on a great stretch of fallow land, at the edge of which stood the twisted shape of a copper beech. He trotted over to the dogs, who stood around the foot of the tree barking inexplicably up at the great branches. A boy with mauve eyes crouched there in the fork, holding on with both hands.

"I'm frightened of the dogs!" he shouted to Tiffauges as soon as he was within earshot. "Call them off!"

Even if he had wanted to, Tiffauges couldn't have driven away the eleven Dobermans kicking up hell's delight around his feet. He got Bluebeard up against the trunk of the tree and tried to stand up on his crupper. As if he understood the meaning of the phoric rite about to be performed, the gelding stood still as a statue in spite of the hounds leaping up and down around him like black waves. Lothar, still crouched in the tree,

tried to kick Tiffauges away. Finally the hunter succeeded in
getting hold of him by one leg, and pulled him toward him. At
the moment the boy fell into his arms his joy was so violent he
didn't feel his prey sink his teeth in his hand until it bled.

*

S.W.   The horse is not only the animal totem of Defecation
and the phoric beast par excellence. The Anal Angel can also
become an instrument of ravishment and rape, and, as the
rider carries his prey phorically in his arms, rise to the level
of *superphoria*. More: ravishment can come even after superphoria—for example if a superhuman being snatches the
child away from the rider who is carrying him off, as in the
poem of *The Erl-King*. Goethe's ballad, which shows the father fleeing over the moor on horseback, clasping under his
cloak the son whom the Erl-King is trying to lure away, and
whom he finally seizes by force, is the very charter of phoria,
which it raises to the third power. It is the Latin myth of
Christopher and Albuquerque lifted to a paroxysm of incandescence by hyperborean magic. To the hunt, in which the
Anal Angel tracks down and brings to bay the Phallophoric
Angel, my particular genius adds the metamorphosis of the
stag into a child and the superphoric rite that follows. This
development opens a new era in the play of essences and will
achieve fulfillment at Kaltenborn.

*

For a long time Raufeisen wondered what the commandant
wanted with Tiffauges when he sent for him urgently and kept
him in the castle, sometimes for hours. His dignity forbade him
to ask the Frenchman; his sense of hierarchy prevented him
from asking the general. The truth of the matter was that since
their encounter at the side of the road and their drive back to
Kaltenborn in the cart, the old aristocrat had found in Tiffauges's universe of signs and symbols a field of inquiry at once
close to his own preoccupations and sufficiently novel to in-

terest him. He lived strictly isolated in his suite, out of the daily
life and work and celebrations of the Napola, and he was
pleased by Tiffauges's deference and attention, and by the significance of some of the things he had to say, which made one
forget he was a Frenchman, an enlisted man, and a commoner.
For Tiffauges, for the first time in his life, had departed from
the absolute secrecy he had always maintained about his joys
and fears and discoveries. He didn't take the commandant entirely into his confidence—for instance he didn't say anything
about his ogreish origins or the collusion between himself and
fate—but, in the hope of finding out more about them, he did
tell the old man about inversion both malign and benign, saturation, phoria and the heroes who embodied it.

In the course of these conversations the commandant spoke
of his own memories—his childhood and youth at the military
academy at Ploen, where the Kaiser's sons had been fellow pupils; life in the garrison at Koenigsberg, so stifling even for a
Junker who had been brought up to it that he had been glad to
seize the opportunity of escape offered by the Boxer Rebellion.
As a newly fledged lieutenant from Potsdam he was one of the
international expeditionary corps commanded by Field Marshal
von Waldersee which avenged the murder of Ketteler, the German minister, and freed the foreign legations being held prisoner in Peking. He threw himself into the 1914 war with an
enthusiasm that could no longer be accounted for by his age,
but that appeared to be justified by the first successes of the
German offensive. But when the cavalry regiments were dis-
banded and cuirassiers mingled with infantry in the mud of the
trenches, he saw that some essential element in the order of
things had been destroyed—its most agile, subtle and brilliant
source of strength. The setbacks and finally the defeat that followed were the inevitable consequence of that initial fault.

Later he looked on at the abdication of the Kaiser and the
Socialist agitation with the detachment of one prematurely aged

by the disappearance of the world he really belonged to. And ever since, heraldry had acted as a translucent screen between himself and reality.

"Everything is in symbols," he declared. "I realized my country's greatness was over and done with forever when the National Assembly met in 1919 in the municipal theater in Weimar —Weimar! A theater! The right place for complete masquerade! —and rejected the glorious black, white and red imperial standard derived directly from the Order of the Teutonic Knights, taking as the new emblem of the nation the red, black and gold striped flag that had spread like a poisonous flower over the barricades of 1848. It was the official opening of an era of shame and decadence. Whoever sins by symbols will be punished by symbols! Tiffauges, you are a reader of signs—I could see it, and you have proved it to me. You think that in Germany you have found the country of pure essences, where everything that passes is symbol, everything that happens is parable. And you are right. Besides, a man marked by destiny is inevitably bound to finish up in Germany, just as a moth flying around in the dark always ends by finding the light that intoxicates and kills it. But you still have much to learn. Up to now you have discovered signs on things, like the letters and figures one reads on a milestone. That is only the weak form of symbolic existence. But don't go thinking signs are always feeble and harmless abstractions. Signs are strong, Tiffauges—it is they that brought you here. Signs are irritable, and the symbol thwarted becomes a diabol. From being a center of light and concord it becomes a power of darkness and division. Your vocation has revealed to you phoria, malign inversion and saturation. You still have to learn the height of this mechanism of symbols—the combination of those three figures in one, which is synonymous with apocalypse. For there is a terrifying moment when the sign no longer accepts being carried by a creature as a standard is carried by a soldier. It acquires autonomy, it escapes from the thing symbolized, and—this is what is frightening—it takes over that thing. And then woe to that thing! Remember Christ's Passion. Jesus carried his cross for many hours, then the cross carried him. Then the veil of the temple was rent and the sun was darkened. When the symbol devours the thing symbolized, when the cross-bearer becomes the crucified, when a malign inversion over-throws phoria, then the end of the world is at hand. Symbol, no longer ballasted by anything, becomes master of heaven. It pro-liferates, insinuates itself everywhere, and shatters into a thou-sand meanings that don't mean anything any more. Have you read the Apocalypse of St. John? It shows terrible, grandiose scenes that light up the sky—fantastic animals, stars, swords, crowns, constellations, a great chaos of archangels, scepters, thrones and suns. And all that, undeniably, is symbol and ci-pher. But don't try to understand it—don't try to find the thing to which each sign refers. For these symbols are diabols, and no longer symbolize anything. And saturation with them brings the end of the world."

He was silent and walked toward the window, from which the pole of a flag rustling in the night wind could be seen.

"You see me now," he said, "in my own castle, bristling with swastika banners and oriflammes. I admit that I experienced a moment of hope in 1933 when the new Chancellor discarded the three colors of Weimar and restored those of Bismarck's Empire. But when I saw what he did with them—that red flag with a big white circle inscribed with a crooked cross—I sus-pected the worst. For that tottering spider, turning around on itself and threatening everything that comes in its way with its hooked claws, is a blatant antithesis of the cross of Malta, radi-ant with serenity and the desire for peace! The limit was reached when the Third Reich, as part of its policy of restoring traditional insignia, set about reviving the glory of the eagle in the arms of Prussia. You know, of course, that in heraldry right is called left and left right?"

Tiffauges nodded. It was the first time he had actually heard of the rule, but it was so much in keeping with the left-right reversal he had always encountered when symbols took charge that it seemed familiar at once.

"The reversal is given a practical explanation, probably invented after the event. They say a shield has to be read not from the point of view of a spectator facing it, but from that of the knight who bears it on his left arm. Be that as it may, the Prussian eagle has its head turned *dexter,* according to sound heraldic tradition. But now look at the eagle of the Third Reich, which carries a wreath of oak leaves with the swastika inside: its head is turned *sinister.* It's an eagle *contourné,* a genuine variation reserved for bastard or fallen branches of noble families. Of course, none of the Party officials could explain this monstrosity. They tried to put it down to a mistake on the part of the designer in the Ministry of Propaganda. But now Goebbels has found an explanation at last: the eagle of the Third Reich looks to the east, toward the U.S.S.R. it threatens and attacks. But the truth is different, Monsieur Tiffauges."

He came close to the Frenchman to hiss the awful secret they were about to share.

"The truth is that ever since it began the Third Reich has been the product of symbols, which have taken over control. The inflation of 1923 was an eloquent warning, though no one understood it: that cloud of worthless bank notes, monetary symbols symbolizing nothing, which rained down all over the country with the destructive rage of a plague of locusts. And take note that it was in that same year, when one dollar was worth 4.2 billion marks, that Hitler and Ludendorff marched on the Odeonsplatz in Munich with a handful of supporters to overthrow the Bavarian government. You know what happened: the volley of shots, which killed sixteen of Hitler's escorts; Goering seriously wounded; Hitler dragged to the ground by the dying Scheubner-Richter and escaping with a dislocated shoulder. Then the Fuehrer's nine months' imprisonment in the fortress at Landsberg, where he wrote *Mein Kampf*. But all that is of minor importance. As far as Germany was concerned, man was irrelevant from then on. The only thing that counted that day in Munich, November 9, 1923, was the conspirators' swastika flag that fell among the sixteen bodies and was stained and consecrated by their blood. Henceforward the flag of blood—*die Blutfahne*—was the most sacred relic of the Nazi Party. Ever since 1933 it has been exhibited twice a year: once on November 9, when the march on the Feldherrnhalle at Munich is re-enacted, as in a medieval passion play; but above all in September, at the annual Party rally in Nuremburg which marks the peak of Nazi ritual. Then the *Blutfahne*, like a sire fertilizing an infinity of females, is brought into contact with new standards seeking insemination. I have been present, Monsieur Tiffauges, and I can tell you that when he performs the nuptial rite of the flags, the Fuehrer makes the same movement as the cattle breeder guiding the bull's penis into the cow's vagina with his own hand. Then whole armies march past in which each man is a flag-bearer and which are simply armies of flags: a vast sea, heaving and undulating in the wind, of standards, ensigns, banners, emblems and oriflammes. At night the cressets complete the apotheosis, for the light of the torches illuminates the flagpoles, the bunting and the bronze statues, and relegates into the shadows of the earth the great mass of men, doomed to darkness. Finally, when the Fuehrer steps on the monumental altar, a hundred and fifty searchlights suddenly spring alight, raising over the Zeppelin-wiese a cathedral of pillars a thousand feet high to attest the sidereal significance of the mystery being celebrated.

"You say you love Prussia, Monsieur Tiffauges, because signs shine with incomparable brightness in its hyperborean light. But you don't yet see what this awful proliferation of symbols leads to. In the sign-saturated sky a storm is gathering which will be violent as an apocalypse, and which will engulf us all!"

*

S.W.   At three o'clock this morning there was a general alert. For the first time I was present at what the boys call a "masquerade," one of the most revolting tortures ever hatched in the brain of a Prussian non-commissioned officer. Raufeisen realizes discipline is going to pieces at Kaltenborn and that the Napola is slipping out of his control. And he reacts by sporadic but violent blows.

The boys have to be assembled in the courtyard in field uniforms within three minutes. Punishments rain down on any who are late, and subsequently on any whose uniform doesn't pass muster. After they have stood at attention for a quarter of an hour a new order rings out. In two minutes everyone has to be back again in the same place in Jungvolk uniform. They gallop up the stairs, rush into the dormitories, struggle around the cupboards. More punishments rain down on those who speak, then on those who are late, then on those who don't pass the director's inspection. Another quarter of an hour at attention. Fall out. Everyone back in two minutes in dress uniform. Then in gym outfit. Then in parade uniform. They grit their teeth and all try to be little robots, but I saw some of them crying with exasperation.

I could have stayed in bed, but I couldn't have borne to miss them parading in different sorts of dress. I observed eagerly how their personalities altered with each. It is not that they came through the clothes as a voice does through a wall, more or less distinctly according to the thickness. No—each time a new version of their personalities is put forward, altogether new and unexpected, but as complete as the previous one, as complete as nakedness. It is like a poem translated into one language after another which never loses any of its magic but each time puts on new and surprising charms.

On the most trivial level, clothes are so many keys to the human body. At that degree of indistinctness, key and grid are more or less the same. Clothes are keys because they are carried by the body, but they are related to the grid because they cover the body, sometimes entirely, like a translation *in extenso* or a long-winded commentary that takes up more room than the text. But they are merely a prosaic gloss, garrulous and trivial, without emblematic significance.

More even than a key or a grid, a garment is a framing of the body. The face is framed, and thus commented on and interpreted, by the hat above and the collar below. Arms alter according to whether sleeves are long or short, close-fitting or loose, or whether there aren't any sleeves at all. A short tight sleeve follows the shape of the arm, brings out the contours of the biceps, the soft swelling of the triceps, the plump roundness of the shoulder—but without any attempt to please, without any invitation to touch. A loose sleeve hides the roundedness of the arm and makes it seem slimmer, but its welcoming ampleness invokes a caress that will take possession of the arm and go right up to the shoulder if need be. Shorts and socks frame the knee and interpret it differently according to how low the first come and how high the second. A knee narrowly framed in a longish trouser and a longish sock is reduced to the harsh and tedious role of a crank-head. It expresses rigor, efficiency and indifference to the flesh. But if the sock is not long, or if it is allowed to fall down in wrinkles over the shoe, the tenderness of the calf comes into its own and contradicts the knee's claim to austerity. The image conjures up the idea of a discipline imposed from without on some careless and charming creature who unconsciously defends himself and foils the disciplinarian by the spontaneous way his body deals

with the clothes handed out to him. A more harmonious com
position is obtained from a very long sock coming up to o:
even partly over the knee, and very short trousers that leav
most of the thigh uncovered. Then it is the thigh that i:
framed and exalted, and the knee appears as its unobtrusiv
support. This is the royal formula, uniting rigor in the gar
ment with lyric celebration of the flesh, a respect for orde:
with praise for the fullest, softest and most inviting portio:
of the leg. By a sure instinct this is the formula most favore
for the boys' various uniforms, particularly the Jungvolk an
sports outfits. But long socks often fail to do what they ar
supposed to do. If they are not long enough or not pulle
up properly, they leave the leg too bare and deprive it o
interpretation altogether. Then the only hope is in the shoe
which has to be clodhopping enough to redeem the whole
crumbling edifice at the last moment, and stubborn and face-
tious enough to provide it with the strong plinth it needs.

*

S.W.   Lothar Wuestenroth. Born December 19, 1932, a
Baerenwinkel. Height: 4 feet 9 inches. Weight: 77 pounds.
Chest: 30 1/2 inches. Horizontal cephalic index: 72.

He is slim and vibrant as a bow, and his thinness brings
out his surprising muscularity. The thoracic notch is a wide
pointed arch. This is a characteristic Blaettchen didn't think
of, though the whole architecture of the torso depends on
it. In poor specimens it is as if the thorax is closed by the
ribs almost meeting in front. In average cases the notch is
triangular, in the form of an inverted V. The arms of the V
may curve, but the more they approach a full arch the more
pleasing the shape. On this thoracic opening, even more
than on the height of the brow or the shape of the mouth,
the degree of *inspiration* of the whole being depends. This
is not a play upon words. It is natural that at this level literal
and figurative meaning should merge, though at the same

time one should never forget that "spirit" comes from the Latin *spiritus,* the original meaning of which is breath or wind.

The face is short and as if stylized, a bony mask breached by the small mouth, the as yet unformed nose and the mauve pools of the eyes, and whittled down from above by the heavy helmet of platinum-colored hair with its pudding-basin cut, which is usual in these parts. This exemplary head makes it unnecessary to resort to Blaettchen's anthropometric paraphernalia to discover the golden rule of human beauty. It consists in the relationship between the size of the skull and the face. All the aesthetic superiority of the child over the adult resides in that. A child's skull is already as large as it will ever get. But the surface area of the face will at least double, and thus beauty will evaporate. As the face becomes larger in proportion to the skull, the head gets nearer to the animal type. The proportion of skull to face is the opposite in an animal of what it is in a human being. A dog's or a horse's head is all face—forehead, eyes, nose, mouth—and the skull is reduced to almost nothing. I note that the men and women usually admired for their beauty all retain something of this childish proportion, or disproportion, between the skull and the face. On the line connecting animal and man the child lies beyond the adult and must be considered supra- or superhuman. And aren't we obliged to come to the same conclusion about intelligence? If we define it as the ability to learn new things, to find solutions to problems encountered for the first time, who is more intelligent than a child? What adult would be capable of learning to write if he hadn't already done so when he was a child, still less of learning to speak from scratch, without starting from any other language?

As I finish these notes he waits meekly, at ease, with his weight on the living, fragile column of the left leg, a contrast

with the right thigh, soft and inert. Pyriform sex: the glans
and testicles are three almost equal masses joined by a net
work of folds converging toward the narrow peduncle grow
ing out from the pubis.

I look up, and he smiles at me.

*

The boys were assembled in the knights' chamber in the
castle, transformed that evening into a huge dark amphitheater
rustling with whispers and stifled laughter. A low podium was
lit by four torches, which made the vaults of the ceiling, with
their ribs swooping out to the pillars that supported them, seem
to stir in the shifting light. As usual, though everything had
been planned in advance, the secret had been well kept, and it
was in wondering silence that everyone suddenly saw the com
mandant appear in full general's uniform on the platform. His
retired life in the shadow of the Napola, his unimpressive civil
ian dress, the mystery surrounding someone who, as even the
youngest boys knew, possessed prestige and titles that eclipsed
the macabre vainglory of the SS—all this lent his speech that
evening an extraordinary significance. When he spoke the
silence grew deeper still, for his voice was low and scarcely
audible. It was as if the crowd of children leaned forward in
the darkness to listen to him. But gradually his tone mounted
his voice grew firmer, and the great figures he invoked peopled
the room.

"Jungmannen," he said, "tonight we are going to perform a
ceremony that is the culmination of your careers so far. Hajo
Haro and Lothar, from now on you will carry on your left the
sword whose dual invocation, 'Blood and Honor,' will dominate
your life and death. Nowhere does this ceremony take on such
significance as under these vaults, built by my ancestor Hermann, Count von Kaltenborn, knight of Christ of the Two
Swords in Livonia, prior of the Order of the Knights of the
Sword, elector of Pomerellia and Courtdoctor of Riga. He is

your patron and master in so far as you are or become this evening young Knights of the Sword. Therefore you must know what he was like and how he lived, so that in no matter what situation you can answer the question: 'What would great Hermann have done if he were in my place?'

"Like all the knights of his day, Hermann von Kaltenborn first forged his courage in the terrible sun of the East. He had known all the sufferings and also all the joys of the great Crusades. But he was not content, like most of his companions, to cleave the infidels in twain. He was a Hospitaller and knew how to tend the sick and wounded, and he brought back to this part of the world secret remedies and electuaries he had learned of from the wise men of the Levant, which made him famous at the bishop's court at Riga. At the beginning of the thirteenth century he took part in all the battles that made the Knights of the Sword masters of the hyperborean borders, from the shores of the Baltic to the banks of the Narva and of Lake Peipus. There were only a few Knights of the Sword, a few hundreds, just like you Jungmannen gathered in this room. But they were giants! They possessed nothing, neither wealth, wife, nor a will of their own, having taken the vows of poverty, chastity and obedience. They slept under arms, their swords beside them. Their sword was their only wife. The rule was so strict they were not allowed to kiss even their mothers or their sisters. Two days of the week they ate only milk and eggs, and on Friday they fasted. They might have no secrets from their leaders, and receive no messages that were not passed on to them. They went to war on horses big as elephants, and their arms and armor were so formidable each one looked like a traveling fortress. But secretly, under their coats of mail, their shoulders and backs would be bleeding, for they scourged each other before they went out to fight. . . .

"At their head was the greatest among them, Hermann von Kaltenborn: the light of his saintliness was such that the ancient oaks in the pagan forests knelt as he passed by. He preferred the winter to more clement seasons, because the rigor of cold symbolizes that of morality, the bareness of the forests recalls that of a holy life, the purity of the cloudless windswept sky evokes that of the soul freed of the flesh by faith. And the hard earth, the frozen lakes and marshes, made the way easier for his wagons and artillery.

"The tree he liked best was the fir, because it is thick and straight, green and shiny, rising in regular tiers like an edifice of justice—because, in a word, it is the most German of trees."

The commandant went on for a long while like that, mingling together past, present and future, comparing the child's sword that the Jungmannen wore on the left hip with the titanic swords that threatened the sky on the parapet of the main terrace; the war of the Panzer divisions against the U.S.S.R. with the fight of the German knights against the Slavs; and the two battles of Tannenberg—the first in 1410, when the Teutonic Knights and the Knights of the Sword succumbed to the superior numbers of the Poles and Lithuanians, and the glorious revenge in 1914, when Samsonov's Russians were crushed by Hindenburg's Germans. Finally he contrasted the attitudes of France and Germany toward their Crusading monks back from the Holy Land. At the very moment when the Teutonic Knights were building Marienburg, symbol of the rights over the province given them by their Emperor and Pope, the French Templars, slandered and reviled, were being burned at the stake by Philippe le Bel. Thus, while the spirit of the German knights still lived on this soil and within these walls, France was still expiating the crime of their perjured king. But Tiffauges noticed that the commandant didn't make a single allusion to the buried Telamon who bore the fortress on his shoulders.

After the speech the Jungmannen all stood up and recited Hofmann's poem:

> *"Unfurl the standards steeped in blood!*
> *Send the flame leaping up to the sky!"*[12]

and the old vaults quivered at the assault of their metallic voices. Then the group to which the three novices belonged assembled on the glacis for the solemn vigil.

It was no small matter, for they had to stay there till sunrise, ranged in a semicircle open toward the east. When the globe of fire rose behind the heights of Nickelsberg the Jungmannen would sing a heliophanic hymn. The leader of the group would remind the three catechumens of the absolute fidelity to the Fuehrer they undertook on becoming Knights of the Sword, and adjure them to step down and withdraw if they did not feel themselves strong enough to die without question for the Third Reich. Finally he would hand them their swords in the glory of the first rays of the sun.

*

Perhaps the ceremony which thus grouped them together had something to do with it, but Hajo and Haro became inseparable from Lothar. Wherever he went, whatever he did, Lothar the nervous, the expansive, the indefatigable would be accompanied by the calm, taciturn, inclined-to-be-idle twins. At first the Jungmannen reacted against this triangle, which went against the rules of conduct implicit in any community. But the three newcomers met hints and mockery with such impertubable indifference that the attacks died away and the trio became an undisputed fact.

Tiffauges, who watched them fondly, soon saw that the twins *served* the boy with white hair with tacit and instinctive devotion. Without haste, but without hesitation and with a kind of infallible prescience, they always and everywhere provided an ideal frame to contain and comfort Lothar. At assemblies for saluting the colors or roll call, during mounted gymnastics, apparatus work in the gym, or practice firing with the Mauser HJ reduced to 6-mm., Hajo and Haro would always be there first, and Lothar, light, impetuous and hasty, would take his place between them.

One gray misty morning the director had the boys out in the quadrangle. In the pale light their red jerseys stood out vividly against the white sand. Tiffauges stopped in front of the trio, who were forming a pyramid, with Lothar standing on his hands, held up by Hajo on the right and Haro on the left. All the other Jungmannen were forming similar groups, but theirs seemed uneven and imperfect compared to the perfectly balanced, poised and symmetrical one made up by the white-haired boy with the mirror twins on either side.

"These three! I've noticed them before! Whatever they do they are always together, like the three swords of Kaltenborn!"

Tiffauges hadn't heard the commandant come up, leaning on his iron-tipped stick. He turned to greet him.

"Yes," went on the commandant, "they're so faultless you'd think they came out of some ancient armory!"

At a sign from the director, the middle boy of each group jumped to his feet and stood at attention between the other two.

"Don't these red shapes and white ground remind you of something, Tiffauges?" said the old man, pursuing his own thought. "What would you say if I made you a knight attached to my house, with a coat of arms alluding to mine, in the traditional way: for example, argent, with three pages gules erect on pales?" He laughed. "It *was* you, wasn't it, who recruited these boys?"

The jest came so close to Tiffauges's own preoccupations that he came gradually nearer the commandant, looking at him questioningly, without thinking his attitude might be interpreted as threatening.

"You notice," continued the old man imperturbably, "that though heraldry makes much use of plants and especially of

animals, it very rarely uses the human figure. Why? I've wondered about it. True, Prussian arms include a shield upheld
by two savage men with clubs resting on the ground. And you
sometimes find a Moor's head, or fabulous creatures half animal,
half human—centaurs, sphinxes, sirens, harpies. But as far as
I know, no man, woman or child, or very rarely."

He had turned and was picking his way slowly back toward
the castle. Suddenly he stopped.

"I say, I've just had an idea. Don't you think the inclusion
of a living creature in a coat of arms is implicitly associated
with the idea of *sacrifice?* If you go back to the beginning, a
totem animal is an animal possessed, killed and eaten: that's
how its virtues are transmitted to the bearer of the emblem.
And now please tell me what is the best-known and most sacred
of human emblems? Christ on the cross—symbol par excellence
of the supreme holocaust! So to allude in one's arms to the
ritual sacrifice of an eagle or lion, or the slaying of a monster
like a dragon or the Minotaur, or the mastering of a black slave
or a savage man—all that is only to be expected. But it's better
still to have a warrior, a woman, and above all a child! Do you
see, my poor Tiffauges? With my three pages gules erect on pales
I was going to give you the armorial bearings of an ogre!" And
the commandant laughed.

*

S.W.   Riding back from Ebenrode, I came up to a boy on a
         bicycle.

I reined in Bluebeard and went at an easy trot so as not
to overtake him. What was happening? A bicycle is something with height and length but no thickness. The body
riding it is reduced to a silhouette in which all the lines are
sharpened. It is clarified, purified, reduced to a diagram.
A low relief, a medal. It has only one leg, and we see its
inner side in a mirror. The foot doesn't touch the ground
but is carried along in a perfect circular movement in which

it is joined by the calf, the knee and the long thigh, and which dies away in the touching oscillations of the little hindquarters on the saddle. The play of the muscles is quite visible and as regular and monotonous as in an animated anatomical drawing. The immobile torso, with its shoulders hunched up by the ears, suggests an attitude of scorn or fear.

At the entrance to the village of Ohldorf my little cyclist stopped, propped his bike up on its stand, and walked off. The spell was broken. The third dimension took possession of him again. The irregular motion of walking spoiled his lines. The boy who before had seemed so admirable that I was already hatching plans about him descended to the level of the ordinary when he got off his bicycle. He was still not to be despised, admittedly, but not worth a special effort.

What had happened? The bicycle, though it has no power over adults, acts like a deciphering grid on the body of a child, isolating its essence and beginning to elucidate it. This is a dual illustration of certain somewhat obscure sayings of the commandant. First of all because the bicycle experience brings out the child's *heraldic vocation,* a formidable one if it is to be fulfilled in sacrifice. And secondly because I understand better now the difference between the *key,* which gives us only a particular sense of the essence, and the *grid,* which takes total possession of it and offers it, illuminated, to our intuition. The difference is of a phoric order, because the key is carried by its essence, as an ordinary key by its lock, while it is the grid that carries *its* essence, as the glowing bars of iron carry the body of the martyr. What I still have to understand is the transition from key to grid which the commandant described as the malign inversion changing cross-bearer to crucified.

The old man certainly knows more than he says. It's up to me to take advantage of the familiarity he allows me to make him tell all at the first opportunity.

*

Tiffauges didn't have the chance to question the commandant. After the attempt on Hitler's life on July 20 an unprecedented wave of arrests and executions swept Germany, and
especially East Prussia, where the assassination attempt was
made. The police terror struck blindly not only at the conspirators but also at their families, friends and even most distant
connections. The Gestapo reports came back again and again to
the greatest names of the Prussian aristocracy: Yorck, Moltke,
Wiltzleben, Schulenburg, Schwerin, Stuelpnagel, Dohna, Lehn-
dorff . . .

One morning a car with a sheathed flag stopped outside the
door of the castle. Two men in civilian clothing got out. They
had a secret interview with General Count von Kaltenborn.
Then they came out and went and waited on the glacis. An
hour later, at about eleven, the boys who happened to be there
were surprised to see their commandant come out in full uniform. He walked with a rapid, automatic step, staring in front
of him. He went along the central path without answering
anyone's salute, got into the waiting car with its drawn curtains,
and disappeared in the direction of Schlangenfliess.

Tiffauges was deeply upset by the departure of the only man
in whom he had confided. The commandant's speculations, the
atmosphere he emanated of past greatness, and the way he had
encouraged the Frenchman to think and reflect, had helped to
raise Tiffauges above his appetites. Once the old man had gone,
Tiffauges gave himself up to his instinct for power, sometimes
with farfetched subtleties, as shown in his "Sinister Writings."
The deterioration of the situation also gave him more and more
freedom. Hitler's proclamation on September 26 of the *Volks-
sturm,* the mobilization of old men, women and children in an
attempt to stave off defeat, marked a new phase in Tiffauges's
rise. Raufeisen, who had resigned himself to the departure of
the commandant, now saw his officers, non-commissioned officers, men and civilian staff taken away from him one after the
other. He was furious at being left with nothing but what he

called a "kindergarten." But he was determined that the Jungmannen should at least be trained and armed for the final test.
He made frequent trips to Koenigsberg, and talked of approaching Himmler's staff at Possessern, thus leaving Tiffauges with
carte blanche to run daily life at the Napola as best he could.

*

S.W.   For the last three days, in a basement room, the barber from Ebenrode and his apprentice have been laying waste
the manes of the miniature men with the aid of great electric
clippers which I'd have thought were only for horses. It's true
the barber and his assistant hadn't come for five months, and
the boys had to part their hair with their hands to see where
they were going and even to eat. I was largely responsible for
this negligence, for the thought of this rough collective shearing gave me a pang. Then I resigned myself to the inevitable,
and lo and behold, I see how I can turn it to account.

I observe first of all that hair may be beautiful in itself,
but that in its relation to the face it always plays a *negative*
role: it weakens the expression, blurs the features, takes
away the definition of the whole face. It follows that it has a
beneficial effect on ugly faces, which look better when they
have plenty of hair on top than when exposed naked. And
since ugliness is the general rule, hair is generally preferable
to baldness. But a really beautiful face has everything to gain
from not being stifled by hair. As the boys came up from
the basement, amusing themselves by hitting one another
over the newly razed nape, I was taken aback by the almost
violent revelation of the beauty of their faces. It was a bare,
stripped beauty, clean and sculptural, with something of the
sword and something of the marble mask. And when the mask
is warmed and animated by laughter, how speaking, how
communicative it is!

Seeing all this, I went down to assist at the metamorphosis.
I stood and watched for a long time as the clippers made pale

trenches through the hair from nape to brow. The scalp revealed its secrets, its irregularities, its scars, and above all the way the hair grows. The silky locks fell in a scented harvest on the floor, which the barber, when he had finished, carelessly swept into a corner. I at once gave orders for all that wild gold to be kept. It can be put into as many sacks as necessary. I don't know yet what I shall do with it.

*

S.W.   As I watched the shearing of the boys I noticed that hair usually grows in a spiral from a center situated exactly at the top of the occiput. From that point it spreads in a centrifugal vortex over the rest of the skull. The "tuft" people have is formed by the hair at the center of the spiral, the only hair not caught up in the general revolution.

I remembered the hide of the deer brought back by the Jungmannen last week and laid out on a table in the refectory. In the oblique light you could clearly distinguish different zones of hair going in different directions. They too were in the form of vortices, either centrifugal or centripetal. Elsewhere there were large patches that might meet along a ridge where the adjacent hairs went in opposite directions, or where they might shrink away from one another, leaving a bare parting. I also remembered Dr. Blaettchen saying a man has just as many hairs as a bear or a dog but that, except for certain parts of the body, they are so small and colorless they can be seen only through a magnifying glass. It seemed to me then that it would be interesting to study the geography of the boys' hair and to compare various examples.

I therefore chose the three who seemed most downy, most spangled with gold and silver in a slanting ray of sunlight. I summoned them in turn to the laboratory and examined them inch by inch through a magnifying glass, placing them between myself and the window.

The results were interesting but did not differ from one

individual to the other. Once again the Jungmann emerges as an incredibly homogeneous and undifferentiated species.

The hair on the body as a whole grows in whorls that belong to one of two categories: divergent vortices at the inner corner of the eye, under the armpit, in the fold of the groin, on the inner side of the buttocks, on the back of the hand and instep, and of course at the back of the head; and convergent vortices under the angle of the jaw, on the olecranon, in the navel, and at the base of the sex organs. There is a parting down the sides joining the vortex of the armpit to that of the groin; from this parting the hairs diverge. But down the front and the back of the trunk, along the spine and the sternum, the hairs converge and collide to form a sort of elongated "tuft."

In most cases this geography can be detected only slowly, under a glass, and in a suitable light. But you can get to know it immediately—and how much more touchingly!—by brushing your lips rapidly over the skin. The down then reveals the direction it grows in by the smoothness or resistance of its caress.

*

S.W.   I've shed so many tears over my huge clumsy hands, it's only fair to give them their due when they deserve it. I was wrong to dream of furtive nimble fingers like those of a conjuror, skillful at slipping into the opening of a blouse or a pair of shorts. My big hands may be incapable of that kind of touch, but they have their own talent. It didn't take them long to learn how to handle the pigeons of the Rhine with consummate agility: their vocation was so evident that even a strange pigeon felt no instinct to flee when they were held out toward it.

As for boys, the way I can handle them is simply wonderful! Anyone who watched me at it would see nothing but roughness and carelessness. But the boy knows better. At

the very first touch he knows that under this apparent roughness is hidden a great and tender skill. With boys, even my
surliest gestures are secretly lined with gentleness. My supernatural destiny has given me an innate knowledge of a child's
weight, balance, centers of gravity, all his articulations and
inflections, all the quiverings of his muscles and all the touching hardness of his bones. The mother cat grabs the kitten
by the scruff of the neck and the kitten purrs with pleasure.
What looks like roughness covers an intimate maternal
understanding.

The first thing I do with a new boy is put my hand on his
neck, a little below the nape. This essential root, fragile or
muscular, curly or smooth, flexed or yielding, is the key to
both the head and the body. It tells me straight away what
resistance or submission to expect. The gesture doesn't com-
mit me to anything and can be withdrawn without trace. But
it can also develop, quite naturally, take possession of the
back, spread to the shoulders, and descend to the loins, point
of equilibrium for raising from the earth, lifting, carrying.

My hands are made for carrying, lifting, bearing off. Out of
the two classic positions, prone and supine, only the supine
suits them. It is their habitual position—palms open to the
sky, fingers together out straight. Lying prone makes them
uncomfortable—gives them cramps, in fact. Phoric hands, indeed! And it's not only the hands but the whole body, from
my inordinate height, my porter's back, my Herculean
strength—all things that correspond to the small light bodies
of children. My bigness and their littleness are two elements
perfectly adapted to one another by nature. All of it is pre-
ordained, willed, prepared from all eternity; and so, venerable, adorable.

*

S.W.   There had to be some ritual to manifest complete
enumeration, the exhausting of the category of which the

citadel is a supreme example. This is the sole object of the
roll calls I preside over when the director is away, in the evening in the closed courtyard. I hold them because of my dual
need, of rigor and of chance.

The boys play in the courtyard, which is overlooked by
the terrace with the three swords. I wait thoughtfully in the
chapel; the stained-glass windows filter the last rays of the
setting sun. I let myself be lulled by the symphony of cries,
shouts and exclamations rising toward me like aural incense
and taking me back, through my experiences at Neuilly, to
St. Christopher's. True, the East Prussian voices have a
raucousness, an edge the French ones didn't have, but they
also have the purity of essence that is what Germany held in
store for me, and my reason for being here.

When the time comes, I walk across the terrace, caught
up in the ceremonial. As soon as I appear between Hermann and Wiprecht, the tumult suddenly dies away; when I
put my hand on the point of Hermann, the boys fall into line.
They make forty lines with ten in each, forming a dense rectangle just contained within the limits of the courtyard. It
takes months of merciless drilling to train them to fall in like
that at the bat of an eyelid, and in such flawless order I'd suspect they aligned themselves on the flagstones if I couldn't
see all the four hundred faces unwaveringly turned toward
me, reflecting four hundred times the look with which I em-
brace them all. Then with a wave of the hand I shatter the
silence built in so masterly a fashion by the discipline of my
little soldiers, and release the anthem of East Prussia:

"Lances in one hand, the reins of our stallions in the other,
we, children of the west, ride toward the east to finish the task
of the Teutons.

"The storm howls, the rain drives, the horses flinch. But we
ride on, as knights and peasants did of old, toward the land
of our faith.

"We gallop through the dust, we pass like lightning, our gaze fixed on the east, on the towers of Kaltenborn, keeping constant vigil over the horizon.

"We have forged anew the blade and the sword eaten by rust. Sword in hand, blade in earth, tomorrow the sun rises for us." [13]

The youthful voices rise toward me, metallic, sharp. They pierce me with a painful joy. I feel a pang. For there is blood and death in the irresistible swell of their song. Then comes the lovely long litany of the roll call. This rite involves only Christian names and places of origin, and I have introduced an element of novelty that makes it different every time, leaving to chance the coupling of call and reply. For places in the rectangular formation are not fixed in advance: each is occupied by a different Jungmann every evening. The roll call proceeds as follows: the first on the left of the last rank calls the Christian name and place of origin of his neighbor on the right. The latter answers "Present!" and calls out the name and place of origin of *his* right-hand neighbor, and so on up to the last on the right of the first rank, whose reply brings the operation to an end.

Needless to say, a roll call organized like this does not fulfill the usual function of showing who is missing. In fact, what I want it to do is the opposite: I want it to be a full, entire, circular demonstration of four hundred individuals shut up between narrow walls and absolutely at my disposal. There is no sweeter music to me than those evocative names, uttered by voices always new, each in turn visited by the name belonging to it. Ottmar from Johannisburg, Ulrich from Dirntal, Armin from Koenigsberg, Iring from Marienburg, Wolfram from Prussian Eylau, Juergen from Tilsit, Gero from Labiau, Lothar from Baerenwinkel, Gerhard from Hohensalzburg, Adalbert from Heimfelden, Holger from Nordenburg, Ortwin from Hohenstein . . . It hurts me to have to interrupt this census of my riches, each linking the weight of a body to the smell of a corner of Prussian earth.

The roll call is followed by a minute's silence. Then, as one, the four hundred boys swing around to face east, like me, and all I can see of them is a field of golden tufts and stubble, the hair I have now entered into possession of and for which I must invent a fit mode of celebration. And once again the chorus builds up its hard, brilliant pyramid of sound. They sing of the great eastern plain that draws their souls toward it:

"Raise the standards in the east wind,
For the east wind fills them and bears them up.
Sound the order to march, and let our blood hear the signal,
And the earth with a German face will answer us. So many
have impregnated it with their blood it cannot remain silent.
Raise the standards in the east wind, and let the sound of
them signal new departures!
Let us be strong—no ordeal is spared him who builds in
the east.
Raise the standards in the east wind, for the east wind makes
them greater. . . .[14]

*

S.W.   This morning I stopped in Birkenmuehle, where I'd been told there was a Frau Dorn, a carder by trade, who had a loom on which she would make up pieces of cloth for anyone who supplied his own wool. The war has reduced economic life to such a primitive level that now only people who keep sheep can expect to have any clothes! I haven't any sheep, but I have my young men, and the idea occurred to me of having a cape or a sort of jacket made out of their hair. It would be my golden fleece, a mantle of love and ceremony both, satisfying my passion within and manifesting my power without. I smiled with pity thinking of the bashful lovers who wear a locket containing one lock of their beloved's hair!

Frau Dorn, a great horse of a woman, all legs, arms and nose, showed the greatest mistrust at seeing a rider in un-recognizable uniform stop outside her door. All the time I was talking to her about her weaving, she maintained a hostile silence. Most likely it's regarded as a reprehensible activity—for a long time everything that's not compulsory has been forbidden here! To convey the basis on which I wished to conduct the matter, I brought a bag from under my over-coat and took out a haunch of venison that I laid on her kitchen table. She seemed slightly reassured. Then I brought out the sack, which I had so far kept behind me, and showed her the boys' hair. I explained I had a lot of it and that I wanted her to weave it. Her reaction was violent and in-comprehensible. She suddenly started to tremble and shrank away, repeating, "No, no, no," and making gestures as if to repel the venison, the sack of hair, and me. Finally she dis-appeared though a little back door, and I could hear her heavy footsteps running away through the vegetable gardens.

I wonder what frightened her so much about my sack of hair? I came out again as well off as I went in, with my haunch of venison and my potential golden fleece. I fear it's going to remain potential for some time to come!

*

S.W.   I've had all the hair used to stuff a mattress, an eider-down and a pillow. That idiot Frau Netta wanted me to have it washed first!

I had an extraordinary night wrapped in all that wool, softer but no less musky than that from a lamb's first shearing. Of course I didn't get a wink of sleep. The smell of boys' suint went straight to my head and put me in a state of happy intoxication. Joy, tears, tears of joy! At about two in the morning I could no longer bear the absurd cloth coverings. I slit open the mattress, eiderdown and pillow and emptied them into Blaettchen's fishpool. It had been empty since he left, but now it found its real raison d'être. Then I plunged right into this new kind of nest, as before I had plunged into my down-filled pigeon loft. They were all there, my adored ones; I recognized them one by one as I pressed handfuls of hair to my face. I recognized Hinnerk by his smell of new-mown hay, Armin by the blue gleams of his tufts, Ortwil by the ash-blondness that is his alone, Iring by the impalpable fineness of his curls—cherub's curls, Haro by the ferruginous smell of that hair yellow and tough as brass, and Baldur, and Lothar, and all the rest. Then I mixed, stirred and kneaded them, and caught them all up in armfuls. I was shaken with convulsive sobs and wondered—as I wonder still—if my reason wasn't beginning to go in the stress of this excessive emotion.

I'm like a natural, inveterate, atavistic but so far uncon-scious alcoholic, who's never drunk anything before but some mild little watered-down cider, and who's suddenly given as much 70 proof rotgut as he can swallow.

After my sleepless night I got up this morning and roared.

*

S.W.   They were rushing about the closed courtyard, filling it with their games and their cries. A sudden scrimmage sent one of the little ones flying up against me, and by a phoric reflex I gathered him up on the wing. My two big hands clasped the sturdy round head in which only the hazel eyes moved, looking right and left for escape. I bent over this mir-ror of the soul, clear and deep as a lake. I was a buzzard hov-ering immensely high, but drawn dizzily down by a sheet of water. The mouth opened, cool as a little shellfish.

It was then I noticed deep red cracks in the lips, separated by little islands of dry skin.

"Do your lips hurt?" I asked.

"Yes, sir."

"What about your friends? Do theirs hurt too?"

"I don't know."

"Go and see!"

Free again, but completely bewildered by my strange command, he disappeared into the crowd like a fish released into a fishpond. But a minute later he reappeared with another Jungmann in tow, so like him they must be brothers. The mouth of the second boy was just one big sore: some of the cracks were even oozing serous fluid.

That evening I went to the chemist's in Arys and got a pot of sweet-almond oil and cocoa butter, and after dinner the refectory became the theater of a strange and moving liturgy. The boys filed past me in procession, and I anointed them. . . . Each one stopped in front of me and proffered his mouth. My left hand rose, the forefinger and middle finger held together in regal benediction. Soon it didn't even have to move, my Left, my Sinister, my Genial, my Episcopal Hand: it was they who leaned toward it, taking from it a little of the holy chrism as an evening viaticum, like suppliants kissing the wonder-working statue of their patron saint. There were even some—only a few, just the right number!—who were heresiarchs, who drew back their heads or turned away in refusal.

What marvelous ambiguity, by which, in phoria, you possess and master inasmuch as you deny yourself and serve!

*

S.W.   It occurred to me that the shower room might provide a special opportunity for creating that density of atmosphere that has always seemed to me the antithesis and complement of phoria. It's a big room about forty feet by twenty with a cloakroom adjoining. The paved floor has runnels in it to drain away the water, and the ceiling bristles with sixty showers controlled from the cloakroom. The hot water comes from a boiler with a tank that holds five thousand liters. A mixer makes it possible to have either hot or cold water separately or a mixture of the two.

The boys used to go into the showers by group, but now, to save hot water, they'll all go together. Before, in a spirit of manly comradeship, an officer or non-commissioned officer used to share in their ablutions. From now on they will be accompanied only by me.

As we use wood now instead of coal, the fire has to be kept stoked all night in order to heat the water to forty degrees. I went down five times to stoke the boiler, obsessed by the memory of Nestor: his death from asphyxia in the boiler room at St. Christopher's haunted my ardent vigil. It had been arranged that the boys would be sent to the showers at eight o'clock, before breakfast. I was lying naked under a burning spray, already gasping and blind, when the music of their clear voices and the patter of their bare feet on the stone filled the staircase. Then came joyful commotion; scrimmages and laughter under the furious drizzle; hot clouds of shifting steam enveloping everything in pearly shadow. Bodies merged into and emerged out of it suddenly, as in a dream, only to vanish again. All these children were being boiled in a giant cauldron before being eaten, but I had thrown myself in through love and was cooking with them. Trampled on over and over again, crushed by the weight of the wet bodies falling on me, I met an old acquaintance I'd forgotten for years, since war was declared, to be exact—the angelic. But a braised angelic, and one that had thereby changed its sign. It was no longer an oppression, a difficulty in breathing that plunged me into depths of anguish, but a glorious assumption on eddies of immaculate cloud, which would have been insipid and vaguely religiose had it not been for my swelling heart thudding against my ribs—a dramatic tomtom imposing a rhythm on the pomp of my apotheosis. I thought of the resurrection of the body promised by religion, but of a flesh transfigured, at the highest degree of its freshness and youth. And I spread out all my brown, defiled, adult's skin, I offered my scored and swarthy face to the jets of boiling vapor; I buried my black and ravaged countenance in that wheaten flour; I offered it to those powder puffs of living flesh, to cure it of its ugliness.

*

S.W.   As the nights are getting colder and we can't use the central heating for lack of coal, we've had to abandon the little dormitories of eight beds and turn the great knights' chamber into a general dormitory, heated with iron stoves. The boys welcomed the change—they think it holds out the possibility of large-scale horsing around. As for me, I see it as an opportunity to set against my intent and anguished solitude a great nocturnal communion full of sighs, dreams, terrors and abandon.

The boys took it upon themselves to push the cots up one against the other, thus forming a sort of raised floor, a white padded causeway which I gave myself the pleasure of running about on barefoot in all directions. It's more a hypnodrome than a dormitory in the traditional sense.

*

The hypnodrome has been marvelous. The great frolic that the boys hoped for has unfolded its wonders. It was terrific! A wild chase all over the great elastic plain paved with little white beds. Whirlwinds of eiderdowns and pillows laying low swathes of warriors who fell shouting with glee; fierce pursuits ending up under the beds; furious assaults on a soft fortress of heaped-up mattresses; and all in a hothouse stuffiness, saturated with animal warmth, with thick curtains covering all the windows.

I watched operations from a corner where I'd succeeded in making myself forgotten. I knew the boys had been dig-

ging anti-tank trenches all day and were using up the last of
their strength. Some had already fallen asleep where they lay
in ambush. The tension had already begun to slacken when
I brought the revels to a stop by switching off, all at once, the
seventy-five lamps that lighted the room. At once seventy-
five little nightlights created that blue and trembling dormitory atmosphere more anesthetic than darkness itself. The
hubbub died away quickly, despite the few last-ditchers who
were keeping up rear-guard actions. It was then I felt my
own eyelids growing heavy. I hadn't foreseen that I, the nocturnal, the insomniac, the nightwalker, would be one of the
first to fall asleep, sitting on the edge of a bed with my back
propped against a wall. Perhaps that was the best and most
instructive surprise of the whole evening. Perhaps the reason I usually sleep so badly is because I was born to sleep
always with four hundred children.

But there must have been someone inside me as well
who thought I wasn't there just to sleep, for I woke all of a
sudden in the middle of the night—and, I should point out, as
fresh as a daisy. All those bodies strewn over the great lunar
plateau in every sort of position were a strange and striking
sight. There were groups gathered together as if by fear;
brotherly embraces; whole rows that looked as if they'd been
mowed down by one machine-gun volley; but the most touching of all were the ones on their own, those who had crawled
away in a corner to die alone, or whose last breath had cut
short a vain effort to be with others.

After the joyous tumult of the evening, this scene of
slaughter was a cruel reminder of that trick my fate keeps
suspended over me, which is called malign inversion. The
commandant's numerous warnings were always indirect and
emblematic, but tonight's lesson is frighteningly plain. All
the essences I've unveiled and brought to incandescence can
tomorrow, or even this very night, change signs and burn with

a fire the more infernal the more magnificently I exalted them
before.

But the sadness of these presentiments was so lofty and
majestic it easily merged into the solemn joy I felt as I contemplated my sleepers. I went from one to the other, winged
with tenderness, my feet scarcely touching the hypnodrome.
I noted each one's attitude, sometimes turning a sleeper over
to see his face, as one turns over a pebble on the beach to
uncover its damp and secret side. Farther on I lifted up, without separating them from one another's arms, the twins: their
heads rolled gently, sighing, one on to each of my shoulders.
My big, damp, flexible dolls—I shan't forget the peculiar quality of their dead weight! My hands, my arms, my back, and
each of my muscles all learned forever that quite incomparable specific gravity.

*

S.W.   Reflecting later on the lessons of that memorable
night, I saw that all the different positions adopted by the boys
in their sleep could be reduced to three main types.

First is the dorsal position, which turns the boy into a little
effigy piously arranged with feet together and face looking
heavenward—an attitude, it must be admitted, suggesting
death rather than repose. In contrast to this is the lateral position, with knees drawn up to the stomach and the whole body
curled up in the shape of an egg. This is the fetal posture,
the most frequent of the three, and a reminder of the time
before birth. In contrast again to both these attitudes, one
miming the hereafter and the other the heretofore, is the ventral position, the only one relating to the terrestrial present.
It alone confers importance—and capital importance—on the
surface or bed the sleeper rests on. The sleeper falls down
on this bed—ideally our earth—both to possess it and to ask
for its protection. It is the posture of the telluric lover who
impregnates the earth with his fleshly seed; and also the one

young recruits are taught in order to keep out of the way of bullets and shrapnel. In ventral sleep the head is placed laterally on one cheek, or rather on one ear, as if to auscultate the earth. Finally, for Blaettchen's sake, it may be noted that this position seems to be best adapted to long skulls. One even wonders whether the habit of putting babies down on their stomachs with their heads on one side does not, given the malleability of their skulls, tend to make them dolichocephalic.

*

S.W.   Yesterday I was looking at my Bluebeard, without saddle or bridle, just tied to a ring in the wall with a halter. Without any harness like that, he lets himself go: his head droops, his ears are like a mule's, his back is hollow, he's slack, sloppy, rawboned, broken-down. But as soon as you put a head-stall and a noseband on him, and throw a saddle over his back, he pulls himself together, frisks and paws the ground and lifts his head up with firm eye and pricked-up ears. . . . And in the same way I, sad and awkward, encumbered with my size and strength, legs limp and arms dangling, only become myself, smart and ready for anything, when I'm harnessed by the body of a child, girt by his legs, saddled by his trunk, with his arms for a collar and his laughter for a crown.

*

S.W.   Unlike grownups' buttocks, which are lumps of dead flesh, adipose reserves as sad as the humps of a camel, children's are alive, quivering, alert, one moment sunken and hollow, the next smiling and naïvely optimistic—as expressive as faces.

*

S.W.   Six o'clock, and already the first rays of the sun ignite the painted tiles of the eastern towers. Under its caress the four hundred penises in the hypnodrome lift their little blind heads, dreaming of a possible flowering, of a coming into the light, into the color, into the scent, into the capital branches of the phallophoric angel. But once this morning stir is over, they fall back into their torpor, doomed to darkness and abnegation, condemned to be thrown into the genital dungeons and only come alive for the obscure task of perpetuating the species. Unless . . . phoria, perhaps? Who knows whether this might not be the meaning of St. Christopher's great reward—that for having carried the child-God on his shoulders, his rod suddenly flowered and was laden with fruit?

*

S.W.   The honey secreted in their ears is as golden as bees', but tastes so quintessentially bitter it would repel anybody but me.

VI
The Astrophore

And it came to pass, that at midnight the Lord smote all the first-born in the land of Egypt. . . .

Exodus 12:29

The last fighting in East Prussia in 1944 was for the town of Goldap, about a hundred miles northeast of Kaltenborn. It was taken house by house on October 22 by the troops of the Third White Russian Army commanded by General Cherniakovsky, and recaptured on November 3 by a counteroffensive of General Decker's 29th Panzerkorps. From then until the new Soviet offensive launched on January 13, 1945, there was a lull, during which the civilian population was able to guess at the danger threatening it and evaluate the assurances of the Nazi government. Just to contemplate the possibility of the Red Army invading East Prussia was to be guilty of a criminal act of defeatism and treason. The long procession of refugees driven before the Russians—first White Russian peasants, then Lithuanians from the Memel district, and then the first Germans from East Prussia—were not to be taken by German civilians as a warning. People convicted of making preparations to depart were to be seen hanging from ropes in village squares and city parks. So in the areas abandoned by the Wehrmacht the Red Army took the civilian population completely by surprise. Russian soldiers reported that when they entered farms they found all the animals in the byres or stables, a fire burning in the grate and a pot of soup simmering on the stove. Along the few narrow roads, in the polar cold of winter, refugees of all nationalities fleeing to the west mixed in wild confusion with columns of the Wehrmacht making for the front or for the back areas.

Although for the most part Tiffauges was not affected by external events, he was twice a witness to this pitiful exodus. The first was just before Christmas 1944 on the road from Arys to Lyck. An army column was making its way slowly toward Lyck, and a line of refugees going in the other direction seemed to be paralyzed by the cold. A bottleneck must have formed toward Arys. It was as if the stoppage was dissolving the convoys: the men took advantage of it to check the harness and loads, and the children played about on the banks and in the woods near the road. Tiffauges passed them at a trot in the direction of Arys, and after about a mile came on the cause of the trouble in a group of soldiers and civilians gathered around two vehicles entangled with one another. An army wagon drawn by two horses had skidded on an icy slope and collided with a peasant's cart in such a way that the pole of the latter had been driven like a pike into the chest of one of the army horses. The dying animal had fallen to its knees, held up on the right by its teammate and on the left by the horse pulling the peasant's cart, both of which were rearing and shying to try to free themselves.

Tiffauges was deeply impressed by the sight of the exodus. He thought of the flight of the French in June 1940, an embarkation for Cythera in comparison. He repeated the line from the gospel: "Pray ye that your flight be not in the winter." The picture of the impaled horse engraved itself on his mind unforgettably: he suspected it contained a symbol, indecipherable alas, or better still a heraldic figure unknown but with some affinity with the Kaltenborn arms. But what he saw when the stream of refugees was able to move again bore no symbolic aura. It belonged simply to the most naked horror. It was a human corpse flattened into the frozen road, run over again and again by the treads of tanks, the tires of trucks, the wheels of carts, or just people's boots, till it was as thin as a rug, a rug roughly cut out in the shape of a human body, and in which one could just make out a profile, an eye and locks of hair.

A few days later, on the road from Loetzen to Rhein, Tiffauges had another encounter that affected him even more
deeply. He had seen them coming a long way off, all these prisoners, their heads swathed in scarves and forage caps, their feet
in strips of cloth or newspaper, dragging behind them on a string
a case of tin or cardboard fitted on little wooden sleds. There
were hundreds of them, perhaps a thousand, not silent and pre-
occupied like the other refugees but chatting and joking and
carrying bags stuffed with provisions. Tiffauges realized at once
who they were, but the first words of French still pierced him
like a thorn. He opened his mouth to greet them, to question
them, but something resembling shame left him tongue-tied. He
suddenly remembered, with a nostalgia that surprised him,
Ernest the driver, Mimile from Maubeuge, Phiphi from Pantin,
Socrates, and above all mad Victor. There was really nothing to
stop him from joining these men marching gaily toward France
and proposing to cover nearly two thousand miles of war-torn
country, in midwinter, in boots made of rags and paper. He
looked down at his own boots, the fine soft shiny black boots of
the lord of Kaltenborn, which he had waxed and polished with
his own hands that morning. The prisoners were going past him
now. They lowered their voices, taking him for a German, except for one little dark chap rather like Phiphi, who called out
as he went by:

"Fritz kaput! Sovietski everywhere, *überall!"*

The Parisian impudence even in this fleeting contact recalled
to Tiffauges the insurmountable distance that had always separated him—heavy, taciturn and melancholy—from the affable
race who were his companions. He turned Bluebeard, who had
shown his impatience by tossing his head and whinnying loudly,
and started to ride back to Kaltenborn. He soon forgot the encounter, for he now belonged to the Prussia crumbling all
around him. But all the way back to the castle he was haunted
by the image of the Erl-King, buried in the swamps and pro-

tected by a heavy layer of mud from all assaults, that of mar and those of time.

*

S.W.   Was in Gumbinnen this morning. Outside the shoe-maker's was a line of women and old men, each holding a piece of old tire. Inside they took their shoes off and waited while the cobbler nailed on the old rubber to make a new pair of soles for the dying shoes.

As my own power grows, I watch with anguish and delight the simultaneous disintegration of the German nation. The small children have been evacuated to the rear. The older ones are asked to be anti-aircraft assistants, so schools are closing down one after another. Only the post offices in the towns still function, and you have to go miles to mail a letter or a parcel. In the town halls some old man acts as mayor, deputy and clerk all at once, attending only to what is indispensable. This includes not only the distribution of ration cards and the announcement of deaths in action to next of kin, but also, at the Gauleiter's insistence, the celebration of marriages. The great Reich, even though it is crumbling, wants its descendants to be legitimate. There's not a doctor left for fifty miles around.

Sometimes you hear people complaining that life gets more and more complicated. The fact is that it gets simpler and simpler, but the simpler it becomes the harder and harsher it grows. The administrative, commercial and other networks of modern life were like little springs that absorbed the friction between men and things. More and more, now, people are confronted with crude reality.

This place touches me more and more deeply because it is collapsing. I see it falling naked at my feet, weak, exhausted, reduced to the greatest indigence. It's as if, as it falls, it suddenly shows its hitherto buried foundations in the light of day. It is like an overturned insect, waving its six legs in the air around its soft white exposed belly, suddenly deprived of the dark protective proximity of the earth. It's as if one could smell the odor of damp earth and living corruption that comes from the livid belly of the nation overthrown. Here lies the great defenseless body of Prussia, still warm and living, but with its tender vulnerable parts exposed beneath my boots. It had to be, in order that the country and its children might be subjected to my imperative tenderness.

*

Raufeisen disappeared for a week and returned one evening at the head of a convoy of Wehrmacht trucks, which unloaded into the courtyard three thousand Panzerfausts and twelve hundred anti-tank mines. The Panzerfausts, little individual rocket-throwers of great efficiency despite being light and simple, had turned up in the nick of time as an ideal weapon for isolated snipers against the tanks of the invader. The rocket exploded on impact, releasing a jet of burning gas and a charge of molten metal that traveled at a speed of several thousand yards a second and had a temperature of several thousand degrees. The metal shot through the hole in the target, wounding or killing the crew and igniting the vapors present inside the tank. But the Panzerfaust's range was only about eighty-five yards, and instructors insisted on the need for the person who fired it to get as close to his target as he dared. Sixteen yards was the ideal distance, they said, but it was also a heroic one, and to get as near as that to a heavy tank called for a sang-froid that was almost insensibility.

So Raufeisen, in the theoretical training given in a room in the castle with the aid of a blackboard, set about trying to domesticate the armored monster in the eyes of the boys.

"A tank is deaf and half blind," he would rap out. "You understand—it can't hear anything. The noise of the engine even prevents the crew from knowing what hit it, whether automatic weapons, artillery, or bombing from the air.

"And it can't see very well. The sighting mechanisms have
a very limited field and cannot cover their immediate vicinity
The unevenness of the tank's motion makes observation ever
more difficult. At night it is forced to travel with its turret and
flaps open.

"It cannot fire everywhere at once, nor in its own immediate
neighborhood. The blind areas, and the fact that it takes the
turret at least thirty seconds to perform a complete revolution
should enable a really resolute infantryman to attack withou
risk. The blind angle of its cannon varies from eight to twenty-
two yards and that of its automatic guns from six to eleven yard
according to the type of tank. Finally, it is impossible for a tank
to take exact aim when it is moving. To fire its cannon accurately
it has to stop, and that gives the infantryman his cue."

Then he listed the six vulnerable points at which the attacker
should aim: the tracks, the deck, the ventilation system, the
engine, the gorge of the turret, and the sighting mechanisms

As he spoke, the tank became for the boys a sort of fabulous
beast, of terrifying strength but slow, noisy, clumsy, myopic
and deaf, and they compared it with the red and black game
they were used to hunting. A tank was certainly a more dangerous quarry than a stag, but easier to approach and bring
down; in short, no more than a superior sort of wild boar. And
they laughed with pleasure to think of the exciting hunting parties in store for them.

Actual firing practice on the Panzerfaust, which was held on
the Eichendorf moor, with brick wall targets in the rough form
of tanks, brought them back to a somewhat ruder reality. The
explosion of the shot and the jet of flames that sprang at the
back of the firer's neck; the ululation of the rocket ricocheting
through the snow when it failed to explode after hitting the
ground at too sharp an angle; the impact, with its tongue of
flame scattering the bricks like confetti—all these quickly
showed the boys that they had been given a diabolical toy, and

that a new age was beginning for them. The first accident occurred two days later, and cost the life of one of the Jungmannen, Hellmut von Bibersee.

The Panzerfaust's firing charge, on the principle of the recoilless gun, was divided into two equal pressures, one acting forward to launch the rocket and the other backward, to be lost in the air. The chief danger for the firer and his "numbers" was this last tongue of fire shooting out from where one would least expect it. If, after leaving the barrel, it encountered too near an obstacle, it shot back deadly fragments at the firer. But it was the one who found himself behind the firer who was normally exposed to the greatest risk, for the flame was lethal for a distance of about three yards.

When Tiffauges heard that Hellmut had been completely decapitated by the rear flame of a Panzerfaust, and that his body was on a stretcher in the chapel, he went at once and stayed there alone for part of the night.

*

S.W.   It wasn't until the first glimmers of dawn that I could tear myself away from contemplating the thin body, outlined as if in India ink on its white sheet, a bony structure covered here and there with round masses of muscle, like mistletoe in the bare branches of a tree. But does this bizarre image sufficiently convey how there was nothing human left about that decapitated body? I mean by that, nothing left to link it to the bustle of adults. Hellmut von Bibersee was no longer Hellmut, and came from nowhere. He was the essence of being, fallen from the sky like a meteorite, and destined to merge into the earth. Death gave his flesh a fullness it had never known in life. The tendons, the nerves, the viscera, the blood vessels, all the secret machinery that warms and irrigates it had become one hard homogeneous mass, which was only form and weight. Even the thorax, raised as if by a deep breath, and the gentle valley of the abdomen, proclaimed plenitude and absolutely excluded any suggestion of respiration. My meditation, of course, revolved around the notion of weight—dead weight—and of the phoric act that was to crown my reverie.

I've always suspected the head of being just a little ball filled with mind (spiritus, wind), which lifts the body up and holds it vertical, and thereby relieves it of the greater part of its weight. By the head the body is spiritualized, disincarnated, shirked. But when the body is decapitated it falls to the ground, suddenly restored to terrific incarnation and endowed with incredible weight. The phenomenon of twins, which is accompanied by a dividing up of the mind and a proportionate increase in the weight of the flesh, had given me a relative instance of this; death now gave me an absolute example. Hence that apparent increase in plenitude, despite the inertia of the flaccid body, which had lost all that moved it.

I lifted up the small effigy in my arms, gazing at the horrible wound of the neck. In spite of my strength and the fact that I was expecting what happened, I staggered under my burden. I solemnly swear that headless body weighed three or four times its live weight.

As for the phoric ecstasy, it bore me up into a black heaven pulsating with the cannons of the Apocalypse.

*

S.W.   The middle of the night. They are all there, gathered in the hypnodrome, reduced to the most complete submission. What shall I do? I flit clumsily from one to another like a great velvety moth, not knowing how to vent my desire, the plaintive thirst that also concerns the heart. The moth flies on wings of love toward the electric light bulb. And when he gets there, close to it, as near as he can be to that which attracts him irresistibly, he doesn't know what to do. He doesn't know what to do with it. For indeed what can a moth do with an electric light bulb?

I keep pushing away a suspicion that haunts me so insistently I'm going to let it write itself down on this page in the secrecy of the night. Could it be that my vigil by Hellmut's body has given me forever a taste for a flesh more grave, more marmoreal than that which is snorting and snoring sweetly in the hypnodrome?

*

S.W.   One of the heaviest fatalities that hangs over me—or should I say one of the brightest benedictions?—is that I can't ask a question or form a wish without fate sooner or later taking it upon itself to provide an answer. And that answer often surprises me by its force, long accustomed though I am to such blows.

What am I to do with the children I've imprisoned in the retort of Kaltenborn? I know now why the absolute power of a tyrant always ends by driving him mad. It's because he doesn't know what to do with it. Nothing is harder to endure than the imbalance between infinite power and limited knowledge. Unless fate shatters the limits of an indigent imagination and takes by violence the vacillating will.

I've known since yesterday the atrocious and magnificent use to which my children are to be put.

Raufeisen hasn't relaxed his efforts to make Kaltenborn obey the Fuehrer's repeated instructions to resist to the death. Hellmut's death has caused no slackening in the Panzerfaust training. And every other group works according to a roster on the setting up of anti-tank minefields. They use flat Teller mines, which are comparatively safe to handle because they explode only under a weight of over eighty pounds. But each one weighs over thirty pounds itself, and it's a grueling test of the Jungmannen's strength and endurance to have to carry them from the trucks to the emplacements—the "inevitable tracks" of a hypothetical attack by enemy tanks. They are placed in quincunxes along a belt two or three hundred yards long, in such a way that three mines bar a strip two yards wide.

Without a qualm I'd been bringing the mines along in one of the army trucks which the Wehrmacht is letting us have for a few days more: it had five hundred Teller mines in it, enough to blow up a whole town. Two previous loads had already been distributed, and only about twenty boys were waiting for me this time. According to the rules, each man has to take one mine and one only and carry it on his own to a distance at least forty yards from the nearest of the others. I supervised the distribution, then followed the last of the boys, out of a mixture of idleness, curiosity and friendliness.

It was Arnim, of Ulm in Wurtemburg, one of those little Swabian peasants, short and strong-backed, with round heads and hard skulls redeemed, for the SS selectors, by light green eyes and golden hair. Blond Auvergnats, in short, and the more so as in the rest of Germany, like natives of the Auvergne in the rest of France, the Swabian has the reputation of being grasping, vindictive, plodding and dirty. But I like Arnim for his strength, concentrated mainly in his legs, which appear too sturdy for his weight and yet lend him a light, almost skipping gait, as if at every step they laugh at having so little ballast to carry.

But now he didn't have his usual elastic gait, Arnim from Ulm, for in his right hand he was hauling along the heavy disc of death, an ironclad pebble that made him lean to one side, his free arm stuck out horizontal to balance him. He was walking along taking small steps, and I went after him, vaguely thinking of helping him, instructions or no. After going about a hundred yards he stopped and changed hands, adjusting the piece of cloth wrapped around the sharp and slippery handle to make it easier to carry. Then he tottered off again, this time with his right arm stuck out. Then he stopped again and, seeing me, smiled and puffed out his cheeks to show he was tired. Finally he adopted a technique that was probably easier but quite different from anything we'd been taught about laying and taking up mines. He held it clasped to his stomach in both hands, his shoulders thrown slightly back. His two halts had brought me quite close to him, and I was only about ten yards away when the explosion occurred.

I didn't hear anything. I just saw a white flash where the boy had been, and immediately afterward a gust of red, a squall of gaseous blood, enfolded me and threw me to the ground. I must have lost consciousness for a bit, for I seem to remember having people around me and being carried away almost at once, which is scarcely possible. In the infirmary they were astonished to find me unharmed: of all the blood that covered me from head to foot, not one drop was mine. Arnim pulverized into a mist of red globules only left me bespattered.

This ferocious baptism, coming after my vigil by Hellmut, has turned me into a different person.

A great red sun suddenly rose before me, and that sun was a child.

A crimson hurricane threw me in the dust, like Saul on the road to Damascus, struck down by the light. And the hurricane was a boy.

A scarlet cyclone buried my face in the earth, as the majesty of ordinant grace pinned to the ground the young Levite. And the cyclone was a miniature man of Kaltenborn.

A mantle of purple weighed with unbearable weight on my shoulders, attesting my dignity as Erl-King. And the mantle was Arnim the Swabian.

*

S.W.   Though I'd long been perfectly fit, I malingered on, with no avowable reason, in the soothing hands of Frau Netta. On reflection, it's surprising I didn't venture sooner into this region of basements converted into an infirmary, where the sweet aggressive scent of ether throws me into strange transports. Flesh open and wounded is more flesh than flesh intact, and has its own garments, bandages, deciphering grids more eloquent than ordinary clothes. This atmosphere of mingled anguish and ecstasy took me back all at once to the infirmary at St. Christopher's, where I had to stay for a while after Pelsenaire made me wash his wounded knee with my own mouth.

Now, thank God, I'm strong enough and lucid enough to bear the whole truth about that unfortunate but vastly significant episode. It has taken me all these years to be able to get the admission out of what's most reserved and shy in myself. But let's be accurate and avoid any anachronism: when fever and convulsions felled me at Pelsenaire's feet it never occurred to me to analyze what was happening to me. I experienced the events of my life too immediately to try to explain them. And even if I had tried, all the many troubles that were weighing down on me would have been enough to account for my nervous collapse. But afterward came a longish rest in the infirmary, about a fortnight, which ought to have opened my eyes if a dim fear of learning too much about myself had not kept them obstinately closed.

So it's only now that I'm in a position to write down the truth about that crisis, and I do so in as few words as possible: what ravaged me when my lips encountered those of Pelsenaire's wound was nothing but an excess of joy, a joy of unbearable violence, a searing more fierce and deep than any before or since, which was pleasure. It was quite impossible for my virgin constitution, still closed on its own tenderness, to endure such a lightning stroke.

The days that followed in the infirmary were in fact only a repetition, toned down, diluted and, so to speak, made more tender, of that intolerable ordeal. The sickly ambiguous smell of ether, which stuck to everything and even got into the food, made me live in a sort of slight intoxication at once happy and uneasy. But what most of all warmed and illuminated those feverish hours was the attraction dressings exercised on me and the avid curiosity with which I followed the removal of first the bandage, then the wadding, then the gauze, to come at last, in the middle of the white puckered skin, upon the visage of the wound itself. A piece of sticking plaster held in place by a cross of adhesive tape excited me more than the most abundant swathings. As for the wound itself, its shape, depth, and even the stages of cicatrization fed my desire more richly and strangely than a mere naked body however appetizing! The stages of healing were marked by the scabs, sometimes scratched off to open a new wound oozing blood, sometimes falling by themselves to reveal a newborn skin, pink and translucent. Even the disinfectants lent the wound a provocative air of sophistication. Iodine made fantastic, henna-like designs on the milky hydrogen peroxide. But there was nothing to equal the glaring vermilion of a new product called mercurochrome, which was suspected of being useless because it was painless. Some wounds had the sober, stern rectitude of thin-lipped truthtelling mouths, but they were the exception. The majority were laughing, grimacing and made up like the chops of a whore.

*

S.W.   This morning the four hundred boys assembled in close formation on the glacis. They had just finished their workout and despite the cold wore only their black shorts: their bodies and legs were bare. Raufeisen, who was due at the command post at Johannisburg at eleven, was dressed up in uniform, cap, boots and monocle, and walked nervously to and fro with his stick under his arm. I could tell, just from seeing him decked out like a June bug in front of all that defenseless innocence, the ignoble feeling that had taken possession of him. He gave a brief order, and all the ranks fell forward like dominoes: there was a vast scattering of bodies arranged as neatly as swathes of wheat or hay after the reaper has passed. Then he advanced into their midst, not between the bodies but on them. His boots had the temerity to walk on that human carpet, crushing at random here a hand, there a buttock or a neck. He even stopped in the middle of the field of mown-down children and lit a cigar, legs straddled, stick stuck under his arm.

By diabolical instinct you have found precisely the recipe for the anti-phoric act par excellence, and for that, Stefan of Kiel, I give you notice of a cruel and imminent death!

*

They came from Revel and Pernau in Estonia, Riga and Libau in Latvia, and Memel and Kowno in Lithuania, and attracted less attention than the other refugees because they traveled mainly by night, under an SS escort who kept people well away. An old peasant woman who saw them pass in the moonlight in ghostly silence said that the dead from the cemeteries in the east had risen from their graves and were fleeing before the enemy, desecrator of churchyards. Other witnesses confirmed that their shaven skulls and faces were like those of skeletons, but said they moved like scarecrows inside striped pajamas, and that they were sometimes chained to one another. When one of them fell from exhaustion, the nearest guard came up and finished him off with a bullet in the back of the neck, so the secret exodus left no trace behind.

Tiffauges never met any of these columns from the death factories, mines, quarries, ghettos and concentration camps in the east, which had to be evacuated in haste before the Red Army. But one day when business had taken him as far north as Angerburg, he stopped Bluebeard and found a corpse hidden in the ditch under an old shepherd's cloak. It was the body of a being without sex or age, with no means of identification except a number tattooed on the left wrist and a yellow J on a red star of David sewn on the left front of the clothing. Tiffauges remounted but stopped again a couple of miles farther on by a heap of sacks leaning against a post. This time it was a child. It was wearing a cap made of three pieces of felt sewn together. It was breathing; it was still alive. Tiffauges shook it gently, trying to make it speak. In vain. It was deep in a torpor that seemed close to death. When Tiffauges lifted it up in his arms, it pierced his heart to feel how incredibly light it was, as if there were nothing inside the coarse wrappings from which the head emerged. He rode back at a walking pace toward Kaltenborn. The citadel was still a good twelve miles away; he would get there, he hoped, before sunrise.

An hour later the clear hyperborean night enveloped him in its twinklings and its mysteries. Bluebeard went at a peaceful, regular pace, and the ice on the road fractured into stars beneath the tranquil beat of his hoofs. This was not the wild ride that used to bring Tiffauges back to Kaltenborn after a successful hunt, clasping a fresh, blond quarry. He was not borne up by the usual phoric intoxication that issued in roars and wild laughter. Above him the great bestiary of the stars turned slowly in the circus of the sky about the pole star. The Great Bear and its Wain, the Giraffe and the Lynx, the Ram and the Dolphin, the Eagle and the Bull mingled with sacred and fabulous creatures like the Unicorn and the Virgin, Pegasus and the Twins. Tiffauges rode along with solemn slowness, feeling somehow that he was inaugurating an absolutely new era by performing his first astrophoria. Under Tiffauges's big cloak the child Star-Bearer sometimes moved its lips, to utter words in an unknown language.

Most of the roofs of the castle were covered with loosely fitted tiles that allowed a whole population of night birds to fly in and out. But in the corner of one attic there was a little garret where heating and drainpipes converged, and where it was possible, with the aid of a primus stove, to keep up a hothouse temperature. It was here Tiffauges installed his protégé, on a camp bed snatched up at random from the odds and ends in the lumber rooms. Then he went down to the kitchens and came back with a bowl of cream of wheat, which he tried without success to feed to the boy.

From then on his life was divided between his usual occupations inside and outside the castle and the padded, overheated cell where he tried desperately to bring Ephraim's broken body back to life. It was impossible to tell his age. He might have been anything between eight and fifteen, and his physical weakness contrasted with his intellectual precocity. In the infirmary Tiffauges found a cake of pyrethrum, and with it he gently washed Ephraim's head, which was covered with a nauseating cap of hair stuck together with scabs and lice. But what was most worrying was his dysentery, with its torturing colics that twisted the skeletal body, ejecting whitish, blood-streaked stools into the bowl Tiffauges put under him. Afterward he would keep on asking for something to drink, and if Tiffauges wasn't there he would drag himself over to the big brass tap, which was surrounded by the fire-fighting equipment, hoses, axes, sprinklers and buckets. Then he would fall into a sleep interrupted by nightmares and struggles against imaginary enemies. Tiffauges set up a little stove in his room on which he could prepare meat and vegetable broth for his patient.

He had to wait two days before the boy began to speak to him. He spoke in Yiddish mixed with words of Hebrew, Lithuanian and Polish: Tiffauges could understand only those of German origin. But they had unlimited time and inexhaustible patience for getting to understand one another, and when the boy turned toward him his thin scabby face with its huge dark eyes, Tiffauges listened with all his ears, with all his being, for he could see an edifice rising that reflected his own with terrifying fidelity, and reversed all its signs.

He discovered that under the Germany exalted and polarized by the war there lay a network of concentration camps forming a subterranean world with none but accidental connections with the superficial world of the living. Over all Wehrmacht-occupied Europe, but chiefly in Germany, Austria and Poland, nearly a thousand villages and hamlets made up an infernal map of its own that subtended the ordinary country and had its own centers and capitals, and also its own subprefectures, junctions and sorting offices. Schirmeck, Natzviller, Dachau, Neuengamme, Bergen-Belsen, Buchenwald, Oranienburg, Theresienstadt, Mauthausen, Stutthof, Lodz, Ravensbrueck . . . Ephraim spoke of these as familiar landmarks in the world of shadows which was the only one he knew. But none shone with such black brilliance as Oswiecim, twenty-five miles southeast of Katowice in Poland, which the Germans called Auschwitz. It was the Anus Mundi, the great metropolis of degradation, suffering and death on which convoys of victims converged from every corner of Europe. Ephraim had been so young when he went there it seemed to him he'd been born there; he appeared almost proud of having grown up in the depths of that abyss, which enjoyed a sort of funereal prestige among the people of the concentration camps. He and his parents had been arrested by the "Special Services" in 1941, soon after the Wehrmacht invaded Estonia, and sent directly to Auschwitz. All he could remember clearly of their arrival there in cattle trucks were the captive balloons that formed a string of sausages in the sky. SS men controlled the great herd of people with big sticks. Then came showers, head-shaving, disinfection; the children were delighted when everyone was told to dress again by taking clothes from a heap of odd rags.

"We played at dressing up as women. Some could only hop

because they'd taken two right or two left shoes. You'd have thought it was Purim!"[15]

Ephraim couldn't help giving a little cracked laugh as he described this farcical arrival. After that he was separated from his parents, whom he never saw again, and put in the blocks for children under sixteen, where there were even a few babies. An ex-teacher came to give them lessons, and he would never forget a question they were asked one day. They were asked, What would happen to you if the force of gravity ceased to operate? The answer was, We should all fly up to the moon. Ephraim had to laugh at the thought! Often the SS were nice to them. The children were allowed to keep their hair. They were given a ping-pong table, and even a parcel of clothes from Canada.

When Ephraim first uttered the word "Canada" Tiffauges realized that the great malign inversion had just been proclaimed. Canada had been a province of his own personal dream, the refuge of his Nestorian childhood and of the first months of his Prussian captivity. He asked for details.

"Canada?" said Ephraim, surprised at such ignorance. "It was the treasure house of Auschwitz. You see, the prisoners used to carry around with them whatever valuables they had left, precious stones, gold coins, jewels, watches. When they'd been gassed, their clothes, and whatever had been found in the pockets and the linings, were put in a special hut that was called Canada."

Tiffauges couldn't accept without a murmur this horrible metamorphosis of all that had been for him most intimate and happy.

"But *why* did you call those huts Canada?"

"Because for us Canada is wealth, happiness, freedom! I've always heard people say, 'If you want to be happy, emigrate to Canada. Your Great-uncle Jehuda owns a clothing factory in Toronto. He's rich and has lots of children.' I used to dream of going to Canada too. I found it at Oswiecim."

"What else was there?"

"Rooms full of clothes, others where there were only glasses, lorgnettes and even monocles. Or women's hair—it had to be at least eight inches long to be usable. In order to be able to recognize women who escaped they used to shave their heads in a thin strip down the middle of the head. They used to bring the hair by the truckful. I think they made it into felt, for over-shoes for the German soldiers in Russia."

Tiffauges could not hear this without seeing himself holding a sack of hair in one hand and offering Frau Dorn a haunch of venison with the other. He remembered how the tall clumsy creature backed away, making negative gestures with her head, her hands, her whole body. She must have heard about the hair at Auschwitz and thought she was being asked to take part in that vast and macabre manufacture.

Then Ephraim told about the agonizing roll calls that might last up to six hours, during which the prisoners had to stand motionless whatever the temperature. And Tiffauges recognized at once the diabolical inversion of his rite of total exhaustive-ness, which he used to carry out by the loving enumeration of all his children. After that the Dobermans of the concentration camp, trained to hunt and tear the prisoners to death, seemed almost a light touch, designed to finish off the monstrous anal-ogy, the *countersemblance* that was his personal hell. But the description of the gas chambers disguised as shower rooms was a revelation that completed his despair.

"In the end," went on Ephraim, "about twenty of us chil-dren formed a 'raiding party,' with a cart. We were the horse! We used to pull the cart all around the camp, galloping down the main paths. I was always the one who went in front and guided the cart to right or left with the pole. We used to carry linen, blankets, wood. Like that we could go all over the camp and see everything. I was present sometimes when they sorted people out. Once I gave a woman some rouge to put on her

cheeks so that she wouldn't look so ill. One day in winter a corporal let us go into the gas chambers to get warm. They were
fixed to look like shower rooms. They made the people who
were going to die get undressed and told them to remember
where they put their clothes so as to be able to find them again.
They even handed out towels. Then they pushed as many men
and women as possible into the room. In the end the kapos had
to shove the doors shut with their shoulders, and they threw
the children in on top of the others. The sprinklers of the showers were imitation: I saw they didn't really have holes in them,
they were only made to look as if they had. When the doors
were opened after the gassing, you could see that the stronger
ones had trampled on the others to escape the vapors that came
up from the floor. The dead formed a heap reaching up to the
ceiling, with the children and the women at the bottom and the
least feeble men on top."

In spite of the possibilities offered by his age and his raiding
party, Ephraim hadn't actually seen everything that went on in
the huge metropolis of death. But he had ears to hear, and rumors spread fast in the camp. He knew of the existence of B
section, where Dr. Mengele conducted medical experiments on
the prisoners. Mengele, he told Tiffauges, was passionately interested in the phenomenon of twins and watched the arrival of
fresh batches of prisoners in order to select for his own use any
pairs of twin brothers or sisters among them. It was of major
importance to be able to make a simultaneous autopsy of dead
twins, and chance alone practically never offered the opportunity. The hand of Dr. Mengele remedied the deficiency of
chance. It was also said that experiments were carried out at
Auschwitz putting prisoners to death in a vacuum, in order to
find remedies for the physiological effects of accidental depres-
surization in planes flying at high altitude. The human guinea
pig was put in a chamber from which all air could be instanta-
neously withdrawn, and through a window blood could be seen

pouring from the victim's nose and ears, while he slowly clawed the flesh off the bones of his face.

Thus, through Ephraim's long confessions, Tiffauges, steeped in horror, saw an infernal city remorselessly building up which corresponded stone by stone to the phoric city he himself had dreamed of at Kaltenborn. Canada, the weaving of the hair, the roll calls, the Dobermans, the researches into the phenomena of twins and atmospheric densities, and above all, above all, the mock shower rooms—all his inventions, all his discoveries were reflected in the horrible mirror, inverted and raised to hellish incandescence. He still had to learn that the two peoples the SS persecuted and whose extinction they were working for were the Jews and the gypsies. Here he encountered once more the immemorial hatred of the sedentary races for the nomads, now carried to its paroxysm. Jews and gypsies, wanderers, sons of Abel, the brothers he felt so close to in heart and soul, were falling in thousands at Auschwitz beneath the blows of a Cain who was booted, helmeted, and scientifically organized. The Tiffaugean deduction of the death camps had been achieved.

While Auschwitz was the terminus of death for most of the prisoners who crossed its threshold, over which was written the heavily ironic slogan, "Work is freedom," for others it was a junction from which they were sent to other camps, or to mines or factories, by an administration that wanted both to destroy and to get the maximum amount of work out of them. In the spring of 1944 Ephraim set out with a small convoy for his native Lithuania; their destination was the camp at Kaunas. But they did not stay there long, for in August the camp was evacuated before the approaching Russian army, and there was a new exodus to the southwest, this time on foot. The pitiful band wandered from one temporary camp to another, finally crossing the province of Angerburg. It was here that Tiffauges had taken Ephraim in.

*

The Nazi authorities tried to stave off as long as possible a measure that was bound to be interpreted in East Prussia as sinisterly symbolic. This was the transfer to western Germany of the ashes of Field Marshal Hindenburg, reposing in the Tannenberg mausoleum among the standards of the Prussian regiments he had commanded. But it was done in January 1945, when, after a lull of two and a half months, the Russians launched a vast offensive against the German lines. On January 13, when a cold wave had made lakes and marshes negotiable by armored vehicles, two brigades of heavy tanks supported by three hundred and fifty artillery batteries broke through the German defenses between Gumbinnen and Ebenrode, followed up by thirteen infantry divisions. The forest of Rominten was invested and the hunting lodges burned down. When wild-eyed horses were seen galloping with flying manes over snowy fields and frozen lakes, branded on the right quarter with a stylized elk's antler, everyone in the countryside knew that the imperial stud at Trakehnen was no more. On the twenty-seventh, with the Russians at the gates of Koenigsberg, German engineers blew up the bunkers and installations of Hitler's Wolf's Lair at Rastenburg. It was said that at Varzin the old Baroness von Bismarck, daughter-in-law of the Iron Chancellor, had obstinately refused to leave the castle and lands given by the Kaiser in 1866 to the victor of Sadowa. She stayed on alone with one old servant, asking only that the others dig her grave before they went. And she waited there, frail and intrepid, with her white braids and her lorgnette, for the red tide she knew she would not survive.

But the Russian advance consisted of thrusts exploited to the utmost, and sometimes covering hundreds of miles, rather than of one continuous line sweeping forward across the country. Countless islands of resistance remained in the victor's rear, and held out there all the longer because of Hitler's continued orders to fight to the death and refuse all surrender. The North

Army Group, for instance, stationed in Lithuania, cut off from East Prussia since the beginning of October 1944, and only supplied by sea through the port of Libau, stood out until the armistice. The fortress of Koenigsberg itself did not surrender until April 10, and at the general capitulation of the Wehrmacht on May 8 there were still large pockets of resistance in such areas as the Hela Peninsula and the east coast of Danzig.

The role of the Napolas in these apocalyptic days had been already fixed by their chief, SS Major General Heissmeyer, in a circular dated October 2, 1944. This said that the Napolas, almost all in isolated situations in open country, must not count on the protection of the army if the enemy came, and all necessary measures must therefore be taken to turn them into independent nests of resistance.[16] It seemed quite natural that the commandant of Koenigsberg should send a unit of boys into action, hampered by helmets that fell over their eyes every time they fired a shot, and issued before the attack with sweets and chocolate instead of cigarettes.[17]

During the night of January 22-23 a great glow lit up the horizon visible from the eastern terrace at Kaltenborn. It was the town of Lyck burning. For the next couple of days and nights troops streamed in disorder past the walls of Kaltenborn. Old M 2 tanks from the beginning of the war towed along four or five trucks, overflowing with wounded, which tried to help with their exhausted engines and skidded in the icy ruts. Motorcycles with sidecars that had served in the campaign in France; buses stripped of their bodies; covered carts drawn by horses shaggy as bears who tossed their heads and breathed out a double jet of steam at each step; single foot soldiers pushing their gear along in baby carriages—all streamed by in an inexorable crescendo of disintegration. Raufeisen thought it best to confine the Jungmannen within the citadel to spare them the spectacle of the wreck of the Wehrmacht.

Then came emptiness and silence. At last on February 1 there was enough information to draw the new front on the map: it ran from Kulm to Danzig, passing through Graudenz, Marienwerder and Marienburg, which were two hundred miles to the west of Kaltenborn. It was now clear that the citadel was cut off in the rear, in a pocket where fighting had for the present come to an end.

*

Tiffauges paid only distant attention to these events. He spent most of his time with Ephraim, who had now gotten a little life back in him, a little flame of life that was curiously frisky, sometimes even gay. One day Tiffauges had perched him on his shoulders and taken him for a walk through the attics of the castle, a vast chaotic scene oddly lit by small round windows, at which Tiffauges stopped to let the boy see the vast expanses of forest, lake and marsh that surrounded Kaltenborn. Ephraim had enjoyed it, and every time he saw Tiffauges now he asked for another ride.

"Steed of Israel," he would say, "carry me off and show me the trees. I must look out for the thaw that will herald the night of the fifteenth of Nisan."

It was dangerous, and Tiffauges didn't conceal the risks the Star-Bearer ran in the midst of that brood of blond beasts of prey. But the hell Ephraim had already gone through made the threats that still hung over him seem pale.

One night, however, when the Steed of Israel had just taken the boy for a ride into the north wing of the castle, he found himself face to face with SS man Rinderknecht, who had come up to put some mattresses away in the storerooms. There was a moment's hesitation on both sides, then, without stopping to put Ephraim down, Tiffauges got hold of the SS man by the lapels of his canvas jacket, lifted him up, put him against the wall, and squeezed his chest in the hempen vise till his ribs cracked. His struggles were growing weaker and his contorted face was going blue, when Ephraim gave a shrill cry and started to beat his mount on the head with both fists and jump up and down as hard as he could on his shoulders. Tiffauges, blind with fear and anger, would have taken no notice, but the boy struggled so wildly that he fell off on to the floor, where he crouched, sobbing nervously. At this Tiffauges abandoned his prey, who stood leaning against the wall puffing like a seal, and came and knelt down by the boy.

"Don't kill him, Behemoth!" Ephraim kept saying between his sobs. "The soldiers of the Lord will come and deliver the people of Israel, but don't you kill, no, don't kill! I swear he won't say anything!"

Tiffauges carried him back to the garret without bothering any more about the SS man. Ephraim might be right, but it was a great risk. This was the first time Ephraim had imposed his will on Tiffauges on any important point. Tiffauges had no doubt that he would now abdicate more and more before his protégé, and he resigned himself to it, feeling that the boy was inhabited by fate even more than he was himself. But he wanted to know who Behemoth was, and why the boy had called him that. He asked him the next day.

"Because of your strength, Steed of Israel," he answered. "One day God spoke to Job out of the whirlwind, and said:

'Behold now Behemoth, which I made with thee; he eateth grass as an ox.
Lo now, his strength is in his loins, and his force is in the navel of his belly.
He moveth his tail like a cedar: the sinews of his stones are wrapped together.
His bones are as strong as pieces of brass; his bones are like bars of iron.
He is the chief of the ways of God; he that made him can make his sword to approach unto him.
Surely the mountains bring him forth food, where all the beasts of the field play.

He lieth under the shady trees, in the covert of the reed, and fens.
The shady trees cover him with their shadow; the willows of the brook compass him about. . . .'"

Ephraim had chanted these verses from the Book of Job in a Talmudic singsong. He ended his recitation with his elfin laugh.

Tiffauges, who was immediately struck by the image of the Erl-King "lying in the covert of the reed, and fens," admired Ephraim's certainty of the final triumph of his God, and drew near him, as to a glowing fire, to feel the radiance of his prophetic faith. One day there wasn't any water, because the sluices of the local reservoir had been bombed. Then it began to trickle out of the taps again, but tinged with red and leaving streaks of rust on basins and sinks. Ephraim was not surprised. Didn't the first plague of Egypt turn all the water in the land to blood? The time was ripe, he repeated, and deliverance approached.

*

At the end of March the cold suddenly ceased. A storm of wind and rain swept the country, driving before it flocks of starlings, plovers and lapwings, whipping the thawed lakes into furious waves, flooding the streets of low-lying villages. Then the wind dropped, and V-formations of wild geese could be seen flying high overhead. The boys on the anti-aircraft gun couldn't restrain themselves from opening fire on the living targets flying across their field. When a shell exploded in the middle of one close formation, all the birds disintegrated in a cloud of feathers. The boys shouted exultantly.

Raufeisen was glad about the early thaw, which must, he thought, delay any Russian attack. But that same evening, through the quiet of a night once again full of buds and scents, there could be heard for the first time, in the distance, the precise, staccato, terrifying click of Russian tanks. If any doubt remained, it was removed by the arrival of a young peasant riding bareback on a little chestnut Trakehner, his bare feet clad in nothing but spurs. He came from Arys, a small town about twelve miles away and almost completely evacuated, where he had stayed behind with a few old men and some animals. The Russians had reached there three hours ago, and must be close behind him. Raufeisen at once ordered the manning of all the battle emplacements he had organized: the Jungmannen were assigned to them in groups and columns.

The wait would have been long if the signature tune of the tanks, multiple and unremitting, had left anyone time to think. At last two tanks appeared in the twilight on the glacis and advanced, all lights extinguished, toward the rampart. They were T 34s, the great pachyderms made by Siberian peasants, incredibly rustic with their ill-fitting armor full of gaps you could put your thumb into, their tracks wide as escalators, and their low tapered lines; but they were impervious to cold and mud, and they had been rolling heavily from the confines of Asia, crushing beneath them Hitler's Panzer divisions.

They stopped, switched on their lights, and swept the blind-looking wall. They were followed by one of those little amphibious cars of American origin so useful in these regions of lakes and swamps. An officer got out and went and stood in front of the tanks so that he was silhouetted sharply in their headlights. He had a megaphone in his hand. It was Lieutenant Nicholas Dimitriev, veteran of Stalingrad, decorated on the Minsk front, legendary among his men and among his friends for his temerity and for his luck. He put the electric speaker to his face and spoke a few words of German in his singsong Ukrainian accent.

"I am unarmed! We know there are only children here. Surrender! No harm will be done you. Open the gates—"

His sentence was interrupted by a volley of machine-gun fire from one of the flanking towers. The megaphone rolled in the snow, and Lieutenant Dimitriev clutched at his chest. But the lights of the tanks went out, and he couldn't be seen as he fell. The darkness was immediately pierced again by the flash of rockets being launched to converge on the tanks. Their diesels began to shriek, and the two great monsters attempted to beat a hasty retreat. But the tracks of one of them had already been shot away; it swerved and hit the other tank with a clang. They both stood still like two bulls confronting one another, under a hail of fire that shot away every projection and left clouds of black smoke pouring out of what remained. Then there was a lull lasting half an hour, and the air was rent by the thunder of a 155 firing straight at the ramparts. This was followed by the crystalline music of all the windows in the citadel shattering. A moment later the anti-aircraft battery could be heard farther off: it must be raking the Schlangenfliess road, which was no doubt jammed with Russian columns.

It was not Raufeisen's intention to defend the ramparts to the bitter end. His idea was to evacuate them after the first engagement and concentrate his fire on the entrance, or on whatever breach the Russian tanks attacked through. But there was one thing missing from his calculations, and that was an accurate appraisal of the enemy's firing power. He was surprised by the amount of artillery directed against the ancient walls. Instead of making a small breach, easy to concentrate on, it set about the systematic destruction of the citadel, knocking down whole stretches of the ramparts on to the buildings within. An hour later, two heavy quadruple machine guns mounted on trucks took up position in the shelter of the outbuildings and directed their fire at all the openings in the façade of the castle. At the same time sections of howitzers—difficult targets for the Panzerfausts—dotted themselves about the other buildings. The positions of the defenders would soon be untenable. There was nothing for them to do but try to join the snipers scattered outside the citadel to harass the enemy tanks and mechanized artillery.

Tiffauges had almost finished exchanging the handsome clothes of the master of Kaltenborn for his old castoff prisoner's uniform with the huge letters POW on it when the first mortar shells began to fall on the roof. He hurried up to the attics, spurred on by a fleeting glimpse, around a corner, of the bodies of three Jungmannen sprawled over the carriage of a submachine gun pointing toward the black square of the window. In one of the attics a heap of mattresses was emitting clouds of thick, choking smoke, which still hung over the floor in spite of the great jagged openings in the roof. Tiffauges rushed into Ephraim's cubbyhole.

The little Jewish boy was sitting in front of the rickety table, which he had covered with a square of white cloth. On it he had set out some slices of bread, a mutton bone, some herbs, and a glass holding water reddened with wine.

"Ephraim, we must go," shouted Tiffauges, running in. "The Russians are destroying the castle!"

"How is this night of the fifteenth of Nisan different from every other night?" asked Ephraim gravely.

"Come on, there isn't a minute to lose!"

"Behemoth, chief of the ways of God, answer, 'On that night came we out of the land of Egypt.' How is this night different from every other night?"

"On that night came we out of the land of Egypt," said Tiffauges meekly.

But an earthquake tremor shook the floor under his feet, and a hail of debris fell from the ceiling.

"Come with me, Ephraim! We must get away!"

"All right, we'll go," said the boy, pushing the table aside. "The soldiers of God are striking down the eldest born of the Egyptians, but they will protect our flight. But if you won't sit with me at the table of the seder, at least let me say the first verses of the Haggada."

He lowered his eyes, and his lips began to move. Some more

grenades went off, then followed a silence even more agonizing than the firing. Tiffauges grew impatient.

"You can finish your Haggada sitting on my shoulders," he said. "Come on, up with you on to the Steed of Israel!" he commanded, kneeling by the boy.

When he left the garret, stooping to let Ephraim past the door, the stutter of machine guns from all quarters and the persistent silence of the artillery seemed to indicate that the Russians were storming the castle. He had to turn back; the attics of the left wing were ablaze. He would have to use the central staircase and risk going into the main part of the building, from which the sound of the fighting came. At every step Tiffauges came upon Jungmannen who had been killed. Some were not visibly hurt and looked as if they had fallen asleep, alone or in groups—Tiffauges thought with a pang of the hypnodrome. Others were mutilated, torn, unrecognizable. Shouted orders in Russian and revolver shots forced him to go up one floor again. A door was open: it was the commandant's office. Tiffauges rushed in. The big window overlooking the terrace with the swords gaped open. Tiffauges leaned against a tapestry to get his breath back. It was then that he heard the cry. He recognized it at once, and knew he was hearing it for the first time in its absolute purity. That long, modulated, guttural plaint full of harmonics, some of a strange joy, others breathing the most unbearable sorrow, had never ceased ringing out ever since his sickly childhood in the icy corridors of St. Christopher's, up to the time it greeted the death of the great stags in the depths of the forest of Rominten. But those more or less distant echoes had been only a series of gropings toward the transcendent chant that had just arisen with unendurable clarity from the terrace of the swords. He knew he was hearing for the first time in its primitive form the clamor suspended between life and death which was the fundamental sound of his whole destiny. And once again, as on the day he met the retreating French prisoners, but with a persuasiveness incomparably greater, it was the peaceful and disincarnate face of the Erl-King, wrapped in his shroud of peat, which presented itself to his mind as the ultimate resource, the ultimate retreat.

"Did you hear?" he said. "I think there's someone dying on the terrace. Can you see anything?"

By leaning forward Ephraim could see the parapet, and he told Tiffauges what he could see through the darkness starred every so often by explosions. Yes, the three swords were there, but they seemed to be bearing dark, heavy shapes, as if they had become the poles for three standards of thick brocade with drooping folds.

Tiffauges went back to the main staircase. He was just approaching the first-floor landing when he was forced by detonations close by to shelter in a corner. Some Russian soldiers—the first he'd seen—were pushing along in front of them a man who staggered, fell, and was kicked on to his feet again. A push sent him flying nearer, and for a moment Tiffauges saw turned toward him a swollen face with one eye running down the cheek in a mixture of blood and aqueous humor. He recognized Raufeisen. The SS man fell once more and tried to haul himself up by the banister. He had got himself on to his knees when a soldier put the barrel of his revolver to the nape of his neck. There was a muffled explosion, and Raufeisen's head shot forward and hit the side of the banister. Then his lifeless body slid down on the stairs. Tiffauges took Ephraim's thin knees in his hands and drew his thighs forward around his neck, as if to make more sure of their protection. As he did so a phrase from his childhood was ringing through his brain: "that in their common fortune the child's innocence might serve him as warrant and recommendation to God's favor, to bring him safely through."

There was no going down the stairs now. He would have to go up again, perhaps to the chapel, and hide on the main terrace. Tiffauges scarcely stopped to think. He was acting on the spur of the moment. Part of the ceiling of the chapel had come down, but the door on to the terrace gaped open. Tiffauges rushed through it, took a few steps, and was frozen to the spot by what he saw.

The flags of the terrace were covered by a carpet of spotless snow untouched by the thaw. The balustrade was also white, save at the foot of the three swords where it was stained red, as if a crimson mantle had been thrown under each. All three of them were there, Hajo, Haro and Lothar, the red-haired twins faithfully flanking their friend, the boy with white hair—pierced from omega to alpha, their eyes staring into space, the three swords making in each a different wound. In the case of Hajo the point came out over the left shoulder blade, so that it looked as if he were lifting one knee and throwing back his head to regain his balance. One great toe, frozen in a spasm, was linked to the parapet by a thread of congealed blood that shook in the night breeze. Haro leaned his head to the right as if toward Lothar, but really because the blade emerged from the right of his throat and went up to the ear. His fists were clenched and his knees slightly flexed like those of a jumper in full flight, rising upward. Lothar's head was thrown back. His mouth was open, his teeth gripping the point of the sword emerging between the jaws. He was impaled right through, legs together, arms at his sides, like a perfect sheath for the ancient blade. The stars had gone out, and the Golgotha of boys stood out against a black sky. "Argent, three pages gules erect on pales, with sable chief," murmured Tiffauges.

An explosion that shook the terrace brought the chapel crashing down, and Tiffauges and Ephraim were covered with debris.

"Ephraim," said Tiffauges, "I've lost my glasses. I can hardly see. You'll have to guide me."

"That's nothing, Steed of Israel. I'll hold on to your ears and guide you like that!"

A string of tracer bullets burst in tears of fire above the trees.

"Ephraim, I see a closed fist in the black sky. It clenches, and from it well drops of blood."

"Let's go, Behemoth—I think you're becoming *meschugge!*"

"Ephraim, doesn't it say in the sacred books that his face and hair were white as snow, his eyes like flames of fire, his feet like copper reddened in a furnace, and that a two-edged sword came from his mouth?"

"Behemoth, if you don't turn around I'll pull your ears off!"

Tiffauges obeyed meekly, and from then on he was only a child in the hands and between the feet of the Star-Bearer. They hadn't gone ten yards before they were stopped by a group of Russian soldiers who turned their machine guns on them. And it was Ephraim's shrill voice shouting *"Voïna prani! Franzouski prani!"* that made them fall back and leave the way open to the Child-Bearer.

Fighting had stopped inside the castle; only the left wing, with the Telamon tower, seemed to be intact. But detachments of Russians must have been reducing one by one the Jungmannen commandos scattered among the woods and moors: every so often there were volleys of firing. Tiffauges made his way along by the burned-out buildings, past the fence of the kennels, where the eleven machine-gunned Dobermans were the last bag ever laid out at Kaltenborn, and started out on the road to Schlangenfliess, which went more or less toward the redeeming west. Like someone shipwrecked in mid-ocean, who swims by instinct, without any hope of being saved, he went through all the motions that might have brought him to safety, without for an instant thinking he might escape. He went through Schlangenfliess, lit up bright as day by the houses burning like torches and throwing columns of smoke and sparks high into the sky. He went on for a few more minutes, blinder than before, and then Ephraim suddenly tugged on both his ears.

"Stop, Behemoth! Listen!"

He stopped and listened. Through the silence of the night

there came the silvery, multiple click of a column of Russian tanks, advancing with menacing precision. A rocket, fired from scarcely a mile in front of them, hissed through the sky, leaving its red curve written on the darkness. And almost at once the first shells streamed whistling over the road. So the anti-aircraft battery had not yet been wiped out and was replying to the snipers' signal.

"We shall have to leave the road," Ephraim decided. "Go left over the moor, and we'll work around the column of tanks."

Without arguing, Tiffauges went over to the bank on the left of the road, plunged into the muddy drifts of snow, then felt beneath his feet the soft and treacherous soil of the moor. His face was scratched by a bush, and after that he went with his hands outstretched like a blind man. He went along like that for a long time, until the shelling of the road was only a dim and stormy murmur. Gradually the ground grew spongy, and he had to make an effort at every step to overcome the suction. Then his hands encountered the trunks and branches of a little wood, and he recognized the black alders of the marshes. He tried to stop and turn back, but an irresistible force bore down on his shoulders. The deeper his feet sank into the waterlogged swamp the more he felt the boy—so thin and diaphanous—weighing down on him like a lump of lead. On he went, and still the mud rose around his legs, and the load that was crushing him grew heavier with every step. He had to make a superhuman effort now to overcome the viscous resistance grinding in his belly and breast, but he persevered, knowing all was as it should be. When he turned to look up for the last time at Ephraim, all he saw was a six-pointed star turning slowly against the black sky.

Notes

1. Quoted in *Pétain et de Gaulle* by J.-R. Tournoux (Plon).
2. *Erle* = alder in German.
3.
THE ERL-KING

O who rides by night thro' the woodland so wild?
It is the fond father embracing his child;
And close the boy nestles within his loved arm.
To hold himself fast, and to keep himself warm.

"O father, see yonder! see yonder!" he says;
"My boy, upon what dost thou fearfully gaze?"
"O, 'tis the Erl-King with his crown and his shroud."
"No, my son, it is but a dark wreath of the cloud."

(*The Erl-King speaks*)
"O come and go with me, thou loveliest child;
By many a gay sport shall thy time be beguiled;
My mother keeps for thee full many a fair toy,
And many a fine flower shall she pluck for my boy."

"O father, my father, and did you not hear
The Erl-King whisper so low in my ear?"
"Be still, my heart's darling—my child, be at ease;
It was but the wild blast as it sung thro' the trees."

Erl-King
"O wilt thou go with me, thou loveliest boy?

My daughter shall tend thee with care and with joy;
She shall bear thee so lightly thro' wet and thro' wild,
And press thee, and kiss thee, and sing to my child."

"O father, my father, and saw you not plain
The Erl-King's pale daughter glide past thro' the rain?"
"O yes, my loved treasure, I knew it full soon;
It was the gray willow that danced to the moon."

Erl-King

"O come and go with me, no longer delay,
Or else, silly child, I will drag thee away."
"O father! O father! now, now, keep your hold,
The Erl-King has seized me—his grasp is so cold!"

Sore trembled the father; he spurr'd thro' the wild,
Clasping close to his bosom his shuddering child;
He reaches his dwelling in doubt and in dread,
But, clasp'd to his bosom, the infant was dead.

Johann Wolfgang von Goethe
Translated by *Sir Walter Scott*

4. Quoted in *Generation im Gleichschritt* by Werner Klose (Stalling).

5. See *Elite für die Diktatur* by Horst Ueberhorst (Droste), the standard work on the Napolas.

6. *Nuremberg Trials*, Vol. XX, pp. 566ff.

7. See Alfred Rosenberg, *Der Mythus des XX. Jahrhunderts.*

8. See Werner Klose, op. cit.

9. Quoted in *Elite für die Diktatur.*

10. A. Pardun. *Nuremberg Trials*, Vol. XXXIII, p. 70.

11. *Heuaktion: Nuremberg Trials*, Vol. XXV, p. 88.

12. K. Hofmann. *Nuremberg Trials*, Vol. XXXIII, p. 71.

13. Eberhard Marschall. Quoted in *Der braune Kult* by H. J. Gamm (Ruetten & Leoning).

14. Ibid.

15. Purim: Jewish feast during which the children dress up. De-

tails taken from document CCCLXI-32, Centre de documentation juive contemporaine, Paris.

16. Letter from Heissmeyer quoted in *Elite für die Diktatur*.

17. See *Der Kampf um Ostpreussen* by Diekert-Grossmann (Graefe & Unzer).

About the Author

Born in Paris in 1924, Michel Tournier has unusually close ties to Germany: both his parents were German scholars, and he studied at the University of Tübingen. He holds master's degrees in both law and philosophy, and worked for some years at a large French publishing house. He is fascinated by photography, and has produced his own programs for French television. His first novel, *Friday,* won the Grand Prix du Roman of the Académie Française. His second, *The Ogre,* is the only novel ever to win France's most prestigious literary prize, the Prix Goncourt, by a unanimous vote. Like his two subsequent novels, *Gemini* and *The Four Wise Men,* they received enthusiastic reviews around the world.

A bachelor, Michel Tournier lives near Paris. He acts as a cultural consultant for French television, but devotes most of his time to writing.

PANTHEON MODERN WRITERS ORIGINALS

THE VICE-CONSUL

by Marguerite Duras, translated from the French by Eileen Ellenbogen

The first American edition ever of the "masterful novel" (*Chicago Tribune*) that Duras considers her best—a tale of passion and desperation set in India and Southeast Asia.
0-394-75026-8

MAPS

by Nuruddin Farah

The unforgettable story of one man's coming of age in the turmoil of modern Africa, by "one of the finest contemporary African writers" (Salman Rushdie).
0-394-75548-0

NELLY'S VERSION

by Eva Figes

An ingenious thriller of identity by the author of *Waking* and *The Seven Ages*.

"A taunting, captivating novel."—*Times Literary Supplement*
0-679-72035-9

DREAMING JUNGLES

by Michel Rio, translated from the French by William Carlson

"A subtle philosophical excursion embodied in a story of travel and adventure...it succeeds extremely well."—*New York Times Book Review*
0-394-75035-7

BURNING PATIENCE

by Antonio Skármeta, translated from the Spanish by Katherine Silver

A charming story about the friendship that develops between Pablo Neruda, Latin America's greatest poet, and the postman who stops to receive his advice about love.

"The mix of the fictional and the real is masterful, and...gives the book its special appeal and brilliance."—*Christian Science Monitor*
0-394-75033-0

THE SHOOTING GALLERY

by Yūko Tsushima, compiled and translated from the Japanese by Geraldine Harcourt

Eight stories about modern Japanese women by "a subtle, surprising, elegant writer who courageously tells unexpected truths" (Margaret Drabble).
0-394-75743-2

YOU CAN'T GET LOST IN CAPE TOWN

by Zoë Wicomb

A "superb first collection" (*New York Times Book Review*) of stories about a young black woman's upbringing in South Africa.
0-394-75309-7

ALSO FROM THE PANTHEON MODERN WRITERS SERIES

A PAINTER OF OUR TIME
by John Berger

John Berger's artistic detective novel, a complex and powerful portrait of an artist at odds with his time.

"Fresh and inventive."— *New York Times*
0-679-72271-8

PIG EARTH
(the first volume of the projected trilogy *Into Their Labors*)
by John Berger

An exquisite fictional portrait of life in a small peasant village in the French Alps.

"Lovely, lyrical, haunting…a masterpiece."— Todd Gitlin, *New Republic*

"A work of art."— *Washington Post*
0-394-75739-4

ONCE IN EUROPA
(the second volume of the projected trilogy *Into Their Labors*)
by John Berger

A linked series of love stories, set among the peasants of Alpine France.

"Berger is one of our most gifted and imaginative contemporary writers [and] *Once in Europa* contains what may be his best writing to date."
— *New York Times Book Review*

"Marvelous stories."— Angela Carter, *Washington Post Book World*
0-394-75164-7

THE MARRIAGE SCENARIOS
by Ingmar Bergman, translated from the Swedish by Alan Blair

The film scripts for *Scenes from a Marriage*, *Autumn Sonata*, and *Face to Face*.

"A terrifically moving piece of writing."— *Los Angeles Times*
0-679-72032-4

ALL FIRES THE FIRE AND OTHER STORIES
by Julio Cortázar, translated from the Spanish by Suzanne Jill Levine

"One of the most adventurous and rewarding collections since the publication of Cortázar's own *Blow-Up*."— *Los Angeles Times*
0-394-75358-5

BLOW-UP AND OTHER STORIES
by Julio Cortázar, translated from the Spanish by Paul Blackburn

A celebrated masterpiece: fifteen eerie and brilliant short stories.

"A splendid collection."— *New Yorker*
0-394-72881-5

Ask your local bookstore for other Pantheon Modern Writers titles.